A Haunting DECEPTION

BOOK ONE IN THE ASCENSION SERIES

MICAH BRIARMOON

In Loving Memory of Anne Topp

Her passion inspired me
Her love encouraged me
Her expertise guided me

Anne played an integral role in bringing this book to life. We spent countless hours together reading and discussing. With her guidance, from word choice to added details and restructured paragraphs, she helped shape the flow of this story with love, patience, and insight. Her presence lives in these pages.

Late-night discussions and rewrites with Anne helped me become the writer I am today.

I miss her deeply.

Prologue

Nagasaki, Japan

August 12, 1945

How many newly dead will I count today?

Emerging from the skeletal remains of a building, Damarkus Jones stepped onto the street, radiating strength—the rotten, unnatural kind that carved shadows beneath eyes and devoured flesh. He leaned back and stretched his stiff muscles as his gaze swept across the eerie pink clouds. The atomic blast from three days earlier had swollen the heavens and imbued them with a sickly afterglow. The unseen poison loomed everywhere, evident in the stench of death carried by the evening breeze off the sea.

Damarkus had spent his day forcing souls to transcend, feeding on the dark energy left in the wake of a spirit's passage into the realm of oneness. Weary from work, he headed for the center of town, eager to find more silhouettes cauterized into the streets, stone stairways, and walls of shattered buildings. He loved stories, especially the ones the blackened portraits whispered.

"Damarkus Jones," a woman called.

The voice yanked him upright, tightening his spine as if a rabid dog were barking his name. Yoona stood in the street in front of him, flanked by two pale men wearing long black coats. Damarkus clenched his hands into fists, then shook his head. "I guess I should have expected you." He circled the trio, holding Yoona's gaze. "There are plenty of souls here. There's no need to fight over them."

Glancing to his left and then his right, Damarkus saw his fellow Banishers, Jarec and Pavlo, appear from behind piles of rubble. "Ah, Yoona. You're out-matched."

A sly grin crept across Yoona's face. "Damarkus, we need to take you into custody."

"Why? I haven't killed anyone. The war has given us a plethora of souls. I have no need to kill. They are everywhere. I am doing this world a service by sending them to the ultimate dimension. Think of all the hauntings and suffering I am preventing."

"It's not your action that concerns me. It's the purpose for which you act."

"These souls are in shock. They have no idea what happened. Whatever this weapon was, it has disrupted the rhythm and flow of energy. These souls need to be pushed to transcend. Your 'counseling' them won't work."

Yoona tilted her head. "So, love and compassion are what motivate you?" Her eyes glinted with amusement. "Tell me more."

"There's nothing more to tell. I suggest you and your friends move along." The corners of his lips curled into a sinister grin. "Before something unfortunate happens."

With soft eyes and a honeyed voice, Yoona said, "Damarkus, I am here to help you."

Damarkus hardened his gaze. "I have not requested nor do I require *your* help."

"Your soul reeks of dark energy," she shot back.

He chuckled, savoring the sharpness in the Shaman's voice. "Yoona—known for your calm wisdom... You should let your composure slip more often. It highlights your true nature."

She took a slow breath. "How long have you been consuming the residue of forced transcendences?"

"Are you jealous?" He stepped closer, testing her. "To partake in the fruit of one's labor is not a crime."

Yoona didn't flinch. "It's not too late for you to cleanse your soul," she replied. "Come with us."

Lowering his voice to a growl, Damarkus responded, "I'm not going any-where."

The two gentlemen next to Yoona removed their long coats to reveal priests' cassocks.

A surge of panic coursed through Damarkus. Yoona wasn't here to play. The priests with her meant his very existence was in jeopardy. A fleeting doubt crossed his mind—*if I were to fall here today, would anyone truly care?* He shook away the self-defeating thoughts and took a defensive position, readying himself for battle. He would not die today. He was the hero; his daughter's eyes had told him so.

Drawing in his chin, Damarkus intensified his stare. Yoona's skills were legendary, but he had plenty of dark energy. Jarec and Pavlo could deal with the priests.

"Consider this carefully. I have not taken a life. I've committed no wrong-doing. If you insist on trying to capture me, or worse, shred my soul, I will defend myself. I don't wish to harm you, Yoona."

She shook her head. "You won't be able to stop your consumption. Your thirst will drive you mad, as it did your friend in Germany. I cannot allow you to continue absorbing dark energy, and I am prepared to take whatever action is necessary to that end. Please, Damarkus. For your safety and well-being, come with us." She stressed the final words, her eyes sweeping over everyone as they surrounded him.

Damarkus looked at his companions, his face grave with understanding. "You're siding with *her*? When did you decide to betray your own kind?"

"Damarkus, the war is over," Jarec said in a firm voice. "We have made an alliance and created a council, installing checks and balances to prevent any one of us from ever rising to power again."

"By working with the Church?!" Damarkus spit. "They believe us to be devil worshippers."

"You have crossed a line and are traveling a dangerous path. Let us take you to the temple," Jarec insisted.

"I've crossed a line?" Damarkus almost choked on the words as a bitter laugh escaped him. He gestured to the smoking ruins of Nagasaki. "Look around you. The city is completely leveled: forty thousand people vaporized! Another ten thousand have died from their injuries, and thousands more will drop from atomic bomb disease. Ghosts are everywhere! More will come in the following days. And *I've* crossed the line?!"

Pavlo put both his hands in the air to show he meant no harm. He moved slowly toward Damarkus, holding his gaze, as he pleaded with his estranged friend. "Why don't you drain the energy you're holding? Let it go. Show us you haven't become addicted."

Damarkus smirked. "Sure." Extending his arms out to each side, he discharged two powerful energy waves at both his colleagues. He forced his hands together and separated his palms, pushing them forward to fire a giant blast toward Yoona.

Jarec and Pavlo turned sideways and raised their right arms to cover their faces, creating a forcefield to protect themselves. The energy waves pushed both men back in opposite directions, knocking them to the ground. Jarec's head bounced off the pavement as he clutched his ribs. Pavlo rolled onto his knees, coughing up blood.

Yoona put her hands together and pointed them forward like an arrow before separating them. The blast aimed at Yoona and the priests diverted, flattening the dead, brittle trees behind them.

Yoona ran straight toward Damarkus. He threw a folly of forward punches. She blocked and dodged, fending them off. Twisting and turning, he used a combination of jabs, elbow strikes, and kicks to the knees and stomach. Yoona struggled to match his speed, and the strain of blocking his powerful blows was breaking her defenses. Damarkus landed a knee to her side, followed by a hook to the chest. Yoona stumbled backwards. His eyes blazed. Jumping into the air, he spun to deliver a kick to Yoona's head—but Jarec collided with him mid-turn.

He screamed, landing awkwardly and stumbling. Pavlo came from behind and struck Damarkus in the kidney. He fell to the ground and rolled to his knees.

Wincing, he clutched his lower back. With darkening eyes, he stood and faced his allies-turned-betrayers.

The two priests with Yoona brandished their crosses and holy water, chanting in Latin, "*Pater noster, qui es in caelis, sanctificetur—*"

Damarkus roared, blasting Pavlo into the only remaining wall standing in a ten-block radius. He moved for Jarec. Water droplets struck his shoulder, burning him. Then came the priests' unseen fingers, groping for his soul. Damarkus had to end this now. With a quick strike, he grabbed Jarec by the throat and flung him into the air with enough force to clear a three-story building. Whipping around, he fixed his scowl on Yoona and balled his hands into fists—then froze.

The priests had him. Damarkus had lost.

Yoona held out her hands, grunting as she slowed Jarec's descent. He landed on the ground, unhurt.

Damarkus couldn't move. His face was red in torment as the priests restrained him, his soul on the edge of being ripped from his body.

Yoona stepped to him, and they stood face to face. "Will you consent to cleansing your soul?" she asked.

Damarkus's eyes pierced Yoona's. "I..." He started, his voice gruff.

Placing her hand on his cheek, Yoona whispered sweetly, "Let me help you."

His jaw clenched.

Her eyes pleaded with him as her thumb rubbed his cheek. "It doesn't have to end this way."

Damarkus relaxed his body.

Yoona let out a soft sigh.

He understood her reaction—she misinterpreted his softening for concession. But he couldn't. The mere thought of confinement brought sweat to bead on his brow. His skin flushed. A throb behind his eyes spread like wildfire, making his hands twitch. Isolation meant hours of meditation, throwing up, fevers, headaches, and desperate cravings—thirsting for the power. He wouldn't go through that again. The non-stop pacing alone would drive him crazy. Dark energy had permeated his cells, rewiring them. His body wouldn't function without it. His identity had fused with the phantom burnt residue, granting him strength, speed, and a weapon. This confinement meant death—either for him, or for the people guarding him. He would try to escape. He would kill for a fix.

Damarkus couldn't let himself become the evil villain in his daughter's eyes. Suzi had been right to take her from him. Everyone had left him: his mother yelling, "Don't come back." His sensei's disapproving stare, saying, "I can't teach you anymore." His life had come to an end. His lip quivered, and his eyes watered. "I can't."

With quiet resignation, Yoona gave him a consoling nod. "I'm sorry, then." Stepping back, she removed her hand as a tear rolled down his cheek. Yoona's head dropped, a weak gesture for the priests to proceed.

They pulled their arms back in midair.

Demarcus shrieked as his essence was ripped from his body, the threads of his soul snapping from his flesh like fabric torn at the seams.

His body collapsed, but his formless being hovered in the wind—cold and naked—bound by the priests' phantom grip.

In his final moments, before they shredded what remained of him, Demarcus summoned the last of his will and sent a telepathic message to his daughter, Ruth. He poured what memory he could into his words: "I love you."

PART ONE

A Haunting Deception

Day One—Wednesday
Spring 2025

Three hours southeast of Portland, Oregon, nestled into the side of Bobcat Mountain, stood a mansion overlooking Lake Valley. From the floor-to-ceiling living room windows, the residents could admire the city's bustling parks, local wineries offering daily tours, and the sandy beach on the edge of the lake, a popular summer destination. Hiking trails ran through the city, winding between houses and through parks before disappearing into the lush green forest where they led to spring fed waterfalls. The fine restaurants, local theaters, and jazz clubs which sold out nightly livened the city with dancing lights. Around the bend and out of view from the mansion was the casino run by the nearby native reservation. It attracted famous entertainers and added culture to the city with yearly festivals, Powwows, and a wilderness camp.

The mansion, an award-winning architectural achievement, had once drawn tourists to the area. They had flocked to view the main feature of the house—the west wing set into the rocky hillside, where a natural stream flowed onto the roof into a second-floor pool. From there, the water cascaded into a pond on the ground level and followed its natural path through the front lawn.

Now, though, twelve years after the mansion's construction, the city had all but forgotten it, allowing this grand building to become a jail cell—for one.

Nong Ekamai stepped into the kitchen with slumped shoulders and heavy shadows hanging under her eyes. Her black pants carried a streak of dust, picked up somewhere between the office and the library. Wiping her hands on her apron, she glanced around the room and muttered, "Still dirty. Always is."

She reached for the broom and began sweeping along the baseboard, gathering tiny crumbs and traces of flour that had settled in the seam. She noticed a splatter of red sauce on the wall, crusted over like dried blood. Oh, the joys of cleaning up after someone who never cared. Endless and thankless.

Nong filled a bucket with water, added vinegar and soap, then dabbed at the spot and left it to soak. After she finished sweeping and mopping, she knelt beside the wall, dipped a rag into the soapy water, and scrubbed. A faint, barely visible line remained, outlining where the sauce had landed.

With a weary sigh, she removed a toothbrush from her apron. Her fingers curled around it, and a hallow pain spread through her chest as her thoughts went to her daughter.

"I hope Ploy is brushing her teeth every day," she murmured to herself. Nong set the brush against the wall and gently worked the area, praying Ploy was with her parents. "She has to be." The words escaped her without thought, the way they often did when silence became her only companion. "Because if she's not and ends up with a cavity, she won't complain."

Gripping the toothbrush, Nong tapped her fist against the wall. What worried her most was how quietly Ploy carried pain. With the back of her wrist, Nong wiped her eyes and resumed her chores.

When she finished, she rinsed the bucket, mop, and rags, and put them away. Then she switched off the light and pulled the door closed. But before it latched, she froze.

A voice, low and calm, drifted from the darkness behind her. "That wasn't loving enough."

Nong's hand tightened around the doorknob, and she squeezed her eyes shut.

"I need to *feel* the emotion. Do it again."

Nong didn't move. She clenched her jaw and her voice caught in her throat, trapping the scream that was ready to burst from her lips. Her chest heaved, angry breaths through her nose whistling like steam through a valve.

"Do it again," the voice repeated in a sharper, commanding tone.

Turning the light back on, Nong entered the kitchen, filled the bucket, found a brush, and kneeled on the floor. She stared at the door with reddening eyes.

"Not loving enough?" she seethed through gritted teeth. She yanked the brush from the soapy water and slammed it to the floor. "Is that loving enough for you?!"

Nong scoured the kitchen floor with wild, erratic force. "You want loving? I'll give you loving."

When she reached the other side, she seized the bucket and hurled it across the room. The bucket hit the wall with a whack, sending soapy water everywhere.

"Is this clean enough for you?" Nong yelled. "Does it *feel* any better? Or would you prefer I use my tits to wash the floor?"

Dropping to her knees, she wept. Her extended confinement and lack of human contact had broken her. "I can't do this anymore. I can't." Lifting her head to the ceiling, she screamed, "I'm done! Do you hear me?" The term companion tickled her tongue, but this wasn't love. It was entrapment. "I refuse to be your *slave*." She doubled over and cried.

After several minutes, she sat back up and tucked her feet beneath her. She picked up a sponge and set it in a small puddle on the floor. As the porous foam soaked up the water, Nong absorbed the hopelessness pooling inside her. Four years of pleasing, submitting, and compromising had not gotten her any closer to freedom or to seeing her daughter.

In a soft, defeated voice she quivered, "I can't love you like he did. I'm not him. You must let me go."

Nong thought of Ploy, snuggling close, her warm breath on her neck as she read her favorite bedtime story—*Skippyjon Jones*—and heard her giggles as she played with her pink bunny slippers.

Tears fell. She could only imagine how Ploy must have felt waiting for her after school, only for her to never show.

The Apology

Eighteen miles from the mansion, a Freightliner P700 step van rumbled its way to the entrance of the Go Express delivery hub. The driver stood, descended two steps, and slid open the door of the fourteen-foot rectangular truck. His badge read: "Jared Davenport, Delivery Driver." Looking at his hands, blackened with the dust and dirt from the 217 packages he had delivered that day, he scanned his badge to open the gate. He was tired, his sore muscles tight as he turned the large wheel and drove to bay door 400. Conscious of the orange poles protecting the building, he backed his truck into its designated space, 429. He rubbed the knot in his shoulder before releasing a deep, tortured sigh.

The contract stared at him, lying on the island console beneath his half-eaten Power Bar and a stack of door tags. He paused the audiobook, *Mexican Gothic,* and glanced around the quiet terminal. The morning's commotion replayed: clattering conveyor belts moving boxes, storage carts screeching across the floor, and computer terminals beeping. He reached over, unfolded the form, and stared at the numbers. A modest increase.

What am I doing? Jared thought. *Am I really going to sign this?*

Today was the end of three years—two and a half longer than he had planned and three more than he had wanted. Yes, the job was low-stress compared to running his own architectural firm with high client demands and strict deadlines. Yes, he was able to pay the bills. Yes, he got a workout every day. And, yes, he had finished a long list of audiobooks he'd wanted to read: *Wheel of Time*, *The Book Thief*, and *I Take My Coffee Black*, to name a few. But the mindless repetition sucked the life out of him.

His eyes drifted down to his new route number: 511—the Bobcat Mountain neighborhood. *An easy area*, Hossain had told him. He stared at the page, rolling his pen between his fingers. *One more year*, he thought, then signed the contract.

"Jared," Hossain called as he crossed the aisle towards him. Jared's boss, born in Türkiye but raised in Germany, spoke with a thick accent. He was a compact, muscular guy with short black hair, brown eyes, and wrinkles that showed his age and experience. "Hey, your new truck is waiting for you. I just parked it. It's got new brakes and tires. It's all ready to go for you, man."

"Great. Thanks."

"Did you sign the contract?" Hossain asked. "Nice raise, yeah?"

Jared handed him the form, then gathered his belongings from his old truck: his cooler, water bottle, dog treats, first aid kit, and phone charger.

"Here. Let me help you." Hossain grabbed the cooler and water bottle. "You're looking scruffy." That was Hossain's way of saying he needed a haircut.

Jared's light brown hair fell below his ears, and his bangs would have covered his blue eyes if it wasn't parted to the side. He rubbed his chin, confirming his need to shave.

They walked to the next loading dock, passing workers installing charging units.

"The first electric van will be here next month," Hossain informed him. "We'll have five of them by the end of the year." Then reassuringly, he proclaimed, "You're going to love this new route, man. Really. It's mostly residential, with only two apartment complexes, a small strip mall, and one office building—easy,

easy. Just be careful out there. It's an expensive neighborhood. Most of those houses cost five million or more. I don't want any accidents, y'know."

"Hossain, I've been driving for you for three years without an accident. Knock on wood."

"Knock on wood? What's that?"

They rounded the end of the belt, the green truck with yellow logo waiting for him like a prison sentence.

"We say that so we don't curse ourselves," Jared said. "It's supposed to ward off evil spirits, so our good luck stays with us."

"Ah, right. I know. I know what you mean. Okay, knock on wood."

Jared stepped into the truck and situated his things.

"Hey," Hossain called. "You're working every day this week, right? I need you, man."

Jared heard the guilt in Hossain's voice. His boss hated asking him to work on his days off. Exiting the truck, he said, "I remember."

"I appreciate that, man. Thank you. I owe you."

When Jared arrived home, he grabbed the mail and shuffled through it as he walked toward the house. The first letter was from his attorney, informing him that the lawsuit against him for damages, medical expenses, and personal losses had been finalized and that additional hours were incurred beyond the retainer fee. The amount due was $5,500. He looked up at the gray clouds that threatened more than they acted. He exhaled, sharp and tired. "So much for my raise," he muttered.

Thumbing through the envelopes, Jared saw one from a wealth management company addressed to his daughter—Leah Davenport, 2143 SE 46th St., Lake Valley, OR. He knew exactly what that letter meant. Leah would start receiving her trust fund payments once she graduated high school—a monthly allowance, plus access to additional funds to pay for tuition, books, and rent.

His chest contracted in pain. From regret? Disappointment? Because *he* was a failure? Tossing the mail on the coffee table, he dropped onto the brown leather sofa, the life he had lost rolling through his mind—his Mercedes, the yearly trips to Europe and Asia, the private school for Leah, the tutors and nannies.

And Stacy.

Laying his head back, he ran his hands through his hair, guilt clinging to him like a cat that refused to let go, its sharp claws buried into his flesh. Eight years had passed, and he still couldn't move forward. The divorce had shattered his life—his dreams, his business, his family, and his very reason for living.

He glanced around the room, feeling the emptiness. The bare wall stared back at him, having once displayed a family photo taken at a Scottish castle. So did the lonely corner, where a rabbit foot fern she had cared for had grown, and the refrigerator, now devoid of notes reminding him to buy Oreo cookie ice cream. He needed Stacy's decisiveness—the way she threw together shepherd's pie without glancing at a recipe, how she picked the arboretum for their weekend outing, the way she handled chaotic travel sites to plan their trip to Rome. He missed her affection—how she slid her arms around his chest and pressed a kiss to his ear. There was a hook in his heart that pulled him to her. She was everything he loved. And everything he had taken for granted.

Condemned. The notice nailed to the building still haunted him. *Condemned.* The missed meetings with contractors, unapproved sketches shoved into corners, and hollow words—*Next month, I promise. Condemned.* The divorce that ended his marriage and his career. *Condemned.* Their project. Stacy's dream.

He closed his eyes, trying to push past the ruin. He needed to find the man he had been before his life fell apart, when he had felt alive and had hopes, ambitions, and dreams. One night embodied this whole emotional package: the awards ceremony where he had met Stacy. He remembered the roller coaster of emotions—nerves at dinner, tense conversations, unexpected introductions, putting his foot in his mouth, and then ... their walk.

He replayed that night, searching for a piece of himself he had lost.

Staring at his distorted reflection in a thirty-foot-high glass panel in the two-story atrium of the New York Convention Center, Jared smoothed his rumpled brown hair that was longer on the top than the sides. His smile—the result of his parents shelling out a small fortune in orthodontia, and of him suffering through four brutal years of high school in braces—was as confident as ever. Behind his reflection, on the building's exterior, hung the massive American Institute of Architects banner, heralding the annual convention and awards ceremony. It swayed gently in the evening breeze coming off the water.

Jared felt a surge of gratitude for the discomfort and countless adjustments he had endured, knowing the insult-attracting wires that had once filled his mouth had given him a fabulous asset. He was ready to captivate and inspire his audience. After he glanced at his speech one last time, he slipped it into his pocket.

Taking a deep breath to calm his nerves, Jared turned slowly to appraise his surroundings. *Why do they always make convention centers look like this? All glass, modern and edgy, like something a second grader drew and considered cool.* But after winning this award... Jared imagined the headlines: "Daring Architect Ushers in New Era of Cool That Benefits the Environment." He heard the cheers and the cameras clicking at press conferences, congratulating him on changing the world.

He felt her hand on his shoulder before she spoke. It startled him out of his reverie, in which stars like Morgan Freeman shook his hand in gratitude.

"Enjoying the view?" she asked warmly.

Turning around, Jared gasped. She was stunning, the kind of stunning seen at a Hollywood awards ceremony, not at an architectural convention. The word "ethereal" came to mind—her skin luminous. Was that a trick of the light coming in from the city? Her gown was captivating, a designer, for sure. It was an empire-cut, creamy silk sheath, with gauzy mint-green layers cascading over it. The silver accents sparkled, drawing his eye.

"Oh, I'm sorry." She reached out with the grace of a ballerina to delicately touch his sleeve. "I didn't mean to alarm you," she apologized, her voice sincere.

Jared gawked for a moment. Her chocolate eyes held his while he tried to think of something—anything—coherent to say. "Oh... ah..." he mumbled, "You're fine. I came out to get some air and calm my nerves." He held up his hand momentarily, displaying his shakiness.

"Winning an award can do that," she said, her gaze attentive.

"Yes. My partner, Jeremy, and I won for Innovation in Design: Historical Site."

"Yes," she said, with a practiced smile. "The museum expansion. That was a work of art."

"Thank you," Jared replied. "I'm still in awe. Not only because I won the bid, but it turned out better than I had imagined."

"It is absolutely magnificent. How did you manage it?"

"Winning the bid? Well..." Jared explained that he couldn't let a once in a lifetime opportunity—building an addition onto a museum built by the Carnegies—pass him by. "Never mind that the ink hadn't even dried on our business license yet. I didn't care. This project deserved special care and attention, a dream come true from a design standpoint, so we intentionally underbid it, knowing the name recognition would more than make up for the losses we would suffer. But also, it was that important to me. And look, it made a name for us—boom—right out of the gate!" He paused. "I'm sorry. I'm rambling."

"It's okay. I'm interested. Tell me about some of the struggles you had with the project." She leaned closer to him and grazed his arm.

"You can't even imagine the crap we had to deal with," he began, thinking about which examples would be best to share.

"Oh, I can," she exhaled.

"I didn't know..." Jared stopped, remembering how they had gambled everything on this one project. "I hadn't anticipated how many hours I would spend chasing down impossible shit. For example, there was the stone flooring to match rock cut from a quarry that closed twenty years ago. Or finding a blacksmith to recreate the door pulls. A blacksmith? I mean, jeez, this isn't 1880!" He grinned. "I worked on this project twenty hours a day, while my partner, Jeremy, worked his financial magic to keep the lights on. But we did it."

She tilted her head, her smile softening. "I love a man who takes risks and follows his dreams."

Her words lit a fire. He felt that she understood him—the thrills and anxieties of allowing oneself to be vulnerable, while striving to achieve the impossible. He wondered who she was. Had she had similar success with challenging ventures? He imagined her as a visionary entrepreneur who had revolutionized sustainable energy and garnered international acclaim. Perhaps she was now looking for an architect to build the housing for her crowning accomplishment.

"I, for one, am grateful," she added. "God knows anyone else would have built a monstrosity like this." She gestured at the soulless atrium.

"That was my exact thinking as well. I was driven to win the contract."

"I'm so glad you did." Shifting her weight to her back foot, she sized him up. "What are your future plans? What's next for J&J Architects?"

"Next?" This was a loaded question. The truth was, he had been arguing with Jeremy about next. "To be honest," Jared began, but then noticed his partner rushing toward them, panic in his eyes. He pointed, saying, "My partner, Jeremy."

The woman turned to meet him, but Jeremy ignored her and said, "Sorry, will you excuse us for a moment?"

Not waiting for a response, Jeremy tugged Jared a few steps away. "You cannot give the speech we've prepared!" He dug into his pocket and handed Jared a new one. "Read this one instead."

"Why? What's wrong?" Jared asked. They had agreed that this moment would be used to address the unsustainability of the building industry and how it was destroying the planet. They designed the speech specifically to create controversy, hoping for extra press coverage, mainly to bolster their name, but also to propel the issue into the limelight to prompt a serious discussion.

"Look." Jeremy pointed to the woman to whom Jared had been talking. "She's wearing a genuine, one-of-a-kind Issey Miyake from Milan Fashion Week! That dress cost more than your Dodge. There are people here from Fortune 500 companies, and they didn't get there by trying to save the whales. If you give a speech about ethics and sustainability like a pompous prick to *this* roomful of people, we'll never work again."

"You're overreacting."

"I'm not. There's a CEO in there who is known for constructing buildings that are environmental disasters—polluting streams and ruining farmland. If you go up there and lecture, we're done."

"That's all the more reason for me to give the speech we've prepared."

"You don't understand. We can't pay next month's rent. We are broke. This acceptance speech has to win us a new contract, or this gamble was all for naught. We have to play it safe. You can give your sermon at the next awards ceremony."

"If there is a next ceremony."

Jeremy's eyes pleaded with Jared. "We will sink."

Rubbing his forehead, Jared sighed. He was surprised by Jeremy's sudden reversal—he'd never seen him panic before. Jared understood the stakes were high, and his speech would annoy many of the conservatives in the room. But would that really harm their chances at future contracts? The institute had recognized their work as the best. Still, there was the politics of business, a game his partner played too well.

Jeremy thrust the paper toward Jared.

Maybe Jeremy was right. They were on the brink of bankruptcy, and if he offended the one business here to hire them...

Jared grabbed the new speech and mumbled, "Sure. Okay."

"Thank you." Jeremy exhaled loudly and repeated, "Thank you."

The woman wearing the Issey Miyake approached the men and said, "They're ready to start. We should head in."

The staff had transformed the main conference room with soft lighting, circular tables draped in white linen, and a jazz quartet playing in the corner. Waitstaff moved between guests in suits and evening gowns, topping off wine glasses and removing dessert plates. Two projection screens flanked the stage, displaying photos of nominated projects. Jared took his seat as the host stepped onto the stage.

Forty-five minutes later, Jared approached the podium, his mouth dry, his nerves a wreck. *What to do?*

He placed Jeremy's speech in front of him, pressing his hands flat on top of the podium to keep them from shaking. He glanced at the crowd before starting. Angst gripped him. He didn't want to look back on this moment ten years from now and regret missing this chance to speak on what truly mattered to him. But he also didn't want to close the door on any business opportunities. Jeremy was trusting him to make the "right" decision—the one that resulted in money. The silence was uncomfortable. Sweat beaded on his forehead as he shifted his weight from one leg to the other.

With a thumbs up from Jeremy, Jared smiled and began the speech. Then he saw *her*. Regal. Poised. Angelic. He heard her voice in his mind: *I love a man who takes risks.* She was ready to be wowed. If he didn't deliver, he'd become another lost face sailing in the sea of safe choices. No! Take the risk, grab the reward.

"Oops. This is the kid-friendly speech." Jared removed his speech from his pocket and placed it on top of Jeremy's. "*This* speech will blow you away."

Jared saw his partner's horror-stricken face. He was mouthing, "Please, don't."

The enchanting princess straightened and adjusted her seat in anticipation.

Jared began. "Our industry designs settings for life. We mold the faces of communities, give hearts to cities, and determine how and where people interact. In a competitive atmosphere, we rush to build bolder, fresher, and jazzier places that grab attention. And in this mad frenzy to grow, we don't stop to think about the devastation we leave behind. We rape the land for the raw materials, polluting the air and the water. We disregard nature, build on floodplains, and fill in wetlands.

We bulldoze our history, disposing of valuable materials and destroying the stories and memories that define us..."

When Jared finished, the applause was minimal. He grabbed his award and left the room, feeling the complete fool. Reaching the staircase, he grasped the railing, dizzy and breathless; his heart spewed radioactive chemicals. He sat on a step and replayed the speech in his mind, wondering if his delivery had been off. The mood had shifted shortly after he began, and heard the gasps of disbelief as he shamed his colleagues for choosing their ego-driven visions over environmental considerations. He saw Jeremy bury his head in his hands and the beautiful woman staring at him, expressionless, assessing each word he spoke. Jeremy had warned him, and the lack of applause made it clear—he had made the wrong choice. Jeremy was going to kill him.

Leaning the award against the edge of the staircase, Jared placed his head in his hands, feeling sick. He had wanted to make a positive change, but ended up sabotaging his life's ambitions. His company would fail, and he would be stuck working for a boss, forced to be a yes-man in someone else's company, powerless.

"Fuck!" he shouted.

"May I join you?" came a woman's voice from behind him.

Jared turned to see ... her—*I love a man who takes risks.* Her upswept golden-brown hair framed her face. She was calm and bright, and her eyes held a hint of excitement. Did she love the speech? Jared stumbled to his feet, stammering, "H—Hi."

"That was unexpected." She moved a water bottle from her right hand to her left as she reached out and touched his shoulder. Her head tilted to one side, and her silver tiered earrings grazed her collarbone. Their eyes met, and she studied him.

She hated his speech. Pity had brought her here. Even she knew he was done. "I've likely been labeled the World's Most Ungrateful Architect. They'll never invite me back again," he said and gestured toward the conference room door behind her, periodic bursts of conversation escaping as people exited the event.

"I can think of several industries more destructive than ours: agriculture, energy, transportation."

"That guy's got a pair of balls. Where does he get off telling us how to run our business?"

"That speech was a masterclass in arrogance."

"No shit. He just won the 'Burn Every Bridge' award."

Jared returned his gaze to Stacy, shoulders sagging.

She disguised a wince as a smile. "It certainly was ... a moment," pausing before the last word, as though searching her vocabulary for something lacking negative connotation.

He bent over, putting his hands on his knees, feeling weak. "I think I'm going to pass out."

She handed him the water bottle. "Drink this."

Jared accepted it.

She smiled reassuringly before saying, "Look, I'm no life coach, but what you did in there..." she paused, considering her words. "You pointed out some unfortunate truths to a group of people who needed to hear it. Was there *maybe* a more delicate way to mention that the building industry was killing the planet and that these awards—how did you put it—'celebrated the never-ending stream of dump trucks to our overburdened landfills'? Yes. Undoubtedly. But it's true. We all know construction debris is the number one contributor to our landfills." She finished with a tentative smile. "And I can assure you, your life is not ruined." she gestured at the plaque and confidently said, "you will absolutely work again."

"Thank you. I needed to hear that. But I'm not sure I share your optimism." He sighed heavily, shoulders slumping. "I'm afraid Jeremy was right. Our career is over. You saw what happened."

She smiled empathetically. "I did. I also know some people in that room took note of what you said. You planted a seed. You used your platform—maybe not in the way you originally envisioned, but you did a good thing today. Who knows, maybe in twenty years, there will be an award celebrating sustainability. And your work speaks for itself. You didn't preach environmentalism, you practiced it. I know you reused absolutely everything you could on that project and sourced reclaimed materials to blend the new addition with the existing museum. That speaks volumes."

Jared took the first deep breath he'd taken in hours. "Right. Yes." He stood taller. "You're right," he went on, more to himself than to her. He held the high ground. Now was the time to double down. *Embrace positivity, keep pushing forward. Risks have paid off in the past.* "I've always taken chances. When I was a teenager, I put everything I made into a single stock. Everyone said I was crazy, but the returns covered for my tuition, books, and housing at university. And when

I cashed out, I used that money to put a down payment on the commercial space where J&J Architects was born." He smiled, his confidence returning. "I'm sure you're invested in the company, too. Stillen Corp."

She sucked in a breath and narrowed her eyes, as though attempting to keep her expression neutral.

"Anyway, I knew the museum expansion was going to be a huge risk, but I had to take it." He pointed at his plaque. "And it paid off."

"So, what made you care?" Stacy asked. "Most architects I've met aren't worried about landfills."

"My professor, Mr. Grothy," Jared answered without hesitation. "He lectured about the speed at which we are destroying our planet, and when I saw the devastation firsthand, I knew I had to say something. Tonight was that time. I needed to honor the protest that lives here," he said, poking his chest with his finger, "before it was beaten out of me."

He paused, gazing across the atrium at the knots of people in small circles, laughing and chatting. He caught Jeremy's glare, arms crossed, jaw tight. Jared exhaled and rubbed the side of his head.

"I had this hope, a dream really, that tonight was going to change my life. That this moment would open people's eyes to what the industry is destroying, but..." he sighed. "Well, who knows? You seem to understand."

She nodded with a knowing smile, "And on that note, I have—" a boisterous laugh filled the atrium and reverberated off the walls, cutting her off. "Shit," she mumbled under her breath as she looked down. "He's with me."

"You're with *him*?" Jared blinked and spied the man who had come out of the conference room and was laughing uproariously, holding court with a handful of people. He was old enough to be her father, with a full head of salt-and-pepper hair. His rotund belly, screaming of excess, was tightly framed by a suit that was clearly designer—perfectly tailored and reeking of old money. "Because ... of course you are."

She drew back. "Excuse me? What is that supposed to mean?"

Jared was startled. "I mean, you're wearing an Issey Miyake."

"And?" Her question burned.

"It's luxurious. Stunning."

"Wait! So because I'm a woman wearing an expensive dress, I'm obviously tied to an old rich guy?" Her face was tight, anger in her eyes.

Jared's mind raced to find an escape. He understood her disgust completely. "No. I didn't—I am so sorry. I know you're not arm candy or simply a luncheon lady." His face reddened. "May I offer a feeble explanation?"

"Please do. I'm all ears," she fumed.

"When you said you were with him, I—"

"I didn't say I was with him. I said, he was with me."

Understanding smacked Jared in the head. "Right. You did. Of course he is. I see that now."

She narrowed her eyes. "What are you playing at?"

"Look at him. He's clearly not an architect and probably knows little or nothing about the industry. The only reason he would be here is if someone dragged him here."

Her mouth dropped open. "Huh?" she rolled her eyes with a shake of her head.

He cringed, her reaction stinging. "*You* are clearly knowledgeable and obviously enjoy being here. I'm guessing you are business partners?" he speculated. "And your company is looking for a new architecture firm?" That sounded right. That made sense.

She tapped her foot and pursed her lips.

"My small brain was so occupied with my colossal downfall that when you made the comment that he was with you, an image, force fed to me by the media, flashed in my mind. That man," Jared flung his hand as if tossing an apple core to the side of the road, "is so disruptive, I was shocked. I know that a young, beautiful woman with money doesn't need to be tied to a rich guy. I was wrong to think that. I'm really, really sorry."

"I liked you a lot more before you opened your mouth."

Jared rubbed his temples while closing his eyes briefly to think. There was no recovery. Extending his hand, he gave her his best puppy face. "Can we start over?" he pleaded. "Hi, I'm Jared Davenport. Nice to meet you."

With a stern stare, she replied, "Wait one moment." Turning her back to him, she took a deep breath. Facing him again, she was all business, expressionless. "Anastasia Stillen. You may call me Stacy. The pleasure is all mine."

Jared froze, and his face turned white. This was none other than THE Anastasia Stillen, architect and voting member for the AIA awards.

Stacy's face brightened. Crossing her arms, she smirked with a subtle shake of her head. Stepping aside, she said, "I would like to introduce you to my father,

William Montgomery Stillen of Stillen Corp. He goes by Bill." She gestured to the big, bellowing beast.

Jared's eyes doubled in size. He looked at Bill, back at Stacy, and at Bill again. *That man*, Jared recalled himself saying. Stacy must think he was a complete ass. Torn between being star-struck and completely embarrassed, Jared wasn't sure how to respond.

Stacy called, "Bill, come meet Jared Davenport."

A booming, confident voice, just short of a bellow, called out, "Jared Davenport! If it isn't the man of the hour!" Bill made a beeline for him and extended his hand. "I'm a big admirer of your work, young man. What you did in there?" He let out a full-body laugh, his head tipping back. "Woohoo, you know how to ruffle some feathers!" Mr. Stillen took a firm hold of Jared's hand and shook it, meeting his eyes and holding them for a moment too long.

A pulse of sensation crept up Jared's arm as he shook Bill's hand. Pressure, awe, nerves, sent his heart racing. "It's an honor, Mr. Stillen," he managed, still reeling.

"Such a pleasure to meet a real changemaker like yourself. You know, I couldn't let an opportunity to meet you pass me up. Whenever I see a gem, I have to seize it. You know what I mean? That's the kind of man I am!" He laughed, apparently amused with himself, finally releasing his hand.

"I believe I do," Jared squeaked.

"I'm sure Stacy told you all about the plan. Expect my secretary to call your office to set up a time for you to meet the whole team. Nothing formal, just a little sit-down dinner at my place to get acquainted. I want to make sure you're a good fit," he said, smiling with encouragement. "The VP of real estate and the VP of acquisitions will be there." Grabbing Jared by the shoulder, Bill pulled him in closer and lowered his voice, "Between you and me, I need someone like you on the team. I'm surrounded by ass-kissers who keep getting me into hot water—how was I supposed to know the land we bought for that factory was an orphanage? The press ate me alive for that gaffe."

Patting Jared on the back, he returned to his boisterous self, looking around the room, making sure he had everyone's attention. "Your ethics talk in there about doing something good for the planet really spoke to me. Your vision is exactly what Stillen Corp needs." Turning to his daughter, Bill shouted, "Anastasia, darling!"

Stacy nodded regally.

"It's all settled then, sweetie. Great find in this kid! You really did your homework and brought us someone worth our time."

Stacy smiled demurely. "Bill, you have an appointment with Major General Cros this evening to discuss Extended Life," she said.

"Right! Right! Yes, this one is always keeping me pointed in the right direction. Call the car for me, please." Putting his hand on Jared's shoulder again, Bill leaned in close. "If I get this defense contract, you are going to be a very busy man. You might want to start thinking about expanding. I have a feeling you're going to need help. Biotech is the future."

As Bill stepped away, he added in his booming voice, "I look forward to doing business with you, Jared." Then he was off, glad-handing the circle of admirers who had been milling around.

Stacy stepped toward Jared.

"So..." he started tentatively. His world had shifted and turned so many times this evening, he was feeling shaken. "To recap: you are Anastasia Stillen, architect, voting member for AIA awards, daughter and personal assistant to Bill Stillen, and you headhunted me for your company."

"I think the word you're looking for is scouted—as in, I scouted your firm."

"I feel like your dad was under the assumption we had discussed details. Perhaps I could buy you some ice cream as an apology, and you could bring me up to speed."

With a warm smile, she said, "I know the perfect spot. It's only a few blocks away." She linked her arm with Jared's. "Shall we walk?"

They crossed over onto the Empire State Trail that followed the shoreline of the Hudson River. The restless city hummed with noise and motion, filling Jared with the thrill of New York. Passing the Hudson Yards skyscraper and Chelsea Piers, they made their way into the park, which offered a calm respite from the rush of traffic. During their stroll, Stacy informed Jared of all the missteps (atrocities) Stillen Corp had committed in the name of share value and the almighty dollar—little things involving child labor and a series of environmental disasters.

"I've taken the helm and am determined to transform Stillen Corp," Stacy asserted. "I need people who are committed to working honestly, with consideration for human dignity and the environment, without compromising the overall quality of the projects. That's how I found J&J."

Jared listened, noting Stacy's passion and finding himself admiring her even more. "So my role is not only that of an architect, but also a touchstone for keeping the company from further PR disasters."

"And shifting karmic balance," Stacy joked.

They reached the ice cream parlor, the warm smell of fresh waffle cones spilling from the building. Jared paid for their pistachio ice cream, and they slid into a booth next to the window. Stacy scraped the softening ice cream along the edge of her bowl and took a bite.

"I want you to understand why I am so determined in transforming Stillen Corp," she said, her spoon hovering over her ice cream. "It's not about correcting past mistakes or preventing future disasters—it's about improving people's lives."

She told him how her dad had a tendency to view people as a numbers problem. To think that business was all about production and profit. "But life is more than that. I believe creating emotional bonds fosters trust, loyalty, and commitment, and I know that starts with the architect."

Jared's gaze was locked on Stacy. Her words, her conviction, her humanity—they struck a chord in him. He leaned forward, nodding. "I couldn't agree more."

"I've seen the toll greed takes," she continued. "Workers who feel undervalued, communities that suffer from negligence and corruption. It's painful. Your work shows a deep respect for both people and the planet, and that's exactly why I need you."

"Thank you," Jared replied. "I can help you create spaces that uplift and inspire."

"Yes, that's it. Functional doesn't mean drab and lifeless." She leaned forward, her spoon still in hand, gesturing like a professor making a final point. "Just so we're clear. You are preserving and repurposing the buildings we acquire. Your designs will minimize environmental impact. And we build for people—workers, neighbors, communities. Nothing about this contract is going to be easy."

"I'm with you," Jared said. "Let's create something amazing."

Stacy leaned back, studying Jared for a moment. A smile crossed her lips. Then, with a nod, she reached over and took his hand. "I want to show you my favorite building."

Jared glanced at her hand in his, her touch sparking a rush of adrenaline that sent his heart racing. "Okay," he mumbled, nodding like a little kid accepting candy.

She called for the car, but instead of driving them to the airport to fly to Paris or Rome, it took them to a depressed section of the city. They stopped in front of an older, run-down building.

She rolled down the window, the breeze catching her scent—warm, like sun on stone with a touch of rose—and wafting it gently through the car. "Here," she said, delight brightening her face. "I know it doesn't look like much, but I have big plans."

It was a simple mixed-use building, constructed pre-Civil War, with commercial space on the ground floor and three stories of residential space above. It wasn't necessarily unique—there were buildings like it in every town across America, many with former lives as general stores or post offices where the owners lived above their workplace—the commute enviable.

"Do you see it?" she asked, searching his eyes.

Jared scanned the building. If ever a structure could speak, this one did. *My weathered walls wait for eager hands of renovation*, it seemed to say.

"Of course," Jared replied, "but tell me what you see, and we'll share it together."

Her smile spread across her face, and she pointed. "The old hitching posts are mounted directly into the brick." She paused, assessing his expression.

Recognition dawned in his eyes as he realized she had seen something he hadn't.

"This is where Alexander M. Grieg started the City Despatch Post in 1842. He created the first adhesive stamps issued in the United States. Ellen Stillen, my great-grandfather's mother, worked at this very store. The business was so successful, the government bought the post and kept Grieg and his team on as agents."

An image glided through Jared's mind—Stacy in a taupe floral gown with an apron. The two of them loaded boxes of letters into a wagon and then unhitched the horses from those posts to send their deliveries off.

"I see it," he whispered and added, "Most of these old buildings are razed and thrown in a landfill."

"All of the history lost in the name of progress," Stacy bit. "But not this one. This one is mine." Her voice filled with enthusiasm. "I'm going to bring this piece of history back to life—a tiny museum next to an architectural office on the ground floor and my home above."

"It's going to need new pipes," Jared said. "The current ones are probably lead."

Stacy agreed. "And new wiring. It's still a knob-and-tube. And the flooring is going to need patching with new hand-milled boards to match the existing floor."

"Those remained intact? That's a miracle."

"Remarkably intact. Also, we'll need to do some patching to the lathe and plaster. Do you know a good plasterer?"

We? Jared's heart stirred.

"Did you meet anyone while doing the museum project?" she asked.

"Yes." He looked into her eyes.

She matched his stare.

"We'll need to meet seismic code," Jared said.

"Then let's come up with a plan to retrofit the building that keeps as much of it intact as possible."

"I have a feeling you have an idea about how to do that already," Jared chuckled.

"An idea, yes. But I would like your help making that plan a reality. Are you ready for us to take on this project?"

Us. He was thrilled.

"I believe *we* can take on this challenge."

She beamed. "I look forward to it."

Jared's phone rang, the guitar strum informing him his brother Tim was calling. Answering, he failed to sound normal. "Hey, Tim, what's up?"

"Did I wake you?"

"No, just a rough day."

"Want to talk about it?"

Jared grunted. "It's stupid. Leah starts receiving her trust fund payments after she graduates."

"And you're kicking yourself. This wouldn't feel like such a punch in the gut if you had moved on and started dating. You have to get out there."

"I know," Jared responded uncertainly.

"Great! I have the perfect woman for you."

Jared groaned, "No. Please, no."

"The lady who hired me to remodel her kitchen is single. Let me introduce you."

"I'm not ready."

"Come on, bro. She's an artist and a damn good one, too."

Jared didn't know how to respond. The idea made him anxious. "I'm going to pass."

"Just meet her. I need your help moving the appliances anyway. What are you doing Monday?"

"I'm working," Jared replied.

"I thought you had Mondays off."

"I usually do, but we're short a few guys and I'm starting a new route, so they asked me to work extra this week. But I might be able to help you in the evening."

"Can you be there before five?"

Jared paused. A new route meant meeting new people and navigating unfamiliar delivery points. His first week would involve driving back and forth as he fine-tuned the optimal sequencing. Businesses had designated areas for picking up and dropping off packages, with specific time windows for each. It would take him time to find hidden houses and addresses that didn't match the city formatting. Then there were the lengthy driveways to traverse. He needed to assess each one for safe turnaround spots. Calculating the extra time needed, he answered, "Probably not. Six-thirty or seven is safer."

"You couldn't start your day earlier, finish before then? She wants me out of the house by seven."

Jared hesitated. This was his one escape, but he didn't want to leave his brother in a bind. "Sure. Monday routes are business-heavy, but this new one's mostly residential. I might be able to make it by five."

"Why don't you call me Monday morning and let me know."

"All right."

"Cool. And hey, you are going to love this lady. She's attractive and funny, so try to smile." Then Tim added as if he almost forgot, "And get a haircut. You look like a bum."

"Are you still coming to dinner Friday?" Jared asked.

"Yeah. Patty's ladies' night is still on, so I'll be there. Beetlejuice is the next movie on our list?"

"I think so. I'll have to ask Leah."

"All right, bro. See you Friday," Tim hung up.

Jared sat still, the phone resting in his hand. He thought about Tim and meeting this new woman. Something about smiling across a table at someone, pretending he was interested, didn't feel right.

What would the Jared of old do—the one who bet everything on his visions?

Leaning forward, he rested his elbows on his knees and held his phone in both hands. His thumbs played with the contact list, moving the names up and down. Stacy's number appeared, along with an image of the building and the guilt tied to it. He hadn't apologized. Not really. He'd given her a bunch of excuses, but never a real apology.

Chewing on the inside of his lip, Jared inhaled slowly. He needed to say it. *I'm sorry.* He had to let go of this guilt. With a final nod, he hit the call button.

Stacy's voice, firm and deliberate came through the speaker. "Hello?"

"Hey. It's me," Jared said.

"Is everything okay? Is Leah—"

"She's fine," Jared responded. "I'm calling because I got a letter today about Leah's trust fund."

"Okay," Stacy said. "Any news from Stanford?"

"Not yet, but Columbia's still on the table."

"Columbia? Sure, it's on the table. Just not *her* table." Stacy chuckled. "Jared, you still haven't changed."

"I have," he insisted.

"Have you?" she shot back. "If you'd been listening, you'd know Columbia's not what she wants. *You* want her to go there, because it's here in New York. Look, I have a meeting to attend, so—"

"Wait," Jared blurted. "I wanted to talk to you about Leah. Prom's next month and then graduation. I thought ... maybe you'd want to be here for those."

"Of course I'll be there."

21

"Right," he said, hesitating.

"Were you planning something special that I need to know about?"

"No." He took a breath. "The real reason I called ... is to apologize. About the building."

"Jared—"

"I know I messed up," he interjected. "That place was your dream, and I failed you. I'm so, so sorry."

"The building?" Stacy's pitch rose. "Jared, I can summarize our entire marriage in one afternoon, Leah's tenth birthday. The three of us were together, but you were glued to your phone, texting, emailing, working." She gave a tired sigh. "I'm not having this conversation again. Take care of yourself, okay?"

The line went dead.

Jared stared at the phone, then set it on the coffee table. He'd said what he needed to. Holding on to that guilt hadn't done him any favors.

Stacy... He shook his head, scattering his thoughts. Thinking about her wasn't doing him any favors either. Picking up the remote, he turned on the television and leaned back to forget.

The Cold Case

In the police station downtown, Detective Brandon Spencer of the Lake Valley Police Department worked at his desk. It was his designated night to stay late until the overnight detective arrived at eleven. With the night officers out on patrol and the phones quiet, the only sound in the room was Brandon's rhythmic click-clacking at the keyboard as he entered witness statements into the database for the Mitchell case.

Pausing momentarily, Brandon ran his fingers through his curly black hair and stretched. His notes were strewn about his desk, and he took a moment to regroup as he reorganized and reviewed each one.

The case involved Stephanie Mitchell, a twenty-year-old who had called her mother to get a ride home from her friend's house. Her mother, Monica Mitchell, arrived at the friend's house, only to learn her daughter wasn't there; Stephanie had already left.

Sifting through his notes, Brandon remembered Stephanie's nervousness—her constant fidgeting. When he asked why she left before her mother arrived, she first said the movie they had been watching was boring. Later, she changed her statement, claiming her ex-boyfriend had showed up.

Brandon felt skeptical about Stephanie's explanations and found her interaction with her mother that night peculiar.

Monica had driven around the neighborhood and eventually spotted her daughter walking alone along the street. When she pulled over, they began to argue. Witnesses had seen Monica grabbing Stephanie and trying to pull her toward the car. She later claimed she was simply trying to protect her daughter. Stephanie said she couldn't remember what the argument had been about.

Brandon rubbed his chin. He wished he knew why they had fought, because he was stumped by Stephanie's behavior. She had called her mom to come, so why hadn't she waited or simply gotten in the car when Monica found her?

Picking up another note, Brandon winced. Monica's bloody, broken body appeared in his mind. She had been arguing with her daughter when a guy on a motorcycle rode up and viciously attacked them. The daughter had sustained a cut on her lip, while the mother had suffered multiple broken bones.

Brandon pressed his palms to his forehead, trying to release the vision of her in the hospital. He shook his head and grabbed the next set of notes.

Both women had accused a man named Dimitri, alleging he attacked them in retaliation for refusing to star in one of his sex films.

But Brandon had doubts. The injuries she sustained told a different story. He picked up two notes, reading the eye-witness accounts.

Witness 1: "No. He came at her screaming mad. Called her a two-timing bitch, yelling something about his house. And just beat the shit out of her."

Witness 2: "He was pissed, yelling, 'You stole it from me.' Just pounding on her."

The witness statements seemed to suggest the attacker and Monica were possibly dating.

When Brandon visited Dimitri, the first thing he noticed was his red sweater. Given that the CSI team had collected red fibers and DNA at the crime scene, Brandon took a few fibers from Dimitri's sweater to compare them. Dimitri's sickly figure and soft hands, however, told Brandon he probably wasn't the attacker.

Dimitri was visibly shaken. Initially, he denied knowing Monica. Then he admitted they had met. Finally, he conceded they were acquainted but mentioned he hadn't seen her in several weeks. As for the attack, he claimed to have been home all night, having two witnesses—his sister and his friend.

However, neither the sister nor the friend could be found—the sister, Alysia, being a drug addict, and the friend, Spud, having an outstanding warrant for his arrest. Brandon emphasized that it was in Dimitri's best interest for his alibis to contact him.

The final blow to the Mitchells' credibility had been a boy who had seen Stephanie's broken lip before the attack. This contradicted Stephanie and Monica's claims that the motorcyclist had attacked Stephanie.

Brandon rose from his chair and paced the room. He believed both the mother and daughter were hiding something. But why? His initial guess was that the daughter had been sexually assaulted before calling her mother and that the man attacked the mother to ensure their silence. Were they hiding the truth because they feared further acts of violence if they didn't? But the words "two-timing bitch" and "you stole it from me" gave Brandon pause. There was more history behind this attack.

Brandon needed to talk with Stephanie again, but not until he verified a few details first: namely, had she actually been at her friend's house?

Finally—a case that demanded real detective work. Brandon felt relieved and a little excited. As a rookie, all the cases that came his way were straightforward: person A did something to person B, like a robbery or vandalism. He would document the damage and injuries, collect statements and evidence, make an arrest, write the reports, and send it to the prosecutors.

The Mitchell case initially appeared to be the same: a simple case of battery. But it had turned into a complex mystery. This investigation would showcase his abilities and, hopefully, earn him some respect.

Due to his previous career as an elementary school teacher, the other officers saw Brandon as naive. Despite that perception, he remained confident that his experiences living in foreign countries had equipped him with an advantage in understanding people. He was determined to let that knowledge shine through in his work and demonstrate his ability to tackle tougher challenges. Could he finally earn the dignity his peers had yet to afford him?

Returning to his work area, he pressed his lips together and shook his head. A *Kindergarten Cop* poster had been taped to the front of his desk. As the newest member of the force, he endured constant teasing from the other detectives, like the small plastic barrettes that he had pushed aside when he found them littering his desktop. Was he still in elementary school? This was ... childish. He rolled a pink one with a yellow butterfly on it around in his fingers, a slight ache developing in his chest. Putting the barrette in the palm of his hand, he squeezed it, taking several deep breaths. This particular prank hurt. But he reminded himself: *they don't know what happened.*

Rubbing his temples, he recited, "I am here. I am now. I am enough. Let the past go." He suppressed the burning emotion in his chest and buried it deep down. Depositing the barrettes in the top left drawer of his desk, where thirty or more he had already thrown, he sat down at his computer.

The phone rang, startling him.

"This is Detective Brandon Spencer. How may I help you?" He rested the phone on his shoulder and continued typing the report.

"Detective, this is Dr. Nathanial Jackson at Sunnyside Psychiatric Hospital. We have a patient named Tyler Jiles. Do you know him? Are you familiar with his case or his situation?"

"Good evening, doctor. I'm not aware of a Tyler Jiles. No."

"Tyler's case is connected to Nong Ekamai's and Amanda Bowman's cases. All three of them are believed to have been abducted. Does that sound familiar to you?" the doctor asked.

Abducted? That caught Brandon's attention. "I'm sorry, doctor. It doesn't."

"Tyler has been with us for the past four years, suffering from a condition known as unresponsive wakefulness syndrome. It means that he is living inside his own head. He's unable to communicate or care for himself. He needs someone to feed him, walk with him, and meet all his other basic care requirements. We believe this condition was caused by the trauma suffered from the abduction."

Dr. Jackson cleared his throat. "Tyler has emerged or regained consciousness and would like to talk with a detective. Can you transfer me to someone familiar with his case?"

"I'm sorry. I'm the only one here. I'll have someone contact you. Let me get your name and number." On a notepad, Brandon documented the information.

The doctor continued, "Tyler's been awake for about three hours. I've been with him, and we've talked. He's confused and asking questions. Would you be willing to talk with him? He needs reassurance that someone will help. I need to reduce his anxiety. His mind is fragile."

"Sure, I understand."

"Perfect. One moment."

Brandon logged into the police files database as he waited for Tyler to pick up.

"Hi. Can you tell me what the hell's going on?" Tyler's voice was clouded by confusion, stinging with urgency.

"Yes, but let me start with your name. I am recording this conversation." He clicked the record button on the computer.

"Okay. I'm Tyler K. Jiles."

"J-I-L-E-S?" Brandon questioned.

"Yes."

Brandon typed "Jiles, Tyler" into the search bar.

"Good evening, Tyler," he said, waiting for the results. "I'm Detective Brandon Spencer with the Lake Valley Police Department. Can you tell me where you are right now?"

"I'm at the Sunnyside Psychiatric Hospital," Tyler said.

Tyler's file popped up on the computer and Brandon clicked on the icon. "And who is with you?" he asked.

"Dr. Jackson."

"Great. Thank you, Tyler. What has the doctor told you so far?"

A strained moan came through the line. "He's been telling me about the last seven years." There was a pause. "Apparently, I was kidnapped and then in some kind of coma."

As Tyler spoke, Brandon skimmed the information on the computer screen. Every detail lined up. Tyler had been abducted and missing for three years. A parent discovered him in the parking lot of an office building in a vegetative state. For the past four years, he had been at Sunnyside Psychiatric Hospital, living in this vegetative state. Tyler's file referenced two other cases believed to be linked to his. The first case was Ms. Amanda Bowman, and the second was Ms. Nong Ekamai.

"The last thing I clearly remember," Tyler continued, "was talking to a lawyer about the possibility of bankruptcy. I have other memories, but they aren't clear. Not like a dream I can't remember, but like there's something on the tip of my tongue."

"And physically? How are you feeling?" Brandon asked, jotting down Nong Ekamai's and Amanda Bowman's names and case numbers.

"I... It feels like I'm stuck in a thick fog. My memories are barely visible. Anyway, I would like to know about my case."

"I understand, Tyler. We can have someone see you tomorrow morning."

"Tomorrow?" Tyler gasped. "No, please, not tomorrow. My head hurts. I only needed to know someone was working on my case. Give me a few days before we meet."

"I believe we can work out a schedule with Dr. Jackson if that's okay with you."

"Yes, please," Tyler said. "Thank you. Here's the doctor."

The line went quiet, and Brandon returned to the search bar, typing "Bowman, Amanda."

Dr. Jackson came back on the line. "Hello, detective. Can you come Monday morning? In the meantime, we'll take Tyler to Northside Medical Hospital and run some tests, work with him on regaining some memories, and have his family visit."

"I'll inform the captain, and we'll have a detective there first thing Monday morning. Have a good evening, doctor."

"Thank you. Good evening." Dr. Jackson hung up.

Brandon read through Amanda's file. She had been the first one abducted, two years prior to Tyler. She had turned up the same day Tyler had gone missing and in the same vegetative state. Amanda eventually regained consciousness. However, she had no memories of what had happened to her or where she had been.

Nong's case remained unresolved. Four years before, she had gone missing the day Tyler had been found. The police suspected the same person who took Amanda and Tyler had taken Nong, making this a serial case. The FBI had taken control, creating a task force to find Nong and catch the abductor. They failed and labeled the file a cold case.

Brandon went to the storage room and found four boxes of documents and information on Nong's case. He flipped through interview notes and official statements from people close to Nong. No one had requested money. It didn't look like a sexual obsession. Sitting down, he thought, *This is a lot of information.* A challenge worthy of a true detective. Tyler might know something that would help find Nong and catch this elusive abductor. Brandon wanted this case.

Something's Wrong

Leah Davenport parked in front of Barb's house and turned off the car. She flipped down the visor and opened the mirror, checking her hair and makeup. After taking a deep breath, she got out of the car, hoping Barb's brother, Dan, was home.

Leah had met Barb last November while volunteering with the school play. Barb often worked on the stage sets, listening to *Phantom of the Opera* or *Into the Woods*. After rehearsals, they would walk to the parking lot together, singing their favorite show tunes from *Les Misérables, Cats,* and *The Book of Mormon*. For Christmas, Leah received two tickets to see *Phantom* at the Majestic Theater on Broadway and invited Barb to go with her. Leah's mom flew them to New York, and they stayed at her apartment for the week. Exploring the city, they had gotten lost on the green line, ate coal-fired pizza at Grimaldi's—crispy, crunchy, oh so good—and gave the leftovers to a homeless man living under a bridge. They'd also visited a convenience store at three in the morning to buy powdered donut holes, popcorn, and ice cream sandwiches. Relying on each other in a crazy city made them best friends. But Leah still had so many questions she wanted to know. Had Barb dated? What did her tattoo mean and why did she get it? It was an infinity symbol with a heart and butterfly between her collarbone and her breast. The biggest question she had, though, was how did her parents die? It was the subject Barb avoided most.

Leah knocked, and her heart skipped a beat when Dan opened the door. Her cheeks flushed. "Hi."

Opening the door wider, Dan said, "Hi, come in. Barb's showering. She'll be out in a bit."

"That's okay. I'm in a bit of a hurry. I stopped to grab a book. Barb said it was next to the door."

Dan reached over and pulled *The Girl with Seven Names* off the table. He handed it to her, saying, "Barb said she has a newfound respect for the South Korean government after reading this one."

Studying his hands, Leah saw the strength they conveyed. She longed to feel them wrapped around her body. Taking the book, she explained, "It's on the list for our world literature class."

Dan nodded. "I'd be interested in reading it. The three of us could discuss it then. I could help you put together your presentation."

Leah was captivated by his light-brown eyes. Their warmth welcomed her, and their clarity was so vivid she could make out every detail—the clear, brilliant white framing the dark rings circling irises flecked with amber. The shimmer entranced her.

"You..." she murmured, unaware she had spoken.

"I..." Dan said, drawing the word out, giving her time to finish the sentence. Leah blinked, realizing she had lost herself.

"...am such a great guy for helping you?" Dan finished playfully.

Leah shook her head. "No, you have your own schoolwork."

"I have time. It'd be fun. I'd love to help you."

Looking down, Leah nodded. "Okay," she said and pulled at a strand of hair.

After a long, awkward pause, Dan broke the silence, "Are you sure you don't want to come in? I can get you something to drink."

Leah took a step back. "Sorry. I have a doctor's appointment, and I'm taking my dad out."

"Ah."

Leah half-turned and then stopped. "Umm. Are you ... free tomorrow?" she asked, looking back at him.

"Tomorrow evening? Yeah."

Leah twirled her hair around her finger. "My dad is going to be working late. I was thinking about ordering pizza for dinner. Do you guys want to come over?"

"Yeah."

"Cool. I'll call Barb and set it up," she said. Walking back to the car, Leah glanced behind her. He was watching her. She grinned and waved.

Driving home, she groaned, gripping the leather steering wheel. Man, was he handsome!

Dan was two years older. He attended community college and worked at the movie theater. He played baseball and wrestled. He was tall and muscular, with wavy brown hair. His eyes held knowledge and experiences that mystified her. The pain behind them was like a light drawing her in. She had to force herself not to stare at him when he hung out with her and Barb, the pull like a car out of alignment.

Turning up the volume on her car radio, she sang along with the Righteous Brothers to "Unchained Melody." She rolled down the windows, allowing the words to escape, letting the world know exactly how she felt—she hungered for his touch and his love.

As she pulled into the drive, Leah felt the familiar pinch of guilt—the same guilt whenever she saw her father's older model Honda Civic. She drove an Audi S7 luxury Sportback that her grandfather Bill had given her for her sixteenth birthday. However, the guilt left as fast as it had come, as always. She parked in the garage and entered the house through the kitchen door. Her dad sat on the sofa in his work clothes, having fallen asleep watching TV.

The television was loud; Father Joseph was soliciting funds with his famous line, "I fight the devil."

Leah scoffed at the idea that anyone would send Father Joseph money. She found the remote and pushed the power button. Her dad didn't care for this priest either.

Setting the remote on the arm of the sofa, Leah stared at her dad. She cupped her hands, covering her mouth and nose as she breathed deeply. What was she going to do with her father? She couldn't shake the futility that washed over her. Her dad was struggling, and she didn't know how to help him.

Leah had called her Uncle Tim about it; he believed her dad needed to start dating.

Sitting on the edge of the coffee table, Leah contemplated her father. The first time he had fallen asleep on the sofa in his work clothes was when Mom had sent him divorce papers. Then there was the time Uncle Tim had laid him off. And the time he was depressed because he hadn't received any interview requests from architectural firms. The time he had re-applied for insurance coverage to open his own firm, only to be denied. Time and time again, she had sat with him, hugged him, and encouraged him. How long was he going to continue being like this? She loved her dad, but coddling him like a little boy was ridiculous. Had agreeing to another year as a delivery driver really been this depressing? Whatever it was, she needed to knock him out of this funk. With a momentary flare of anger, she shook her father's shoulder.

"Dad, wake up. What happened?" she asked, her voice harsh.

Jared stretched and gave Leah a warm grin, accompanied by a longing stare. "Welcome home."

Leah had seen that look before. It was usually followed by, "You have so much of your mother in you—her golden-brown hair and chocolate eyes." He'd gush about her being "outgoing, athletic, and a straight-A student" saying, "How did I get so lucky? My boss can't believe how confident and independent you are." She didn't want to hear it again. She needed him to wake up, both figuratively and literally.

"What's wrong?" she pressed.

"Nothing," he answered sleepily.

"I know something's wrong. Tell me."

"Nothing's wrong, really." He pointed to the mail on the coffee table. "Your trust fund payments will start soon."

A burst of excitement filled her. "Oh, yay." She grabbed the letter and opened it. Her eyes widened as she read. "Fifteen hundred a month plus rent. Awesome!" She kept reading. "Okay. Cool. I hope I get into Stanford." She was thinking about majoring in cognitive science. She was fascinated by the differences in personalities between the members of her family. Her mom was sure and quick, while her dad was introspective and creative. Her grandfathers were polar opposites: Bill being so proud and Jim being so humble. In particular, she was curious about the interplay between nature versus nurture. The whole situation with the divorce made her wonder how the brain perceived and processed information. No matter how things played out, she envisioned herself working with her mom. Of course, she also had the option of joining her grandfather's company in the marketing department.

Looking back at her dad, she questioned, "Were you upset about this?"

"I wasn't upset. Only reliving mistakes."

Leah's gaze softened as she studied her father. She saw him now, not just as a parent, but as a man burdened by regrets. The divorce haunted him, and she had a feeling he hoped her mom would magically return and they'd be a family again. She reached out, squeezing his hand. "It wasn't your fault. Mom made the choice that was best for her." As she recited those words, she was twelve again, hearing them flow from her father's lips as his loving blue eyes embraced her. "I know you still have this idea of us being a family, but that idea is dead for Mom. She followed her dreams and created a life she loves for herself. You need to do the same."

Jared lowered his head. "I know," he said, with all the energy of a sloth.

Her dad's crestfallen face gave her a sting of frustration. He had been so strong and confident, so bold and outgoing. Add that to the fact that he had asked her to do what he still wasn't able or willing to do, and... she snapped, "I can't believe you're acting this way. I mean, you were the one telling me this stuff years ago. What's going on with you?"

Jared shrunk into the sofa, casting his eyes down in shame.

"Will you tell me already? I've heard the whole story from Mom's point of view," Leah said. "Why are you so hard on yourself when we talk about Mom? Tell me."

Scratching his head, he brushed his hair behind his ear and rested his chin in the palm of his hand. He sighed.

"So dramatic," Leah said, widening her eyes.

Lifting his head, he straightened. After taking a giant deep breath and blowing it out, he asked, "Do you know what your mom's original dream was?"

Leah tilted her head with a quizzical look. "Yeeaaah," she said, drawing the word out. "Horses."

"No, I mean her first dream."

"I'm eighteen, not eight. She's loved horses since she was a little girl."

"Oh," he mumbled.

Leah saw the revelation in his eyes. *Maybe Mom was right. He didn't know.*

"Did she tell you about the dream she had for us?" Jared asked.

Leah searched her memory. She shrugged when nothing came to her. "No."

Jared swallowed hard. "There was a building your mom wanted. We were going to live on the upper levels, and she was going to start her own business on the ground floor. We had planned to renovate it together, but I kept putting it off, delaying the project until the building was condemned and torn down."

Leah was confused. "The historical one in New York City? With the hitching posts built into the brick? The city had condemned it, but she rescued it. She submitted her plans and a timetable, and her friends in the city allowed her to proceed. It's gorgeous!"

Jared froze, his face contorted in a Picasso of perplexity. "Wha...What? Really?"

Leah jerked her head back, blinking. *Seriously?* How could he be stunned by this news?

"I don't believe it." Jared inhaled sharply. "Why didn't she tell me? I thought she joined the circus."

"She did, kind of. She owns a horse farm outside New York and trains them to perform. She also owns that building and has an apartment there. She rents the other two units and owns the architectural office below. How could you not know that?"

"Owns a farm? Really?" He sat looking dumbfounded.

Leah felt like slapping him. He couldn't be this out of touch.

"Well, I guess I knew about the farm. But she's always traveling."

"She's managing multiple companies. You can't tell me you didn't know about her New York office."

Jared opened his mouth to speak, but paused. "I... How could I know? She refused to talk about it after the building was condemned. Kept saying I didn't need to be concerned."

"It was in the divorce agreement."

"I didn't read that agreement. We had a prenup, so I blindly signed."

"But still. I'm sure I told you about it. I stay there every time I'm in New York."

Jared leaned forward and placed both hands on the back of his head. "The whole reason for our divorce was that building." Running his hands over his head and down his face, he straightened. Exhaling, he wondered out loud, "She saved it?" He stared at the ceiling before resting his forehead in the palm of his hands, his elbows on his knees. "So why did we get a divorce? I don't get it."

Leah's eyes softened. "Probably because you're clueless."

He shook his head, grimacing. "I'm finding that out."

"Anyway, she's constantly traveling because she's running between the farm, the office, different circus troupes, and competitions."

"That explains why she's so short with me."

Leah shook her head, her voice tender. "Has the building in New York been bothering you this whole time?" Sitting down next to him, she rubbed his back. "I know things haven't been easy for you lately, but, Dad, you have to open up and talk to me. I'm here for you."

Jared's eyes flickered, a mixture of gratitude and sadness. "Thanks, sweetheart."

Leah smiled. Then she turned up her nose and abruptly added, "You smell like boxes. Go take a shower ... and shave. After my doctor's appointment, I'm taking you to get a haircut."

As Jared showered, Leah called Rote's Barber Shop and explained her father's haircut needs to Bob. He commented that Jared was long overdue and squeezed his appointment in as his last client.

At the doctor's office, Jared sat in the waiting area while Leah went into the examination room. The nurse explained that this would be Leah's last visit with Dr. Thomas. Since she was now eighteen, he would recommend a primary care physician for her. As Leah slumped in her seat. Dr. Thomas was more than a doctor—he was a trusted confidant and a source of solace. When she saw him, he spoke in soothing tones, had soft, deliberate movements, always explained what he was doing and why, and made funny animal sounds to distract her before administering shots. He listened to every update about her life and always encouraged her to talk about her feelings. She trusted him and looked forward to her appointments.

When Dr. Thomas entered, she saw a friend. A smile bloomed on her lips, and they greeted each other. As he checked her ears, eyes, reflexes, felt her stomach, and listened to her heart and lungs, Leah told Dr. Thomas about her trust fund, her hopes of being accepted to Stanford, and her dad's increasingly somber mood, especially now that he had reluctantly agreed to continue working as a delivery driver.

"Which area does he work?" Dr. Thomas asked.

"His new route is in the Bobcat Mountain neighborhood," Leah said.

Dr. Thomas paused, his eyes retreating into thought. "I see." He turned his chair and wrote in his notepad. Clearing his throat, he said, "Walking up and down those steep hills will provide a great cardiovascular workout for him." Then, Dr. Thomas gently broached the subject of Leah's mother. "I know your mom being away is tough. How have you been feeling about her absence?"

Leah hesitated, torn about her parents' separation. She understood why her mom had left and often felt closer to her because of it. They were best friends. But she missed her mom's presence at home—the motherly doting, comforting, and guidance that could only come when they were together. She explained all of this to Dr. Thomas and gave him the details of her last visit with her mom—riding horses, sailing in the Keys, and shopping at the Coconut Grove Arts Festival.

When Dr. Thomas finished the examination, he gave Leah a clean bill of health and followed her into the lobby. He shook Jared's hand and asked, "Are you feeling okay? Any behaviors or thoughts you want to talk about?"

Jared glanced at Leah, his discomfort evident in the furrow of his brows. She flashed a reassuring smile. With a nod in Dr. Thomas's direction, she indicated her confidence in his ability to help.

"I appreciate your concern, doctor," Jared replied, guarded. "But I'm working it out."

Dr. Thomas's dark, calm response was unnerving. "Do you feel manipulated or influenced by forces beyond your control?" The subtle edge in his voice provoked an eerie discomfort.

Jared remained silent, his eyes narrowing in confusion.

"Voices whispering to you... feelings of paranoia, or distrust towards those around you?"

A chill crept down Leah's spine. The questions and manner in which he delivered them, struck her as odd. Why was he talking to her father in this way? She was glad he was trying to ascertain the depth and possible causes for her father's deepening gloom. However, for him to speak with an undercurrent of menace felt strange and uncharacteristic.

Jared took a step back. "No, I'm fine. How is Leah?"

"I didn't mean to make you feel uncomfortable." He put his hands in the pockets of his white coat. "But my colleague has encountered patients who have struggled with similar feelings, and I want to make sure you get the help you need. If any of these concerns arise, I can recommend you to her."

"That's okay. Thanks." Jared motioned to Leah. "She's good?"

"Yes. She's in excellent physical health," Dr. Thomas said. "But I am concerned about Leah's emotional well being."

"How so?" Jared asked.

"Her mother being so far away is worrisome. Emotional stress can lead to physical ailments."

"She has a great relationship with her mother."

Dr. Thomas moved closer, putting his hand on Jared's shoulder. "Take this advice," he offered in a murmur.

Leah stepped closer to hear.

"The stress from unprocessed trauma can affect you mentally, emotionally, and physically. The mind has a strange power to both create and distort, manifesting shadows and twisting reality. Therapy will untangle your guilt, your mistakes, and the pain you keep buried."

Leah turned to her dad, seeing him swallow.

"Therapy?" he said. His body sagged and drooped as if the doctor's words had injected him with a sedative. The stillness in the room felt deadly, the only sound coming from the hum of the purifier in the fish tank.

Dr. Thomas took Jared's hand. Her dad stared down at his grip. The doctor pressed his thumb into the back of his hand.

"It's not just stress I'm worried about," the doctor said. "The area you're working in..." He trailed off, keeping his grip strong, far too long for comfort.

Leah's stomach tightened.

"Call me if you start experiencing any strange anomalies," Dr. Thomas said.

Leah stepped next to her dad, providing solace. "Well, that was a little dark and creepy," she remarked, attempting to lighten the mood. Offering her hand to Dr. Thomas, she said, "Thank you, for everything. I enjoyed having you as my doctor. I'll miss you." Then, in an afterthought, she asked, "Can I have a sticker for old times' sake?"

Dr. Thomas chuckled softly. "Of course, Leah. It's been a pleasure taking care of you these past few years." He went behind the counter and handed her a tray full of colorful stickers. She chose a butterfly sticker that read, *Flying to Success.*

The doctor handed Jared a folder. "Here are Leah's medical records. I've included the names of two family physicians for Leah as she transitions into adulthood," he said, "along with a therapist that she would benefit from seeing—although I hear Stanford is a possibility. Congratulations, Dad."

Jared gave a wary smile. "Thanks." They shook hands again and said goodbye.

As Leah and Jared left the waiting area, she asked, "Did any of his questions or advice feel relevant to you?"

"No."

"I've never heard him speak like that..." Leah trailed off as she thought about the doctor's words to her dad. She hadn't said her dad was losing his mind, just that he wasn't himself. Did he misinterpret her?

In the elevator, her dad put his arm around her. "I know you're worried and for good reason. But I promise, I'll turn things around."

At Rote's Barber Shop, Jared tipped Bob $15 in advance, and they caught up. Leah ate yakisoba at the Japanese cafe while she waited. She thumbed through her social media accounts, commenting, and posting a photo with the caption,

"Best way to spend a spring evening—yakisoba at my favorite Japanese restaurant! #foodie #seniorlife."

On their way home, she said, "Mom has a boyfriend, you know."

"I know."

"Then why haven't you started dating?"

Jared stared at his hands, locking his fingers together. "I guess I didn't want to hurt you."

Leah kept her eyes on the road, not looking at her dad. The comment stung a little, but she didn't want to talk about that now. At the same time, however, she didn't want to let it pass unaddressed. She simply said, "You did hurt me, both of you. But you made it better." She glanced at him. "And Mom knows that, too. You both did."

"I'm sorry."

"Yeah, yeah. We need to talk about you," she said. "Do you remember teaching me about the stock market—how to read analyst ratings and place puts and calls? I bring this up, not because I miss it, I don't, but because you were so passionate about it."

Their eyes met briefly.

"Leah."

"Dad, where's your bravado? I almost don't know you anymore. I think this moment is the perfect time for a new start. You have a new look. You're starting a new route." She paused. "I think it's time you found a girlfriend. Start dating."

Jared gave his daughter a sideways look. "Are you and Uncle Tim tag teaming?"

Leah grinned. "Did he already say something?"

"He has someone in mind, too. I'm going to meet her on Monday when I help him move appliances."

"What time Monday?"

"Around five. Why?"

"Dad! Dan and Barb's Grandma Carol, is having her birthday dinner on Monday. We're making lasagna. You're going."

"Shit, I forgot." Jared took a second to think. "Tim is coming for dinner on Friday. We can talk to him about rescheduling for Tuesday."

Leah nodded in agreement.

"By the way," Jared added, "you and Dan seem to be getting close. Are you two dating now?"

"No, we're not dating," Leah shot back defensively. "Well, not yet," she amended, her voice hopeful yet confused. "I don't know. It's complicated because Barb's my best friend."

"I see," he said in a lower pitch, tinged with relief. "It's probably best that you don't start."

"Why?"

"You're leaving for college after the summer."

"So? Ever hear of FaceTime?"

When they arrived home, Jared said, "I'm going to bed early. Starting a new route is always a pain in the ass."

Under her breath, Leah responded, "Getting you to start over is a pain in the ass." She watched him turn for his room, then called, "Dad?"

He stopped and looked back. "Yes?"

"Thank you for fighting for me. I didn't want to go to a boarding school in England. But now I need you to fight for yourself."

"Thanks, sweetheart," he said with a tired smile. "I will. I promise."

Day Two—Thursday

The Doorbell

Jared arrived at work ten minutes late. Waking up in the morning and getting ready for work had become a challenge. His body ached from various accidents over the years—a twisted ankle, a strained rotator cuff, and a sore knee. At the terminal, he began looking through the truck. It was still being loaded by the package handlers who sorted the packages for the different routes. Jared inspected the bigger packages for damage: two carpets, four window blinds, a bed frame, a couple of shelving units, and two chairs. These would need to be loaded by Jared himself after the sort was finished. He hated large heavy packages.

After studying the map of his route for the day, Jared rearranged and turned boxes so that they were in order of delivery and easy to find. As he flipped a medium-sized box, he read, "LuvNailz.com." Taking out his phone, he snapped a photo, sending it to his brother. "Check it out!" he typed. Tim's wife, Patty, was a professional nail tech who shipped products to her clients. He sent the text. The next box he flipped had "Stillen Corp" stamped in bold red and gold letters. He pressed it, anger filling his veins. "Uugh." He thought of Stacy's father—an arrogant, self-righteous ass. He drop-kicked the box to the back of the truck.

"Be careful, that package might press charges."

Jared jerked his head up, but upon seeing Dustin, the previous driver for route 511, he sighed in relief.

"You saw it attack me, right?" Jared quipped.

Dustin grinned. "Hossain wanted me to go over the route with you."

"Any tricky businesses I should know about?" Jared asked.

"The grocery mart stops taking deliveries after 1 pm, the dentist in the little strip mall is closed on Tuesdays, and the Education Center has a mailroom. The person at the front desk will sign for any packages."

"What's the Education Center?"

"It's similar to a community center, but privatized. It offers classes in art, music—like guitar and piano. You can learn cooking, computers, woodworking, swimming... Group and private classes are offered. You haven't been there?"

"No. I've heard about it, but didn't really know what it was."

"It's an impressive building. A lot of people think the place is haunted, but they offer some great classes. My sister took a prep class for her SAT's there."

"What are their hours?"

"They close at eight or nine. You'll have deliveries there every day, but it's easy."

"Cool. What else do I need to know?"

Dustin handed Jared index cards connected with a ring that had addresses and four-digit codes written on them. "These are the gate codes for houses and gated communities. Be careful about the driveways, especially the steep ones; the owners tend to get angry if you leave tire marks or if your truck is leaking oil."

"Got it."

"It's an easy route. Take your time and get to know the people; it pays off come Christmas."

"Okay, thanks again."

"Yep. See you 'round."

After filling his water bottle and using the restroom, Jared stepped into his truck and drove toward his route. The traffic was light, and he arrived at his first stop in under thirty minutes. Route 511 was in a mountainous area, and Jared quickly found himself driving up and down hilly streets and walking up and down steep driveways. Hossain's voice ran through his head, "Easy."

Not so. He huffed and puffed up a driveway, careful not to slip and fall on the light green evergreen pollen that had dusted everything. Trudging up a flight of stairs, Jared dropped a package at the front door of a multi-level, three-car garage house, with a large balcony off the second story. Hossain was right about one thing. This neighborhood is expensive. The houses were immaculate with fresh paint, new roofs, professionally maintained lawns, no garbage anywhere, and Teslas and Land Rovers in each driveway.

Jared's day proceeded smoothly as he scanned packages, closing each stop after a delivery. At the businesses in the little strip mall where he delivered, Jared got signatures for each stop as required by his company—at the gas station and the daycare across the street. Then he headed back into the residential area closer to the mountain and steeper hills.

Jared was a little more than half done when he climbed into the truck after a stop and leaned back in his seat, feeling tired. He wasn't used to walking up steep hills. He took a deep breath and let it out, trying to slow his breathing and relax. He looked at his scanner for the next stop, which was on 175th. Opening the map, he checked to see where that was. He noticed he was at the edge of his route because the Sukiya reservation was beyond this point. Next to the reservation was Bobcat National Park. He loved how a trail system through the city connected to the paths that went into the park.

Jared closed the map and started the truck, turning down 175th. His shoulders tightened and his head began to ache. "Note to self, 'Stretch before doing excessive exercise.'"

As he drove up the street, he saw a large home that stirred his memory. He knew this place. In fact, he had studied this house! He remembered first seeing it in an architectural magazine. It had won several awards—best in interior design for flexible spaces, innovation in incorporating environmental features with exterior design, and first place for Masterclass Architectural Design. This was the Bellevue House.

Approaching the home from the southwest, Jared drove over a bridge, which crossed a stream and continued around the circle drive. Built into the side of the hill, the house had a waterfall flowing off its roof. The stream then wound around beds of tulips, primroses, and daffodils. Small vegetable patches of cabbage, parsley, and radishes lined a maze of paths and ornate bridges that snaked along the stream. The second-floor deck, along with the waterfall and pool, supported a pergola covered with lavender wisteria. A rock stairway leading off the deck and up the hill created the image of the house being a part of the land. Stepping out of the truck, Jared walked along the path. He stopped and closed his eyes, reveling in the melodic rhythm of splashing water and the sweet jasmine scent of the flowers. "Magical," he whispered, with a smile.

The south side of the house was a wall of windows overlooking the valley. He paused for a minute to admire the view. From where he stood in front of the house, downtown looked like a miniature city with a small model train chugging through it. He marveled at the highway, the tied arch bridge, the Topp Tower, and the boating docks. The sun glistened off Lake Evelin, highlighting the homes along its borders. Mt. Champion's snowy peak was on full display from sixty miles away. Jared stared at the endless green, feeling hope that nature had a chance. He took photos and texted them to Leah.

"The house certainly lives up to its name—Bellevue—beautiful view."

He turned back to face the house. Turrets, arches, and a glass canopy walkway connecting the lower west wing to the east wing gave the house a combination medieval, Gothic vibe. The magazine photos didn't do it justice. Jared couldn't believe he was seeing this architectural masterpiece; hadn't the house burned down several years ago? He remembered reading about the fire, which was why he had never ventured to see the house in person.

As he took a minute to appreciate the framing and arches, he found himself transported back, reliving lectures on spatial design and context. In that moment, he yearned to be back at his drawing table, sketching designs, feeling the surge of creative energy, and experiencing the magic of conceived solutions. Oh, how he longed to bask in the satisfaction of a successful project.

Jared allowed himself to dream about opening a downtown office. With Max-Micro Innovations stimulating the local economy, there was lots of work. *I could be designing green buildings that were completely self-sufficient.* He would have respect, self-dignity, and validation. Leah could feel proud to call him, Dad. Stacy would see that he was successful and making a difference.

Turning toward the delivery truck, he stared, then drooped his head. *What am I doing?* He closed his eyes as his mind flipped through the wreckage of his career: gross negligence, lawsuit, denied insurance. Jared clenched his jaw and balled his hands into fists, thinking about the blueprints he had approved. How had those building plans passed the multiple layers of validation—the city, the inspectors, the zoning board, and the environmental agency? How was it he had taken the brunt of the blame? "Damn! If only things were different."

Jared trudged back to the truck and retrieved the package for this stop. He carried the box to the front door, set it down, and rang the bell. Returning to the truck, he closed the stop on his scanner. But the stop didn't close. His scanner read: *Error. Signature Required for Business Stop.*

Jared stopped and grunted. "They must run a business here."

He returned to the front door and rang the bell a second time. He waited briefly before filling out a door tag that read, *Sorry, we missed you.* Ringing the bell a final time, he placed the tag on the door, grabbed the package, and headed back to the truck.

Nong Ekamai stood in front of the sink, glaring at a plate and a knife. "I must wash these now? I can't wait until after dinner?" Her captor demanded cleanliness above all else: *Not a hint or trace of your activities should ever be visible!*

For lunch, she had made a tomato, cheese, cucumber, and spinach sandwich. She had washed the cutting board and wiped the counter immediately after use. Only then was she allowed to eat. Now she had to wash the plate and knife. *I'll do it later,* was never an option. She would receive swift punishment if this procedure wasn't followed every time, all the time.

Nong, however, didn't move. Her anger simmered as she clenched the sponge in her hand. Yesterday's outburst had created tension, and she was determined to continue her rebellion, her only path forward. By keeping her captor in a state of perpetual agitation and distress, Nong hoped for a mistake that would allow her to escape.

Ding dong. The sound assaulted her. She jumped in fright, arms raised in anticipation of her punishment.

Nothing.

Lowering her hands, Nong narrowed her eyes and wrinkled her brow as she listened.

"Was that the doorbell?" she asked, as a shimmer of hope filled her heart. In her four years here, she had never heard the bell ring, not once. Her nerves stood on edge as she waited for confirmation, and then directions, or for the opportunity to run.

The air was still. She held her breath, praying this opportunity wasn't a soldier marching off to war, never to return. But when there was no follow-up ring, no knock, no voices asking if anyone were home, she let herself exhale. Her hope sank as she drowned in the reality that this new punishment was perhaps the cruelest of all.

The mechanical chimes rang again. Nong's heart leapt with renewed hope. "What should I do?" she called out. "Can I answer it?"

Her jaw tightened. Her muscles tensed. She wanted to run, but fear held her in place, too afraid the bell was a trick, or a test.

"Can I answer it?" she pressed. The clock ticked in her ears, sounding like a jailer's tin cup clanging against the bars of her cell—tick, tick, tick. Panic swelled.

The bell rang a third time. Sweating and gasping for air, Nong stole the opportunity to run for the door. Her body shook as tears welled in her eyes.

As Jared returned to the truck with the package, the front door swung open, and a woman in her late twenties or early thirties appeared. She was short, with long, silky black hair and radiant brown skin. Jared's breath caught in his throat. Then confusion cut through his awe—her face was consumed by fear.

The woman froze at the threshold, her stare pleading for help. She shot a terrified glance over her shoulder, then turned to Jared. Her lips moved in a silent scream, but he heard no sound. Bending over, she clutched her head with both hands.

"Are you okay?" Jared quickened his pace to help the woman. Who else was in the house? Was she being abused? Her strong, athletic build suggested she could defend herself, if need be, but something was wrong.

Jared reached her and set down the package. "You okay?" he pressed.

The woman brushed a tear from her eye, straightened, and gave a tired grin. Jared scanned her arms and face for cuts, bruises, and blood, seeing none.

She lifted her gaze to him through her bangs, extended her hand, and laid it on his chest, gently, like a whisper. Her touch was warm, powerful, and communicative.

They looked at each other for a long moment. Her dark brown eyes softened, melting into tenderness. He relaxed, the tension in his shoulders easing as her touch lingered. The small mole below her right eye caught his attention, its imperfection highlighting the smoothness of her skin.

"Hi, I'm here," she said.

Her voice was sweet and layered; Jared could almost hear a harmony within it. "Yes, you are," he murmured.

"I'm so glad I caught you." Her lips flowered into a gentle smile.

A tingling sensation flowed from her touch, straight into Jared's heart. He glanced at his chest, and she dropped her hand, dragging her finger to his belly like a match being struck, igniting his senses. Jared trembled. She pulled her arm back, and the vacancy left him cold. He wanted to grab her hand and place it where it belonged. Closing his eyes, he captured the memory. And as he did, he heard his heartbeat synchronize with hers.

"Now we're connected," she said.

Jared opened his eyes, and she bowed her head, blushing.

"It feels that way, yes," he voiced.

An electrifying pause followed. She slid a strand of hair behind her ear as her eyes met his again. His pulse quickened. He didn't understand the visceral pull she had on him. Trying to ground the swirling emotions, Jared reminded himself he was working.

"It looked like you were in trouble," he said. "Is everything all right?"

"Yes. Sorry. I was washing up from lunch. I wasn't expecting a package. I mean, I am. I was. But not until tomorrow. I was startled and bumped my head on the door. Silly of me."

Jared couldn't believe it. She was flustered, yet excited. Her stammering pulled him closer. He was a helpless ship being dragged in by her tug. Jared became aware of his breathing, deep and heavy. Biting his inner lip, he attempted to flirt himself, saying, "Actually, the package doesn't require a signature, but the scanner lists your address as a business, so I need to get one." Lowering his voice, he asked, "May I have your signature?" He felt like a goofy teenage boy.

"Yes, I can give you that."

He re-scanned the package and asked, "Do you run a business out of your home?"

"A business?" the woman questioned. She took in a quick breath and answered, "No. Not exactly. I don't run one here."

"What about your husband? Maybe through the Internet?" Jared enjoyed flirting, but if she were in a relationship.

She turned her cheek, displaying dimples. The innocence was seductive in the most beautiful way. "I don't have a husband." She lowered her head while keeping her eyes fixed on him.

Goosebumps followed the chill that ran through his body. He took in her petite, muscular frame—pure art. "Oh. That's ... that's umm." He paused, then asked, "No boyfriend selling vitamins?"

She laughed. "No."

"Roommate?"

She took a second to think about that, seemingly unsure about how to answer.

Jared used that second to mentally slap himself. *I'm being creepy. Stop!*

"Yeah, you could kind of say I have a roommate, but, no business," she reassured him.

"I see." Jared switched the setting to residential and closed the stop. "I guess I don't need a signature after all. I fixed this, so I won't bother you again."

"No!" the woman shot back. "No," she repeated in a soft defeated voice.

Jared frowned.

"I mean, no, it's no bother at all," she emphasized. "In fact, I want you to bother me. I can sign. I want to sign..." she trailed off, touching her forehead with a slight grimace.

"You don't seem okay." Jared veered his head to steal a glance inside the house. Was someone watching them? He wondered if she wanted to sign because she needed to convey a message. He grabbed the notice off the door, turned it over, and handed it to her with his pen so she could write him a note.

She lifted her hand and placed her fingers on the pen, but then hesitated. "Actually, I'm fine, really," she managed, forcing her smile to return. She pushed the pen back, her finger brushing against his.

Jared's whole body shivered with desire.

"I would like you to knock, ring the bell, visit if you have time," she said. "I would love to see you again."

A brief, stunned silence gripped him. "Sure," he stammered. "I'll make sure to do that. I won't bother your roommate?"

She withdrew her hand, a satisfied glint flickering in her eyes. "No."

"Are you in trouble?"

"I—I desire the company. And you won't bother my roommate. We aren't really roommates anyway, so no, absolutely no bother. I get lonely. That's all. My name is Nong by the way. Nice to meet you."

Lonely? Jared swallowed. *This is moving fast.* "Your roommate's a gamer? Lives in the basement glued to the computer?"

Nong raised her eyebrows and nodded. "Yeah, something like that."

"I'm Jared. Pleasure." He wanted to ask what nationality her name was but didn't want to sound rude. "Nong is a lovely name."

"It's Thai," she said. "My dad was an executive with Ford. After they built a large factory in Thailand, he transferred here as a culture and language consultant. I was three at the time."

Jared tried to remember the names of the cities he had visited ten years ago. He was about to say, "The land of smiles," when Nong asked, "So, are you the regular delivery guy?"

"Yes, it's my first day, but this is my route now. I've been a delivery driver for about three years, but I was an architect. Actually, I can't believe you own this house. I remember—"

"Studying this house at university?" Nong said, finishing Jared's sentence and they both giggled.

"I remember first seeing it in *Exploring Architecture*."

"I had a subscription to that magazine as well."

"Really, you're an architect?" Jared asked in amazement, feeling strangely relieved.

"Yes, I am, or was. I haven't worked in the field since I bought this house."

"What happened—if you don't mind my asking."

She opened her mouth to speak, but stopped. She glanced at the second-floor window. With a forced exhale, she articulated, "Ah. I think that's a tale for another time. But I am curious about your story."

Jared focused on the same window, wondering if she was being held against her will. "I hope you like tragedies," he said. "My story has all the bells and whistles." He returned his gaze and saw Nong fidgeting with a button on her blouse.

"Mine is a horror story with all the bells and whistles," she voiced. "I'm not sure you would understand, but I'll tell you someday."

"Can't say I'm a fan of horror, but I am intrigued."

Nong motioned her head back, asking, "What do you think of the house?"

"The house? Are you kidding me? I love it! The dynamic massing fits perfectly with the shape of the land, and the scale... I envy you so much right now."

"You can live here. As you can see, the house is much too big for me." She pointed to the upper level. "Lots of rooms. There's even an indoor pool."

"I'm sold. When can I move in?" Jared quipped.

They laughed together.

Jared wanted to ask about projects she'd worked on, where she had studied, and how she became interested in architecture, but he needed to get back to work. He still had half his route to finish, and he was bleeding time.

"It was so nice meeting you, Nong, but I have to get going," he said.

"Oh yes, please. I'm sorry for keeping you. Will you come see me often?"

"If you order lots of packages. Yes." Jared chuckled.

Nong's shoulders slumped, and her eyes flickered with disappointment.

"Don't worry. I'll see you again soon."

As Jared backed away, Nong's eyes sparkled with sudden inspiration. Her voice sprang to life. "I can give you a tour of the house sometime, if you'd like."

His heart skipped a beat. To tour this house had been a dream, and now a beautiful woman was offering him a private showing. "Oh..." His voice was just above a whisper. "I would love that."

The two of them stood quietly for a moment, wanting each other. Jared blinked and forced himself to say, "Ok, so I'll see you again soon."

"Can't wait," replied Nong, a devilish smile dancing at the corners of her lips.

Turning, Jared practically floated back to his truck, his steps light with new-found energy. He glanced at Nong again. She hugged the door frame, admiring him. He waved, and she waved back.

In his side view mirror, Jared saw Nong watching him as he drove away. He turned the corner, and she was out of sight.

"Wow!" exclaimed Jared. He stopped the truck to breathe. Closing his eyes, he put his hand on his chest where she had put hers and let the electricity of the encounter dance through him. His heart was tied in knots, and Nong was in his head to stay. After taking a few minutes to decompress, he looked at his scanner for the next stop. Turning off the street, his body relaxed, and a broad smile crossed his face. Nong was a dream.

Nong watched the delivery truck turn the corner and drive out of sight. She glanced longingly at the package, sighing as she closed the door, leaving it outside. "Are you happy? You'll soon have a new mouse to play with." Her outward disdain, however, didn't mask her true excitement for her impending release. It was finally happening. If she played her cards right, she would soon be free. A sting of guilt poked her, knowing what that meant for Jared. Would she be able to do to him what Tyler had done to her? Who would he miss? Who would miss him? She couldn't think about that. It didn't matter.

Permission Granted

"Hey, Brandon, the captain will see you now," Detective Rodriguez told Detective Spencer, as he walked past his desk. Brandon grabbed the file on Nong Ekamai and entered Captain David Crandle's office.

"Morning, Brandon. I have a letter here from Hope's Heart Residential School. They wanted to let me know how much they appreciate your volunteering there. How long have you been doing that?"

"Five months, I guess."

"That's great. It reflects well on the department. Those kids need a positive role model. Maybe I should have Freeman go in your place." The captain chuckled. "So, what did forensics come up with?"

"I'm not here about the Mitchell case."

"Oh, okay. What can I do for you, detective?"

"I received a phone call last night from Tyler Jiles. Do you remember him?" Brandon asked.

The captain didn't hesitate. "Tyler Jiles. Oh yes, I know the case all too well. He's connected to the perp who kidnaps people and scrambles their brains."

"Yeah, that's the one."

"Okay, so? Does he remember anything?"

"That's unclear. I would say he's struggling. They want a detective to go see him first thing Monday morning. I want to go with whomever you send, and I want to reactivate the Nong Ekamai investigation."

"Wait a second. Do you even know anything about that case?"

"I got the call, sir. It's technically mine now. I scanned the files last night. I'm a fresh set of eyes—someone who can see it from a different perspective. I'm ready for a challenge," Brandon asserted.

"Look, detective, we followed every lead in her investigation. Let's find out if Tyler remembers anything first before we start reopening cold cases." The captain pointed to a stack of folders sitting on the edge of his desk to emphasize he had plenty to do.

Brandon was taken aback by David's comments. Surely Tyler regaining consciousness was monumental. It increased the hopes of finding Nong, and as a result, the perpetrator. There were now two victims who could collaborate, giving the department new clues. "When was the last time we spoke with Amanda Bowman?" Before David could respond, he continued, "I believe it would be beneficial for Amanda and Tyler to sit down together. Their discussion may trigger memories, helping them recall crucial details about their abduction. Nong is most likely still alive, and their conversation could assist us in finding her."

The captain didn't look convinced and was about to counter, but Brandon spoke first.

"How long do you think it'll take for the press to find out Tyler is responding? We have to get in front of this."

"Detective," the captain began, his tone initially firm, "I'm not convinced you're ready for this case." He paused, his expression softening as he continued, "However, your point about the press is valid. Before I agree, I need to know what your plans are for the Mitchell case."

Brandon interlocked his fingers, bringing his hands to his mouth before speaking. "I need to verify the suspect's story. Dimitri has agreed to cooperate. I'm waiting on the forensics results, which will be a few days. I want to confirm that the daughter was actually at her friend's house the night of the attack, so I'll petition for Stephanie's cell phone records. I can work both cases."

"And the Turner case?"

"Tod owed Joe money. Joe's prints were found at the office. His truck was identified as the vehicle parked in the lot, and he doesn't have an alibi. The arrest will be made today."

"What about the hit and run case?"

"The video from the ATM and the paint samples we collected at the scene both match the vehicle we found at the schoolyard. It's currently being wiped for prints. The owner of the car informed us that his son had been using it. I'm driving to the college dorms to speak with him today."

Sighing in resignation, David nodded. "Okay." He picked up the phone and dialed a number, looking at Brandon. He pointed one finger in the air, signaling him to wait. He spoke quickly, informing the person on the other end about

Tyler. Putting down the phone, the captain said, "You remember Sam Marvin, right? You took over his desk. He was the lead detective on these abduction cases. He's coming in tomorrow morning to brief you. Get the files from the back room, and familiarize yourself with the cases so you can ask some intelligent questions. Then interview Tyler alone. Call Amanda and interview her alone before you connect the two of them. If you find any leads, I'll consider giving you another detective to work the case. Let me handle the press."

"Thank you, sir," Brandon said as he turned and opened the door.

"Try to keep this quiet for now, ok?" the captain added.

As Brandon left, Maggie, the office secretary, stuck her head into the room and said, "Captain, there's a reporter on line three. It's regarding a story that will run in Sunday's paper about Tyler Jiles."

Returning to his desk, Brandon felt a whirlwind of emotions swirling in his chest—encouragement, excitement, and nervousness. He now had two cases that were intriguing, and investigating Nong's was huge. It offered him a chance to have autonomy over his future, throwing away the shackles of being assigned the "leftovers." Respect, honor, and prestige were within his grasp. He had worked so hard for the title of detective, and this was his moment to prove he was worthy of the badge. But beyond any personal gain, what truly motivated him was the opportunity to find and rescue a woman abandoned by the department—a woman he firmly believed he could save.

Eager to get started, he filled out the court documents required to obtain Stephanie Mitchell's phone records. After filing the petition, he would head to the college to interview the student and then return to unpack what was perhaps the biggest puzzle the city had ever faced.

The Photo

Leah sat hunched over her notebook, scribbling out equations when the doorbell rang. *Yay, they're here.* Closing her calculus book, she ran out of her room and down the short hall to answer the door.

"Hey, girlfriend." Barb and Dan came in, carrying pizza.

"Thanks for getting that," Leah said.

"Sure," Dan answered. "When's your dad coming home?"

The question excited Leah, and she took a quick breath, stealing a moment in his eyes. She was dreaming—We can be alone all night. Clearing her throat, she answered, "Not until late. It's his first day on this new route."

Dan set the sausage and mushroom pizza on the kitchen table as Barb grabbed plates, and Leah pulled root beers from the fridge.

"Hmm..." Dan vibrated, as he devoured his slice.

His moan reminded Leah. "Holy crap, Barb. I have a book you have to read—*Erotic Stories for Punjabi Widows*!" Leah grabbed her arm, and they rushed to her room.

A guilty smile crossed Dan's lips at the mention of the book. When the girls returned, he was eating his second slice as they chatted. "Yes! But, no. It's a drama. It has mystery, romance, tradition, new love, old love, renewed love, and is about empowering women. It's also funny."

"Okay. I'll read it," Barb promised.

"Can I read it when you're done?" Dan asked Barb while looking at Leah.

His gaze made her warm. Trying not to blush, she picked up her phone, pretending to check her messages when she remembered the photos her dad had texted.

"My dad sent some scenic shots from the mountain. Want to see them?"

"Na. Scenic photos from your phone are never that good," Barb replied, sitting at the table. She lifted a piece of pizza, the melted cheese stretching before she used her finger to wrap it up.

"I'll look at them," Dan said. He stepped close to Leah, studying her features. Leah noticed him smell her hair and turned slightly toward him.

"Are you two..." Barb questioned, seeing the interaction, "into each other?"

Leah stepped away. "What? He's your brother."

Laughing, Barb proclaimed, "Holy shit, you are!"

"We aren't. We're friends. Stop blowing things out of proportion."

"Hey, it's cool with me. I don't mind."

Leah's face was red. She glanced at Dan, who glared at Barb before turning his gaze on her. They all fell silent.

"Let me see your dad's photos," Dan said, trying to ease the tension.

Barb laughed. "I love it."

Lifting her phone, she showed Dan. He paled, stumbling back. "Whaa... whea..."

"What is it?" Leah asked, turning her phone to study the photo.

Barb abruptly became curious. "Let me see."

"No! Don't look at it!" Dan exclaimed.

"Why?" both Barb and Leah shot back.

Putting her hand on Leah's arm, Barb turned the phone to look and froze. Her nostrils flared, and she turned away.

Dan didn't say anything. He was ghost white, his jaw tight as a steel trap.

Leah spoke hesitantly, "I... I don't understand."

"I need some air," Barb said. She spun out of her chair and headed straight for the door. "I'm going for a walk. I'll be back." She hurried out the door.

Leah had no idea how to interpret Barb's abrupt departure. Turning to Dan, her eyes begged for an explanation.

His hand was on his mouth, covering his nose.

"Why are you upset over a view of the city from the mountain?" Leah asked. "I don't understand."

"It stirred a memory. Shook us, that's all."

Leah nodded. "Okay." She turned and headed for the door. "I'll go talk to her."

"No!" Dan said, holding up his hand. "She'll be back. Trust me on this."

Leah saw that mysterious pain alive in Dan. He was hurting. She knew a little bit about pain—the knot in the chest that ached and festered, the thoughts that swam round and round in the mind, stinging, telling you that you were to blame. She moved close to him, wrapping her arms around him.

His body was warm and firm. She could feel the strength in his muscles. Feeling like she was stealing candy, Leah backed away, but Dan grabbed her and held her tight.

They stood locked in each other's arms, suspended in a timeless embrace. Leah lifted her head, and Dan kissed her.

Leah held her breath, eyes wide, heart electrified. A surge of excitement thrummed through her as her pulse raced. Closing her eyes, she pressed into him, her desires to kiss Dan satisfied. But confusion followed. Why was he kissing her? What had happened to Barb? What did that scenic view represent or mean to him? Pulling back, she searched Dan's face, silently pleading for answers.

"Is it okay that I kissed you?" he asked.

Leah nodded. "Yes."

He leaned in and paused.

She met him, and they kissed again.

As their lips mingled, Dan's mouth painted a picture. Each turn, press, and linger became a brushstroke, conveying his longing for connection, his yearning for passion, and a sense of comfort in her embrace. She soaked in the experience, filling her with newfound intimacy. A soft moan escaped her as she gently pulled back.

"Do you want to see my bedroom?" Leah was thinking that if he came for movie night, it'd be the perfect opportunity for him to become familiar with her father and uncle.

Dan took a breath in, raising his brows and widening his eyes. "Umm."

"I can show you my collection of 80's movies that I've watched with my dad and uncle."

"Okay," he agreed.

She took his hand and led him across to the living room first. On the shelf near the TV were twenty VHS tapes. She smiled, thinking about how the shared experience of watching movies with her dad and uncle gave them common reference points to language, quotations, and expressions—"Hey you guyyyys!" "Do. Or do not. There is no try." "Inconceivable! You keep using that word. I don't think it means what you think it means." It was more than tradition; it was bonding. She wanted Dan to be a part of that. "These are the movies I haven't seen. We're watching Beetlejuice next." Dan looked at the titles—*When Harry Met Sally, Beverly Hills Cop, Flashdance, Ferris Bueller's Day Off*...

A giant grin spread across Dan's face. "This one is good," he said, pointing to Purple Rain. "You haven't seen this, yet?"

"I will. My Aunt Patty hosts a ladies' poker night on Fridays, so my uncle comes over, and we pick one to watch. Come on, I'll show you the ones I've already seen."

"I have two movies you need to add to this shelf," Dan said.

"Oh?"

"*The Natural*, with Robert Redford, and *Major League*, with Charlie Sheen."

"*Major League*? Is that a sports movie?"

"They're both baseball flicks."

"I see." Taking Dan's hand, she led him down the narrow hall past the bathroom door, turning into her bedroom. Leah's heart pounded, making her skin sensitive. Her breathing quickened as they stepped next to her bed.

Leah watched as Dan surveyed her room. A white IKEA desk with open shelves held notebooks, a jar of pens and pencils, schoolwork, and a lamp. On the wall above the desk hung a calendar and two cork bulletin boards. The first board held notes and inspirational sayings. The second was full of photos, receipts, and a vast collection of ticket stubs from venues like *Dr. Strange*, a Taylor Swift concert, Macbeth, *Phantom of the Opera*, *The Magic Flute*, and Six Flags. She had a rosary draped on her mirror. Her dresser was long and littered with makeup, lotions, and perfumes. A rack held a variety of hats, Midi Mayfair purses, and Cartier sunglasses. Leah noticed she forgot to put her Advil away and felt embarrassed, hoping Dan wouldn't understand what that meant. Does he even think I'm cute? She felt naked and vulnerable, as he examined her room—the things that showed experiences, memories, and beliefs that made her who she was. He was peeling away the layers of her identity, and her body responded with a mix of nerves and longing. His kiss and his presence in her space left her feeling both exposed and exhilarated.

He picked up a small vial of essential oil, reading, "Peppermint." Placing it next to her water bottle, he glanced at the book entitled, *The Energy of Prayer* laying next to her laptop on her bed. Two bookshelves—one next to the closet door and one at the end of her bed—were crammed full of hardcover books, paperbacks, and VHS tapes.

"Here." She pointed to the bookcase devoted to the movies she'd seen over countless Friday nights. "The ones on the top shelf are my favorites."

Dan leaned in, reading the titles. "*Back to the Future, Highlander, Dead Poets Society, Goonies, E.T., 9 to 5*..." He picked up *Dirty Dancing*. "How was this one?"

Leah allowed a fantasy to creep into her head: Dan was shirtless, and he picked her up, laying her on the bed. "It was fabulous—one of my top five."

"Would you watch it again?"

"With you? Absolutely." Her voice was alive with excitement. She thought of sitting next to him in a dark room watching a sexy, romantic movie while their hands explored each other's bodies.

Dan glanced at her, a hunger in his expression. "That would be nice." He looked at titles on the second shelf: *Bill and Ted's Excellent Adventure, The Breakfast Club, Say Anything*...

Leah sat on the bed as he fingered the titles. What would those fingers feel like on me? She imagined the sensation as he traced her skin, sending a shiver down her spine. The room held its breath as her musings danced with anticipation of what could be.

The lowest shelves held titles like *Die Hard, Airplane, The Thing,* and *Top Gun.* Dan tilted a cassette forward. "*Aliens.* I could never watch this movie."

"It's pretty intense. More action than horror."

"I've lived horror. I don't need to watch it." He scrunched his eyes, shaking his head.

"That's quite a statement. I'm willing to listen, if you want to share."

"Another time?"

Leah nodded. Dan moved to her bulletin board, looking at the receipts in foreign languages. "Can you read this?" he asked, pointing to one.

"That's in Arabic." Leah moved next to him, pointing to other receipts. "Japanese, Thai, Korean, German, French."

"How many languages do you speak?"

"Dos. Español y inglés. Y tú?"

"What did you say?"

"Two. English and Spanish. My nanny was from Mexico."

Dan pointed to a photo of a Mexican woman. "Is that her?"

"Sí. Su nombre es Paulina."

"Paulina. And this is your mom?" Dan asked, pointing to a photo that was taken at a fairground. Stacy had a giant smile on her face which was covered in a layer of dirt and grime, streaks of sweat carving paths down her face.

"Yes. I love this photo. I see her strength and determination shining, and it reminds me that anything is possible."

"I can't get over her smile. It's magnetic. And she has this rugged beauty that…" Dan blushed. "Your mom seems pretty cool."

Leah took Dan's arm and turned him to her. "I need you to know that when my parents separated, they tried to hide it from me. I was ten, and they often left for business. Paulina was the one who basically raised me. I understood fairly quickly though that my mom wasn't coming back. Everything was wrong—the way Dad behaved, the way Paulina spoke to him, and how my mom always kissed and hugged me when I went to visit. It wasn't normal. I thought I had done something wrong to make her go away. Do you know how that feels? I mean, did they think that because I was so busy and had so many people around me, that I wouldn't notice my mom was missing? It wasn't until after my twelfth birthday, when I started getting into trouble that my dad finally sat me down. I know that's nothing compared to what happened to you, but I want you to know that you can talk to me."

Dan hugged Leah. They squeezed each other tightly and then kissed and kept kissing. His tongue touched hers, making her shiver. He ran his hand through her hair, his thumb playing with her ear. She twitched, producing a soft moan.

Barb's voice rose from the living room, the level just shy of a shout. "Hello, Mr. Davenport. Welcome home. How was your new route?"

Leah pushed Dan away. "Oh shit, my dad's home." Then she giggled, taking his hand. "Sorry. Come on."

"Are we going to get into trouble?"

"No. My dad's cool."

As they headed down the hall, they heard Jared ask in an investigative tone, "Where are Dan and Leah?"

Walking into the living room with Dan, Leah said, "Hey, Dad."

Jared spied the two of them. "Umm," he started, but then hesitated. He looked at Barb, pointing to Dan and Leah. "So... ?" Jared dragged the word out, questioning.

"He wants to know if we're dating and probably wants to check my sheets." Leah giggled.

"Eww," Dan blushed, putting his hands in his pockets.

Barb's face cringed, giving Leah a sideways look. "Don't worry, Mr. Davenport. Leah's my best friend, and Dan's my brother. I absolutely won't allow things to get out of hand."

"That makes me feel so much better," Jared said sarcastically, heading for his bedroom.

"Dad? Are you feeling ok?" Leah asked as her father brushed past her.

"I'm tired. My head feels funny. I'm going to sleep early."

"There's pizza in the kitchen," she called.

"I grabbed a burger on my way home."

"Good night, Dad." Grabbing Dan's hand, she led him out. After they left, she leaned back against the door, her hands clenched to her chest, a smile plastered on her face. Then she stomped her feet and shook her hands, squealing softly. He's so firm. She replayed their interactions. Does this mean we're dating now? She wondered if she should text him. No. Not yet. With long, deep breaths, she fanned her face to cool her emotions. A dark thought crept into her. *I hope he didn't kiss me to forget about that photo.*

Unboxing the Clues

In room 4 of the police station, Brandon lay back against the chair, asking, "Nong Ekamai, where are you?"

Having taken all of the boxes from the three abduction cases out of the storage room, he sat surrounded by a mountain of paperwork. He had spent the last two hours skimming and organizing the information. He had perused binders dedicated to single individuals. He had looked at interview statements, stake out reports, CD's labeled "security tapes," affidavits, search warrant reports, maps of searched areas, photographs, audio cassettes, officer reports and notes, doctor reports, thumb drives—all spanning a total of nine years. Brandon felt a bit overwhelmed, although the puzzle pieces in this case should be easy enough to solve. "A chief fire inspector, a developer, and an architect and landlord—what do these have in common?" But he needed a framework before putting those pieces together. He decided to wait until after his talk with Sam Marvin before he truly began to dig in. *Tyler will provide the missing piece,* Brandon thought. In his gut, he knew he would find Nong.

Closing the boxes, Brandon grabbed his notepad, where he had written questions and observations, carried it to his desk, and closed it in the top drawer. Heading home, he hoped his mom had come into town and left him some dinner.

After finding no food, Brandon ordered delivery. He sat on the floor in the middle of the living room, focusing on his breathing. He felt the stale air pass the walls of his nose and fill his lungs. He held his breath shortly before exhaling, feeling the warm moist air leave him. Breathing in—he felt calm. Breathing out—he acknowledged this moment—the soft carpet, a distant barking dog, and his too-long fingernails—a spark of disapproval flashed, followed by grief. He quickly repositioned himself, wiping the emotions away. Refocusing, he continued with his mindful meditation, which centered him in the here and now. Breathing in—he smiled. Breathing out—he cherished this moment. Now is when life happened. In, and out—he cleared his mind, released his stress, and felt at peace until the delivery driver interrupted his calm by ringing the doorbell with his dinner—cashew chicken and rice.

Before bed, he clipped his nails, laid out a clean suit for the morning, and allowed himself to revisit his cases—the Mitchells, Nong, and the college kid, Marc. He gave his subconscious permission to aid him as he set his pen and paper on his nightstand. Insights he gained while dreaming were often very useful.

He closed his eyes thinking about Nong. This was why he had become a detective. He could find her. He had to...

Rolling onto his side, he tried not to cry. If he could save her, maybe then, he could face his demons.

Day Three—Friday

Five-Day Pattern

Detective Spencer arrived at the station, powered on his computer, checked his emails, and began typing up Marc's statement—the hungover student who claimed he had no idea who'd taken his car in the hit-and-run case.

"Morning, Brandon," Maggie, the secretary, said, on her way to her desk. "Detective Sam Marvin is in Room 4 waiting for you."

"He's here already?" Brandon replied, a bit surprised. "Okay, thanks." He grabbed his notepad and headed down the hall.

When Brandon opened the door, he saw Sam sitting at the table looking at his laptop. Sam had opened several of the boxes and pulled files. "Good morning."

"Good morning. Have a seat." Sam gestured to the chair on the other side of the table.

"Thanks for coming. I wasn't expecting you so early." Brandon sat.

"Yeah, well, I got a little excited," Sam said as he clicked the mouse, pushing the computer aside. "Look. These cases have really baffled us. Even with the FBI's resources, we weren't able to solve them. I know you're itching to make a name for yourself, but unless Tyler is able to give us something new to go on, I'm afraid you're going to be disappointed."

Brandon nodded his head. "If you could give me an overview and point me in the right direction, I'd appreciate that."

"I'm tempering your expectations, but to be honest, I am more than a little excited to solve this thing."

"Okay. Let's start with Amanda Bowman's case," Brandon said.

Opening several folders, Sam slid them to Brandon. He listened as Sam explained that Amanda had been the Chief Fire Inspector. Nine years ago, she drove to an empty lot near Bobcat Mountain, two days before the construction of the Education Center began, and was presumed abducted. Two years later, she was found wandering the parking lot of the now-constructed Education Center, the same place from where she was thought to have been abducted. She fell into a vegetative state for three years, unable to communicate. "When she regained consciousness, she suffered from memory loss and wasn't able to help us with the investigation."

"She was missing for two years and in a vegetative state—known as unresponsive wakefulness syndrome—for three years. What has she been doing for the past four years?" Brandon asked.

"She's been living with her mom. After taking a year to recover and readjust, she went back to the fire department. She's currently working as a firefighter."

"She hasn't been able to give you any information about what happened?"

"It's been a few years since we've talked, but no," Sam said matter-of-factly.

"Tyler Jiles was next." Brandon closed Amanda's folders and pushed them aside.

Sam detailed Tyler's case, opening folders as he spoke. He told Brandon that Tyler was a building contractor and that seven years ago, he left his office, drove to the Education Center, and parked his truck. He had gone to see a woman with whom he was romantically interested. Sam explained that not everyone agreed Tyler had been abducted. He'd expand on that point later. Tyler was missing for three years and was found in the parking lot of the Education Center in the same state as Amanda. "He's been in that state for four years, and as we now know, he came out of it two days ago."

"He was missing for three years and in a vegetative state for four. The length of the abduction and the unresponsive wakefulness are a year longer than Amanda's," Brandon observed. "Okay, and Nong?"

Sam exhaled and said, "Nong Ekamai." He pointed to the four boxes resulting from her investigation. "The FBI had us working over-time after she went missing." Sam started by showing Brandon photos of her properties and her downtown office, describing her as a successful architect and respected landlord. He outlined the events that led to her disappearance, including the fact she had ridden her bicycle to the Education Center to see a guy about a property she was interested in buying. She was presumably abducted, still missing after four years. "The FBI have nothing."

"No ransom demands or anything of that nature?"

"These are not your typical kidnappings."

"I see that. Nong's been missing four years, a year longer than Tyler. There's a pattern. Amanda was missing for two years, Tyler was missing for three years, and Nong has been missing for four. That pattern must mean something." What were they using these people for? Whatever it was, the increased time felt like they were coming closer to reaching their goal.

Sam shrugged and continued, "Amanda was found the same day Tyler disappeared. Tyler was found the same day Nong went missing. They all vanished in the same place, the Education Center. Amanda and Tyler were also both found at the Education Center."

Sam turned his computer and clicked on a video file to show Brandon footage from a security camera. "This is from the video camera outside the front entrance of the Education Center seven years ago, the day Amanda was found, and Tyler went missing." Sam pointed to the screen. "Here you see Tyler entering the building at 11:27 am."

"Do you have feed from the other cameras? Do we see who he meets or where he's going?"

"The camera in the lobby was being repaired, and Tyler didn't appear on any of the other cameras. He wasn't found in the building, and we have no footage or evidence showing him leaving. But it gets better. Look here." Sam clicked on a second clip. "At 3:12 pm on the same day, the camera captured Amanda coming out of the Center." They watched as Amanda stumbled out the door and stopped. She stood in place for over a minute and then headed into the parking lot.

"Do you have video of her entering the building?" Brandon asked.

"There was only video footage from twenty-four hours prior, and she isn't seen in any of the security footage from any of the cameras."

"That's odd. But the abductor was there. Surely someone knew something." Brandon's voice rose.

"Don't get excited. No one knows anything or hasn't talked. At that time, there were only a few cameras on the premises. Whoever brought Amanda there and then abducted Tyler knew where the cameras were and how to get around them. Fifteen additional cameras were installed after that day, and we investigated everyone coming and going from the building over the next month. Nothing," Sam said. "But it gets even better." Sam clicked on a second video clip. "This feed is from four years ago. This is Nong Ekamai here." Sam pointed as they watched.

Nong walked to the front door and stopped, staring blankly, her face a pale white.

"What's she doing? I don't understand."

"Just a second. Watch this. It gets weirder."

As they watched, Nong snapped back to life, smiled, and waved. She looked happy as she turned away.

"This video was captured five days before she was abducted," Sam said.

"That's very odd. Who was she waving to?" Brandon asked, more as a rhetorical question.

"Was she hallucinating? Was she meditating? Could it be a seizure? I don't know. But look, it happens again the next day." Sam clicked on the next clip.

Nong walked to the door again, standing with a blank stare and a pale face. But then the door opened, and she entered the building.

"Please tell me you have feed from the other cameras," Brandon pleaded.

"We don't," Sam said. "There was an electrical storm the evening prior, and a few of the breakers were fried, including the one for the front lobby. She doesn't show up on any of the other cameras either. But here she is leaving the building an hour and twenty minutes later."

The video showed Nong walking out the door, turning, saying something, waving goodbye, and heading off, smiling.

"She is obviously talking to someone," Brandon said.

"I don't think it's so obvious. She could be seeing things."

"But the door opened."

"This next clip is from the day she was abducted." Sam played the next video clip.

Nong rode her bike, parking it next to the door. She touched the wall, as if ringing a doorbell, took off her backpack, and removed a leather legal folder. She wrapped the backpack strap around her bike seat waiting for the door to open. Smiling, she walked into the building.

"Let me guess. The camera inside isn't working," Brandon sighed.

"Exactly. And this is the last time we see Nong. She doesn't leave. However, guess who does leave three hours later?"

"Tyler!"

Sam clicked on the next clip, which showed Tyler Jiles leaving the building. "He walked in circles around the parking lot for almost two hours before someone called the police," Sam said.

"We don't have any video showing Tyler entering the building before Nong?"

"We have five days of video prior to Nong's abduction, and Tyler isn't in any of the footage," Sam said.

"But we don't actually see them abducted. Are we sure that's what happened?"

"You're right. It was decided later that these were abduction cases."

"Who made the decision?"

"Someone above me," Sam said. "I didn't ask. It seemed logical based on the evidence."

"Who else saw Nong coming and going? She arrived during office hours, what did the employees say?"

"They never saw her. None of them recognized her photo."

Brandon scratched his head. He was struggling with the fact that all three people disappeared without a trace. How does someone simply vanish?

"What about Tyler?"

"Same. No one at the Center had ever seen him."

"How is that possible?" Brandon asked.

"I don't know. But like I said before, the abductor obviously has another way in and out of the building," Sam said. "The FBI went over all the footage, and everyone has been investigated."

Sam paused. Brandon took a deep breath, sitting in thought. He put himself into Nong's shoes—I arrive at an office building during business hours. I greet someone who manages to avoid being seen by cameras and walk into the building. I have a folder with legal documents and am ready to discuss purchasing a house. We find a quiet place to sit. And then, someone comes up from behind. The same person who distracted the employees. "There must have been more than one person who abducted Nong."

Sam nodded. "Sure. Could be. We have no evidence suggesting there's only one person."

"And that fact doesn't change anything?"

"It might, if Tyler can give us something new to go on."

"Let's go back to Amanda's case," Brandon suggested.

"What questions do you have?"

"When Amanda was first reported missing, what did you know, and what did you do?"

"Because she was the Chief Fire Inspector, we feared the worst, most likely murder. Perhaps someone who had to close their business or maybe a hate crime."

"Hate crime?"

"Amanda likes women."

"Okay. And?"

"We talked with everyone she knew and had had appointments with during the two weeks prior to her disappearance. We checked phone records and cell tower pings to show her whereabouts. We sent search parties along the trails and into the park and the mountain. We didn't rule out the possibility that Amanda was doing something illegal, and we checked her bank records, personal records, and social media accounts. What we found was that Amanda was a hard-working, honest woman who people respected. She simply disappeared without explanation." Sam waited for Brandon to respond.

"What happened when she reappeared?"

"The media created a lot of attention for the case," Sam said. "When a popular official in a demanding position goes missing and is presumed dead, then suddenly shows up and in a vegetative state to boot—that's a story every news outlet wants to report. We sent Amanda to the hospital, where she received medical attention. Physically, she was completely healthy—no signs of abuse of any kind. Mentally, she was... that's a different story."

"She was a vegetable."

Sam pushed the computer aside and moved two folders in front of him. "I'm going to tell you exactly how it was explained to me."

Sam opened the first folder containing several images of brain scans. "Do you know the headgear the doctors put on people to measure brain activity? It records the parts of the brain that are active, creating an image, a map that highlights those parts of the brain."

"Yes, I've seen them before."

Sam put the first image in front of Brandon. "This brain scan is of a person taking an algebra exam. See the areas here?" Sam pointed to a part of the brain that was red. "This is the active area." Sam laid down the next image. "This one is of a person painting a design on a vase. The active area of the brain is over here in red."

"I see it."

Sam began to display several pictures of brain scans in a row. "This is a person dreaming, a person tripping on LSD, an architect designing a floor plan, a guitar player composing a piece of music, and so on and so on," Sam said as he laid down five more images.

Brandon looked at them, fascinated by how various activities stimulated different areas of the brain.

"This next image superimposes all of these onto one brain." Sam showed the next one.

"Wow, it's all lit up. What does this mean? Where are you going with this?"

"Here's the mystery. This next image is Amanda's brain scan two days after she reappeared while still in a coma." Sam showed Brandon the picture.

What the hell? Brandon was staring at a visual he wasn't sure how to interpret. He was expecting to see no activity, but instead was looking at... "What is this? It's all lit up." He felt like a comic book character looking at the brain of a super—villain or hero. "This doesn't look like she was in a coma to me."

"Yes, she was in a coma. It's a fifteen-minute brain scan."

"Jesus!" Brandon gasped, trying to wrestle his mind around the possibilities. Had she been drugged? Was something inserted into her brain to stimulate it? Was it psychological trauma—some crazy Clockwork Orange brainwashing?

"I said the same thing."

"Any scars?" Brandon asked. "Any indication of surgery?"

"No."

"No foreign objects in her body, her ears? Traces of drugs?"

"Nothing. Now look at Tyler's," Sam said, laying his scan next to Amanda's.

Brandon was looking at two identical images. His face tightened, and his heart dropped. "What's going on here? What's the explanation?"

"The doctors have never seen anything like it before," Sam said. "Here is the last image. It's Amanda's scan after she regained consciousness."

The image looked like a typical brain. It couldn't have transitioned from one state to the next overnight. "How many scans were taken while she was in her vegetative state? I'm asking because there must have been some kind of progression back to normal."

"She wasn't normal. I'll get to that later." Sam rifled through the folder for the other scans. "Here. Three total. They all look the same."

"Do we have a professional's opinion on that?"

"Yes. There is no change from one scan to the other."

Brandon grappled with this fact, unsure of what to make of it.

"You can now understand why people began to speculate that her abductor had experimented on her brain," Sam said. "Some crazies suspected it was an alien abduction. One of the officers thought she was possessed by a ghost."

"It reminds me of a movie I saw. The guy takes a pill, activating his whole brain, which makes him super smart. Maybe the abductor is a drug researcher."

"Let's keep going. What other questions do you have?" Sam asked.

"Amanda showed up the same day and place where Tyler went missing. What were the connections between Tyler and Amanda? Who were the main suspects?"

"A few of the detectives believed that Tyler's going missing the same day and in the same location was purely coincidental," Sam said.

Brandon snorted. "You're kidding. Why on earth would they think that?"

"Tyler had separated from his wife five months prior. His business was on the verge of bankruptcy. The guys at the office said he was romantically involved with a rich woman and that he had joked about running away with her. Some in the department believed that's exactly what he did."

"Did you think that?" Brandon asked.

"I didn't. He didn't take any of his belongings. There was no credit card activity and no withdrawals from his bank account. The limited information from the Education Center video feed indicates he didn't disappear of his own accord."

"Now wait a minute. I'm not sure about that," Brandon said. "The video footage is mysterious, for sure, because it lacks evidence that should be there. But to say he didn't disappear of his own accord is a stretch."

"At any rate, it turned out I was right."

"Looks like it. So, who was this woman Tyler wanted to run away with?"

"No one knows. Tyler never mentioned a name or showed any photos. The only thing we do know about her is that she owned an expensive house in the Bobcat Mountain area."

"So how did the investigation proceed? What connections did you find between the two cases?"

"We followed missing-persons protocol. Nothing came of it. He vanished. The investigation lasted several months. We combed through the security footage from the Education Center, paying extra attention to the security guard and the patrons. The camera being repaired seemed too convenient. The few connections between Tyler and Amanda led nowhere."

"Ok. So Amanda goes missing. Huge ordeal. She's presumed dead. Two years later she turns up a vegetable, but her brain lights up like a Christmas tree. That got lots of attention which didn't help. How much media play did Tyler's case get?" Brandon asked.

"Some. However, his abduction was overshadowed by the news coverage of Amanda being found. And like I said before, many thought that he ran off and didn't want to be found. He left what little he had to his wife and called it a day."

"Right." Brandon looked at his notes.

"The next media frenzy came when Amanda recovered. It was a whirlwind of activity."

"Explain."

"Amanda started talking five days before Tyler was found and Nong was abducted. Then the FBI declared this a serial case."

"Five days before?" Brandon repeated.

"Right. We thought Amanda could now shed light on where she had been, who had taken her, what horrors had happened to her. However, she had memory loss and was struggling with anxiety and depression. She found it difficult to think and speak. She complained of frequent headaches. She really couldn't tell us anything."

"Going from genius to normal may do that. When you say memory loss, what are we talking about? Complete amnesia?" Brandon asked.

"No. What we were able to determine is that five days prior to her abduction, her memory began to fragment. We collected information to outline the two weeks of Amanda's life leading up to her disappearance. She couldn't remember most of it, starting five days before she had gone missing, including an argument with the city clerk and a retirement party she had attended. She also had no memory of the two years she was gone."

"Convenient for the abductor. What happened next?"

"She went back to the hospital for tests and met with different specialists, but she didn't give us any leads."

"Do we know why or how she regained consciousness?" Brandon asked.

"No. It's a mystery. One day she woke up."

The phrase, "she woke up," resonated with Brandon, in particular, the excitement that had followed, the anticipation and hope that came with it. "I'm wondering if the media circus played a role in Nong's abduction," Brandon said. "Hear me out. If we look at it from the abductor's perspective, Amanda wakes up with information that might lead to an arrest. So, they, I'm thinking at least two, release Tyler Jiles and abduct Nong Ekamai in an attempt to create more confusion and chaos. Am I reading too much into that?"

"Why would they release Tyler? Tyler may have information we could use."

"But Tyler, too, is in a vegetative state," Brandon said.

"Why abduct another person?"

"From the brain scans, we know something is happening. At any rate, the added chaos buys them time to move, change appearance perhaps."

"Sounds like a possible theory," Sam replied.

"How was Tyler after his release?"

"Same as Amanda. You saw his brain scan. Although, now that he's awake, it sounds like his memory may be a bit better than Amanda's. At least I hope it is."

"Me too," Brandon agreed. "Ok, so after Nong was abducted, you said the FBI took over. What did they do?"

"We had surveillance warrants. We had stakeouts. We executed search warrants. We followed all leads and looked at every connection. It's as if she was literally abducted by aliens, which I'm not subscribing to, but it's really dumbfounding." Sam shook his head, clearly frustrated.

"There has to be some connection. They all work with buildings. No one at the Center knew them?"

"No one."

"Same school? Clubs? Online chats? Shopping at the same hardware store? There has to be some connection, and it must tie to the Education Center somehow," Brandon said, a bit aggressively.

"I feel your pain. Imagine how we felt every time a lead turned up empty."

Sam and Brandon sat silently. Finally, Brandon spoke, "Now that Tyler is awake, he'll generate media attention. I think the pattern will continue—Nong will be released in five days, and someone else will go missing. We should make sure those surveillance cameras at the Education Center are working."

"I wonder if the perp will go back there," Sam said.

"I believe they will, if it's a pattern."

"I don't think it's a pattern. The abductor knows Amanda wasn't able to give us any information after she recovered. We know Tyler's memory is questionable."

"I don't think they'll risk that chance. The added chaos worked last time. They'll do it again," Brandon said confidently.

"Regardless, we've got to find Nong and make sure no one else gets hurt."

After Sam left, Brandon lined the eight boxes of documents and tapes along the wall. He scanned his notes reviewing the puzzle. They vanished at the Center. No witnesses. No video showing the abduction. No suspects. They reappeared at the Center. They were in a coma with strange brain activity. No signs of surgery. No traces of drugs. Memory loss when they wake. There seemed to be no connection between them other than working with buildings.

Brandon grabbed the first box and set it on the table. He removed the contents and spread them out. The first thing he needed was the connection that brought all three of the victims together—why the Education Center? Was it a specific building they had visited or worked, an activity they shared, a class, or a teacher? That connection is the starting point. If he could find that, he could solve this case. And according to his calculations, he only had three days before someone else went missing.

Gateway Bite

At the Go Express terminal, Jared opened his scanner, scrolling to see if Nong's address was there. She had said she was expecting a package today. Jared paused and smiled. There it was. 4871 175th. Feeling giddy, he jumped up on his toes, acting more like a teenager today than yesterday.

As he delivered packages, Jared thought about Nong—her touch, her excitement. He recalled her saying, I want you to bother me. Picturing her smile and stumbling over words while with him, made him feel virile, coveted. He reviewed questions he would ask her. Where had she studied? Which architectural style did she prefer? What projects had she worked on? How did she use context when designing? And how did she feel about repurposed materials? He missed his discussions and debates with Stacy—the collaboration they engaged in. Could he and Nong have the same?

Jared thought about Nong so much that he forgot what he was doing and where he was going. More than once, he had to turn the truck around and go back to deliver packages he'd skipped.

Nearing Nong's address, Jared felt an adrenaline rush. His heart pounded with excitement, and his body tingled. His palms moistened, and a drip of sweat rolled down the inside of his armpit.

Once he arrived on Nong's street, his shoulders tensed, and he got a headache. Jared put his hand to his head, grabbed his water bottle, and took a swig. He dismissed the discomfort to the adrenaline running through his body, turning his focus to Nong.

Jared entered the driveway, admiring the house. This is awesome, he said to himself, hoping Nong was serious about giving him a tour. I need to ask for her phone number.

Stacking four different-sized packages from the back of the truck, Jared carried them to the door, put the boxes down, and rang the bell. His stomach roiled like an eddy. His fingers numbed. A fire raged in his heart. Reaching for the bell again, he stopped. How long had it been? A second? Two minutes? Time had divorced him.

The door opened.

Nong stood smiling felicitously. She held a small plate of treats. Her hair was up in a bun, revealing her soft neck and delicate ears. She was wearing a low cut, sleeveless white blouse. Jared forced himself to look at her eyes so as to not embarrass himself.

"Hi. I'm so happy to see you today. I made you some sweets." Nong held up cake pops covered in chocolate.

"Wow, I would love to try one." Jared reached for the plate.

But Nong pulled back and said, "No, let me." She took one of the sweets and reached her hand to feed him.

Nong put the cake into his mouth, sliding her finger in between his lips, touching his tongue. Jared's knees became weak. He felt his cheeks and ears redden as his chest warmed. He wrapped his lips around her...

An electric shock surged through him, making his muscles tense and stiff. His eyes rolled back. Jared saw nothing but white. His head throbbed with an intense irritating pain, as if a sliver had been embedded in his brain. And then Jared began to have visions. Memories of himself with his babysitter, Jenny, played in his mind like a movie, starring him as a character.

Jared's heart danced with excitement as Jenny prepared chocolate ice cream, topped with whipped cream and a cherry. Then they drew stars, planets, and spaceships, hanging them on his bedroom wall, pretending they were flying through space using his bed as their very own ship. After that, they sang and danced to Pink Floyd's "The Wall."

He saw himself standing next to her hospital bed, holding her weak boney hand as confusion and fear tore into his seven-year-old heart. Cancer! What was cancer?

Puzzled, Jared heard a strange voice ask, "Do you really love me?" It came from inside him, a low soft whisper that had a melodic feel. There was a hint of an accent that he couldn't place.

Nong's finger left Jared's mouth, releasing him from the shock and pain. Emotions flooded him—sensual electricity from Nong and grief from losing his caretaker. They abandoned him—the finger's impression faded, and the vision disappeared.

Jared stared at Nong. Her sweet smile and loving eyes gave no indication that she knew what had happened. "Well? Do you like it?" she asked.

Jared was confused. What had happened? Her touch caused his senses to scream with lust. This reaction was completely unexpected. Not knowing what to say, he replied, "Yes, it's delicious."

"Did you like all of it?" Nong asked alluringly.

Jared grinned. "Oh yes." Nong putting her finger in his mouth was so erotic that he had truly lost his mind.

"Would you like another?"

"No, thank you. I don't think I could control myself," Jared replied, with a playful reluctance and genuine uncertainty.

"Maybe next time you won't need to."

His heart jumped, speeding double time, turning his face red. He would make love to her right then and there, if she invited him in. Her lips parted slightly, asking him to kiss her. He lifted his hand, reaching for her, but dropped his scanner. It bounced on the concrete. Jared picked it up; work had robbed the moment. He couldn't, shouldn't do anything. He turned the conversation back to the house. "How long have you lived here?"

"I've been here four years," Nong replied. "When I first saw this house, I knew I had to have it. So I talked with the owner and bought it from him." Her eyes lightened. "You are quite taken by this house, aren't you?"

"I remember you offering me a tour. Maybe I could bring treats for that?" Jared suggested.

"Oh? Yum." Her smile was wicked. "I look forward to that."

They looked at each other for a long second, the energy between them building. Then Nong's face lit up.

"I can't wait for you to see the inside! You are going to love the spatial definition. Living here has really changed my ideas about what I can do with space. When I get out—I mean, back out—into the field, I have some great ideas I want to try. Are you free Monday night?" Nong asked.

"Yes, I'm free," Jared blurted but then remembered Leah. "Ah, actually, I have to attend a birthday party on Monday."

"Let me know when you're free."

"How about Tuesday?"

"Sounds perfect. But don't be a stranger. If you are in the area, please stop by."

"Absolutely."

"Bye," Nong said, waving as she abruptly went back inside, leaving the packages outside and Jared confused and wanting.

He grabbed his chest, pressing it hard with his palm. When he reached the truck, he lifted the scanner, closing the stop. *Error. Signature Required for Business Stop.*

That's odd, Jared thought. *Why did it reset?*

He changed the setting again, closed the stop, and drove away. After leaving Nong's street, he felt his headache disappear, but a fog in his brain remained, making him tired. He took a deep breath to relax, but had difficulty concentrating. His head didn't hurt, but he felt like he hadn't gotten enough sleep.

Jealous?

Standing in front of her puke-green locker, Leah slid her homework into her bag as she tried to block the loud chaos of after school. "Hey, Leah," Becky said, stepping behind her. "A bunch of us are going to the mall to look at dresses. Do you want to come?"

"I can't. I have dinner plans with my dad. Next time?"

"Cindy's coming along. We're meeting Abram and Eric. Tell your dad you need some friend time."

"Na. You go ahead."

"Okay, but you're missing out on some fun." Becky's eyes widened as she flashed the brightest smile she could.

Leah gave a weak smile in return.

"Do you have a date for prom?" Becky asked.

"Hmm... maybe." Leah's smile animated as she twirled her hair.

"Really? Who? Tell me."

"I'll tell you later after it's official."

"I want to know everything...youth group, Wednesday. You are coming, right? I missed you this week."

"Yeah, sorry. Model UN had a meeting on Wednesday," Leah replied.

Cindy, Jane, and Sally joined them, giggling. "Hey, Lea. Ready?" Cindy asked.

"She's skipping this one," Becky said.

"You got a date?" Sally teased.

"It's unofficial," Becky said gaily.

"Do tell," Sally said.

"Spill the beans," Jane said, expectantly.

Leah rolled her eyes. "Movie night with my dad."

The girls groaned. "Come on, Leah. We're looking at prom dresses."

"You guys go ahead. I'll go with you next time."

Sally pulled on Jane's shoulder. "Look. There goes Derric. I'm going to ask him to join us. Come with me."

Cindy put her hand on Leah's shoulder, conceding with a sigh, "All right. But you are coming with us next week. No excuses."

"See you Monday, Leah," Becky said, the four of them prancing after Derric.

"Yep, Bye." Leah closed her locker and put her bag on her shoulder as Dan came around the corner. A volcano erupted in her chest as the memory of her lips on his, their tongues touching gently, replayed in her mind. Instantly, her cheeks blazed a brilliant ruby. He didn't take his eyes off her as he glided straight for her and took her hand.

"What are you doing here?" she asked earnestly, searching the halls to make sure the gossip queens had vacated.

"I still have friends that go here. Plus, my girlfriend is a senior here," Dan explained, as they slowly made their way toward the doors.

A giant smile crossed Leah's face as she looked away. Squeezing his hand, she asked, "Won't she get jealous if she catches you holding my hand?"

"She's not the jealous type."

"Oh really? She must have caught you in compromising situations for you to learn this."

"No. She loves who she is. She's the catch, not me."

"Is that because she's beautiful?"

"She is, but that's not the reason." Dan stopped and faced her, lowering his voice, "She's incredibly smart, well-traveled, and empathetic." With emphasis, he added, "She sees people for who they are." He paused, taking her in with his gaze. "She feels cozy and makes my heart melt."

Leah stood silent, eyes locked, connecting to him. "She sounds like a nice person," she whispered.

"More than you know." Then Dan abruptly asked, "Are you excited about movie night?" He turned, and they continued down the hall toward the exit.

"Am I ever excited about watching old movies?" she asked, turning to avoid being bumped by a boy rushing to the locker room for track practice.

"You loved *Back to the Future*."

Leah's expression changed. With a goofy grin and one eyebrow higher than the other, she asked, "Did I, though?"

Dan smiled, "I liked it."

"Yes, I did, too. And I'm told tonight's movie will be equally entertaining. We'll see."

"Any chance I can join you? I'll help cook."

The question burned. She wanted to say, yes, but..., "Let me feel my dad out first. He seemed... agitated last night."

"So, he's not cool with us seeing each other?"

"No. It's not that." Leah played the encounter in her mind—her father brushing past her in a dreary state. "I think something happened at work. Maybe he lost a package or had an argument with a customer. He hasn't been himself lately, and I don't want to push him."

"Okay." Switching the subject, Dan asked, "Are you picking me up tomorrow, or am I picking you up?" He often asked that when he wanted Leah to drive.

"Can I pick you up?" Leah didn't care for Dan's car. There was a funky smell in it. She thought something was molding under the seats.

"Of course," he said with clear relief.

"I still have no idea what to get your grandma for her birthday."

"I'm sure we'll find something. I'm thinking Bath and Body Works or a gift certificate to Janet's Spa."

"I can't imagine going to a spa at the mall. It seems like an oxymoron to me."

When they reached Leah's car, he kissed her before saying, "Enjoy your night. Call me before you go to bed."

Leah smiled. "I will."

A Familiar Name

Jared sat on his couch with his eyes closed. His head was still foggy, and his memories of the past few days seemed lost. Nong, however, was crawling in him. Her smile, dimples, sexy mole, golden complexion made his emotions dance. His urge to kiss her neck below her ear panted for relief. He played the image of her lips parting over and over in his mind, wishing he had been bolder.

What was it she had done to him? Oh yes, her finger on his lips, touching his tongue, and then the pain. Intense pain. Memories. And that voice. It was addictive. The pain, the headache, the adrenaline rushes, and the feeling of intense passion and desire. Jared was addicted.

He sat, spellbound, as he replayed their encounter. Then an image began to materialize. It was Nong standing on a chair, dusting a cobweb from the corner of the room. She paused and turned. "Jared?"

"Jared," Tim called from the dining room.

Jared's mind went blank as he returned.

"Dad?" Leah said, touching her father's shoulder.

Jared opened his eyes, feeling unnerved. "Yes?"

"Uncle Tim is here. Dinner is ready. Let's eat," Leah said.

Jared got up, heading into the dining room. "Hi, Tim. Nice to see you. Glad you made it." He hugged his brother. Tim was shorter than Jared, but much more muscular, with a beer belly.

"I love the new look," Tim said, gesturing to Jared's haircut, a fade which had been buzzed around the ears.

"When are you going to cut your hair?" Jared asked, pointing out Tim's long blond wavy hair pulled back in a ponytail.

"This is by design. I'm a Greek god."

Jared snorted. "Yeah, a regular Russell Crowe," he quipped.

Leah laughed. "It's true. You look just like Zeus."

Tim stood taller and and looked at the table. "The spaghetti looks fantastic. I'm starving."

They sat down and dished up.

"So, how is the new route?" Tim asked, hoping for good news.

"I should be able to help you on Monday. I only have a few businesses in a tiny strip mall."

"Awesome. I can't wait for you to meet this woman."

"Actually, I met someone."

"What? Really? Yeah, Dad! When?" Leah jumped in. "This is so great. Maybe we can go on a double date?"

Jared turned his body and faced Leah full on. "What? You started dating? Who?"

Leah backed slightly. "Dad! Dan, of course. You caught us making out yesterday." Her head tilted forward, her eyes digging into his own.

He touched the side of his head. "You were what? When did this happen?" Jared was frustrated with this nagging fog that was clogging his memories. He had suspected that Dan and Leah might hook up and was mentally preparing himself to give her the "take precautions" talk. Had he really seen something and not registered it?

"Uh, last night, when you came home from work. Barb was here. Remember?" Leah sighed.

Jared vaguely remembered coming home. He did see Barb. She stood quickly and had spoken loudly.

Tim interrupted by patting his brother on the shoulder. "Come on, bro. Who is she?"

Jared shook his head. "Barb?"

"No. I've met Barb. This woman you met?"

"Right. Do you know the Bellevue House near Bobcat Mountain? She lives there," Jared said.

"The Bellevue House? I thought that house burned down."

"What's the Bellevue House?" Leah asked.

"It was an expensive house that won some awards," Tim said, "but the guy who built it was a certifiable nutcase."

"You knew the guy?" Jared inquired.

"Yeah, I did some work for him. The first time I went there, he wanted me to replace a corner trim board on the house. Someone had hit the wood and put a crack in it. The repair should have been easy—put some wood putty in it, paint it, done. But he wanted the board replaced. Turned out to be a tricky job. I had to cut all the caulking, pull the trim board, align the new board with existing cuts, re-caulk it, and then match the paint. It was too much and unnecessary. I didn't want to do it, so I told him it would be $4,000 instead of the $1,500 it should have cost. He paid it."

"I did three or four crazy jobs like that for him," Tim added. "He's actually the reason Patty and I were able to afford that beach house. I'm telling you, the guy was possessed or something. He talked to himself, obsessing over the house being clean and looking new. And he was always touching it—the walls, the floor. He knew exactly where a spider was or when and where a rodent had entered the house. And he cleaned those places immediately. It was weird."

"Why did you take advantage of him?" Leah asked. "If the guy was crazy, you should have been nicer. Was his family looking after him?"

"He was a rich guy who was asking for perfection. I didn't take advantage of him. I'm not sure about his family, but his wife seemed kind of crazy, too. I could tell she was upset about her husband's obsession with the house. One day when I was there," Tim paused, apologized to Leah, and kept going, "She took me upstairs to the bedroom. She wanted to make her husband jealous, but he didn't care. He looked at us and said, 'Have fun.'

"I think it was the next day that she burned down that house, killing him. She died later of guilt, shot herself, I think. Anyway, the police took me down to the station and interrogated me for almost three hours."

"When did that happen?"

"Oh, ten years ago, I guess."

"When was the house rebuilt?" Jared asked.

"I didn't know it was," Tim said. "But if she's living there, she's pretty well off. I'd love to see that house again. Does she need any work done?" Tim chuckled.

"You didn't know it was rebuilt?"

"Enough about the house. Tell us about her, Dad," Leah said.

Jared picked up his glass and drank some water, collecting his thoughts. "I met her yesterday. Her father's an executive for some big company. I can't remember which one. She's an architect and quite charming." Jared's voice trailed off as he pictured Nong in his mind. Her eyes, so intense and inviting. Jared felt as if he could feel her. She was sitting in her living room, music playing. He closed his eyes to get a closer look at the room.

"An architect? That's great." Leah said. "Maybe she can help you get a job."

"When can we meet her?" Tim asked.

Jared opened his eyes, smiling. "I'm going to her place Tuesday to get a tour of the house and have snacks," Jared said.

"Hey! That reminds me, Uncle Tim," Leah cut in. "About Monday. My dad had dinner plans with me. Can you reschedule your appointment for... Sunday or Wednesday?"

"Dinner plans?" Tim asked.

"My friends and I are cooking lasagna for Carol's birthday,"

Tim put his hand to his lips in thought. "What time is the party?"

"Six," Leah returned.

"I could go in early, leave as soon as the sort is finished," Jared offered. "I bet I could be done by 4:00, maybe?"

"No. I'll try to find someone else. It'll be okay."

"What if my boyfriend and I help?" Leah offered. "Then you can join us for dinner, too."

"Hmm...maybe. Let me think about it. I'll let you know tomorrow."

They finished dinner, cleaned up, and watched their movie. Jared put his arm around his daughter. She snuggled next to him, snacking on popcorn. His heart warmed when she laughed, he squeezed her when the movie frightened her, and he giggled when she commented on the cartoonish nature of the special effects.

When the movie ended, Tim said, "It's still pretty good. I remember the first time I saw it. I always loved the scene with the Handbook for the Recently Deceased. Makes you wonder what's really out there, doesn't it?"

Leah giggled. "'Reads like stereo instructions.'"

"Did you know the practice of shrinking heads was a thing?" Tim said. "Tribes in South America took the heads of their enemies, shrunk them, and kept them as trophies."

They chatted for a while more. Leah and Tim sang *"Jump in the Line (Shake, Senora),"* while doing their own funny dance moves. Jared watched blissfully.

As the night grew later, Tim headed for the door, and Leah gave her uncle a hug. "Can Dan come and watch with us next time?" she asked.

"I don't see why not," Tim said.

"Sure," Jared said.

Before Tim left, he wished them a good weekend, saying he'd call Leah if he needed her help.

Jared closed the door. "I'll clean the living room, if you do dishes."

Markets and Cocoa Puffs

Leah finished the dishes and retreated to her bedroom to call Dan.

"Did you have fun?" Dan asked.

"Tons," she answered sarcastically.

"That bad?"

"No. It was good, a goofy ghost movie," Leah said. "I loved the music. You can come over next Friday."

"Cool."

"How was your dinner?" Leah asked.

Dan had pork chops, and the conversation turned to how four farmers started a business to mix manure and food waste to create energy and sell it. Dan was researching the topic for a paper he had to write about the environment. Vanguard bought the company and built biodigesters that created the renewable energy, which benefited farmers and the environment. Leah thought the topic was interesting and brought up the Sunrise Movement, a youth group dedicated to stopping the climate crisis. She had seen a Tik Tok video about it and was thinking about joining. From there, the conversation turned to travel.

"The air pollution in Bangkok can be so bad that when I blew my nose it was solid black crud," Leah said.

"How many countries have you visited?" Dan asked.

"I don't know. A lot. When I was young, I went somewhere with my parents twice a year. When I got older, my grandparents would take me somewhere over summer and spring break. It's funny, because with my mom's parents, everything is first class and high end, but with my dad's parents, we go economy. I hate flying coach, but I don't mind taking buses, trains, or walking when I'm in another country. You really get to know what life is like there. I especially love street food, which my Grandpa Bill never lets me eat. Where have you been?"

"We've been to a lot of places here in the states," Dan said. "The Grand Canyon, Chicago, New Orleans, Disney in LA. That was fun. My dad was considered rich, but he put everything he had into his house. My grandma wasn't rich at all. The money she got from the insurance and the sale of the land went toward raising us and paying off her own house. She did take us to London for a week. I loved how diverse the city was. Hearing a different language being spoken every ten minutes was pretty awesome."

"I love your grandma. She's so—real. I love that she says exactly what she's feeling."

"Right?" Dan agreed.

"My dad's parents are like that," Leah said. "No superficial politeness. They welcome me and start talking like we've been in the same house for years."

"Where do they live?"

"In Green Bay. They own a cheese and sausage shop near Lambeau Field. They make good money during the football season."

"You're a Cheesehead?" Dan laughed.

"I have one of those hats at their house. But, no, I'm not a sports fan. How about your other grandparents?"

"I don't know them. My dad didn't get along with his parents very well."

"I'm sorry."

"It's nothing."

During a long pause, Leah could hear Dan breathing, and it gave her comfort. She imagined lying next to him, wrapped in his arms, his warm breath tickling her ear. "Tell me something you like."

"Something I like?" Dan repeated. "Hmm... I like cookies dipped in milk. I like adding vanilla ice cream to a bowl of Cocoa Puffs. I love sitting in the shade of a tree on a hot summer day, listening to the world happen around me while I nap. I also love climbing that tree and sitting in the branches while I read a book."

"Sounds nice."

"It is for about an hour, then your butt gets sore," he laughed. "How about you?"

"I love markets and festivals."

"What is it you like about them?"

"Everything: the food, music, art, people." Leah took a moment, recalling the emotions she had felt while standing in La Boqueria in Barcelona, Spain. "The thing I like the best about markets is watching people. There's a unique energy that I only find in a market. The spirit lightens and people shine. The excitement of shopping, seeing new things, finding a special object or a great deal—it creates joy. The interaction between shopkeepers and customers is binding. Taking delight in art with others forms a strange bond that leaves me feeling connected. I walk away from a market happy and fulfilled. They're amazing places."

Dan was quiet for a moment. "You really see people, don't you?"

Leah smiled into her pillow. "I try."

"Oh, I'd say you succeed," he whispered. "The way you described the atmosphere... I've never thought about markets like that before. Makes me want to go to one with you and follow you around—see what you see."

She chuckled. "You'd have to keep up. I get excited and wander."

"Then I'll hold your hand," he said. "That way I won't lose you."

Leah's heart warmed. "That sounds nice."

"Yeah," Dan agreed. There was a pause and then he said, "I love watching people at the beach—seeing what they bring, the way they set up their space, how they treat each other—it can be romantic or comedic."

"We have to go people-watching this summer," Leah concluded.

"It's a date," Dan confirmed.

Cuddled in bed, Leah thought about seeing Dan's half-naked body in the sun while he lusted over her own nearly naked body. She could picture herself holding his hand, feeling his gentle touch as he rubbed lotion on her back, and grabbing each other while splashing in the water.

"What are you thinking about?" Dan asked.

"I'll tell you another time. I should sleep. I'll see you tomorrow."

"I'll see you tonight in your dreams."

"That's sweet. Good night."

"Good night."

The House in Question

Detective Spencer sat in Room 4 at the police station in front of a table full of papers stacked in small piles. He had been reading through statements and interrogation reports, listening to interviews, and looking at documents used to prove a person's innocence. He hadn't gone through half of the materials and was feeling exhausted and no closer to a clear motive, connection, or suspect. Sitting back and closing his eyes, he let the information play in his mind like a mini movie which brought up several questions.

Nong had been planning to buy a house, but there was no information on the house—no address, no asking price, no offer to purchase, no realtor. So where was this house? Who owned it and who was selling it?

Amanda had gone to take photos of a house. What house? Where? Why did she park in an empty lot? Why wouldn't she simply park in front of the house?

Tyler had gone to visit his love interest. She lived in a big fancy house. Where was that house? Why hadn't they met at her house? Why did she ask to meet him at the Education Center? Were they hiding something? Their affair wasn't a secret.

Was this mysterious house the same house in question for each victim?

Brandon needed answers before he interviewed Amanda and Tyler. He would need to walk them through what had happened, helping them remember, jarring their memories. He had the weekend to finish reading, listening, and learning, but it seemed unlikely the answers to solving this case were in these boxes.

Brandon felt uneasy. More experienced detectives had poured over this information and yet, the cases remained unsolved. Sam said every connection had been investigated with no results. But everything Brandon was reading and hearing was focused on the victims' adult lives. Perhaps the connections between them went further back, from childhood—a friend, a club, a field trip, or a sleepover.

Brandon decided to visit their parents. With some luck, learning about them as kids might reveal this elusive connection. Also, better understanding who Amanda and Tyler were would make the interviews with them more personal and effective.

Picking up the phone, he called Sally Bowman. A woman answered.

"Good evening, Mrs. Bowman. My name is Detective Brandon Spencer with the LVPD. I was wondering if I could visit with you sometime this weekend."

"A detective? Is Amanda in some kind of trouble?"

"No, ma'am. I'm looking into her case and am hoping you'll talk with me about her."

"Amanda won't be back until Monday."

"That's all right. I was hoping to talk with you."

"Have you learned what happened to her? Have you finally caught the person who caused us such heartache?"

"No, sorry, nothing new to report, but I have reopened the case, and I would like to ask you about your daughter before I talk with her directly. Would that be okay with you?"

Silence hung heavy. Mrs. Bowman's pause likely spoke to the weight of painful memories. "Why do you need to see me? It's been nine years since she went missing and four years since she woke. I don't know anything new. I told the police everything already. You still don't know anything?"

"This is a very mysterious case, ma'am. I assure you we are working diligently. I am hoping for your help."

"I'm not sure I can help you. Why are you asking me now? Has another person been taken?"

"No one else has been taken. I'm trying to make sure no one else will be."

She mumbled something, paused, and then continued in a softer tone. "Thank you for that. No mother should ever have to go through that devastating trauma."

"I agree. Which is why I would like to speak with you."

"I suppose. Tomorrow morning will be fine."

"Thank you for your willingness to meet with me. Would nine work for you?"

"I'll be here. Good night, detective."

"Thank you very much. I'll see you tomorrow."

Brandon made his second call to Tyler's mother and a third to Nong's parents, making appointments with each of them.

As Brandon locked the room, he thought about the Education Center. Checking the security cameras to make sure they were working properly needed to be added to his agenda. Perhaps a tour of the building as well.

Day Four—Saturday

A Clue

At 9 am, Detective Spencer knocked on Sally Bowman's door. She answered and invited Brandon inside.

"Thank you for meeting with me, Mrs. Bowman."

"Amanda isn't home like I said on the phone. I'm not sure what help I can be." Sally led Brandon into the kitchen.

"I want to know a little bit about Amanda before I talk with her. The more I know about her, the better chance I have of uncovering something new."

"Like I said, not sure what help I will be, but I'm always happy to have company. I heated water for tea or coffee. Which would you prefer?"

"Tea would be great."

"Please sit down. Help yourself to a cream cheese Danish." She set a plate on the table. "I got them fresh at the bakery this morning. Lemon and honey for your tea?"

"Yes, please. Thank you."

She handed Brandon a steaming cup and sat across from him with her own. "What would you like to know?"

"Tell me about Amanda. What was she like as a little girl?"

Sally took a sip of her tea and smiled. "Amanda was strong willed and physically fit; she excelled in sports."

"Which sports did she participate in?"

"Gymnastics and track. She especially enjoyed pole vaulting. Outdoor activities were her thing—hiking in the woods and climbing trees. She loved building little houses for fairies. When it rained, she would build a fort in her room and spend all day inside reading. In the seventh grade, she won an award for building the best structure from toothpicks. It held nineteen textbooks. She was so proud of that moment, talked about it for months, even built a whole village of toothpick homes that lined her windowsill.

"One of our favorite activities to do together was to browse antique shops. Amanda was fascinated with historical objects, which led to her love of old buildings and architecture."

"Amanda loved architecture?" Brandon repeated.

"That's right. She was a self-study. Bought all kinds of books about it and even a college textbook. Come, I'll show you."

Brandon followed Sally into the living room to a bookshelf which held twenty or more books about architecture. Brandon ran his finger along the spines. The books ranged in subject from Ancient Rome to Southeast Asia to modern cities.

"Here." Sally handed Brandon a portfolio.

"What's this?"

"They're pictures of Amanda's favorite buildings. She had them on her walls."

"May I look at them?"

"Absolutely. Please sit."

Brandon sat on the sofa looking at photos and drawings of world-famous buildings in plastic sleeves. Some of the photos were 4 X 6s of St. Basil's Cathedral and Potala Palace. Others were 11 X 14s of The Blue Mosque and Fairmont Le Château Frontenac. There were pictures cut out of magazines that included Angkor Wat and the Parthenon. Others were hand drawings of Casa Milà and the Taj Mahal.

"Did Amanda draw these? They are quite good."

"Yes. She was there when she drew these. She had plans to go to all of these places and draw each one but never got the chance. Now she doesn't care. A part of her soul has been lost since her abduction."

"Why did she become a firefighter instead of an architect?"

"She was going to be an architect until her best friend's house burned down. Then she felt it was more important to become a firefighter. She blended her love for architecture with her firefighting experience to become a fire inspector."

Brandon continued flipping through the photos until he paused, admiring several images of the same house. Among them were professional photographs, amateur snapshots, magazine clippings, and hand-drawn sketches. Pointing, he asked, "What is this place? A mansion in the Alps? It's gorgeous."

"You must not be from around here," Sally said. "That's the Bellevue House. It won a couple awards. It was built, oh, maybe fifteen years ago. Amanda said it was the best house she had ever inspected. She was so excited when she found out someone had rebuilt it after the fire. She was going to inspect it again, but I don't know if she ever got the chance. She went missing later that day. And, of course, she doesn't remember that now. So sad."

"It's my understanding she was on her way to take photos of a house when she disappeared. Was it this house? Do you know?"

"I'm not sure, but I would think so. She talked about the Bellevue House for a few days. She kept wanting to get photos of it, but her old camera wasn't working, so she bought a new one. I'm not sure she ever used it, but I know she wanted to get those photos, so I think that was the house where she was going, yes."

"It's called the Bellevue House? Do you know where it is?"

"No. I tried to find it after she went missing, but I guess it was built somewhere else. I never found it."

Brandon's phone rang. It was Captain David Crandle.

"Excuse me, Mrs. Bowman. I need to take this call. I'll step outside."

"Not a problem. I'll wash up in the kitchen. You can stay here."

Brandon answered the call. "Good morning, captain."

"Brandon, your appointment with Tyler has been canceled. The FBI is sending an agent to see him."

"Come on, captain. You can't be serious."

"You can still talk with Tyler, but not until after the FBI has. Keep reviewing the files. I imagine the bureau will ask for a detective to assist them, so be ready."

"Yes, sir," Brandon replied. "Did you know Amanda studied architecture on her own? Tyler and Nong both studied architecture at university. This is our connection."

"Yes, we knew. Yes, that connection was an exciting lead. Yes, we followed up on it. Is there an angle you believe we missed?" David asked.

"Sam gave me the impression the victims didn't have much in common. This seems like a solid connection."

"It was. The list of people we interviewed following that lead is extensive. Comb through the reports, see if you can find something we missed. We'll talk Monday morning." David hung up.

Brandon had seen the stacks of reports from university classmates, professors, colleagues, and work associates. It would take him time to go through. He'd need to look at enrollment rosters to cross check... Whoa. That work had already been done. Best to stay on his current line of thinking—was there a connection from childhood? Amanda's interest in this mysterious mansion also felt important. Walking into the kitchen, Brandon apologized for having to take the call.

"You're a busy man. I understand."

"So you were telling me how Amanda loved the Bellevue House."

"She did once," Mrs. Bowman asserted, her eyes narrowing. With a hint of anger lurking in her words, she continued, "before being taken by some crazy lunatic." Sally paused, steadying her breathing. "I'm sorry, detective. Talking about dreams my daughter had before her abduction is rather upsetting to be honest. I'm not comfortable talking about it anymore." With a sense of exasperation, she added, "I don't see how any of this is helping you catch the man!"

Brandon was taken aback by her sudden frustration. He leaned forward slightly, speaking in a soothing tone. "We do have some good news regarding your daughter's case. Tyler Jiles has regained consciousness. He was the man who was abducted the day Amanda was found. I would like Amanda and Tyler to sit down together. I believe they may be able to help each other remember details. I came to you first so I can understand Amanda better before I question her."

Mrs. Bowman pursed her lips, clenching her hands. "Have you talked to Amanda about this? Does she know?"

"Not yet, no. I'll call her after I meet Tyler on Monday."

"I should tell you, she's not open to discussing what happened."

"But this is an excellent opportunity to make some real progress. Amanda knows what Tyler experienced, and I believe they could both benefit from sharing their experiences."

"I understand, but...Did you want me to tell her about Tyler?"

"It's probably best if you do. Tyler's story will be in the morning paper tomorrow."

"Very well. Thank you for informing me. I hope your meeting with Tyler goes well." Sally led Brandon to the front door.

"I really appreciate your seeing me today. I look forward to meeting with you again."

"Good luck, detective."

Sitting in his car, Brandon opened his phone and typed "Bellevue House" in the search bar. He scrolled through articles about protests and the fire, then saw an article titled, "Professor Helps Student Create Award-winning Home." Brandon opened the link, reading the article. Calling the station, he asked for the phone number and address for Professor Yun.

Diamond Creek. Brandon mused. My mom has been wanting me to visit.

Brandon called Professor Yun and made an appointment to see him. Then he called his mom.

"Hi, Mom. It's me."

"Brandon, it's so good to hear your voice. Are you coming for a visit?" she asked.

"I've got a lot happening, but I recently took on a new case which, oddly enough, is taking me to Diamond Creek, so yeah, I thought I might swing by for a few minutes if you're free."

"Absolutely. It'll be great to see you. When will you be here?"

"I'm in the car now, so I'll see you in an hour and a half or so. Oh, by the way, is there any chance I could meet your guy?"

"Yes, I love that idea! I'll call Jae and see if he can come over."

"You guys are getting serious."

"Yes. We've been dating for a few months now. You know, we've driven down to your place a few times to see you. If I didn't know any better, I would say you've been avoiding me."

"I know. I know. I'm sorry. This past winter was hectic."

"It's ok, dear. I don't think he's busy today, so hopefully we can have a quick lunch together."

"All right. See you in a bit."

As Brandon drove, he reviewed what he had learned. Amanda loved sports, hiking, and antiques. She had traveled and was an artist. Did Nong or Tyler have these same interests? Had they been to any of the sights Amanda had visited? Architecture was something all three of them had in common. Did they attend the same middle school? Perhaps the same teacher inspired all three of them. His interviews with Tyler's mom and Nong's parents weren't until tomorrow, so he'd read more of the files tonight. He was curious about this Bellevue House. What would he learn about it from the professor? There was no mention of the mansion being rebuilt online. Maybe he would know about that.

Spiked Strawberries

Jared stopped by the grocery store during his route to buy fresh strawberries and cream. He wanted to have something to give Nong when he saw her, and strawberries were the fruit of love. Jared also wanted to ask her something, but that foggy feeling in his brain persisted, and he couldn't remember what it was.

Something I said at dinner last night, he thought. Oh yes, he was going to invite her to dinner and get her phone number—he needed to get her number.

As he worked, Jared's heart pounded. He was feeling impatient and jogged to and from the houses as he delivered packages. How would she respond to his asking her out? At that moment, Jared was unsure if what was happening between them was real or imaginary. His brain wasn't working right. He didn't understand where the strange headache and visions were coming from—a chemical imbalance? His body was out of whack. He was infatuated with Nong—he knew that much—just as he had been with Stacy. However, this new obsession felt different. With Stacy, he felt inspired by their mutual creativity. They had similar goals, interests, work ethics, and a shared vision and passion for sustainable development. But, with Nong, he felt compelled by her enchanting touch—as if he had been drugged. Who was she? He wanted to sit and talk, but hadn't had the opportunity.

Jared continued to work quickly, and by midafternoon, he had reached Nong's street. As he turned the corner and headed towards her house, his shoulders tensed, and the headache returned. Reaching for the first aid kit, he popped two aspirin.

As he drove along the driveway, he marveled at the architectural beauty in front of him. Parking, he grabbed two packages and walked to the front door, placing them on the step. Ringing the bell, he waited, popping his scanner in and out of his side pocket.

Nong answered the door wearing a white T-shirt and green shorts. Her hair was pulled back into a ponytail, and she had a radiant smile.

"Hellooo." Nong pursed her lips into an exaggerated kiss. "Did you miss me?" She raised her eyebrows, turning her head slightly to the right and then to the left. It was a cute gesture.

"I did. I can't stop thinking about you." Jared handed Nong the bag of strawberries and cream, hoping she would invite him in. "I brought you a treat."

"A treat? What a wonderful surprise. Will you be joining me then? Maybe I won't be able to control myself this time." Nong bit her lower lip as she reached for the bag.

The minute Jared saw her bite her lip, he instantly became erect. "Sure, I would..." he started to say, but Nong's finger ran along Jared's hand as she took the bag, making his body sensitive. Suddenly, he stiffened as an electric pulse pushed a fat needle into his brain. The intense pain turned his eyesight white, and visions followed.

Jared's heart brightened, emitting warm, loving fondness, a consistent dependability that always came when he thought about his grandmother. They had packed the canoes with camping gear and drifted down the river, singing, eating campfire-cooked dinners, and sharing raindrop poems written in the night. In the warm summer evenings, while discussing future plans, they ventured into the garden, picking green beans and tomatoes until their buckets overflowed. The vision transitioned to Christmas: eating her famous lasagna, getting a toy semi-truck, playing Monopoly, and laughing as she told stories about Jared's mom, aunts, and uncles.

His chest tightened as he saw her lying in the hospice bed, wracked with dementia—weak, disoriented, and cranky, ready to pass away. As Jared sat in the funeral service, crying, Leah held his hand and asked, "Dad, why are you crying? She didn't even know you."

Coldness gripped Jared's heart as he recalled his grandmother's final words to him, "Who are you?"

That strange voice came back, "I'm so glad you like me. We are going to have a wonderful life together. And I will never forget you."

Nong had taken the bag from Jared, withdrawing her touch. The pain, visions, and voice disappeared. Jared was worried, not knowing what to say or do. He didn't understand why this happened. He looked at Nong hoping again for some clue from her.

"Oooh! Fresh strawberries with cream. You have to eat some with me," Nong said, reaching for Jared's hand to lead him inside the house.

Jared jerked away, not wanting to experience the pain again. "Actually, I have to go. Work is busy today," he blurted.

"I see," Nong said. Then she gestured for Jared to come closer. He bent over, and Nong kissed his cheek. Closing his eyes, he held his breath, waiting for what he knew was coming—a shock, pain, and visions. But nothing happened.

When Jared opened his eyes, Nong touched his nose. "Go to work. I'll see you Tuesday, for sure, but hopefully sooner." Ignoring the packages, she went back into the house.

Jared felt the warmth of her kiss on his cheek. The touch on his nose gave him a happy fuzzy feeling. But what just happened? The intense pain, the visions of his grandmother, and that eerie voice—none of it made sense. Was it some kind of hallucination? Or did Nong have something to do with it? He rubbed his temples, trying to shake off the lingering confusion.

As he walked back to the truck, Jared replayed the moments in his mind. He needed to understand what had triggered those visions. Had Nong somehow caused them with her touch? Or was it his own mind playing tricks on him? The warmth of her kiss contrasted sharply with the earlier pain, adding to his bewilderment. He closed his eyes briefly, taking a deep breath. Whatever it was, he couldn't shake the feeling that something profound was happening.

Jared reached the truck, and the scanner's screen read, *Error, Signature Required for Business Stop.*

Ugh, I'm going to have to talk to Hossain about this, Jared thought, making a mental note. He changed the setting to "Residential" once more, wondering if he should get the signature instead. He faced the house, seriously considering going back, but the pain in his head was real. The visions of his grandmother were still raw. His head was foggy. He turned his back, jumped into the truck, and drove away.

After he turned off Nong's street, his headache vanished; however, he couldn't concentrate or think. These visions! The pain—he missed it, had a strange craving for it, or was it the soft touch of her hand? When she bit her lip, oh my god! He wanted to turn the truck around and go back to see her, but he had to finish working. He would see her tomorrow.

Blueprints and Connections

Stepping up to his mom's front door, Brandon paused. Why had he stayed away for so long? It had been six months since he'd last seen her—when he bought his house. Guilt engulfed his excitement at being home, and he was also feeling anxious. Brandon knew his mom wanted to discuss his past. For some reason, she couldn't find closure unless he would talk with her about it, but he had buried it, in the past, where it belonged. He had moved on. Brandon chortled, allowing himself to feel good about visiting his mom. He had missed her. Knocking, he waited.

Judy opened the door, smiling broadly. "Ah, look at you. Give me a hug."

"Hello, Mom," Brandon said, laying his head on top of hers as he gave Judy a hug.

"I've missed you so much. It's been too long." Judy backed away to look at her son.

Brandon grinned and touched her hair. "Letting it go gray. I like it."

"I got tired of having to dye it. How was the drive?"

"Good." Brandon followed the delicious smells into the kitchen.

"Come, sit down." Judy said. "I've got hummus with carrots, broccoli, apple slices, and pita chips. I made grilled cheese sandwiches with tomato, avocado, and cilantro. And I have some coconut milk curry soup. I already put some of the soup in a container for you, along with some other dishes." She pointed to a large grocery bag full of Tupperware bowls.

"Did you cook for me again?" Brandon knew she had but wanted to sound surprised and grateful.

"You know I did. Chickpea spaghetti, eggplant parmigiana, and salad greens from the garden." She had told Brandon that cooking for him made her feel connected and reassured her he was eating something healthy.

Brandon was genuinely shocked by how much she had prepared. "When did you cook all this?"

"Leave the containers by your door. I'll pick them up next time I'm in town." Her pride was alive and well.

Brandon dipped a pita chip in the hummus and grabbed an apple slice. "So is the new love of your life coming over?" He was genuinely curious about the guy he had kept missing the opportunities to meet. "What's his name? Jay?"

"Jae is busy this afternoon. If you can stay, he'll be by later."

Brandon frowned. "I can't. I have appointments. I'm busy with this new case."

Judy lay her hand on top of his in full-mom mode. "I know you are, son." Her voice was full of concern. "But drowning yourself in work isn't going to—"

"Mom. I'm fine. I've accepted what happened." Brandon grabbed her hand and squeezed it to reassure her. Changing the subject, he asked, "How are your paintings selling? Got any hot new designs?"

She studied him thoughtfully. "Please talk to me. If you bury the pain, it will only fester and blow up later."

"I've dealt with it in my own way," Brandon replied, with a hint of anger.

"Have you talked with your father about it?"

"Mom! Seriously," Brandon intoned, with a forceful edge that couldn't be ignored.

"Tell me you're at least doing your meditations."

"I am."

"Good." Judy watched him, waiting.

"What?" Brandon snarked.

"When's the last time you spoke with Larry?"

Brandon relaxed his shoulders, recalling his last conversation with his dad. It had been at least two years. His dad had divorced his mom three months after Brandon left home for college. He had quit his job as a teacher and moved to New Mexico, where he bought a small plane, flying the *Santa Fe New Mexican*, a daily newspaper, to surrounding communities. He rubbed his lip. "After he sold his Cessna and bought his hot air balloon."

"So he doesn't know about Korea."

"No. And I'm done talking about it. If you want to call him, go ahead."

"No, you're right. Your father doesn't deserve to know."

Brandon struggled with the realization that his mom was never going to stop asking. "Mom, I've come to terms with this; you need to, as well." Frustration lingered in his voice and on his face.

Judy offered a weak smile and nodded. "If you had dealt with this, you could talk about it. *You* are coping. It's called avoidance. And it's not healthy."

A knot tightened in his chest. He closed his eyes, hearing the hum of a lawn-mower, smelling the curry, feeling the smooth finish of the table, and tasting the sweet remnants of the apple. The knot loosened. He opened his eyes feeling fresh and calm.

With a sigh, Judy said, "Okay. Grab a sandwich. Come see my new paintings."

Brandon picked up a sandwich as they walked outside through the garden to the work shed. He looked at comedic drawings of animals doing silly things. He laughed at the one with two dogs looking in the toilet bowl, telling each other, "No, you go first." She had captured the perfect expressions on their faces that said, "Something nasty is in there."

"This one is great! When did you paint it?" he asked.

"Five months ago. I got the idea from a stray dog sniffing a bowl of something behind a restaurant downtown. The dog clearly didn't want to eat it, but it wouldn't walk away either. Poor thing."

They talked about Judy's art fairs and her interest in traveling to a few shows out of state before heading into the house.

"When will I see you again?" Judy asked, wiping some food crumbs from the corner of Brandon's mouth.

He thanked her and replied, "I'll try to come next weekend."

Judy carried the bags of food and walked him to his car. He hugged his mom again, seeing a small tear fall from her eye. He kissed her cheek and headed off.

Driving ten minutes across town, Brandon pulled up to a white, A-framed clapboard house with blue shutters. The mailbox read—Jae Yun. "This must be it." The yard had been freshly mowed. Blooms of vibrant daffodils and tulips adorned the well-tended flower bed. The dogwood tree added elegance to the spring landscape. Meanwhile towering oaks and magnolia trees provided ample shade for the professor, who was on his knees, weeding. Neatly pruned hydrangea and azalea bushes framed the entrance of his house. The overall picturesque setting validated Brandon's preconceived ideas of a professor of architecture.

"Good afternoon. Professor Yun?" Brandon asked.

"Yes, you must be Detective Spencer."

Offering his hand, Brandon replied, "Yes, that's right. Please call me Brandon. Nice to meet you."

"I'd shake your hand, but as you can see, I'm pretty dirty. Come on in," the professor said.

They walked toward the house. "Are you, by chance, related to Judy Spencer?"

"She's my mom. Why do you ask?"

"I'm Jae Yun. Your mom and I have been dating for a few months now. I thought you were her son, especially after she called me to say you were visiting."

Brandon stopped. "What?! You're Jay." He looked back at the mailbox feeling shook by the unexpected coincidence. *Oh, Jae! Professor Yun is my mom's boyfriend.* "What a small world. I'm so happy to finally meet you." Brandon followed him into the kitchen, his mind still buzzing. "I wish I would have known you were her boyfriend. We could have had lunch together."

"Next time."

"Absolutely. Maybe next weekend?"

"Sounds great," Jae said. "So, how can I help you?"

"I'm curious about the Bellevue House. It's come up in an abduction case I'm working, and I understand you helped the man who designed and built it."

As the professor washed his hands, Brandon looked at a wall that was dedicated to the Bellevue House. Drawings, sketches, blueprints, and photos, matted and framed, covered the walls of the living room. Brandon felt as though he were in a museum.

"Yes. That's right. He had most of the design finished when I met him. I helped him flesh it out and make it viable."

"This display is amazing. May I take pictures?"

"Sure. But I have extra photos if you want. I'll give you some."

"I'd appreciate that. Thank you. You must have been devastated when the house burned down."

Jae entered the living room, standing next to Brandon. "Oh, I was. What a tragedy that whole thing was." He shook his head. "The needless deaths and the poor kids." He brought his hand up to his mouth, squeezing his lips.

"What happened?" Brandon asked.

"That house was John's lifelong dream."

"John? Who is that?"

Jae motioned for Brandon to have a seat on the sofa. "John Mills. He was one of my students. He approached me with a plan that he had been obsessing over since childhood. He told me he'd been saving every penny to make it a reality. It was brilliant. I found myself obsessing over it as well, spending all of my free time working on it. After the plans were finished, he hired a team to build it. He loved that house more than anything, including his family. One day, his wife burned it down. She killed him, and then took her own life, leaving the kids orphaned."

Brandon's face numbed from the shock. "That's terrible." His heart went out to the kids. He knew how this trauma affected them—the times they had come home to find ghosts standing at the stove preparing dinner or phantom lectures from their father. He shared the empty silence that filled their hearts. He thought he should find out who they were and visit. The meditations he engaged in helped him, helped the kids he worked with at Hope's Heart Residential School, and would probably help these kids as well.

"That house really was something special," Jae reminisced. "It had a way of pulling at your heart. I really miss it."

"How so?"

"Well, John's passion and excitement for the house was infectious. But more than that, it seemed to breathe life. I felt connected to it—like a long-lost lover who had returned. I understand why John loved it so much, but I can't, for the world, understand why his wife burned it to the ground."

"Were you happy when it was rebuilt?"

"Rebuilt?!" Jae leaned forward and raised his eyebrows. "I didn't hear about that. Who rebuilt it? When?"

"Oh, I'm not sure. I haven't found any information about it yet."

"Who told you it was rebuilt?" the professor asked.

"Amanda Bowman's mother. Amanda was abducted a few years back. Her mom said she was excited about inspecting the house. She was headed to see it the day she went missing."

"I know all about Amanda's case. She went missing nine years ago. The police came to talk to me. They didn't take her mom seriously because the house was never rebuilt," the professor stated plainly. "If you want to know more about the house, you could ask the kids who lived there. They're with their grandmother now."

"What are their names?"

"Barbara and Daniel Mills."

Recalling the Fire

Barb, Dan, and Leah walked across the warm black asphalt of the enormous mall parking lot searching for their car. Dan handed Leah a bag. "Open it."

With a cross look, Leah asked, "What is it?"

"Just something I thought you'd like," Dan said, grinning with anticipation.

Opening the bag, Leah held up a *Back to the Future* T-shirt. "I love it!"

Barb smiled at Leah's reaction and gave her brother an approving nod. Then she held up her own bag. "Mission accomplished. I got Grandma a pair of pearl earrings."

"Perfect," Dan and Leah agreed.

Pointing, Barb said, "I see your car over there." They changed direction, walking toward Leah's car, parked next to a red pickup two lanes over. "Where should we go next?"

"Let's find my dad," Leah said excitedly. "I want to show him my new T-shirt, and besides, it'll be fun to surprise him."

"Isn't he working today?" Barb asked.

"Yeah, he works near Bobcat Mountain."

"I know where he works. I don't feel comfortable going over there," Barb said.

"Really? Why not?" But as soon as Leah asked, she remembered the photo that had caused them to recoil.

Dan put his hand on Leah's shoulder and spoke softly, "It's because we used to live in that neighborhood with our mom and dad."

"Sorry." Leah grimaced. "Let's do something else." She pressed the button on her key, unlocking the doors.

"No, let's go. We can eat at that teriyaki place in the little strip mall. If we're lucky, we'll see your dad, jump in the car, and chase him down. Come on, sis...." Dan stopped talking.

Barb's sharp scowl made Leah's inside clench.

In the gentlest voice she could manage, she asked, "What happened to your mom and dad?" Leah needed to know if she was ever going to fully understand who her best friends were. She had a feeling the photo on her phone had something to do with their deaths. Did their car roll down the side of the mountain?

Obviously, the topic was painful—could she help them heal? But, if for no other reason, she wanted to avoid upsetting them in the future.

Barb put her bag in the car and closed the door. "I'm going to buy a smoothie. You should tell her. I'm not ready to remember that right now." She turned and headed back to the mall.

Leah softened her expression and raised her eyebrows. She looked into Dan's eyes, trying to discern if he was okay with telling her.

Dan took a deep breath. "I... I need to sit down."

Looking around, Leah pointed to some grass and a tree at the end of the parking lot. "How about over there?"

Dan walked with his head down as they held hands. She glanced into his eyes, which had dulled. Sitting in the shade, Dan picked at the grass.

"My dad loved to tell this story—in middle school, the math, art, and English departments created a cross-curricular assignment to design a house. In math, the teacher gave him graph paper, told him the price per square foot, and how much he could spend. He had to design the floor plan using the allotted money. In art, he sketched the house. In English, he had to write a fictional story that included the house. Kind of a fun assignment, right? He started dreaming and drawing and never stopped. He excelled in art and math, using his skills to perfect his house. By eleventh grade, he had a box full of drawings—each room, every angle. In college, he majored in computer science, but also took a couple of architecture and graphic design classes. He planned and designed that house down to the tiniest detail."

Dan paused, swirling his finger in the dirt from where he had pulled out the grass. He clenched his jaw, breathing heavily through his nose.

Putting her hand on his leg, Leah hoped he could draw strength from her.

"You know," Dan continued, "I remember him being a cool dad before he built that house. We played with my Black Sky action figures, and he read to us. We went camping once a month. It was so much fun. But after he built that house, nothing. He even stopped going to school events." Dan gave a half snort, half laugh and shook his head.

Leah watched him press his eyes closed. He turned, looking up at the white cotton clouds. Then he lifted his hand to his face before returning his gaze to the grass. His focus was distant through glistening eyes.

"He won awards for building his house. They called it the Bellevue House because of the beautiful view of the valley. Lots of people came to look at it and take pictures, so the first year we lived there was crazy because of all the cars and people knocking on the door. Dad finally hired a security guard to keep the crowds off the property."

Leah saw the corner of Dan's lips raise. She knew he could tell her some fun stories, perhaps about a crazy lady trying to climb the deck and falling into a rose bush. She'd have to ask him later.

"Besides the gawkers, he invited monks, priests, and rabbis to bless the inside and outside of that house." Dan smiled, likely remembering the ordeal of each ceremony.

"Which religion was he?"

"I honestly don't know. We never went to church or temple. That's why having those religious people in our house was so weird." Dan twisted his mouth and turned away.

Moving closer, Leah put her second hand on the back of his shoulder, rubbing him.

Dan faced Leah. "My dad's behavior was bizarre. He would sit in his den and read out loud, as if reading to the house. He would hug the door frames and say, 'I love you.'" Rolling his eyes, he added, "It was weird."

Then Dan's face turned red, and he balled his hand into a fist, his voice rough. "The worst thing though was when I crashed my bike. I was riding in the driveway and forgot how to stop. I rammed into the house near the door and fell. My bike landed on top of me, cutting my leg. I was bleeding all over, and my dad started yelling at me over the stupidest little crack I made in the siding. I mean seriously, no one could even see it. My dad hired a guy who worked all day to replace that board. He was mad at me for weeks—didn't even care that I cut my leg."

"I'm sorry that happened."

Wiping his eyes, he asked, "Can I tell you a secret?"

"Of course. You know you can tell me anything."

Dan exhaled loudly. "Whoa. Why is this so hard to talk about?"

Leah leaned her head against his arm. "You're okay."

The corners of Dan's mouth raised in an almost smile. "So, I had an imaginary friend. He talked and played games with me, telling me everything was ok. He helped me cope with my dad."

"That's great. Totally understandable."

"He made me promise never to tell anybody about him. After the fire, he disappeared."

That's a weird promise. Predators do that, Leah thought. She dismissed the notion. "I'm glad you found a way to get through it. I never had an imaginary friend. What was it like?"

"Kind of fun, actually. We pretended to slay the monsters under the bed and took encyclopedias off the shelf pretending to read and do important office work."

"Sounds fun," Leah said. "I had nannies and tutors who were always with me. I don't think I was ever left alone. I was always doing something—riding, swimming, golfing. When I first moved here with my dad, I didn't know what to do. I was so bored. I ended up joining a church group. One day, we took a trip to Bobcat National Park, and I wandered off into the woods by myself. It was my first time being truly alone. I became aware of my body, my inner voice, and my own thoughts that day."

"Interesting. We both had rich parents, but totally different experiences."

Leah nodded. "My dad didn't come from money. He and his brother have some fun stories to tell." She paused. "My uncle was the one who replaced that board you cracked. He talked about it last night."

"Really? Your uncle knew my dad?" Dan asked.

"He said your dad was," she hesitated, softening her tone, "possessed or something."

Dan stared blankly out at the cars parked in the lot. "I think that's why my mom started the fire. My dad was at work; she didn't expect him to rush home and run inside. But he did." Dan's face grew tight again. He was trying not to cry, but the tears came rolling down when he added, "He died in the flames. When we got home from school, our mom saw us, grabbed a gun from one of the officers, and shot herself right in front of us."

Leah's eyes grew. Of all the scenarios she had envisioned, car crash, home robbery gone bad, or accidental fire, a murder-suicide was not one of them.

Dan was heaving, unable to talk, bent over.

Leah shuddered at the scene in her mind—the gruesome act of his mother shooting herself. She tapped her head, trying to get it out. She understood why Barb refused to think about that day. Taking in a quick breath, she kneeled beside

Dan. She wrapped her arms around him and repeated, "You're okay. I'm here." His heavy sobs brought on her own tears, which melted into his shirt.

After several minutes, he stopped, apologizing profusely, while Leah kept telling him it was okay.

Finally, she asked, "How old were you when all this happened?"

"I was nine," he sniffled. "Barb, almost eight."

"A year younger than I was when my mom left. I can't even imagine how I would have felt if she had died. And you lost both parents."

They sat in silence for several moments, holding hands, leaning against each other. A car alarm beeped in the distance, and kids were shouting joyously, "Can we go to the Lego store?" They jumped up and down as their parents held on to their hands, making their way toward the mall.

Leah raised her head from Dan's shoulder and said, "My dad knows the lady who lives in that house now."

"No, that's not possible. The house burned down," Dan stated flatly.

"My dad thought so, too, but someone rebuilt it. My dad was an architect for years and knows that house. He likes the woman who lives there."

"Your dad was an architect? Why does he work for Go Express as a delivery driver?"

Leah raised her eyebrows. "It's a long story."

"Let's hear it."

She nodded. "He met my mom at an awards ceremony." Leah went on to explain how her mom and her grandfather, Bill, had gone to hear Jared's acceptance speech before deciding to contract with his firm. After her parents separated, her grandfather ended his business relationship with Jared. The financial hit, combined with his emotional struggles, sent Jared in a downward spiral. He approved plans for a housing project drawn up by his junior staff that contained flaws. During a storm, one of the houses partially collapsed.

"Because both the architect and the engineer worked for my dad, and the plans had his signature on them, he was sued. Now he can't get the insurance coverage he needs to work, and no one will hire him, believing he's too much of a risk."

"That sucks."

"It does. But I'm with you. I'm not sure why he became a delivery driver. It's like he lost his will to live and has decided to coast through life."

"Maybe he needs a physical job to get over the trauma. That's why I got into wrestling."

"Perhaps." A couple kids sped past on skateboards, and one tossed a half-eaten hotdog at parked BMW.

"Dude, that was so weak! The alarm didn't even go off."

Dan took Leah's hands and stared into her eyes. "Thank you. I feel better."

"Thank you for trusting me. I know it's not easy talking about this."

"Yeah, not easy."

As Dan turned to watch the crows fight over the hotdog, Leah turned her thoughts inward. Counseling had helped her. The sessions gave her different perspectives for thinking about the things that had happened.

She recalled her twelve-year-old self learning about different family structures, and that different, didn't mean bad or wrong. Photos of kids being raised by a black woman with a white man, an Asian man with a white woman, two dads, two moms, a grandma, all came back to her. Two photos in particular stood out, burned into her mind for life—one with her and her dad at home, and one with her and her mom at the airport. That was her familial reality now.

The most significant benefit from counseling, though, came from learning how to manage expectations and to verbalize how she was feeling, and what she needed.

She squeezed Dan's hands, bringing his attention back to her. "Have you been to a therapist?"

Dan gave a light chuckle. "A couple of them: The school counselor saw me every day for six months, and Barb and I saw a specialist twice a week, Janet. I really liked her. She helped me set some goals and start living again. Grandma's been my rock—always there, always listening, always hugging and holding me. I don't know what I would have done if I didn't have her."

"She is wonderful. I'm still worried about you, Dan. You really struggled to talk to me about this, and Barb leaves every time it's mentioned."

"With Barb, it's different. If you push her, she gets angry, violent even. It's scary."

"Is there something I can do to help her?"

Dan's eyes glossed over. "We watched Mom shoot herself. That's not something you bounce back from."

Rubbing his back, she said, "I know. Which is why I think you need to continue seeing a therapist. My physician, Dr. Thomas, recommended one for me. Maybe we could see the same person?"

He turned away, nodding his head. "Maybe." Wiping his eyes, he added, "I'll talk with Grandma about it." Standing, Dan offered his hand to help Leah up. Clearing his throat, he said, "Two psychologists meet each other at the coffee shop. One greets the other; "Hello. You're fine. How am I?""

Leah chuckled, "Come on. Let's find Barb." As they walked hand-in-hand, she thought about relationships and marriage, her own family's split, and Dan's family ending in tragedy. Could I be truly happy with myself while living with a partner? Would the expectations a significant other might place on me be too much? Whose job was it to make me happy? She knew her mom had decided it was best to live for herself. Leah wasn't sure that would work for her. But her mom was happy living her dream.

Five Glasses to Clarity

Jared returned home but Leah wasn't there. He couldn't remember where she was. Had she told him? His head was so foggy he couldn't think. He took out a bottle of wine from the cabinet and poured himself a glass.

Sitting with his wine, Jared closed his eyes and visualized Nong motioning him to her. She had leaned in to kiss him... Jared's body shook violently. He opened his eyes, his heart racing, muscles tense. "What the hell is happening to me!" he cried. Headaches! Head pains! Electric shocks! His emotions were running wild. He'd feel extremely giddy one minute and depressed the next. Jared struggled to remember basic things now. "My fucking head!" He drank the glass of wine and poured himself another.

Jared really liked Nong; he was sure about that. Her presence lived in his mind. He felt like a rag doll, completely under her spell. Drinking the second glass of wine in one gulp, he poured himself a third, hoping to drown out the noise pestering him, pulling him toward her and the house.

Jared crumbled, falling to his knees. I failed. Who's to say I won't fail again? He loved Stacy. Her power, charm, and confidence had captured him. Her beauty had been intoxicating. All he had needed to do was be there for her, keep the promises he had made. Why did I give up so easily? Why hadn't I slowed down and given her the time she deserved? He closed his eyes, trying to redirect his thoughts.

Here I am again, losing my mind over another woman. Jared grabbed the edge of the table, pulling himself to his feet. Should I go? Go to Nong's house right now and be with her? I don't have her number. I should tell her about Leah and invite her for dinner. Jared put his hands over his temples and squeezed, forcing himself to relax. I need to get to know her better. But what do I want? A fling? A one-night stand? A relationship? God, I don't even know. What does she want?

Jared's anxiety increased, so he finished the glass, pouring himself a fourth. Dr. Thomas came to mind—his hand resting on his shoulder: Do you feel influenced by forces beyond your control? Voices whispering to you? Jared thought about his mind's enigmatic power to distort reality. Stacy's leaving had been traumatic and his maybe all of this with Nong was his mind processing that pain. Jared stared at the phone, breathing heavily. It's not too late to call. I promised Leah to turn things around. He needed to make an appointment to see the doctor. Opening his phone, he called, but it was Saturday. The office was closed. He left a message, asking for the referral.

Time to shower, cook dinner, and do laundry. He put in a Fleetwood Mac CD, cranked it up, inhaled his wine, and poured himself a fifth.

A Name Redacted

Brandon drove back to Lake Valley, listening to the news. The White House was stirring up trouble with North Korea and Iran. Russia was pledging to defend the sovereign nations from the tyrannical U.S. government. More aid was needed to defend Ukraine from the evil fascist Putin, and Israel continued to use the weapons we supplied to kill innocent civilians, all in the guise of fostering peace. "The war machine keeps turning with no regard to the sanctity of life." The local news caught Brandon's attention. A nearby church was being investigated for sexual abuse and forced conversion therapy. Sam's words bounced in Brandon's head, "hate crime." He thought about the brain scans. Forced conversion therapy. This made him think that maybe someone in the religious institution could be behind these abductions. He wouldn't put it past a crazy zealot like Father Joseph. Brandon didn't remember seeing anything in the police files about a religious organization, so he'd have to look again. The other thought that kept running through his mind was the Bellevue House. He was fairly certain he had seen that name in the police files. It hadn't meant anything to him at that time, but now he wanted to find every mention of it. Was this house the connection?

Brandon drove straight to the police station, headed directly to Room 4, pulled out interrogation and interview statements in Nong Ekamai's case, and began searching for references to the Bellevue House. He knew she had been talking to someone about buying a house. Maybe it was the Bellevue House.

He scanned through the documents he had already read. Most everyone close to her knew she was getting ready to buy a house. Brandon kept flipping pages, searching until he came to a statement made by Mia Lane, who said she was Nong's best friend. There, in the statement, was the house by name, the "Bellevue House." None of the other statements had been this specific, but this person was sure.

Brandon then looked at the files in Tyler Jiles's case, specifically notes on the conversations with his employees about the woman he had met. According to Andy, Tyler's business manager, "She owned a big fancy house." Was it the Bellevue House?

He read through each of those official statements, finding no mention of the place. Brandon sat back in his chair and tapped his fingers on the edge of the table, thinking. Then he looked through the other statements from the rest of the investigation. Nothing.

Maybe he was mistaken, but something felt wrong, missing. Would the officers have omitted the name of the house from the report? Brandon found the bag that contained the officers' notes. Shuffling through them, he came across two mentions of the house. Feeling vindicated, Brandon proclaimed, "I knew it!" The first said, "... house that looked like the Bellevue House..." The second said, "She owned the Bellevue House." Tyler had been there, too.

All three of the abductees had been there. Why hadn't Sam mentioned this? The Bellevue House would have come up in their meetings, no question about that.

Curious, Brandon looked through the files on Amanda Bowman. Had the fact she had gone there been taken out of official statements? He first looked at the conversation she had had with the clerk at the city management department regarding confusion over land being cleared.

Brandon had read the clerk's statements earlier and found the report again. In her statement the clerk had said, "Amanda was positive the land proposed for the new Education Center was not vacant. She was going to take photos of the house and bring them back to us." The house? Had she not said the name of the house, or did the officer withhold the name from the report? Brandon looked through the notes, but didn't find any mention of... wait. As he kept flipping, he found "Bellevue House??," but not from the clerk's interview—rather from Sally Bowman's initial interview.

He wondered if her official statement included the name. Searching, Brandon found the form, but no mention of the Bellevue House was there.

Why were mentions of the house not being included in the official statements? Brandon continued searching.

Finally, in the official statement taken from the janitor who had overheard Amanda arguing with the clerk, he found, "Amanda claimed the Bellevue House had been rebuilt. She was going to get photos."

Nong, Tyler, and Amanda had all gone to this house. Why hadn't Sam or the FBI investigated the Bellevue House? Nothing in the reports considered it. Were they purposely withholding information about it?

Before Brandon called Sam to press him about the house, he quickly looked for any files regarding the church. Not seeing any, Brandon made the call.

A sleepy, irritated voice answered, "This is Sam Marvin."

"Hi, Sam, it's Brandon."

"Brandon, it's eleven o'clock on a Saturday night. Do you really need to talk to me now?"

Brandon hadn't been aware of the time. "I'm sorry, Sam. I have a couple quick questions. Did you investigate a church?"

"Can't this wait until Monday?"

"I haven't seen any files or mention of religion or religious institutions."

Clearing his throat, Sam recalled, "There should be files there. Keep looking. Tyler had been going to St. Raphael Church but quit attending after he bought out his buddies and took over the business. We talked to the priest, Father Joseph, and several members of the congregation. Nothing there. Amanda stopped attending church in her teens. She went to Assumption. Nong is Buddhist. The files are all there, but it's a dead end."

"What about the Bellevue House?"

"The Bellevue House? That place burned down nine or ten years ago."

"Yes, so I've been told, but Tyler and Amanda said they were going to that house the day they disappeared. Nong's friend, Mia, said Nong was planning to buy that house. This is the connection. Do you know if the house was rebuilt or maybe there is another house....?" Brandon was stopped short as Sam interrupted.

"Or maybe there was a misunderstanding, or someone heard something wrong or, or, or—It doesn't matter. Look, you saw the video footage. We know they were at the Education Center. We found their vehicles parked there. The Bellevue House doesn't exist anymore; it's old news and has nothing to do with this case." Sam paused before continuing. "Look, I want to help you. I want this case solved, and I'm hopeful that Tyler will give us something to help us accomplish that. I'm hanging up now, Brandon. I'm retired, which means, I'm tired. Call me during the day. Good night." Sam hung up.

This doesn't make sense, Brandon thought. Is someone in the police department behind these abductions? He had to consider that possibility now. And if so, how many people were involved?

Sally Bowman's voice rang in his memory. "Amanda was so excited about inspecting that house again, but never got the chance. She went missing later that day." Was someone trying to cover up the fact that the house had been rebuilt? Amanda was going to get photographs of the house—even the city clerk had said so.

Looking ahead to the interview with Tyler's mother the next morning, Brandon wondered what new information he would uncover. So far, he knew that the Bellevue House and architecture were two things that connected the victims. He got his notebook to start writing questions he would ask. "Who in the police force did Tyler know? Had he had any connections to the other victims when he was younger? How had Tyler become interested in architecture and why hadn't he become an architect?"

Thinking about other questions he would ask, Brandon wondered, Was Amanda at the Bellevue House when Tyler went there? Was it possible that Amanda was the woman Tyler was seeing? Brandon thought about that for a second. No. First, Amanda liked women. Second, she was being held captive and would have most likely been in her vegetative state by then. Maybe the woman Tyler had met, his love interest, was the abductor.

108

Brandon found Lesley Jiles's taped interview. He wanted to learn what she had known about the woman Tyler was seeing. He inserted the tape and listened to it as he cleaned Room 4 and locked the door. The police had asked her about Tyler's family and his business. He continued listening as he drove home. They had asked about his wife, their marriage, fights, his personal habits, and drinking problems. He listened while getting ready for bed. They had asked about his extramarital affairs, and finally, about the woman Tyler was last known to be seeing.

"I really don't know anything about her. I know he met her at the Bellevue House," Lesley had answered.

"I'm sorry. The Bellevue House? Why do you say that?" a detective asked.

"He was meeting with a lawyer in the Bobcat Mountain neighborhood. He told me he was amazed to have seen the house and stopped because he wasn't sure if it were real or not. That's when he met that woman."

"So not the Bellevue House, but a house he mistook to be the Bellevue House. What did he say about the woman?"

"Nothing. Just that he met her. When I inquired, he said it was nothing. I brought up the fact that I knew he was cheating on his wife, and we had a small argument. That's all."

"Did he give a description of the woman—tall, short, blond hair, black hair?"

"No."

"This was on Saturday?"

"Right. He had come over to fix the greenhouse. He had met her a few days earlier."

"And that was the last time you saw him?"

"Exactly. It was the last time I've seen or heard from him."

"Who was the lawyer he was meeting?"

"I'm not sure, a bankruptcy lawyer, I believe."

Brandon turned off the tape. The officers interviewing her had dismissed the idea that Tyler had seen the Bellevue House and didn't ask any follow-up questions about it. He would make sure not to repeat their mistake.

Day Five—Sunday

Friends to Enemies

As Brandon approached Lesley Jiles's house, he noticed several reporters camped in front of her home. Oh great. This is going to be fun.

Brandon reached the residence, hounded by the reporters who took his photo and called out questions regarding Tyler. One of the reporters called his name. "Detective Spencer, Detective Spencer. It's Brenda Calderwood with the Lake Valley Sun Times. Do you have any updates on Tyler Jiles? Has Tyler been able to identify his abductor?"

He knew Brenda. They had talked several times about past cases he had worked. She was competent and resourceful. She leveraged information to get what she wanted and knew how to push peoples' buttons—friendly one day, a bully the next. "I'm sorry. No comment at this time."

"Brandon. Amanda is my niece."

Brandon stopped. If the police couldn't be trusted, and the files were incomplete, she would have answers he needed.

Brenda pushed her way forward.

Another reporter spoke quickly, "Can you tell us what you've learned? What information do you have about the abductor?"

Brenda faced Brandon. "Give us an update."

"I'm sorry. I have nothing to say at this time. But you and I need to talk." The noise bombarded Brandon as he pushed his way past the sidewalk and proceeded to Lesley's front door.

Brandon knocked. Lesley answered, a fusillade of voices striking them. "Lesley, has your son been able to tell you anything about where he has been? Did you call the detective to come over? What can you tell us about your son?"

Lesley ushered Brandon inside and quickly closed the door.

"Thank you so much for agreeing to see me, Mrs. Jiles," Brandon said.

"Please call me Lesley. I'm sorry you had to walk through that."

"I know it's been a tough few days for you with your son waking up and the media attention. Has it been like this since Thursday?"

"No. I had one reporter visit me from the Sun Times on Friday, and then yesterday, more and more of them began showing up. It's worse at Sunnyside."

"I'm sorry."

"It's okay. It was a lot harder when he first went missing. This time it doesn't seem quite as bad. I really feel for the Bowmans and the Ekamais. Mr. and Mrs. Ekamai are taking care of their little granddaughter. I really hope their daughter returns, but I don't envy the attention they'll get if she does. Honestly, I feel so relieved that my Tyler is back with me."

Lesley led Brandon into the kitchen and handed him a glass of water. They sat down at the table.

"Is this a new police technique? To have detectives work separately?"

Brandon smiled. "It's a bit complicated. But we're doing our best to solve the case, and the information we get and share helps us in that endeavor."

"I see. I'd be happy to help in any way I can, but I only have an hour to give you today. I'm going back to the hospital to be with my son."

"Sure, I understand. As I explained on the phone, I'm new to the case, and I'd like to know more about Tyler before I meet with him."

"What would you like to know?"

"Tell me what he was like as a kid. What kind of things did he do? What interests and hobbies did he have? Did he belong to any clubs or participate in school sports? Did he have any girlfriends? Who did he hang out with—things like that."

Lesley laughed. "Is that all? I'm not sure I have that much time."

"I'd like to learn about your son. Tell me what comes to mind."

Lesley began with Tyler learning how to play chess when he was in first grade. She gushed about how he'd competed and ranked seventeenth in the state by his tenth birthday. In middle school, she was surprised when he lost interest in competitive chess and joined the wrestling team. In high school, he had helped his grandfather build a garage that housed her dad's antique cars. "After that, Tyler loved building things."

"Tell me more about the building of the garage." Brandon felt something of importance was here since this was the catalyst for his desires to build.

"My dad wanted to give Tyler skills to provide him with alternatives beyond college. He believed in empowering Tyler with options. The two of them bonded over the experience." She went on, detailing a barn Tyler helped his friend's family build and then taking a job with a roofing company. "He started his own business as a developer with some of his college buddies. Later, he bought them out and took full control of the company."

"That's when he stopped going to church."

"Tyler was never that religious. He went because of me, but once he owned the business, I couldn't talk him into continuing."

"May I ask you a very personal question about Tyler?"

"Okay."

"Do you know if he liked guys? Maybe he was bi."

Leslie jerked. Her hand went for her mouth, but stopped halfway. "Well, I," she started, clearing her throat. "Tyler was married. He had affairs with several women. If he did prefer men, he kept it a tight secret. Did something in your investigation tell you he did?"

"No. Amanda is lesbian. So I thought if Tyler were gay, then that was a connection I needed to follow."

"I see." Lesley sipped her water.

"Tell me about Tyler's company."

"He bought land in the suburbs, building mostly single-family homes. They secured investors for the contracts and made great money. Then he agreed to build Dr. Thomas' house." Lesley took a deep breath and shook her head.

"Who is Dr. Thomas?"

"Dr. Jeffery Thomas. He works at Northern Medical. He and Tyler were close friends. Dr. Thomas wanted something unique, a special house. He knew Tyler had majored in architecture, so they sat down to design the house together. I don't know all the details, and I'm not sure exactly what happened, but it's my understanding that Dr. Thomas was up against a time limit for capital gains taxes, so they cut corners to expedite the process and avoid fees and red tape. They pulled a few strings to rush the permits to start building the house. I think they proceeded without having an inspector sign off at the necessary stages. The city shut down the project, and Tyler and Dr. Thomas lost the ensuing legal battle. The city leveled the sight and Tyler took the loss. It set him back financially and tarnished his reputation."

"And Dr. Thomas?"

"He lost out, too. Ended their friendship. They were both idiots, if you ask me." Lesley finished her water and added, "Honestly, they both got what they deserved from that ordeal."

Brandon saw another possible connection—the city. Amanda worked with the municipality. Before disappearing, she had questioned the viability of building the Education Center. Tyler had had a legal case brought against him by the city after having "pulled strings," and then went missing. If someone in the police force were covering up these abductions, who were they protecting and why? "Did Tyler know Amanda Bowman?"

"No, I don't think so," Lesley said. "Tyler didn't build around here. He worked mostly in the northern suburbs. She had already been abducted when Dr. Thomas' fiasco happened."

"What do you know about the legal case the city brought against Tyler?"

"Not much. I didn't follow the drama. I thought it was going to work out, and they would end up paying a fine."

"Do you remember who the judge was?"

"No. Do you think that fiasco had something to do with Tyler's disappearance?"

"I doubt it. But I'm going to look into it further." Brandon knew Nong had had a business downtown and owned rental properties. This meant she also had dealings with the city. Had she been interacting with the same person Tyler had dealt with? Was this person corrupt? Brandon was going to do more than just "look into it." He was going to dig.

"The abduction happening so soon after that case has never sat well with me. I remember feeling angry when none of the detectives acknowledged a possible connection."

"They didn't take much interest in the fact that Tyler had seen the Bellevue House either. Can you tell me about that?"

"Right. He said he met a woman there. He was surprised to see the house and went onto the property to look at it. The police insisted it had burned down and basically told me Tyler was mistaken, that he couldn't have seen it."

"Did you fight back on that?"

"No. Tyler said he wasn't sure at first. And I wasn't thinking very clearly then, so I let it go. But reflecting back on it now, I feel certain he knew what he saw. The whole reason for Doctor Thomas approaching Tyler was because he wanted something different and original. They were both inspired by the Bellevue House. Although, he couldn't have seen it, right?"

"He might have. Would you happen to know where that house is?"

"No. Just that it was in the Bobcat Mountain neighborhood."

Lesley and Brandon ended their meeting and thanked each other. Lesley walked Brandon to the door. "Good luck with the reporters."

Lesley closed the door behind him, and he headed to his car. Spotting Brenda, he signaled for her to call him.

Brandon took a moment before starting his car to think about the information he had learned. He went over the list of names—friends, family members, business partners—his eyes returning to Doctor Thomas. A crazy thought came to his mind—the abductor had to be a doctor, maybe one who wanted revenge for losing his house. The captain had said, "The perp kidnaps people and scrambles their brains." When Brandon had talked with Sam, he had said, "There was speculation the abductor was doing brain experiments." Perhaps a pill of some kind caused the vegetative state. It made sense that the kidnapper was a doctor.

Brandon also thought about how both Amanda and Tyler believed they were going to the Bellevue House. But if the house didn't exist, maybe they had been drugged and made to believe it did. Some hallucinogens could be absorbed through the skin. A doctor would have access to such medications. With the right combination of hallucinogens and verbal suggestions, maybe one could be induced to perceive a house that wasn't there. He'd need to talk with a few doctors about this possibility.

Brandon would let the idea roll around his head a bit more. Dr. Thomas was definitely a person of interest, someone with whom he needed to speak.

In his notepad, Brandon wrote, "Case summary for Tyler Jiles and Jeffery Thomas vs City of Lake Valley." He needed to learn what had happened. Had money exchanged hands to expedite the process of building this house? If so, what other corruption might be happening? Blackmail? Imagining possible scenarios for each victim, Brandon thought Amanda would have been in the perp's way, Tyler was going to rat him out, and Nong wouldn't pay his bribes.

Brandon laughed at himself for speculating about outrageous allegations without a single piece of evidence. I should write a screenplay. However, the underlying possibility that there was a bad actor involved in a governmental capacity remained firmly in his thoughts. If this city official was, in fact, corrupt and behind the abductions, that might explain why the police were involved in a cover-up. Of course, this was all a grand illusion at this point.

Brandon's phone rang. "Detective Spencer."

"It's Brenda. Can we meet?"

"Join me for an early lunch."

"Where?"

"Pablo's Cocina, thirty minutes."

Brandon's appointment with Nong's parents was in three hours, so he had time to eat and pick Brenda's brain. What did she know about Dr. Thomas? Was there a corrupt official in the city management? Did she know if the Bellevue House had been rebuilt? He was sure she knew as much about these cases as anyone in the police force. And at this point, she was more trustworthy.

A Cry for Help

Jared loved Sundays. They weren't busy, and drivers could start late. After waking up, Jared took an aspirin and an Alka-Seltzer with some water, then went back to bed for another hour. When he finally got up to get ready for work, he sighed in relief. That nagging fog that dragged on his brain was replaced with a slight hangover. Now that the aspirin had kicked in, he was feeling better.

Getting ready for work, Jared thought about Nong. How would he ask her out? Practicing a few conversations made him feel like a bumbling idiot. He wondered what Nong would think about Leah. He imagined her being happy at the prospect of having a young friend with whom to do fun girl activities. This made Jared giggle. He really didn't know much about Nong, and his imagination was speeding away from him. Besides, would Leah accept Nong? For all her boasting about wanting him to get a new girlfriend, would she be okay with a stepmom?

By the time Jared arrived at the terminal, the sort had been finished. He loaded the large packages and opened his scanner. He scrolled through the addresses, hoping to find Nong's, and did a little celebratory dance after he found it. Jumping into the truck, he began his route.

After Jared left, he cursed himself for not having talked with Hossain about his scanner continually indicating Nong's address was a business. If that happened again, he would get a signature so that he wouldn't get flagged. Hossain could fix it later.

Jared worked quickly and the closer he came to Nong's house, the more excited and nervous he became. Nong wanted him. She kept trying to get him inside her house. He wanted her, too, but every time they were together, something weird happened. Why did he get that pain in his head when she touched him? Why did his memories appear as visions, and why those memories? Finally, who had been talking to him? He didn't recognize the voice. It didn't seem like it came from a memory. He wasn't talking to himself, so what was it?

Possible reasons passed through his mind—was she using some kind of poison in her yard? Was he having an allergic reaction to her perfume? She did live on a mountain, but not that high up. I can't be affected by the altitude. The idea that he had a chemical imbalance came back to mind. Midlife crisis? He had been feeling rather shitty these past few years, which brought him back to Dr. Thomas. Were the things happening to him a trick of his mind? With a deep inhale, he lifted his head, and after a moment's pause, exhaled slowly. He should go back to therapy.

Jared wasn't sure what to make of any of it, or if therapy would actually work, but he was glad he had had that wine last night. It took the weird fogginess that blocked his memories out of his head, and he was able to think again. Jared still wasn't sure what was happening, but he knew he desperately wanted to ask Nong out on a date and tell her about Leah before he went into her house. His emotions for her controlled him though. Would he be able to resist?

As Jared reached Nong's street, he paused the truck before making the turn. He took a deep breath, a moment to check in with himself. Physically, he felt fine. Mentally, his head was clear, but he drank some water anyway and started the truck. Turning the corner, his muscles tensed again, and his headache returned. "Why does this keep happening?" Jared snapped. Stopping the truck, he took three aspirin for his headache and calmed his nerves. This wasn't how he wanted to feel. He needed the passion and excitement. Once he collected himself, he entered the driveway.

After parking the truck, Jared sat still taking in the house, appreciating the genius of it. "You can live here with me," Nong had said. He was starting to hope her words would come true. This mansion was a dream house, and Nong was everything he desired in a woman. Wasn't she smart, successful, talented, and gorgeous? He had a feeling Leah and she would be great friends.

Grabbing the three packages for this address, he headed for the door. Then he took a slow, deep breath, calming the butterflies in his stomach and the pounding of his heart. Jared rang the bell. His emotions took over, and his chest burned. His skin tingled from the adrenaline flowing through his body. Wetting his lips, Jared shook the nervousness from his hands.

Nong stood in the doorway, her bright smile matching her light-yellow transparent shirt. She wasn't wearing a bra. Squeezing her arms toward her chest, she bounced up and down. Her breasts jiggled. Jared's face turned red. He was aroused.

"Hi," she said airily.

"H.. Hi," Jared managed. The only thing he wanted to do was grab her and kiss her. If she asked him to come inside, he wouldn't hesitate.

"How is your day? Are you busy?" Nong asked.

Think about work, think about work, think about work. "No, not too busy. It's an easy day, about a hundred stops. I'll finish early."

"Oh, great. You know, I still have some of those strawberries."

"Actually, I was hoping to ask you something."

"Anything."

Rubbing his lips with his finger, he asked, "Would you like to have dinner with me and take a walk in the park? Then we could meet my daughter for milkshakes." Jared blushed at the abrupt and awkward mention of his daughter.

Nong's eyes twitched. Jared sensed a change in her excitement.

"You have a daughter?" Nong stated, more than asked, with a pinch of worry between her words. "I'd love to meet her. How old is she?"

"She's eighteen. Her name is Leah, and she would like to meet you."

"Fun," she said in a raised voice that meant anything but. Nong turned, putting her back against the door frame and lifting her head until it knocked against the wood.

117

Jared's heart dropped. He was confused by her response. Maybe having a daughter was a deal breaker. His heart quickened as fear turned abruptly into panic, followed by frustration.

Nong added, "You know, I have a daughter, too. She's ten."

"Really?" Relief knocked, asking to calm himself. "I'd love to meet her," Jared said cautiously. If she had a kid and wasn't married, maybe he misread her body language.

"I would love for you to meet her."

"Can she come to dinner with us? Perhaps Leah could join us as well."

"Umm. Maybe."

Nong pushed herself away from the door frame, smiling. She started to speak, but then stopped.

The silence was uncomfortable, and so without thinking, Jared asked, "I was wondering if you would consider having a relationship with me." Suddenly, Jared felt weird. "God, I'm sorry. That was awkward." Why had he rushed that question? But he already knew. The uncertainty of being able to see her stung, and he needed to know she was still interested in him.

Softening her voice, she said, "It's okay. I like surprises." Parting her bangs, she added, "So about meeting my daughter. Can I be honest with you?"

"Yes, please."

Nong looked down at her feet, scuffing the sole of her shoe along the cement. "I need your help to see her."

"My help? Why? What do you need?"

"When I came here to negotiate the buying price for this house four years ago, I left my daughter with a babysitter. I ended up spending the night unintentionally." Then Nong lowered her head, hiding her eyes. "The babysitter left, leaving my daughter home alone. My mother claimed I was neglectful, and I lost custody. She will only allow me to see my daughter once I am settled in a stable relationship. I am fighting for legal custody." Raising her head and meeting his eyes, she stepped forward. "If my daughter likes you, I would totally be open to a relationship. You're handsome and kind and seem honest. I like you, Jared. Will you meet my mom, help me see my daughter?"

Nong's proximity made Jared's nerve endings dance. She needed him. "Yes, absolutely. I can do that."

"Thank you. So, when did you want this date?"

"How about after the tour of your house on Tuesday?"

"That sounds like a wonderful idea."

"Great! It's a date."

"You should get back to work. I was about to eat lunch myself. I'll see you later, ok?"

"Sounds great."

Nong turned to go back into the house. At that moment, Jared had an urge to touch her. He wanted to see if the intense pain and visions he had had before would return. Reaching out, he grabbed her hand.

A twisting, drilling probe sank into Jared's brain creating a pain so intense he dropped to his knees. Visions appeared.

Jared's heart filled with joy as he saw himself and his best friend, Jack, setting bricks on the street with the end of a board lying on them. They measured how far they could jump their bikes. Then they built a city in the sandbox, driving their toy cars along the sandy streets. After that, Jack convinced Jared to try out for baseball.

Jared's heart burst with pride when in the last game, down 3-1 with a runner on second, Jared hit a line drive into center field. The runner at second scored. It was the first time he had helped his team earn a run. Jack came up to bat next and hit the game-winning home run. The team cheered, surrounding Jack, shouting his name.

Jared's joy drained, as Jack was now rarely home. He was off playing with new-found friends. Jared saw Jack at school, a broken nose one week, a black eye the next. Then Jack was arrested for burglary. Jared's heart had hardened, blackened as he sat in the church looking at his friend's casket.

The voice whispered to Jared, "Don't be afraid. I love you. I know you love me, and I won't ever leave you. I'll be your dream forever."

"Stop it! Stop this right now," yelled Nong.

The visions, the voice, and the pain all stopped. Jared gasped for air, looking up at Nong in disbelief. Tears streamed down his face.

She fell to her knees, grabbed both sides of his face, and pulled him close, kissing him. Her bottom lip squeezed between his, and she used her tongue to open his mouth. Turning her head slightly, she fully engaged. The kiss was desperate at first. Forced. But it turned delightful and sweet. As Jared's passion grew, the tension from the visions dissipated.

They finished kissing, and she put her forehead to his. "I need you, Jared. Please don't leave. I really need your help. I'm trapped."

Jared wiped tears from his eyes. "Is this the horror story you didn't want to tell me? Can you explain what is happening?"

Nong stared at him with watery eyes, shaking. "I will tell you everything during our date. I will answer every question you have." Tears rolled down her cheeks. She stood, stumbling back toward the house. "We're still on for Tuesday, right?" she asked, leaning against the door. "Right?" she pleaded.

"Okay. I'll be here."

Nong turned slowly and stepped inside. As she closed the door, she paused to steal a glance at Jared. With hope-filled eyes, she mouthed a silent plea for him to return before blowing a kiss. Then she closed the door softly, the faint click resonating with unresolved turmoil.

Jared sat on his butt, stunned, not knowing what to think. She's trapped? What did that mean? She had yelled, "Stop!" Was the voice he heard real? Her desperation felt scary. His head was foggy. Taking a deep breath, he thought, I'm not sure this is a good idea. But her kiss—so sweet. Let's play this by ear.

Standing, he headed back to the truck and closed the stop on the scanner. *Error. Signature Required for Business Stop.*

"Oh my god! What the hell is going on?" he yelled. Jared turned and took a photo of the house, packages still sitting on the step, to use as proof that this address was, in fact, not a business.

Getting into the truck, he drove away. When he turned off the street, his headache disappeared, but that foggy, nagging drag on his brain persisted.

The Rookie and the Reporter

Pablo's Cocina was known for the best enchiladas in the Pacific Northwest. Brandon stood behind several people who were adding their names to the list to be seated. He saw the busboy pass with his black bin full of plates and noticed the music was barely audible above the sound of chatter. Giving the hostess his name, he waited for his guest and a table. Fifteen minutes later, he and Brenda ordered lunch.

Looking at her, Brandon said, "I'm surprised the paper is allowing you to work this story. I would have thought it'd be a conflict of interest."

"I have a personal stake in finding the truth. And, they aren't willing to fire me. I didn't know you were working this case. I was told the FBI had taken over."

"I was told that, too. I've been instructed not to talk with the press. This conversation is off the record."

"I understand. What can you tell me?"

"How long have you been working this story?" Brandon asked.

"Since day one. This story has haunted me for nine years. Have you spoken to Tyler?"

"I did. We spoke on the phone briefly after he awoke."

"What does he remember? What did he tell you?" Brenda asked.

"He was confused. His last clear memory was talking with a bankruptcy lawyer."

"That was five days before he went missing. That means his memory is the same as Amanda's."

"I don't know about that," Brandon said. "Detective Marvin and I think he may be able to recall more details than Amanda. He said his memories were on the tip of his tongue."

"Will you interview him?"

"Yes. Monday, after the FBI. Right now, he's working with specialists to help him retrieve his memories. I'll interview Amanda afterwards and then sit the two of them together."

"I doubt Amanda will talk to you or Tyler. She's pretty adamant about not talking with anyone regarding what happened."

"That's what her mom said." Brandon took a sip of water and continued. "Let me ask you something else. Has the Bellevue House come up during your investigation of this story?"

"It's been mentioned a few times. Why? What are you thinking?"

"Do you know where that house is? Do you know if it's been rebuilt?"

"The thing that made the Bellevue House special was the waterfall that ran over its roof," Brenda said. "It was also partly built into a hill and had a spectacular view of the lake and city. It couldn't be rebuilt anywhere. The house burned down, and there hasn't been any news about it being rebuilt."

"It was a famous house featured in magazines and textbooks. Lots of tourists. Perhaps the person who rebuilt it made sure to keep it secret so as to not attract attention. He wants to live a quiet life."

"I think you're chasing ghosts," Brenda said.

"Okay, what about Dr. Thomas?"

"He was on my list, yes. But he wasn't involved."

"Why do you think that?"

"The investigation didn't go anywhere."

"Why was he on your list?" Brandon asked.

"He and Tyler had that housing scandal, for one. Also, Jeffery was brought before the board for purchasing and using experimental drugs. He was in jeopardy of losing his license."

"What?!" Brandon searched for his pen. "When was this?"

"Eight years ago. His mother had been battling stage four cancer. The drugs he bought had mixed results in preliminary trials and were eventually ruled ineffective."

"Brain cancer?"

Brenda sat a little straighter, eyeing Brandon. "Lung cancer. But unfortunately, it had metastasized to her brain."

The timeline matched. Amanda went missing nine years ago. If Dr. Thomas was looking for a cure for his mother, he may have needed a guinea pig. That would explain the brain scans in the files.

Brenda looked at Brandon, her expression stern. "When did you learn about this case?"

"Thursday." Brandon tapped his pen on his pad.

The food arrived. "May I get this to go?" Brenda asked the waitress. Turning back to Brandon, she said, "I have to get to Sunnyside. Call me after you talk with Tyler. I need to know what he knows."

"Wait," Brandon appealed. "I need to know who Tyler and Dr. Thomas were dealing with before the city revoked their building license."

"That was five years ago. I don't remember."

"Could you look for me?" Brandon held his hand out in front of him, fingertips touching the table.

Brenda's eyes narrowed, and she lowered her voice. "Listen. I respect you, but you really have no idea what's going on here. You're chasing dead leads. Have you even looked at the police files regarding Dr. Thomas?"

Brandon pulled his hand back and straightened. "I'm not sure I trust the police."

Brenda chuckled. "Okay, rook. I'm listening."

"Do you suspect anyone in the city government or on the police force of being involved in these abductions?"

"Do you? Tell me."

"I'm not sure, yet. Just asking," Brandon said.

"That's a shame. When you make up your mind, let's talk again. I'll print whatever you have."

The waitress returned with Brenda's food, thanking her.

"Let me ask you one more question. What about the church?"

Brenda looked curious.

"The news has been reporting about the sexual abuses and the forced conversion therapy. Could these abductions be related? I thought maybe because of who Amanda likes."

"There's no evidence of sexual assault in the abduction cases. Nothing has pointed to the church, but the police didn't probe that deeply. It may be worth looking into. Keep me informed, and I'll do the same." She placed a twenty-dollar bill on the table.

"Speak with your niece. Convince her it's in her best interest to talk with Tyler."

As Brenda was leaving, she said, "I'll see what I can do."

Brandon reviewed their conversation. Brenda had said, "When you make up your mind." So, she did suspect foul play. Knowing her, she wouldn't tell him about it until after he told her what Tyler knew. Brandon finished eating and drove to the Ekamai residence.

Quiet Panic

Pulling into a picnic area, Jared parked his truck. He was feeling depressed, scared, and worried. *Who is Nong? What is she doing to me?*

Taking a drink of water, he wondered what kind of nightmare could she be living? "I need you, Jared. I'm trapped," she had said. Trapped how?

His head was heavy. His emotions were raw. His feelings for Nong were wavering. She's not being honest. How could a relationship of any kind stand on deceit? Thinking felt like a struggle, so Jared began to talk out loud. "Maybe I should take Leah with me on Tuesday. I would love for her to see this house."

Taking out his phone, he called his daughter.

"Hey, Dad. What's up?"

"I didn't see you last night. Everything okay?"

"I'm on my way home. We're going to play video games."

"You're driving?"

"Yes."

"Okay. Talk later. Bye."

Playing video games. Jared opened a game app on his phone. Ten minutes of mindless entertainment might be exactly what the doctor ordered.

A True Suspect

Sitting on a loveseat across from Mr. and Mrs. Ekamai, who were on the sofa, Brandon pointed to a studio photo hanging on the wall and asked, "Is that Nong?"

"Yes, that's our daughter, Nong, with her daughter, Ploy," Mrs. Ekamai replied.

Ploy stood in front of Nong in her dark blue dress. Nong had her arms wrapped around Ploy, pressing her cheek to her daughter's. It was a touching photo. "They're lovely. You must miss Nong very much." Brandon's gaze lingered on the photo. He felt a mixture of longing and pain. The tenderness of the photo stirred buried emotions. He straightened—touched the love seat, counted the pieces of furniture, recognized the faint smell of rice—then fixed his stoic exterior, remaining professional.

"We think of her every day. I know she will come back to us," Mrs. Ekamai said.

Brandon turned and asked, "Did Nong ever mention the Bellevue House?"

"Is that the house all the tourists used to come to see?" Mrs. Ekamai asked.

"Probably, yes. It was famous for its unique beautiful design," Brandon replied.

"I can't recall her ever mentioning it." Mrs. Ekamai turned to her husband, "Can you, dear?"

"No, it never came up."

Brandon looked at his notes. "In a report I read, it stated that Nong was getting ready to purchase another property prior to her disappearance, but there was no mention of the property she was going to buy."

"That's right," Mr. Ekamai said. "She was excited. Said she was going to surprise us. The owner had a family tragedy and wanted to unload it, so she was getting a great deal on an absolutely beautiful home. We were going to be ecstatic; she had promised."

"That's not an exaggeration," Mrs. Ekamai added. "She was really excited and thought we would be happy and proud of her. But I had a funny feeling about it. It sounded too good to be true."

"Dear, you told her that, remember?" Mr. Ekamai said. "You said she had to be extra careful about the paperwork and make sure everything was legitimate. I remember the conversation you had with her in the kitchen. You said if it had to be rushed and was such a great deal, then it could be a scam, and she should be prepared to walk away. Do you remember that?" He tried to calm his wife before the tears started to fall.

"I do. Yes, of course. But I should have insisted on more information," Mrs. Ekamai said.

Brandon heard the regret in Mrs. Ekamai's voice. He knew that not acting on a feeling that something was wrong could burn and fester, eating one alive. Trying to ease her mind, Brandon said, "Ma'am, your daughter is smart. The purchase of that house and her going missing may not be connected."

"I'm sorry, detective, but that's not true." Mr. Ekamai asserted. "No one ever tried to contact her or us about buying any house after she went missing. She wasn't confirmed missing for two days, and they didn't find a single call, text, or email about the purchase."

"You're right. I'm sorry." Brandon paused. "She didn't have any paperwork on the house? No offer? She didn't use a realtor? Something that would tell us where this house was?"

"I didn't see anything," Mr. Ekamai said, "and the police looked through everything at her house and the office. They didn't find anything either."

"From my investigation, I suspect the house she was planning to buy was the Bellevue House."

"Is that even possible?"

"All the evidence I've found suggests that it is. Mia knew about it. And the two who were abducted before Nong had seen the house."

"Mia didn't tell us," Mrs. Ekamai exclaimed. "Why is this the first I'm hearing about this?"

"It's not substantiated." Brandon knew that Mia had probably been convinced by the police that she had been mistaken. He didn't want to go into that. He quickly moved on. "Nong's car was found at the little strip mall on Bobcat Mountain Way, near the Bellevue House. Do you know why she went there?"

"She often parked there and then either walked or biked." Mrs. Ekamai said. "There's a nice trail system in that neighborhood. She also owns three properties over there, so she often went up that way."

"We did find her bike at the Education Center. Do you know who she may have met or why she went there?"

"No, we don't know why she went there. Maybe she had a class or knew someone who worked there. The FBI looked into all of that," Mr. Ekamai said.

"Do you know if Nong knew a Dr. Thomas?"

"Dr. Thomas is Ploy's doctor." Mr. Ekamai pointed to the photo of Nong and her daughter.

No surprise there, Brandon thought. The pieces were starting to come together. The real question was, how well did they know each other, and who did Nong know in the city government? He needed to uncover the scandal that tied everyone together.

"Why do you ask?"

"I'm trying to find as many connections as possible between Amanda Bowman, Tyler Jiles, and Nong. Dr. Thomas' name has been mentioned. Did they have a disagreement of any kind?"

"Dr. Thomas is a very good doctor and a wonderful man. If you haven't met him, you should do so," Mrs. Ekamai said, sounding defensive. "My daughter thought highly of him. She recommended him to other parents. He's great with kids."

"I see," Brandon said. "He didn't happen to prescribe any medication to Nong, by chance?"

"He's a pediatrician. Nong had her own family physician."

"Did Nong ever talk with him outside of the clinic?"

"No. Not to my knowledge."

"Do you suspect Dr. Thomas knew Nong beyond the parent-doctor relationship?" Mr. Ekamai asked.

"I do."

"You do know that he was a suspect in her disappearance. It's my understanding that the investigation found that there was no relationship outside of the office, and Nong never talked about Dr. Thomas, outside of scheduling an appointment for Ploy."

This made Dr. Thomas seem more likely to be involved. The police had disregarded the Bellevue House and painted Dr. Thomas as innocent. Now Brandon needed to find the second person involved. Scanning his notes, he asked, "Was Nong involved with anyone in the police department or with someone who worked with the city?"

"You mean her boyfriend?" Mrs. Ekamai asked.

She had a boyfriend. And he worked with the city. Here we go. "Who was he?"

"He was the manager at the aquatics department. It operates the beach and public pools. They hadn't been dating that long," Mrs. Ekamai said.

"What was his name?"

"Vance Lancaster. Is he a suspect?"

"Do you think he should be?"

"I didn't know him well. We only met him a few times. He seemed like a nice guy."

"How did they meet?"

Mrs. Ekamai looked at her husband. "Nong had taken Ploy to the pool, right?"

Mr. Ekamai nodded.

"Did they do any business together?"

Mr. Ekamai gave a short laugh, "No, no, nothing like that. They went on a few dates. He was a strong, good-looking man."

A manager, Brandon thought. He'd have to report to city hall. "How long had they been dating before she disappeared?"

"A month, I guess," Mrs. Ekamai replied.

Brandon referred to his notepad and saw Mia's name, Nong's best friend. "Do you know if Mia met him?"

"I believe she did. Mia and Nong knew everything about each other."

Brandon starred Mia's name. He'd need to talk with her for sure. "I need to know who else Nong did business within the city. Do you have her records? Could I look through her files?"

Mr. Ekamai raised his eyes as he sat back against the sofa holding his chin. "The FBI collected all of her business files during the initial investigation. When they returned them, I stored them with her office equipment in a unit downtown. When do you want them?"

"At your earliest convenience. I'll be interviewing Tyler and Amanda this week, and that information is vital in knowing all the connections between them."

"All right. I'll collect them first thing tomorrow morning."

He smiled, thanking Mr. Ekamai. Brandon had a gut feeling that Vance Lancaster and Dr. Thomas knew each other. He felt certain a name in Nong's files was going to match with a name in Tyler's documents, and that that person was in a position of power related to the fire department. He needed the evidence to prove this though. Holding his hands flat, palms down, in front of his chest, he calmed his mind. Let the evidence lead me. I don't lead the evidence.

"Are you feeling okay?"

"Yes. Just thinking." Looking at his notes, he asked, "Did Nong know the Mills family? Barbara and Daniel Mills."

"Our daughter knew a lot of people," Mrs. Ekamai said. "I can't say if she knew them or not." Mr. Ekamai grunted and nodded in agreement.

"How about Amanda Bowman? She was the fire inspector."

"Amanda Bowman went missing when Nong was in college. I don't believe they knew each other," answered Mrs. Ekamai.

"Was Nong involved with a church at all?"

Mr. Ekamai looked to his wife. She shook her head. "We're Buddhist." Then Mr. Ekamai said, "Mia went to church."

"Which church?" Brandon asked.

"I'm not sure, but she did say her pastor was that guy in the commercials. He has that TV program."

Father Joseph. Another person of interest. Brandon found his name and starred it before asking, "Did Detective Sam Marvin ever visit with you?"

"Yes, he talked with us several times. He was part of the task force to find Nong. Why?" Mr. Ekamai asked.

"He's helping me with the case, so I wanted your thoughts about him."

Mr. Ekamai looked at his wife. She shrugged, saying, "I wish they could have given us some answers. It's difficult to hear, 'There's no new information,' time and time again."

"I understand that. Hopefully, we will have answers for you very soon."

"We still have hope."

"Do you know if Nong had any legal trouble?"

"No, none," Mrs. Ekamai responded quickly.

"I just have a few more questions about Nong's past. I'm looking for childhood connections between the three victims—same interests, teachers, sports. Can you tell me what Nong was like when she was young? I'm hoping you can paint me a picture of her as a kid."

Mrs. Ekamai's eyes sparkled. "I'll get the photo albums." She rose and walked around the coffee table, retreating past the kitchen down the hall.

Mr. Ekamai leaned forward and rested his elbows on his knees. "Let's see. Nong was a tough girl. She got into fights when she was in grade school, a real handful."

"Did any of those lead to police intervention?"

"No, she got bullied as a kid and defended herself. The school dealt with it."

"What school was that?" He needed to know the names of those kids. He'd bet money that one of them was now serving in the police department.

"Sukiya Elementary. What are you thinking?"

"Would you happen to remember any of the kids she fought with?"

"You know, I might have some of her disciplinary papers in the attic. I'll look for them today. If I find them, I'll give them to you with her business files."

"That would be wonderful. Thank you." Brandon made a note of the school name in his pad. "What was she like in middle school?"

"In middle school she learned the viola. She was in orchestra and made some friends, became popular by eighth grade. In high school, she joined Deca, played tennis, and was a cheerleader. She excelled in math and art. She took entrepreneurship courses her junior and senior year and loved them."

She was athletic. A case came to Brandon's mind about a bus driver who had assaulted women. All three victims played sports, which meant they would have been on the team bus when traveling. All the schools used the same bus company. He scribbled, "Bus driver?" Next, he asked, "Did Nong cheer at any wrestling meets?"

"Wrestling?"

"Tyler Jiles was on the wrestling team."

"No, she cheered at the basketball and volleyball games during the winter."

"When did Nong become interested in architecture?"

"At university."

"Did she study in Diamond Creek?" He hoped she had studied with Jae Yun.

"She went to Portland State University."

Brandon reviewed his notes.

Mr. Ekamai added, "Nong got pregnant at university. She fell in with the wrong crowd, or so my wife says, and partied too much. I know that's how college is. We weren't happy about the news, but we did get a beautiful granddaughter to love. We took care of Ploy until Nong could get her BA in architecture. And, of course, now, because she is missing."

"Is Ploy's father part of her life?"

"No. He transferred to a different school. Nong never told him about Ploy. We told the FBI about him."

"Good." Brandon wondered if Nong's partying came with a police record. "You said she liked to party? Any issues with the police there?"

"I don't believe so, no. Why?"

"If there was police intervention, then I could read the report. That incident may be a motive."

"I am grateful, truly. I thought you guys had given up long ago," Mr. Ekamai said.

"I believe I'm making progress. I hope to share some good news with you next time we speak."

"Thank you again."

Mrs. Ekamai came back holding five photo albums. Sitting next to Brandon, she opened the first one, and they spent the next hour looking at pictures of birthdays, Christmases, trips to Florida, and orchestra concerts.

The conversation turned to Ploy and how difficult it had been for her to have lost her mom at such a young age. They talked about how well she was doing despite the circumstances. They were so proud of Ploy who would be graduating elementary school and starting middle school in the fall.

"I appreciate your time. Here's my card. If you think of anything that may be helpful, no matter how small, please text or email me."

"We will. Thank you for coming. And please, keep us informed."

"I will. Look for those disciplinary forms. They may be useful. Bye now."

Brandon sat in his car, scanning notes and thinking. Vance Lancaster. Did he still work with the city? If so, in what capacity? Did he know Dr. Thomas? To his to-do list, Brandon added, "Run a background check on Vance Lancaster." Doctor Thomas was now a real suspect. Brandon would read his file next and then set up an interview. He underlined Sukiya Elementary. Hopefully, he could talk with a teacher who might have known Nong. It was a shot in the dark. If Mr.

Ekamai could find those disciplinary papers, maybe they would give him a new lead. Finally, Brandon needed to talk with Father Joseph, who was looking more like a possible suspect.

But first, he needed to find the Bellevue House. Where could it be? If the house had burned down and didn't exist, why would Amanda Bowman be going to inspect it? Brandon called the secretary at the precinct, asking her to email him a list of all the houses built in the Bobcat Mountain area nine years ago. Grabbing the photos of the house that Professor Yun had given him, he carefully studied them so he could easily recognize the house when he saw it.

Time to explore the city and find the Bellevue House. Since it was a beautiful day for a bike ride, Brandon drove home, put his bike in the back of his car, and drove to the Education Center. He opened his email looking at the addresses the secretary had sent. Fourteen houses had been built in this area nine years ago. Mapping out his route, he took his bike out of the car and started to ride.

The Cost of Freedom

Nong sat on her bedroom floor with her legs spread apart. She was stretching forward as far as she could before returning upright. Her hands and fingers rubbed the carpet as if massaging or petting it.

"Can't you let me go? You can find somebody else without me. You did it once before." Nong talked while wearing earbuds.

She kept stretching, the fibers of the carpet running through her fingers. "You don't need Jared. Because of his daughter, he won't come or stay easily," Nong said.

She paused, rotating her body so she could fondle a new section of the carpet. "No! That's not an option. I can't stay."

Shaking her head, she huffed, "Of course I love you, but I cannot stay here any longer. If you insist on keeping me, I will refuse to do anything, and you will have to torture or kill me. I'm done." Nong was serious. Her voice didn't waver, but her heart hesitated. Not because she wanted to stay, but because she could only leave if Jared took her place. Guilt was building, attacking her from all sides. She forced herself to ignore it, bury it. She was too close to winning her freedom. Jared's daughter was eighteen. Ploy had just turned ten. Nong had to get back to her.

A worried expression crossed Nong's face, and she gasped, "Is that really the only way you can capture him? I mean, he likes you. Surely you can grab him another way."

She continued to stretch. Returning upright, Nong clutched her breasts. "I don't want to do that. You said all I had to do was flirt—get him inside the house."

With a blast of anger she burst, "Fine!" She took a breath and in a sigh of resignation repeated, "Fine." Pressing the palms of her hands to her forehead, she added, "I'll do it. He's attractive. A nice guy. No problem."

Nong removed her earbuds, slapped them on the table, and went to shower. She now had mixed emotions about Jared's next visit.

Directions to Bellevue

Brandon biked the trail stopping periodically to ask people for information on the Bellevue House. They responded with strange looks and "sorry's" or ignored him. Continuing, he saw a Go Express delivery truck stop at a house in front of him. The driver jumped out, opened the back of the truck, grabbed a large box, and headed to the front door. If anyone would know where the Bellevue House was or if it existed, it would be a delivery driver.

Brandon cycled to the truck and asked the driver, "Hi, sorry to bother you. I was wondering if you know the Bellevue House?"

The driver looked at him suspiciously. "Yeah. I know it. Why?"

"You do! Oh, that's great." Brandon reached for his badge showing it to the driver. "My name is Detective Brandon Spencer with the LVPD. I was hoping you could tell me how to get there."

The driver looked at the badge and smiled. "Oh, you're a detective. Yeah, the house isn't too far from here. I deliver there every day. Keep heading up this road, and take a left at the light. Bike up the hill for about half a mile and turn onto 175th. You'll pass an apartment complex tucked into the woods, and then where the road bends, you'll see the entrance to the Bellevue House. The drive is lined with driveway lights that lead all the way to the house. You can't miss it. Absolutely stunning."

Brandon thanked the driver and cycled toward the house. That was easy, he thought, wondering why the professor and Sam were so insistent it hadn't been rebuilt. He knew it was near the Education Center, but he was a little surprised it was on the same street. Then again, he didn't remember seeing any apartment complexes, so...

As Brandon peddled, he thought about his next move. Contacting the FBI was probably his best bet. He shouldn't try to talk with the owner without back-up, and he didn't trust Sam or the captain at the moment. The closer Brandon came to the house, the more excited he became about the prospect of solving this case.

Missed Signals

After Jared finished his route and parked his truck at the terminal, he drove home wondering if he should go to Nong's house first. He still didn't have her number, and he was curious about the detective. He suspected he was helping her with the custody case, and if Jared was going to help her, maybe he should know more about it. But he was tired, hungry, and Nong was an enigma. He continued home.

Leah was there with Barb and Dan, listening to music and playing video games. The house smelled of grease from the hamburgers and onions they had fried, making Jared's stomach grumble. He reheated the burger they had left for him and grabbed a glass of wine, hoping it would again relieve that foggy feeling from his head.

Relaxing on the sofa, he watched the kids play. The girls wore headphones and talked with friends online.

"I'm right behind you," Leah screeched.

"Don't shoot me this time," Barb shot back.

Leah laughed, "Yeah, my bad."

"Oh, there goes your mom," Barb shouted.

Jared reached over, tapping Dan on the shoulder. "Stacy is playing?"

"Yep."

He sat up, straightening his back. "Where is she?"

"Hey, Leah, is your mom still in Florida?"

"Umm, no she's... Hey, watch out! To your left, your left. She's, umm... she's in Georgia."

"Hank, give me a sign. Give me a sign, Hank," Barb called.

"Hank? Is that Stacy's boyfriend?" Jared asked.

Dan laughed. "Hank! Are you dating Leah's mom?"

"What!?" Leah shouted back. "Who asked that, my dad? Jeez, Dad!"

"I'm curious," Jared said.

"Hank is my little cousin. He's only twelve," Barb retorted.

"Ha! I gotcha now," Leah cheered. "Oh! Crap. I missed," she groaned.

"Hey, Mr. Davenport. Did you hear the news today?" Dan said. "The guy who was kidnapped and then showed up in that coma syndrome, he's awake. He lost seven years of his life. Seven years! Can you imagine that?"

"Interesting, yes." He wasn't really listening to Dan. He was thinking about how to insert himself into the game rotation so he could play. It was a chance to interact with Stacy. He took another bite of his burger.

"The guy kidnaps people to experiment on their brains. It's scary! I hope the police catch him. They are still looking for that other girl too, Non..." Jared didn't hear the name. The girls screamed and laughed, cutting Dan off.

"Your turn, Dan. Get over here. Dan and Hank will be a team, and Stacy, you and I will be a team," Barb instructed.

Jared raised his hand to get Barb's attention. "Um," Jared said with a mouth full of food. "Can I play?" He mumbled incoherently.

Leah jumped up smiling and came over to give her dad a hug. "How was your day, Dad?"

"Good." Jared returned her smile as he kept eating. "Any chance I could play in Barb's place?"

Leah glared. "No. A new start, remember? I know why you want to play. Don't do this to yourself, Dad." Without allowing Jared a rebuttal, she continued, "Barb and Dan are spending the night. I'll spend the night at their house tomorrow, and we'll go to school together Tuesday. Don't forget Grandma Carol's birthday dinner. If you help Uncle Tim, he can come, too. It's at 6:00. Do you want me to call and remind you?"

"No. I'll be there." Sitting on the sofa with Stacy inches away, with no way of talking with her, hurt. He decided to visit his brother. "I'm going over to Uncle Tim's. I shouldn't be long. Oh wait! Tuesday night." He glanced at Barb and Dan, who were engaged, laughing into their headsets. "I have a date. I was hoping you could meet us for milkshakes at the Creamery afterwards, around 7:30. Or even better, will you join me for dinner?"

"Join you on your date? No!"

"Not so loud," he said, glancing again at Barb and Dan.

Leah chuckled, shaking her head. "I'm glad you're finally going out. You've got this, Dad."

"Join me. She's giving me a tour of the Bellevue House. I'd love for you to see it. It'll be a true educational experience."

"I'm meeting you guys afterwards, right? I can get a tour of the house another time."

A sting of frustration hit Jared. He knew asking Leah to come with him on a date was silly, but he didn't feel safe going on his own. Whatever this horror story of Nong's was, it was affecting him. What could he say to change Leah's mind? He squeezed his eyes tight. Was he really this pathetic? "I'd really like you to come with me."

"I'll think about it. But, yay! I'm excited for you. This is great news, Dad." Leah clapped.

Off Course

Balancing on his bike, Brandon stared at the Education Center. He took out his phone, searching for the Go Express website. Clicking on the link, he found the number and called.

"Our office is currently closed. Regular office hours are from 8 am to 6 pm Monday to Saturday. If you need help tracking your package, please press one." Brandon hung up.

Disappointment lay heavily in his chest. He thought about the directions he had been given and was sure he had followed them correctly—up the hill, past the apartment complex tucked in the woods on 175th. But at the bend in the road was the parking lot to the Education Center. He biked a bit further, looking for a driveway lined with lights, but the road led into the reservation; there were no other houses or driveways. He turned back frustrated. Instead of calling for back-up and raiding the Bellevue House like he had planned, he would have to wait until tomorrow and find that delivery driver to get the address. Brandon hit himself in the forehead, "Get an address! Why didn't I do that the first time?"

Returning to the bend in the road, Brandon thought the house might be tucked into the woods behind the Center or the apartment complex. Brandon rode his bike past the building, crossed the bridge over the stream that was flowing out from the Center, and arrived at the trail next to the Center. Stopping, he admired the view of the valley to the northeast. Behind him, a wall of glass displayed the art center. "What a perfect place for an art room." Brandon continued along the trail that led into the residential area of town, still hoping to find the Bellevue House.

Second Thoughts

Jared arrived at his brother Tim's house, the LuvNailz sign hanging over the door. Walking in, he called, "Anybody home?"

"We're in the living room," Tim called back.

Jared passed the nail salon Patty had in the front part of the house, turned the corner down the corridor to the kitchen, and rounded the bar to the living room. Tim and Patty were watching an NBA playoff game. A small round table with snacks sat next to the reclining sofa. Tim wore a Packers sweatshirt, nursing a beer. Patty was in her pajamas, enjoying a glass of wine.

"Have a seat. Want some chips?" Tim offered.

"Sure, thanks," Jared grabbed a handful of tortilla chips and dipped one in the salsa. "Good game?"

"Pretty good. Round one of the playoffs. Go Bucks! I think they're going to win this series."

As Jared sat down, he was distracted by the sword mounted on the wall next to the television. "Is that the sword you got after Grandpa died?"

"That's the one. Cleans up pretty nice, right? I sent it to a guy who restores Civil War swords."

"Is it worth anything?"

"That was our great-great-grandpa's sword."

"So you didn't get it appraised? It's probably worth a lot since he was a Union officer."

"I did. It's worth about $1,500. Do you want to hold it?" Tim offered.

"No. I was just curious. I thought it'd be worth more."

"I know you were jealous when I got it."

"Not really. It was rusty."

"Lies. I know you were jealous." Tim badgered, laughing. "So, tomorrow. I have a helper. Can you let Leah know I won't need her?"

"Yep. When you're finished, you should join us. Leah is cooking lasagna and invited you."

"Right. At her boyfriend's house."

"It's at Barb and Dan's. It's for their grandmother's birthday. You've met them before."

Tim turned to his wife. "Do we have dinner plans for tomorrow? Do you want to go?"

"Let's go. Absolutely," Patty replied.

"Great." Jared ate a few chips and watched a player slam dunk the ball. The game took a time out, and a news update came on. The President had a new military advisor, General Sam Cros, and an Afghan shaman was accusing the U.S. government of experimenting on innocent civilians at Guantánamo Bay. One of the survivors began spewing nonsense about his soul having been ripped from his body. Jared smirked. His own soul was being ripped out by Nong. He turned to his brother, "I'm going on a date."

"So, you asked her out. Good for you."

"Yeah, we have a date for Tuesday evening, and we're meeting Leah afterwards."

"Great news, bro. Leah's been worried about you. I'm glad you're getting out there."

Jared didn't share his enthusiasm though. The encounters with Nong still plagued him. He felt nervous, even scared. There were too many unexplained occurrences happening. His chest buzzed with panic, and he needed to talk himself out of keeping this date.

"I'm not so sure I should see this woman," Jared confessed.

"Why? What happened?"

"For starters, she sounded worried when I told her about Leah."

"Maybe she's worried Stacy isn't completely out of the picture. It's nothing."

Patty sat up, shouting, "Clean steal. Straight shot to the basket. Nine-point run, baby."

Tim high-fived his wife, then turned back to Jared.

"There's more," Jared stressed. "I keep getting headaches when I go there, and when I touch her, my brain explodes in pain. I have visions. Well, memories that are like visions. I can't explain it."

"I can," Tim said. "It's called—your wife literally ran away with the circus, and you've been in the dumps ever since. Your life turned upside down from losing the business and you probably have PTSD from the whole ordeal. Getting headaches and flashbacks when touching a girl is a part of dealing with the trauma. It'll pass once you know her longer."

Jared nodded. Tim had basically summed up Dr. Thomas' warnings, but it still felt weird. "One more thing. She asked me to help her see her daughter. Her mom has her and won't allow visitation until she is in a stable relationship. She's fighting to get custody and wants me to pretend to be her boyfriend and meet her mom. It feels like she's using me. Plus, Stacy's coming for prom and graduation, and will help Leah move into her college dorm room. I thought I'd try one more time to win her back."

Tim shook his head. "Jared. My brother. My man. Go on this date. Get used. Have fun. Everything will play itself out." Leaning over, he grabbed his brother's shoulder. "Look. Stacy's not coming back. That chapter of your life is over. You need to move on. Leah needs you to move on. I get you're nervous. I understand your body is processing chemicals. Get past it. Get past her." He looked Jared straight in the eyes. "I mean seriously. When's the last time you got laid? It's been what, seven years?"

"That's the thing. I'm so excited when I'm with Nong, I have a hard time thinking. My emotions take control of my mind, and I don't know what's real and what's a hallucination. I feel oddly connected to this woman. She's in my brain and can see my thoughts."

"She sounds perfect. I can hear the wedding bells already." Tim punched his brother in the shoulder. "Get laid. Tell me about it on Wednesday."

Jared left feeling better. He wished he had Nong's phone number. He wanted to call her and learn more about her situation. Had the detective helped her? Was she still trapped? Where was she with her custody case? There was so much he wanted to know about her. She said she'd explain everything during their date, but.... It was fine. He'd call about starting therapy on Monday so he could get his head straight. He'd see Nong tomorrow, get her number, and they could talk for hours on the phone.

You are Loved

After Leah's dad left to see Uncle Tim, the three young adults finished playing their game. Leah said goodbye to her mom and waited as Barb and Dan ended their stream with Hank. She shut down the console and turned off the TV. The sun had set, and the only light came from the kitchen. Barb sat on the floor in front of the coach, her legs stretched under the coffee table that held the remnants of their dinner. Leah sat in front of her, and Dan sat on the sofa next to her. The room was quiet, dark, and an eerie tension hung in the air. Leah turned, seeing Dan motion his eyes to Barb. Repositioning herself, Leah faced her.

Barb fidgeted, glancing back and forth between the two of them. Pointing her finger at both of them, she spit, "Don't you dare try and make me talk about this! I'm doing just fine. My grades are excellent, I participate in extracurricular activities, I have friends."

Leah didn't respond, choosing to remain a spectator for now.

"Barb," Dan started, a serious tone to his voice. "I'm going back to see Janet. In our last session she suggested we visit the site. It's an important part of healing."

Barb's eagle eyes held evil. "And?"

"I want you to come with me."

She scoffed, "Fat chance." Then looking at Leah, she hissed, "Part of the reason I loved being your friend was because you never brought this up. Why are you jeopardizing our friendship?"

Leah didn't respond, giving her best empathetic look. She knew Barb was defensive and angry. Anything she said now was not to be taken seriously.

"Don't look at me like that! What?! You think because your parents got a divorce that means you understand me!" Her voice was sharp, but broke as she ended the statement. Now in a raspy, tear-filled, angry tirade, she hollered, "My mom looked at me and shot herself!" Barb let the words hang in the air as she glared at Leah. "She burned down our house! Murdered my father! Destroyed my dolls! And then had the audacity..." her voice cracked as she stressed, "to look at me." Barb stood to leave.

Dan blocked her.

"Get out of my way!" she screamed.

"No! Talk it out. You'll feel better."

"Ha!" Barb exploded. "You bang a slut, pouring out your heart, and now you're healed?"

Dan grabbed Barb, giving her a bear hug. "Leah," he urged, asking her to join.

"No! Let go of me!" Barb shouted, squirming and kicking.

Leah jumped to her feet, joining Dan, encircling Barb. The two sandwiched her, holding her tight. "You are loved," Leah voiced.

"You are loved," Dan echoed.

Barb struggled for a minute before she completely broke down and started to sob.

Leah grabbed the paper towel, ripping a sheet and placing it in Barb's hand. Leah's heart felt mushy as she held her friend. It was going to be a long process for her.

After a good half hour of silence, petting, and caressing, Barb calmed herself. Leah said, "To set the record straight, Dan and I haven't had sex yet."

Barb chuckled, as she dabbed her swollen eyes. "Believe me, I would have known if you did."

Day Six – Monday

Case Reassigned

Brandon arrived at the station early. He wanted to read the files on Dr. Thomas and then ask the captain about the church investigation. The Bellevue House and interviewing Tyler were also hot on his mind.

Working at his desk, Brandon opened an envelope containing the cell phone records for Stephanie Mitchell. Checking his notes, he verified the date, time, and number for when she called her mother. He found it and cross checked her location with her friend's address. Stephanie had lied. She was on the strip when she called her mom and had made two back-to-back calls before phoning her mother. He highlighted those numbers, when he was told to report straight to the captain's office. He knocked.

"Yeah, come in," the captain said.

"What was Dr. Thomas' role in these abductions?" Brandon asked straight off.

"Dr. Thomas." The captain's voice was flat.

"The abductor is most likely a doctor. You even suggested he messes with people's minds. And Dr. Thomas knows all three of the victims. He has a motive for Tyler and had already been questioned for using experimental drugs. There's a reason he was a suspect, and I want to reinvestigate him."

"First of all, Dr. Thomas knows half the people in this city," the captain countered. "Secondly, he's a pediatrician, not a brain expert. Have you read the files on him? Thirdly, are you on drugs? Why are you asking about the Bellevue House? Did you seriously ask the secretary on duty yesterday to find and email you a list of houses built nine years ago?!"

"All three of the victims were going to the Bellevue House when they went missing. This house is the connection. I think it was rebuilt. Yesterday I met a delivery driver who said he stops there every day, and I'm...," Brandon was explaining when the captain cut him off.

"Wait a second. A delivery driver?" The captain stepped out of the room and called for two officers. "Núñez, Freeman, come over here. You gotta hear this."

The two officers approached.

"This is going to be good," the captain told the two men. He continued sarcastically, "Go ahead. You were saying?"

Brandon cleared his throat. "A driver delivers packages to the Bellevue House."

"Did he tell you where it was?" the captain asked.

"He did, but it led me to the Education Center."

The captain and the officers laughed. "That's because the Education Center is built where the Bellevue House used to be. It's not the connection because it burned down years ago. They built the Education Center in its place."

"I understand that. But all the evidence I have found suggests that it was rebuilt. And when I asked the driver, he said he knew it. I asked for it by name, and he said he delivers there every day," Brandon protested.

"The guy was playing you. Probably thought you were some stupid tourist who read an old tour guide book from nine years ago," Núñez jabbed.

"I showed him my badge."

They all laughed again. "Even more of a reason to play with you," Freeman joked.

The captain excused the other officers, who chuckled as they left. "Ghost house magically appears after burning down nine years ago," Freeman said as they walked down the hall.

"He and the psychic, Choi, should team up," Núñez replied, laughing.

Turning to Brandon, the captain's face flushed with tension. He spoke sharply. "The FBI is handling the abduction cases. I need you to update me on the hit and run from last week. Also, I have a new case for you. It's a burglary involving a hitchhiker. And I need you working the Mitchell case. Have you corroborated the suspect's story?"

Brandon waited, thinking the captain hadn't finished.

"Well?" he barked.

Brandon stammered, "N-not yet, sir. No. Dimitri said his friend left town, and he doesn't know where his sister is."

The captain lifted his hands and turned his palms up and out, mouth slightly open. He raised his eyebrow quizzically—a silent demand, "What are you doing? Go find her!"

Brandon nodded.

"What did forensics say about the samples?"

"Still waiting on the results."

The captain rolled his eyes. "Get down there and press!" He leaned into Brandon, pointing his finger, his words roiling with intensity. "Something doesn't sit right with me. The daughter's story clashes with the damn timeframe. The boy mentioned seeing a cut on her lip before the attack. And have you talked with the ex-husband yet?"

Straightening his posture, Brandon tried to appear composed. "I don't have cause to question the ex-husband, but I did get Stephanie's cell records. She was on the strip when she called her mom."

"So, go and check if there were any fights along the strip that night."

"I will." Brandon lifted his hand, inserting, "You are going to allow me to talk with Tyler and Amanda, right? After I put them together, I promise to drop this. I won't be able to concentrate on the Mitchell case if I can't do at least that."

"The FBI are meeting with Tyler now. Amanda Bowmen is refusing to cooperate. She's blocked my number. I can't even call her." He paused. "Have you listened to her interview tapes?"

"I haven't gotten to it."

The captain raised his eyebrows, his mouth hanging half open. "I know you're still new, but you've got to be smarter than this." The captain sighed. "Look, it's a lot, I know. Maybe too much. If you want closure, listen to Amanda's interview. But I want you to write up your reports and file your notes. You're officially off this case. Dismissed."

The captain returned to his desk and picked up the phone.

Brandon left the office, making his way to Room 4 with a heavy heart. The weight of the captain's words crushed him as he sifted through the tapes. Being belittled by someone he respected was bad enough, but suspecting that same person was entangled in the very case he was investigating created a special kind of frustration. Hurt clung to him as he inserted the cassette and pressed play.

"I ate at Anthony's last night. I think. Maybe," Amanda said, hesitating as she answered.

"That was actually five years and eleven days ago," the officer said. "You ordered the grilled…"

"Grilled salmon salad," Amanda finished his sentence. "Yes, I remember."

"Think about where you slept. What was the room like? The color of the walls, windows? Maybe there were insects."

"Maybe the bed squeaked," a second officer added. "The floor was yellow linoleum."

"My head hurts. I can't remember."

"But you remember something, right? Anything will help us."

"Black. That's what I remember. Pitch black. No lights, no sounds, no floor, no walls, no insects, no bed, no nothing! I was completely alone. I don't know if it was for two hours, two weeks, or five years and eleven days. I remember being angry. My voice was raw from shouting. I remember being defiant, refusing to… I don't even know, but I was alone, in my mind—in dark space. That's it. Then I was at the hospital."

"Was that a dream?"

"A dream?!" Amanda shot back. "No, it wasn't a fucking dream. It was fucking torture!"

No one spoke for several moments.

"I'm tired. I need to rest."

Feeling fairly certain no revealing information was on these recordings, Brandon pressed stop and returned the tape to the box. He was having difficulty focusing. His turmoil—a feeling of betrayal mixed with anger from the insult—suffocated him. He needed to uncover the truth.

Tucking the binder with Dr. Thomas' files under his arm, Brandon decided to study them at home. What connections existed between the doctor, the city, and the police department? Did he know Vance Lancaster? But first, Brandon needed to talk with that delivery driver and find the Bellevue House. Then he had to make sure the security cameras at the Education Center were working. He would have to be careful about continuing with the case, at least until he was sure no one in the police department or the city was involved in a cover-up. Brandon imagined the bloody claws of the underworld rising up and closing its grip. If it gained control of law enforcement, his city would become a cesspool of crime.

Collision Course

Jared arrived at the terminal, looking through the packages he would be delivering that day. He guessed he would probably have 160 stops once the sort was finished.

"Jared," Hossain called. He stood in front of his truck, with paperwork in hand.

"Morning. What's up?"

"You've been flagged, man. It's a red flag, too."

Jared took the two sets of papers. They had tracking numbers, names, and addresses. The first sheet had an orange flag that read, "Failed to collect signature." The second sheet had a red flag that read, "Complaint." He read the complaint. "The delivery driver has been leaving packages outside the building. Please instruct the driver to leave the packages in the mailroom."

"You haven't been getting signatures at this business? And worse, you are leaving the packages outside?" Hossain asked. "What's going on with you, man? Can you explain this?"

Jared looked at the address in question. 4871 175th. Nong's address. "Where is this coming from? This address is not a business. I met the lady who lives there. We talk every day. I have a date with her tomorrow night." Jared took out his phone, looking for the photo of the house he had taken yesterday. "I have a photo of the house to prove it." He couldn't find it. Instead, he saw a photo of an office building—with the packages he had delivered to Nong sitting outside the front entrance. He didn't remember taking that picture. "What the...."

"Jared! Jared," Hossain scolded.

Jared looked up, his face dripping with confusion.

"It doesn't matter. Do your job correctly. If you mess up again, you're going to be suspended. You can't be lazy."

"Lazy?!" Jared lashed out. "I've been working my ass off for you—working on my days off...."

"Yes, yes. I appreciate you so much. I didn't mean lazy like that. I mean you can't leave packages sitting in front of a business. Someone will steal them."

"I didn't. This address...," Jared faltered. He was sure Nong wouldn't have called, which meant there was some misunderstanding. Was this a bad prank? Determined to clear the flag from his file, he said, "Look, I'm going to drive to her house right now and FaceTime you. I'll have you talk to the lady who lives there. She'll tell you."

"No, you don't need to do that," Hossain began to say, but Jared was already walking to his car.

"I'll call you in half an hour," he yelled as he left.

"Stop, come back. You don't have to do this now," Hossain protested, but Jared was already out the bay doors.

No way was he going to get fired. Determined to clear the mistake, he drove toward Nong.

Brandon arrived at the Go Express terminal. He talked to a lady at the front counter who directed him to belt 500 to talk with the manager, Hossain. At the fifth bay door, Brandon saw the 500 belt on his right. He asked a man in uniform where he could find Hossain, and the man pointed to his left.

"I'm looking for a driver who delivers in the area around Bobcat Mountain," Brandon said.

"Oh, you are looking for Jared. He went to run an errand, but he'll be back in about forty-five minutes. Can I help you?"

"I'm Detective Spencer." Brandon handed him his card. "I need to ask Jared a few questions about a case I'm working."

Hossain took the card with a questioning look. "Is this about the complaint?"

"No. Nothing of that nature. My investigation involves the Bellevue House. Do you know it?"

"The Bellevue House? I'm not sure what that is."

"He delivers to that house, and I need its address. Can you have him call me when he gets back? His name is Jared...?" Brandon held the final syllable, waiting for the last name.

"Yes, Jared Davenport." Hossain confirmed. "I'll give him your card."

"Thank you." Heading back to his car, Brandon opened his phone and set GPS directions to the Education Center. "Time to make sure the cameras are working."

Jared pulled up to Nong's house. His headache was back. Turning off the car, he sat, rubbing his left shoulder, while he stared at the house. Five days ago, it was a dream come true—magnificent. Now it was a dark, menacing structure. Nong's words, "Mine is a horror story" and "I'm trapped," echoed in his mind. Rubbing his temples, he thought maybe something more serious was happening to him, like a tumor growing in his head—the ultimate horror! He shuddered at the thought, but knew it was a possibility. His phone rang. Thinking it was Hossain, he grabbed it with irritation, but he didn't recognize the number.

"Jared Davenport, Dr. Thomas, returning your call."

Jared sighed in relief as he explained to the doctor his symptoms: headaches, visions, a nagging fog that blocked his memories, a lack of judgment, and shocks so powerful they brought him to his knees.

"And this is happening at the Education Center." Dr. Thomas said.

Jared paused at the odd statement. "No," he voiced. "I've never been to the Education Center."

"But you deliver in the Bobcat Mountain neighborhood. Haven't you been to the Center?"

"Not yet. This is a new route I started a few days ago. Is it the altitude that's making me sick?"

"No. How about voices? Are you hearing them?"

"Yes. In my head."

"Jared, others have had similar symptoms while working in that area. One of my colleagues' patients was abducted a day after she came in, complaining of the exact issues plaguing you. Other patients, mostly students from the Education Center, have reported headaches and hearing voices. Their brain scans suggest potential neurological abnormalities. I need you to see Dr. Lynn Mathis. Can you come in today? It's urgent, the sooner the better. I'll fit you in right away. No waiting."

"I'm late for work already."

"I'm calling Go Express as soon as you hang up and informing them that this is a medical emergency. Can I expect you in the next half hour?"

A knot of anxiety formed in Jared's chest as he contemplated the doctor's pressing request. Was dropping everything truly necessary? He glanced at Nong's house in front of him, his chest coiling tighter. "Is it really that important?"

"Yes! Get in the car and come now."

Jared wavered. He wasn't going to be abducted, and he hadn't been to the Education Center. But his symptoms had been worsening. "Okay, I'm on my way," he replied, putting his phone down and starting the car. He shifted into first gear when Nong opened the front door and waved. The car jerked to a stop as his foot slipped from the clutch. He was here and still needed Nong to talk with Hossain, so he stepped out of the car.

"Jared!" she exclaimed with a giant smile. "I'm so happy to see you. What are you doing here?" She stood on her tippy toes and gave him a hug, followed by a kiss on the cheek.

"Do you remember when I first came here and 'fixed' your address, changing it from Business to Residential so I wouldn't bother you?"

"Yes, I remember. I freaked out because I wanted you to bother me. Why?"

"The setting was rejected, and I've been flagged. That's bad. I was hoping you could talk with my boss and explain to him that this is, in fact, a residence and not a business."

"Of course. But not in this." Nong smiled, looking down at her clothes. She was wearing a white, spaghetti string lingerie top. "Let me change quick. Come on in."

Nong took Jared's hand and led him into the house. As soon as the door closed, he became dizzy and disoriented. His breathing quickened, fear rose in his chest, and a panic of being trapped enveloped his heart. His immediate reaction was to turn and run, but Nong pulled him close and put her hand on his chest. "Everything is going to be okay."

Once his heart slowed, Nong led him to the living room. Jared felt a tickling in his brain like tiny insects scuttling through his thoughts. Paranoia hit him. He wanted to leave, but his body was weak, and Nong held him tight. Trying to calm him, she ran her hands through his hair, resting her head against his chest.

After Jared relaxed, Nong looked into his eyes, her gaze serious. Lifting her finger to his lips, she said, "Jared, you are going to live here now. This is going to be your new house."

His house? Live here? What did that mean? She wasn't going to steal his car, leaving him here, was she? Jared could hear and understand her, but the termites in his brain were distracting and redirecting his actions. He wasn't able to respond.

Nong took Jared's right hand and put it on her left shoulder. Wrapping her lingerie strap around his finger, she slid his hand down her arm, leaving her shoulder bare. Nong's touch made Jared excited, but he also knew he was in serious trouble. Run! he thought. Followed by, She's so sexy.

"I need you to relax, Jared." Nong now slipped Jared's left hand under the right strap, lifting it off her shoulder, exposing her breasts.

"This is going to hurt, so I will be giving you pleasure until the process is over. It'll help you. Don't fight it, Jared." She began to unbuckle his pants. Her eyes were intense and serious, her movements slow and deliberate.

Lowering his pants, Nong began to fondle him with one hand as her other slid under his shirt and caressed his chest. "I will be able to see my daughter now, thanks to you. I will be able to live my life again. You are my hero, my superman. I love you because of what you are doing for me."

Dropping to her knees, Nong put her lips around Jared's erection and dug her nails into his skin. The electric shock that burned through Jared's body made his muscles contract. His sight turned white, and the termites bore into his brain. Visions flooded him, drowning his ability to do anything, rendering him helpless.

His first kiss. The first time he made love. The first time he met his wife, Stacy. Holding Leah for the first time. Rocking his daughter to sleep. Celebrating her first birthday.

The voice came. "Let me in, Jared. I love you. I want to be with you. I will fill the emptiness in your life. I will take away your pain. We will be happy together."

Jared could feel the voice now. It was inside him, inside his mind. He felt It take control. Fear gripped every fiber of him, and he knew he was in danger. Trying to get the voice out of his head, he visualized a wall protecting the vital parts of his brain. He took back control, forcing his eyes to open and focus.

Jared saw Nong looking at him as she sucked. It felt so good—his head fell back, and his eyes closed, losing himself in the pleasure. Then she bit him, causing sudden pain. Breaking through his wall, the termites triggered a special memory.

Jared sat with Leah inside her tree fort. She was nestled in his arms, holding a hammer and nail as he helped her finish putting the latch on the door. "Dad, can we sleep in here tonight?" she asked. "Mom can come, too. It'll be a family sleep together. Can we, please?"

Jared suspected that the voice was using his memories to control him, keeping him subdued, unable to make his own decisions. Taking the hammer from Leah, Jared crushed termites needling his brain, pushing that memory away. As he frantically pounded them, the rest scurried away. The voice's grip loosened. Knowing he needed to leave immediately, Jared opened his eyes, ready to run, but Nong was on top of him. She was naked, and he felt himself inside her. Her hips moved rhythmically—pleasure vibrating, penetrating his soul, her beauty magical. She bent down, kissing him and he kissed her back. The intensity of the passion washed Jared's fear away until it had completely disappeared, leaving him helpless once again.

Nong dug her nails into his chest, and the shock returned. For the third time, visions filled Jared's mind.

His mom baking sugar cookies and letting him lick the spoon. Winning the 800-meter dash in under two minutes. Watching the value of his stocks soar. Signing his name on the lease to his first business. Holding Leah's little fingers as she took her first steps.

The voice re-entered, strong and in control. "We love each other. Do you feel the pleasure Nong is giving you? The happiness you felt in the past? I can give you this. Our life together will be magnificent, as these moments were for you." Jared wasn't able to fight the voice. He wasn't able to block it. The memories of his life in his prime—taking risks, in peak physical and emotional fitness, surrounded by loved ones—felt good. He wanted that back. Wanted to be that person again. Basking in the greatness of his early days, he surrendered himself and fell into a deep sleep.

Arriving at the Education Center, Brandon parked his car under a tree and took a moment to examine the impressive façade before him. Nestled into the mountain, with towering pillars and grand arches, the ornate architecture of the building exuded academic prestige. It looked the same as yesterday, yet Brandon couldn't shake the sense of foreboding that washed over him. Despite its outward appearance of serenity and majesty, a chill prickled at Brandon's skin. The shadows ebbed and flowed, in and around the corners of the building, emitting unwelcoming vibes. Was it the grandiosity of the building itself intimidating him? Or a subconscious fear of confronting the abductor, only for him to escape? Whatever the reason, he felt an unfriendly push telling him to leave.

Leave? No. He had to check the cameras and make sure they were working. He wanted a tour to familiarize himself with the layout of the building and see all the exits. He needed to put himself in Nong's shoes to understand how she could have possibly been abducted without anyone noticing.

Approaching the entrance, Brandon's shoulders tensed, and a dull ache spread to his head. For an instant, the Bellevue House appeared in front of him. He jumped back with a start and rubbed his eyes, his heart racing. Then two young women walked past him, chatting excitedly about the latest episode of Real Housewives. He took a breath and chuckled. I guess I'm a bit stressed.

At the door, he saw the handicap button. He recalled Nong reaching and pressing. That's why the door opened. Looking around, he found three cameras—one above the door and two on the corners of the building.

Brandon entered. The lobby consisted of the front desk, several sofas, chairs with tables, and a directory naming and numbering the rooms. A beverage station with cookies and crackers sat in one corner, and a play area for small children with toys and Legos was in another.

At the front desk, Brandon checked the young man's name tag and revealed his police badge. "Good morning, Collen. I'm Detective Spencer of the LVPD. I'm wondering if someone could give me a tour of the building, including the security room."

"Absolutely, sir. What is this regarding?" Collen asked.

"I'm investigating the Nong Ekamai disappearance from four years ago and wanted to familiarize myself with the building, interview some of the staff that may have been here during that time, and make sure the cameras are operating."

"Ah, of course, sir. Let me call Charlie. He's the owner of the media center. He's been here since the Education Center opened." Collen picked up the phone and dialed. He explained a detective was here and wanted a tour. "Charlie will be down shortly. Help yourself to coffee or hot chocolate."

"Thank you." Brandon stepped back, searching the room for the security cameras, finding three in the lobby area—one above the front desk, one in the corner, and one above the entrance.

Charlie entered the lobby and offered his hand to Brandon. "Good morning. You must be the detective."

"Good morning, sir. I'm Detective Spencer." After shaking Charlie's hand, he gave him his card. "I would like to check the security cameras and talk to you about the building. Maybe a tour?"

"Sure. Happy to help. Let's start in the atrium. This way."

As they walked down the hall, Brandon noticed how clean the building was. "The place is spotless. Must take a lot to keep it like this."

"That is a mystery," Charlie grumbled, shaking his head. "It's definitely not the janitor; he's not that detailed. I don't know who's been cleaning up after him, but it makes it impossible for us to fire the guy."

Brandon frowned. "Maybe he circles back after everyone leaves—cleans in secret."

Charlie let out a short laugh. "Not this kid. He'd need to have pride in his work for that. This level of clean isn't him."

"You've got a strange little puzzle on your hands." Brandon rubbed his chin. "Speaking of mysteries, what do you remember about the abductions that happened here?"

"It's been a few years. I don't remember much now. You would get better information from the statements I gave before. I believe there is audio, and probably video as well."

"I understand, but what I'm really interested in is your understanding of what happened, now that you've had a few years to reflect and get away from the chaos. Give me your best opinion of what you think happened."

"Sure. You know, I was investigated. Not a pleasant experience. I'm glad I don't have any skeletons in my closet, if you know what I mean," Charlie joked. "Being a suspect because I work here seemed unfair."

Charlie escorted Brandon down the hall. "I had never seen any of the victims before. They never attended any classes here, and aside from the brief footage from the entrance security camera, they've never been seen here."

Stepping from the hallway, Brandon entered a large commons. He was surprised by the grand scale and beauty of the room. "Wow! This place is amazing."

Brandon gawked at the open semi-circular arboretum. The main attraction was a wall of running water on the far side of the room. The stream from the hill outside flowed into the building down a brick wall into a pond before continuing through the middle of the room and under the floor. Benches sat inside a garden space under spineless yuccas, rubber plants, and money trees. The landscape included hydrangeas, African violets, and peace lilies. Chinese evergreens lined the path that went around the pond. Six columns around the room rose from the floor to the glass-domed ceiling three stories high, allowing the sunlight to fill the space. To Brandon's right and left were large staircases that followed the wall to the upper level, where ornate banisters allowed viewers to admire the greenery. Students walked through this exquisite atrium on their way to class.

"It's majestic," Brandon reiterated. "I can't believe how beautiful this is. I had a feeling it was going to be impressive from the outside, but this isn't what I was expecting.

I love it, too. It feels more like a palace than a workplace. I think it's because the Education Center was built with repurposed materials from the Bellevue House. I believe its essence was captured perfectly in this room. This wall, where the water flows, the fireplace in the literature room, and the stone arches are examples where we see the original house."

Brandon gazed, thinking, the remnants of the elusive Bellevue House. Then an eerie shiver ran down his spine. "Do you know if someone built a house similar to or in the likeness of the Bellevue House near here?"

Charlie thought about the question, his eyes rolling up. "I haven't heard anything. I don't think so." He then pointed to the cameras. "We have a total of twenty cameras on the premises. I'm sure you saw the three in the lobby. Five are fixed to the building's exterior. There are five cameras in this area, one above the hall entrance, two on this level, and two on the upper level."

"Would I be able to talk to the security guard and look at the footage for the last few days?"

"You can look at the footage. However, the security guard quit last week. His replacement doesn't start until tomorrow. The security room is downstairs near the pool. I'll take you there after our tour."

Charlie opened a door. "This is the art room."

A teacher was working with a single adult student. "Where are the other students?" asked Brandon.

"This is a private class. Most of our larger classes are in the afternoons and evenings, so we won't see too many people until later in the day."

The art room was an art teacher's dream, with all the supplies needed for a variety of art projects, including paint, colored pencils, chalk, clay, construction paper, and canvases. The workspace had large tables with stools, easels, and drawing desks. Watercolor paintings of fish and flowers, along with pastel portraits, decorated the walls. Cubby spaces and shelving units, storing clay pots and sculptures, lined an entire wall.

Brandon admired the giant windows standing from floor to ceiling. The valley was in full view—mountains, lake, trees, tiny houses, the entirety of the city. "I was admiring this view from outside the other day. It's absolutely breathtaking."

"Right? Inspires the imagination."

"Natural light seems to be a core concept in the design of this building. I love it."

"It is. All the learning areas have plenty of sunlight."

Charlie continued the tour. "I love the fact that parts of the Bellevue House were incorporated into the design and construction of this building, but I'm not sure building the Center here was such a good idea."

"Why is that? It seems like the perfect location."

"The wife set fire to the house murdering her husband, then committed suicide, right? If you want my honest opinion, I think their ghosts are still here. This building is haunted or cursed."

Brandon raised his eyebrows, questioning Charlie.

Opening the door to the next room, Charlie said, "This is the literature room." It was furnished with writing tables, smart boards on wheels, several bookcases full of books, computer desks, a plug-in station with laptops and several printers. An area with sofas, love seats, and sitting chairs surrounded the fireplace where people could gather and discuss. "We have writing workshops, reading and language classes, and book clubs here. Our most popular class is essay writing to prepare kids for college."

"So why do you think the building is haunted?" Brandon asked. He found ghost stories fascinating, but never gave them any credit.

At that moment, both Charlie and Brandon heard rhythmic whispers and muffled gasps. A woman moaned in pleasure. Both men turned towards the noise and Brandon expected to see two young students fully engaged in the act of—no one was there. The sounds dissipated as quickly as they had arrived, leaving Brandon with a pounding headache.

Grabbing Brandon's shoulder, Charlie asked, "You just had to ask, didn't you? You got your answer."

"You heard that?" Brandon put his hand to his head. "I suddenly have an awful headache."

"Me too," Charlie said. "This kind of thing happens here. Not very often, but often enough."

"The sound of people having sex?!"

"No. That's a first. Sometimes we hear music from a radio or piano. Mostly it's a voice mumbling. I'm happy this sexual incident didn't happen during class. Imagine the complaints we would have received."

Brandon investigated the love seats and sofa. The closer he moved to the sitting area, the more his headache intensified until his brain threatened to explode. He became dizzy with blurred vision. "Get away!" a voice growled in his head, followed by the image of a rabid wolf. Stumbling back, Brandon retreated to the door. "Let's go." The throbbing in his head gradually eased as they exited the room.

Stopping, Brandon caught his breath. What had happened? He wanted to go back to reinvestigate, but a strong fear urged against it. He rubbed his head, the image, the growl, the pain, stuck in his mind.

"You alright?" Charlie asked.

"Tell me more about these incidents."

"There have been some interesting ones. Just last week, the kids heard a woman screaming in the Cooking Room. When we opened the door, soapy water was everywhere, no woman. The art teacher said that she had finished a painting, turned to clean up and when she turned back, the painting was hanging on the wall. No one else was in the room. The front door will occasionally open on its own, but the electrician said that's because there's a short somewhere in the handicapped button. What we experienced, hearing something, followed by a slight headache, is the most common."

"Slight? What do you mean slight? It's a slight headache now, but it was extremely painful inside the room."

"Headaches aren't usually that bad and don't last long. First-time students complain, but students who have been here for a while don't even acknowledge them anymore. Anyway, the most expensive problem we have is food going missing," Charlie explained. "I'm not sure ghosts eat food, but the cooking center is the only enterprise to have been sold and resold. Every owner complains about the same thing. Of course, the abductions that have happened are the scariest thing for sure. They have caused us real problems. I was afraid I'd have to close because of them. I've pressed for the owner to have paranormal researchers come to check the building, but she said the events don't happen often enough. I think she's afraid of the negative press."

Charlie finished the tour, showing Brandon the media center, the cooking center, the music center, the woodshop, and the pool.

"That's all the rooms?" asked Brandon.

"The mailroom is upstairs. We didn't see that. There are a couple of storage rooms and then the back stairs."

"I want to see those areas, too."

"Sure. The security room is around the corner. Let's go there first," suggested Charlie.

Brandon went into the room switching on the lights. The monitors were off. In fact, everything was off. "When's the last time anyone was down here?"

"Not since the last security guard was here, I guess. Why?"

"The cameras are off. They aren't recording. Why are they off?"

"I don't know. I own the media center, not the building."

Brandon turned on the board, and the monitor flickered to life. He went to the main screen. "Do you have the login information?"

Going to a small locker, Charlie took out a training book and opened the front cover. He pointed to the password written in black marker.

Brandon logged in, turned on the cameras, and started recording. "Why did the security guard quit?"

"He got migraines. Said it only happened here."

Opening the video files, Brandon said, "There isn't any footage for the past week. The security guard stopped recording last Thursday." He clicked on the last recording. "Has anyone been hanging out in the front of the building? Someone coming by, but not for classes? Anything strange or unusual?"

"Not really."

Brandon fast-forwarded through the footage until he was very near the end when he saw Jared, standing stiff, staring blankly. "Here!" He stopped the feed, playing it back at normal speed.

Jared came to the open front door, set down a package, and then stood, motionless. His facial expression was blank, his complexion pale. He didn't move; then the feed stopped.

"I know that guy. He's the one who gave me directions yesterday," Brandon said, more to himself than to Charlie.

"He's the new delivery guy. We already called and complained about his leaving packages outside the front door," Charlie said, but Brandon was already rushing out of the room, phone in hand, calling Sam. He needed to find that delivery driver right away.

Jared awoke. He was lying on the floor covered with a blanket. He knew that Nong was at the front door but didn't understand how he knew. He got up, put on his pants, and went to her.

"I'm sorry, Jared. I didn't want to do this, but it was the only way for me to see my daughter again," Nong said. "I hope you can forgive me."

Jared was unable to think. He looked at her and smiled.

"I know this is difficult. It's going to be weird for a few days, but it's also going to be wonderful." Nong paused for a moment. "I really do like you, Jared. If you ever get out of here, I hope you come find me. Maybe we can be together."

Nong stood on her toes and kissed Jared on the cheek. Then she was gone.

Jared was exhausted. He could barely keep his eyes open. Walking back to the living room, he lay down and fell asleep.

Brandon exited the Education Center, his headache disappearing. Walking quickly to his car, he talked with Sam.

"Sam, I'm at the Education Center now. The delivery guy has been hanging outside the front door since last Thursday. He leaves the packages by the door instead of putting them in the mailroom and then stands there, stiff, exactly like Nong. He's the next victim."

"Do you know his name? Which company?" Sam asked.

"His name is Jared Davenport. He works at Go Express. I'm heading there now. Can you call and make sure he doesn't leave the terminal?"

"On it."

As Brandon started the car, he saw a woman shuffle out of the building. It was Nong Ekamai! Immediately calling for backup, he ran to Nong. Putting her in his car, he locked the doors, drew his gun, and rushed back into the building.

PART TWO

A Haunting Reality

Day Seven—Tuesday

The Disturbance

"Yoona!" Choi shouted as he jerked awake. Breathing heavily, he took a second to familiarize himself with his surroundings. He let out a soft sigh when he realized he was safe at home in bed.

Jasmine rolled to her side and ran her hands through his hair. "What is it, honey? Bad dream?"

With a sigh, he replied, "I'm sorry for waking you."

Jasmine lay her head on his chest, hearing his heart beating rapidly. "Want to talk about it?"

"It felt more like a vision than a dream," Choi said. "My aunt was in Washington and was struck with some kind of sword. She died."

"I wouldn't worry about her. She has plenty of bodyguards."

Reaching over to the end table, Choi checked his phone. "It's nearly five. I'm going to call my aunt before I start my day."

Jasmine lifted her head craning for a kiss. "Was it that bad?"

Rolling to face his wife, Choi put his hands over her wavy sparkling amber hair and looked directly into her soft green eyes. His thumbs stroked her smooth white cheeks as he locked his lips with hers. When they parted, he said, "It was bad, but I feel better now." Sliding out of bed, he grabbed his phone and exited the bedroom. Turning on the living room light, he called Korea.

Yoona answered straight away, her voice unsettled, "Good morning, Choi. Thank you for calling. I felt it as well."

"What is it, Auntie? What's about to happen?"

"It seems a catalyst for precipitating events that lead to my death has occurred in Lake Valley."

"Don't be so dramatic, Auntie. The future can take many paths. You told me that yourself."

"What has happened in Lake Valley?" Yoona pressed.

"Another abduction occurred yesterday morning, the fourth one in nine years."

"Is there something special or extraordinary about these abductions?"

"They are mysterious," Choi replied. "The FBI are handling the cases, but they have no leads. Rumors of crazy scientists, aliens, and ghosts have been prevalent. I did visit two past victims who were in a comatose state to see if they were possessed. I determined they weren't, although they were connected to a spirit—perhaps a loved one from the other side."

"Why didn't you report it?"

"It seemed natural for the person to connect with a loved one, considering their medical diagnosis."

Yoona paused. "I see. Tell me who was abducted?"

"A delivery driver."

"What do you know about him?"

"Only what the captain told us at the meeting yesterday. He moved here from New York four years ago after losing his architectural business. Seems he was blacklisted from his profession. He worked with his brother, a contractor, for a few months before driving for Go Express. He's the second architect to be abducted."

"And his family?"

"His daughter is a senior in high school. His parents own a cheese shop in Wisconsin. He's divorced. His ex is also an architect and owns a firm in New York City."

Yoona was silent for a long moment. "Choi, I want you to re-establish your connections with prominent energy manipulators. I need you to find someone for me."

"Who?"

"A new user. Seek out individuals who have a strong spiritual core."

"Can you tell me if I'm looking for a man or a woman?"

"It's difficult to tell. Many people surround this individual."

"Auntie, I need more information."

"The person of interest will become either a powerful ally or a dangerous foe, so they have the potential to manipulate energy."

"I think you misunderstood your vision, Auntie. No one here is powerful. The temples and mosques don't house any active users. The psychics are naturally in tune with the energy—they don't manipulate it."

"And yet we both have felt a disturbance."

"A disturbance?" Worry filled Choi's chest. Disturbances were catastrophic events that changed the world—wars, terrorist attacks, violent storms. They forced authorities into action and created change.

"My pending death is certain," Yoona said. "My victory or defeat, however, lies in the hands of this new user. You need to find this person."

Choi's voice was raw with nerves. "Your death? Are you sure?"

"I'm not concerned with that. I am concerned about preventing the corrupt Shaman in the White House from accessing world power. The person I need you to find will be a central figure in that battle."

"This task you are giving me seems impossible."

"Mind your training, Choi. Reconnect with those who have the widest net to get information. I have confidence in you."

Sweat beaded on Choi's forehead. "And this disturbance—how bad is it?" he asked gravely.

"It will attract lots of attention, bringing others who will be looking for this individual, so focus on finding this person."

Choi couldn't believe what he was hearing. "Are you sure a disturbance will happen here in Lake Valley?"

"Yes. I will be called to help and then be led to Washington."

The answer struck like a sledgehammer to his chest. When? How big? Will my family be okay? Then, calm yourself. There is no reason to panic.

"We have time," Yoona insisted. "A month, maybe two. But others will come looking for our new friend, so the quicker you find them, the better."

Choi took a slow, deep breath. "I will make my rounds," he reassured her.

"Call me the moment you know something." Before ending the call, Yoona added, "And Choi, be discreet."

Jasmine joined Choi in the living room. "Is everything okay?"

Choi's mind was flooded with what he needed to do next—make a list of names, call to schedule appointments, request time off work? His dark eyes were unfocused, dancing around in thought.

She placed her hand on his arm and felt him trembling. "Oh my god, Choi. What is it?"

With a quick breath, he focused on her, "It's worse than I thought. I am wondering if it wouldn't be best if you and Jun visit my mom in Korea for the summer. Jun turns seven in a few months, and she would love to see him."

Jasmine laid her hand on his broad chest, feeling his heart pounding. Her eyes widened, and her nostrils flared. "Choi, you're scaring me. What's going on?"

"My Aunt Yoona will be coming here."

Jasmine's mouth dropped open and she froze. Choi knew she didn't care for Yoona, having called her a witch on two different occasions. The first time Yoona talked with Jasmine through telepathy, she screamed. Choi also felt a power dynamic between the two. Yoona often took Choi from Jasmine, which angered her. "When?" she asked.

Choi pulled his wife close to his body. "A month, maybe two."

Holding her husband, she asked, "Are you certain something will happen to bring her here, to Lake Valley?"

"I'm as surprised as you are. I've been tasked with finding someone—an energy manipulator."

"Like you?"

"No. This person will be powerful, an ally or foe to my aunt."

"Shit, Choi!" Jasmine gasped. "This is serious."

"Yes."

"Okay. I'll... uh... I'll start looking for flights to Korea."

Between Homes

Inside the FBI office, Leah waited for her social worker to return and for her Uncle Tim to be released from his interview. She was still convinced she was stuck in a nightmare. Her dad was missing? Presumed abducted? How? Why? He was a grown man. This wasn't the medieval world of Conan. Staring straight ahead, Leah didn't see anything, didn't notice anyone, and felt a dull throbbing ache sitting in the center of her chest.

Yesterday she had been called to the principal's office. When she saw the police officers, she became nervous, her mind racing for possible reasons they would want to see her. They asked if she had heard from her father and then had her call his cell. He hadn't answered.

Uncle Tim stayed with Leah, and they paced all night, unable to sleep, calling her father again and again. Then, this morning, an FBI agent showed up, asking her and her uncle to go with them for questioning.

The woman standing in front of Leah snapped her fingers. "Leah, are you okay?"

"What? Sorry," she said, focusing on the woman who had been assigned to be her social worker.

"I wasn't able to contact your mother. I did talk with Carol, Barb and Dan's grandmother. She agreed to allow you to stay at her house, but I still think it's best if you stayed with your uncle."

"Why do I need your permission? Last I checked, I was eighteen years old."

"Yes, you are. But you're also still in high school and are considered a dependent. Under the circumstances, the police and FBI felt it was in your best interest that I assist you."

"I'll be staying with my friends."

"Your uncle is family. He is responsible for you until we contact your mother. I'm thinking about what's best for you."

"And I'm thinking about what's best for me. I'll be staying with my friends. My uncle has already agreed. So unless you plan to arrest me, stop harassing me."

The woman held up her hands to calm Leah. "No need to raise your voice. I'm here to help you. You can stay with your friends." Showing Leah a business card and a phone, she continued, "This is a burner. The only people who have this number are the FBI and myself. I'd switch your phone to, 'Do not disturb;' you're going to be getting a lot of calls. This is an active investigation, so don't talk with strangers or the press."

Leah nodded.

"I'm adding a therapist's number into this phone. I'll text you the appointment time. If you need to speak with her sooner, call her anytime. She knows what happened. She'll be able to help you process your feelings."

Leah didn't respond.

The social worker squatted to Leah's eye level. "I think it's best if you skip school this week. I'll inform them. Just stay home." She handed Leah the phone.

Leah took it, having no thoughts about going anywhere or doing anything. "Sure."

"Did you tell the FBI agent everything she needed to know?"

The questions Leah was asked blurred together. She couldn't remember what the officer had asked. "Yeah."

"Good. I'll call you after I schedule your appointment. You have my number if you need anything. You'll call if you have questions, right?"

"Yes," she answered dryly, not sure if she would or not.

"Your uncle will be out shortly. Wait for him."

Day Eight—Wednesday

Forming Spiritual Connections

Choi thanked the imam, a prayer leader at the local mosque, ended the call, and added the meeting to his calendar. Taking a sip of coffee, he reviewed his schedule—eight appointments and two services. He shook his head, wondering how he was going to keep them all.

Finishing his coffee, he rinsed the cup in the sink. Jasmine came up behind him, wrapping her arms around him, groping his chest. "You're all set for the day?"

"I am. Any chance you want to come to Mass with me?"

Pressing her head to his back, she asked, "What time?"

"The first one is at 8:00 this morning, and the other is at 6:30."

"I've got to get Jun ready for school, and 6:30 is a bit late for a school night."

Turning in his wife's embrace, Choi faced Jasmine and put his arms over her head and around her shoulders. Rubbing his nose against hers, he kissed her. "I'll be home after nine tonight."

Spinning Choi out of her arms, Jasmine hit him on the rear, saying, "Get going. Be a hero."

As he drove to his first appointment, Choi thought about the people with whom he would be connecting. Religious leaders had special and powerful relationships with the people in the community and were involved with all manners of peoples' lives from birth to death. Religious leaders provided counsel for individuals going through difficulties and prayed with people, helping them connect to their spiritual center. The person Choi needed to find had a strong spiritual core, so this made the perfect starting place. He would spend the day visiting the churches, synagogues, mosques, and temples, meeting these leaders and reconnecting with them.

Haunting Evidence

Brandon watched a news van leave the Education Center parking lot where the team had just finished a live broadcast about Jared Davenport's disappearance and Nong Ekamai's reappearance. Brandon stared at the Education Center. Crime scene tape blocked off the front of the building as the FBI and officers from the department continued to search for evidence. Reporters mingled among onlookers, anxiously awaiting information and answers.

Brandon had read a statement from Dr. Mathis which detailed slight neurological abnormalities in students who attended the Center. Jared had had an appointment with the doctor but had failed to show. Brandon wondered if this detail could explain the next two statements. Jared's manager at Go Express had said: "Jared was adamant that the address was a residence and said he had a date planned with the woman who lived there." Jared's daughter, Leah, had said: "My dad had a date with the woman who lived at the Bellevue House." Did Jared Davenport believe that this building was the Bellevue House because of a neurological abnormality? Brandon replayed his own encounter with Jared. "I deliver to the Bellevue House every day." Jared had given Brandon directions to the Bellevue House, but he had found himself in front of the Education Center.

Staring at the building, Brandon was mesmerized. He recalled the memory of him approaching the Center. Leave! the building had seemed to say, right before the Bellevue House flashed before his eyes. Something about this place was wrong, and it clouded the victims' perceptions.

All four of the victims came here. They all believed this was the Bellevue House. The three who returned, returned here. Nong walked out of this building. Brandon saw her come out with his own eyes. He had been inside the building moments before she came out and hadn't seen her. Where had she been?

His mind wandered for a second, thinking about hidden basements and secret rooms that might be in the building, but then he came back to the main question. How did they believe this building was the Bellevue House? Brandon's thoughts turned to what Charlie, the owner of the media center, had told him and what he himself had possibly experienced—the Center was haunted.

Brandon touched his head, remembering the headache, vision, and the voice. The closer he had walked to the area where he heard two people having sex, the stronger the headache had become. Was that sound Jared and Nong having sex? The doctor's report indicated Nong had engaged in sexual intercourse. He laughed it off as ridiculous, but...

Haunted. For sure, strange events happened here. Many of the employees had quit because of those unusual experiences. Brandon wouldn't have believed such things and still wasn't sure he did, but he had no other way to explain what was happening.

The brain scans. Would having a ghost inside someone create the kind of neurological abnormalities Amanda, Tyler, and now Nong had produced? Brandon wondered if a possessed person would see something that wasn't there, a house, for instance, instead of an office building. After all, the three victims who returned were not themselves. Were they possessed?

Brandon didn't know anything about the supernatural world and wasn't sure he wanted to go down that path, but he wasn't seeing any other options. Did he really want to go find a Whoopi Goldberg and relive the movie, "Ghost?"

While deep in thought, staring at the center, an FBI agent approached Brandon.

"Can I help you?" the agent asked.

"I'm Detective Brandon Spencer."

"Paula Sanders, FBI. Are you part of the task force?"

"This case was mine a few days ago, but no. I was taken off it."

"Any ideas as to who is behind this or where the victim may be?" Paula asked.

"I was thinking about the information again, trying to figure it out. May I ask you a question?"

"Sure."

"Has anybody experienced anything weird today or yesterday? Sudden headaches or hearing strange noises?"

"Funny. I got a headache ten minutes ago—about the time you showed up."

"I'm sorry you feel threatened by me."

"A few of the guys got headaches. Why do you ask?"

"It was something the owner of the media center told me."

"That this place is haunted?" Paula laughed. "Don't tell me you believe that, too. It's enough we have doctors calling and telling us ghost stories even though their own reports suggest the reasons for them."

He was entertaining the idea, but he wasn't going to tell her that. "No, no. But the security guard on duty quit last week complaining about headaches, and I was curious if you guys had experienced any as well."

"We have. The agency is sending a 'specialist' to investigate the cause. They think maybe a chemical leak of some kind is causing them. And until we ascertain the level of danger, we can't enter the building. This delay is frustrating. You understand the time-sensitive nature of abduction cases."

"I do."

"You know, this is our investigation now. If you have any information to share, I'd advise you to do so."

"Absolutely. I've filed my notes and written my reports already. I'm afraid I didn't discover much."

Paula handed Brandon her card. "I'd appreciate it if you could send me copies."

"Sure. First thing tomorrow morning. I'm pretty busy today. If you'll excuse me."

"Call me anytime," Paula called as Brandon retreated.

After getting into his car, he thought, Chemical leak? He didn't buy that. Haunted? Not sure that was a better explanation, but it felt more and more plausible. What exactly had happened to the Bellevue House? He needed to read the files so he had a complete understanding of what had taken place.

Glancing at his watch, Brandon started the car. He had an appointment with a bartender who held key information regarding the Mitchell case, a lead he had obtained through Stephanie's friends. They had revealed that Stephanie had lied about her whereabouts the night she and her mother had been attacked, covering for her to avoid trouble. Calling the bar, Brandon learned that the bartender was well-informed about the family's drama and was willing to share crucial details. Brandon was eager to uncover more about the situation, especially considering Stephanie's mysterious phone calls on the night of the attack—to Dimitri, the suspect, and to her father, Monica's ex-husband. Understanding the family dynamics better would be essential before confronting Stephanie again. After the bartender, Brandon had to find the drug addict, Alysia, who apparently frequented homeless shelters.

On top of the Mitchell case, Brandon had a robbery to investigate and had been handed an existing case involving a string of catalytic converter thefts because that detective had been reassigned to help the FBI on Jared's disappearance. The captain was angry and under a lot of stress, insisting on results. The Bellevue House would have to wait until tomorrow morning.

"Stop!"

Barb drove past Leah's house, seeing several news vans parked out front.

"Keep driving." Dan said. "Let's park on the next street and cut through the backyard."

Barb agreed and drove around to the other side of the block. Parking, they went through the neighbor's yard and jumped the fence. Dan struggled with Leah's keys, trying all four, before opening the back door.

"Her suitcase is on the bottom shelf in the laundry room," Barb told Dan. "Go get it and meet me in her bedroom."

Twenty minutes later, dragging Leah's bag full of clothes, they exited the house the way they had come.

When they arrived home, Barb went into the spare room which had become Leah's temporary home. Leah was curled in bed, eyes puffy and red. Barb's heart sank, knowing exactly what Leah was feeling. How many days, no—weeks, had she been in that same position? Hell, there were still days she struggled to function. Kneeling next to her, Barb gently stroked her hair. "No news?"

"The last guy was gone for three years and then in a coma for four. The lady they just found was missing for four years and will be in a coma for what—four or five more?" Leah sniffled.

"What did the FBI say when they interviewed you?"

"They asked about places we went, people we saw, things we did. They wanted to know more about the woman my dad liked, but I don't know anything about her, not even her name."

"They asked me the same thing." Barb's eyes clouded as she thought about her interview. The man was a first-class asshole and had suggested she had something to do with Jared's disappearance. The man kept twisting her words, making her sound like an accomplice. Her house was mentioned again and again, stirring the memory of her mom shooting herself. Barb had finally broken down and cried.

Thinking about that display of weakness in the face of bold arrogance, made her angry. "I felt like a suspect."

"Why?"

"You said something about our house, and they thought I was involved somehow. The guy questioning me was a real dick!"

"They kept telling me the Bellevue House burned down and that my dad couldn't have been there." Leah's face turned red, and she became animated. "He's an architect! He knows what he saw."

Barb's eyes hardened. She couldn't understand why Leah was so insistent that her house still existed. Barb wanted to scream some sense into her, but held her breath instead. Now was not the time to argue. "Have you called your mom yet?"

Leah raised her eyes, looking defeated. She exhaled loudly, conveying a longing to call, mixed with hesitation. Glancing at her phone, she said, "No."

"Do you want me to call her?"

Shaking her head, slightly at first, Leah's expression slowly animated, until she concluded, "No." Tears began again as she explained. "She left me when I was ten and didn't bother to tell me she wasn't coming back. The first time I flew to visit her, I asked when she was coming home. 'Soon,' she had lied. She stood in the airport, watching me walk away with some strange flight attendant. No, if I call, she'll fly out here. She doesn't get that privilege. It'll just cause more stress and headaches. Besides, the Royal Canadian International Circus hired her for the season. It's a big gig for her."

"Leah, you need her. She's your mom."

"Need her?!" Leah scoffed. "It was my dad who stayed with me. Do you know that she and my grandfather were trying to send me to boarding school? When my dad got sued, my grandfather offered to settle the suit so he wouldn't lose his insurance, but I would've had to attend some school in England in order for that to happen. My mom supported that idea! She approved of taking me away from my dad. No! She doesn't get to come and pretend my dad's going missing is a tragedy."

"Leah, it is a tragedy."

"Yes! For me."

"I thought you and your mom were friends?"

"We are!" Leah yelled before breaking down completely.

Barb held her hand.

Dan peeked in, then retreated.

"I know exactly how you're feeling, believe me," Barb reassured her. She knew Leah would be confused, angry, sad—sometimes all at once. And the nightmares! She closed her eyes, breathing deeply to let her memories subside.

"It's all my fault," Leah said through her tears.

"What are you talking about?" Barb retorted.

"If I would have agreed to go to England, my dad wouldn't have lost his business. I was being selfish."

Barb leaned forward, hugging her. "You are loved," she said, echoing Leah's words from a few days earlier.

"I don't know what to do," Leah cried. "Pray? I've been praying all day."

"You're going to be okay," Barb whispered. "Everything will work out. Look at me; I'm living proof."

After another minute, Leah grabbed a tissue, wiping her eyes and blowing her nose. "I heard a voice while I was praying. It told me to 'follow the path.'"

"I understand that. I've heard voices in my head before, too."

"I have to try to find him. I have to find that house."

Barb's lips tightened and her face tensed. She snapped, "What house?"

"The Bellevue House!" Leah exclaimed.

"God dammit, Leah! My fucking house is gone!" Barb finally burst.

Leah jerked back with a start, staring at Barb with a puzzled expression.

Barb stood and turned to leave. "I'm sorry. But please stop talking about my house as if it still exists." Standing with her back to Leah, Barb waited for a response.

"I'm calling my uncle. My dad knows what he saw."

"He obviously didn't! And you blabbing about it only confuses people. Stop!" Barb left the room.

Unbelievable

Choi entered St. Raphael, a modern church with white walls, brown trim, and stained-glass windows that were very blue. A large cross hung behind the altar, depicting Jesus nailed to it, an image Choi never felt fit with the prophet's teachings. Video cameras, used to televise the service, were visible on either side of the sanctuary. A handful of families shuffled past Choi and joined the twenty or so families already seated near the front. Choi took a seat in the back row to observe.

As the music began, the congregation rose. Father Joseph, a middle-aged man with graying hair, glasses, chubby cheeks, and a large belly, wore a white gown with gold trim. He walked solemnly down the aisle.

When he delivered his sermon, the priest spoke in dark, angry tones. "The devil is among us. He lives in politicians and studio executives who push and promote the worst sin imaginable—homosexuality. The devil has been so successful in infiltrating our society that this sin is celebrated in our streets and shoved down our throats in movies, TV shows," raising his voice, he blasted, "and cartoons!" His face was beat red, and his hands gripped the side of the lectern so tightly, Choi thought he might break off a chunk. "The devil has worked through those Democrats to pass laws that allow this evil to exist in our very communities, tempting our children to accept the devil. Well, I say, 'No more!'" He pounded his fist on the lectern, pausing for dramatic effect. He went on to explain that his new neighbors were a married gay couple and that he saw them kissing one morning before leaving the house for work. The priest shouted, "I am angry!" and called pastors who preached that God hated the sin but loved the sinner, "enablers." He even went as far as to suggest homosexual couples should be murdered.

Choi shook his head, remembering when Father Joseph was one of those pastors who loved all people. Choi thought, If the priest wants to find the devil, all he has to do is look inward.

After reading several passages from the Bible and continuing his homophobic homily, Father Joseph called out several politicians, insisting they were dangerous pedophiles. He ended his sermon by going back to his neighbors, one of whom worked at the Education Center. The priest announced he would fight the devil head on by performing a live exorcism at the Center. "The poltergeist that lives in that building will be vanquished. We cannot allow evil to spread in our city, especially a place our children frequent."

After the service, Choi waited for the priest to mingle with several parishioners before approaching to shake hands and connect.

"It's good to see you again, my son. I'm glad you made it to a service. How is your wife?"

"She's well, Father. Thank you. I'm curious about this exorcism you are performing. Are you certain it's warranted?" Choi understood that this exorcism was simply a ploy to out his neighbor, but he needed to be certain. The Education Center had a presence, but it didn't feel like a ghost as Choi understood ghosts. The energy encompassed the entire building, and Choi thought the energy more likely came from the teachers and students who were passionate about the activities they were doing, creating the feel of a presence. Had Father Joseph felt that presence? Did he believe it to be something other than energy created by the attendees?

With a grave demeanor, the priest intoned, "The building has been known to be haunted for some time now—the strange noises and occurrences, patrons getting headaches, and now another missing person. Evil runs thick through those walls."

"Do you think it's wise to televise the event? I'm worried you will have a difficult time focusing and building the energy required for such a task."

"The public must witness the affair so they can feel safe returning to the building," the priest refuted. "Why don't you join me? It would give the public confidence to see an officer of the law present."

"I'm sorry, Father. I'm rather busy, as you probably know." Choi saw the priest had concerns, but this upcoming event was purely for show. Father Joseph was taking advantage of Jared's abduction to gain viewership.

"Very well." He pressed his thumb to Choi's forehead and made the sign of the cross. "Go with God."

Back in his patrol car, Choi felt like throwing up. He sent a message to his aunt, informing her of Father Joseph's hateful sermon and his plan for the Education Center.

Day Nine – Thursday

Twisted Love

"Jared, wake up," said the voice inside Jared's head. "You need to eat." The voice wasn't his inner voice nor was it a memory. It didn't come from outside of him either, but was rather a distinct and separate voice inside his mind. He had heard this voice before when he had been with Nong, the one that had asked, "Do you really love me?"

"The kitchen has a walk-in fridge. Most everything in there has been prepped. Take what you want, but do not remove the container. If you do, you must return it immediately to exactly where you found it."

"Who are you? Where are you? How are you talking to me in my head?" Jared said out loud.

"First, you don't have to talk. It's best if you don't during the day. I am with you and know your every thought. At night, if you want to talk, you can," the voice instructed. "You can call me Bellevue. That is the name that was given to me. As for who or what I am, I am me," said Bellevue.

"Bellevue?" pressed Jared. He wasn't sure what that meant. "Where are you? Why can't I see you?"

"You can see me," Bellevue laughed. "You are in me. You are living inside me."

"Inside you?" Jared hesitated. "You are the Bellevue House?" he asked in disbelief. "How is this possible? Are you alive?"

"I was once. My one true love created me. He worshiped me from the day he imagined me. He devoted his life to bringing me into existence. His countless

175

years of work, planning, and love created incredibly powerful energy which he poured into me. Thus, I was conceived."

"Conceived?"

"Think of it like a fetus growing inside its mother. I was built and pulsed with life but was not yet alive." Bellevue continued, "Then those who work with the spiritual world gave me a soul and life. The priest blessed me, giving me hope, expectations, and purpose. The rabbi, who put a heart on my door, sanctified me. The monks' chants vibrated throughout the fibers of my being. I began to shiver as the energy resonated in me like a defibrillator, shocking me to life.

"I was a living, breathing entity able to consume energy and expel waste. I could feel people's touch. I felt pain when someone hurt me. I felt love when someone caressed me. I had intimate relationships that were pure and warm. I also had fame and admiration. Tourists came to photograph me. Students came to learn from me. My life was perfect. But then that monster murdered me; I was burned alive, my physical form left in ashes."

Bellevue didn't speak for a long minute. Jared's heart filled with anger and hatred, but those emotions subsided as Bellevue's story resumed.

"To my surprise, I am still here, but different. I can't feel the wind or the sun. I can't feel loving touches or dirty shoes. However, I do have great power, power to control, manipulate, and bring those who have wants and desires inside me. I could bring you inside of me because you wanted Nong, desired her, just as she came inside me because she wanted me. Now you are with me. She is connected with us, and we will be a happy family."

"Wait. You were alive? Living? A living house? How can a house be alive?"

"How can a tree be alive?" Bellevue retorted.

"That's different. They have roots and produce food. They grow."

"They need food because they grow. I'm not growing."

"Trees can't talk."

"Are you sure? Trees communicate. If you are in tune with them, you can understand. I was able to communicate with my family because they were in tune with me."

"What do you mean?"

"I couldn't talk to people like I can now. It was different. Before, I used a person's inner voice. I communicated through ideas and intuition. I presented myself as thoughts. I was an imaginary friend, if you will."

"So you were a living house, which I'm not sure I understand, but now you are—what? I read about the fire. The wife..."

"That monster! She destroyed everything I had, everyone I loved. Took everything dear from me—my physical form, the love of my life, the laughter of my children. They are all gone."

Bellevue's burst of anger filled Jared's chest, his blood burning with hate. Jared put his hand on his heart, surprised by the emotions. "I'm sorry. I didn't mean to upset you." Jared was frightened by the realization that these emotions were not his own.

The tension dissipated slowly during the long silence held between them. Finally, Bellevue spoke, "Continue with your questions. I didn't mean to startle you."

Gathering his thoughts, Jared asked, "So if the fire killed you, that means—you are what? A ghost? The ghost of Bellevue House?"

"I am Bellevue. You need to eat. You have been sleeping for two days, and your body requires nourishment."

Jared grabbed his shirt and rushed for the front door. He opened it, stepping out. But, as he left, he simultaneously returned. "What the hell?" Looking back, he saw the outside and stepped through the door again, only to return to the house once again. "I'm trapped," Jared whispered. Hearing the television, he followed the sound to the media room where he saw his face cover the screen on the evening news.

"Jared Davenport went missing here at the Education Center two days ago. This is the same place where Amanda Bowman, Tyler Jiles, and Nong Ekamai were abducted and where all three were found. Jared Davenport worked for Go Express as a delivery driver and was seen loitering in front of the Center days before his disappearance. Anyone with information is asked to call the 800 number on the screen. Meanwhile, Nong Ekamai has been taken to Sunnyside Hospital, where she continues to suffer from unresponsive wakefulness syndrome, the same condition that plagued Amanda Bowman and Tyler Jiles. The FBI has declined to comment, but have confirmed that all four cases are now considered linked and speculate a single abductor is at large." The television turned black.

"The Education Center? I don't recall ever going there," Jared said.

"I showed you that, so you understand where you are."

"I'm at the Education Center? But I'm in you."

"Think of me as a bubble inside the Center. You are inside my bubble."

"So, I'm a prisoner here? What about my daughter?"

"We both know your daughter will be fine. She has a great relationship with her mother, and you have taught her well. Her stock portfolio is substantial and the money in your account is more than enough to start her career. Besides, her grandfather is a wealthy businessman who has a trust fund that pays her monthly. He has already paid for her college education. He would do anything to make his granddaughter happy."

"I need to take care of her. She needs me," Jared pleaded.

"We are going to take care of each other. I love you and need you, Jared, and you love me," Bellevue said.

"I love you? I don't even know you."

"Look around. You have desired to be here, to live here," Bellevue said. "You have wanted me since the day you saw me in Exploring Architecture. I am the reason you took that night class at university to improve your skills. I reignited your passion. You have studied me. Longed to physically examine me. To look at me unclothed. To see my true beauty. To touch me. Now you are here. Inside me. Come, be with me."

As Bellevue talked, Jared felt his heart stir. He put his hand to his chest, feeling a buzzing sensation. The churning force deep in his soul slowly boiled to the surface, the pressure expanding his chest, deepening his breathing. A raw hunger Jared had only felt with Stacy drowned his anger and confusion. His groin became sensitive, and he had an urge to move his hips. A light sweat beaded on his brow. The need to touch and be touched overtook him. He needed Bellevue. Needed to be with It, to be embraced by It.

Taking off his shirt, Jared walked over to the lounge chair and sank into it. The leather caressed his body, touching and stroking him. He took off his pants, letting himself be taken by the leather.

Pancakes and Kisses

Choi woke early, needing to work a double shift. His plan was to see the other religious leaders while on duty. He could justify his action by saying he was looking for leads to the kidnapper, which was actually the truth. He'd say he had a hunch, and the captain would allow him to go. Choi had earned the nickname "the psychic" for the number of times his "hunches" had come true.

Entering the kitchen, he began making pancakes, slicing strawberries and bananas to add to the batter. When Jasmine arrived home from her night shift at the nursing home, she welcomed breakfast.

Choi leaned into his wife, giving her a slow, sweet kiss. "I hate it when you have to work the overnight shift. I never sleep well."

"I hate trying to sleep during the day. Especially when you have to work a double shift. I'll miss my workout tonight," she pouted.

Choi growled, "I'll give you a workout right now."

"Hey, don't burn my breakfast."

"Is Kim dropping Jun at school today?" Choi asked.

"Yes. Don't worry about me. I'm not doing anything today."

"Good."

Choi finished cooking, cleaned up, and kissed his wife goodbye as he headed for work.

The Invisible Killer

Arriving at the police station early, Brandon typed up his meeting with the bartender. Brandon learned that the attack may have actually been carried out by Monica's brother. He had been renting Monica's former house, which she had obtained through her divorce. But she'd then sold it without consulting him. The brother was furious that she hadn't given him the option to buy it first.

In an email to the Mitchell's divorce lawyers, Brandon requested a meeting. He wanted to understand the specifics of the divorce—in particular this house—before interviewing the brother. Brandon's next meeting was with Stephanie's ex-boyfriend, but first the Bellevue House.

Needing to learn the full story behind the fire, Brandon found the files. He read the officers' reports, the fire chief's report, witness statements, and the autopsy reports. He went online and read all the news articles he could find. Several new facts surrounding the fire and the house came to light.

John Mills had become obsessed with the house he had built to the exclusion of all else. He had a large celebration, posting video of a priest, rabbi, and monks blessing the house. His wife, Debra, was so desperate to get his attention that she had had sex with a contractor while her husband was home. Completely frustrated, but unwilling to leave him, she had poured several gallons of gasoline inside the house, starting a fire. John had rushed home from work, anticipating what his wife was doing. Upon arriving home, he had raced into the house and died trying to put out the flames.

After the firefighters extinguished the blaze, Debra felt extreme pain. She grabbed her head, crying, while she begged for forgiveness. Then she swiped the gun from the officer who was trying to help her and attempted to shoot herself in the head. The bullet tore through her cheek. She died instantly, but not from the gunshot. Her death was from severe brain hemorrhaging, "cause unknown."

Brandon sat back and touched his head. He was remembering the headache he had suddenly experienced while at the Education Center—how it grew in intensity, feeling like a pressure gauge that threatened to blow. Could it have grown stronger to the point it would have killed him?

For the first time, Brandon was frightened.

The Message

Leah barged into Barb's room and fell onto her bed, exhausted.

Barb was sitting on the floor with a basket full of clothes, folding laundry. "Sure, come in," she mumbled.

"I'm sorry," Leah said. "I'm sorry your parents are gone. I'm sorry your house burned down. I'm sorry for all of it."

Barb balled a pair of socks together and tossed them into her open sock drawer. "Did you have a nice walk at least?" Her voice was calm and flat.

Leah sighed, stretching her arms before propping herself up with the pillows. "I guess. The reporters were more of a nuisance than a help. They kept asking about my dad's past with Stillen Corporation and my parents' divorce. Nothing they did or said was related to finding Dad. So annoying."

"Where did you look?"

"We walked the trails in the Bobcat Mountain area all morning. I really thought I'd see a house that looked like..." Leah stopped.

"The Bellevue House."

"Yes," Leah said with relief. "My dad must have parked in the Education Center lot and then walked to the house."

"How many people were with you? It looked like a lot. I saw a clip of you walking on the news."

"No, not too many." Leah thought for a moment, "The press, my Uncle Tim, and some volunteers. Maybe fifteen."

"You didn't find anything?"

"Nothing."

Barb got to her knees. She picked up the pile of folded jeans and put them into her dresser.

"Hey, Barb? Do you think that lady who showed up at the Center, you know, the kidnapped one, do you think she's the lady my dad liked?" Leah asked. The idea had been floating around in her head, but she didn't know why.

"Why would you think that?"

"I don't know. It's weird that she would turn up the moment my dad went missing."

"The news did say that was the guy's M.O.," Barb said.

"I want to visit her."

"Why? You don't know her. I don't think she has anything to do with your dad's disappearance."

"She knows the person who took him," Leah said, matter-of-factly.

"Leah, that lady is a vegetable."

"Yeah, but still, I need to see her. I have to see her." Leah stated firmly. "Let's go."

"What? Now?" Barb protested. "You said you would FaceTime your mom today."

"I will. Later. Let's go. Come on."

"What about the media? Sunnyside is sure to be crawling with reporters. You said they were annoying."

"They are. But I need to talk to this lady."

"The police and your social worker told us to stay put, not to go out or to talk with anyone."

"Barb! It's a little late for that. I've been out most of the day."

"And you're going to get into trouble."

"Are you coming or not?"

"Ugh. This is stupid. Fine, let's get harassed."

The sound of an egg timer dinging in the kitchen woke Jared. "What is that? Is there someone here?" asked Jared as he got up. He dressed and rushed to the kitchen.

It was large and spacious. An island with pots and pans hanging above it covered the middle of the room. Cutting boards and utensils sat on the left side of the top. Shelves underneath held mixing bowls and appliances—food processors, an air fryer, a couple instant pots, several kitchenAid mixers, and more, all state-of-the-art. An eight-burner stove, two large ovens, and three sinks for washing, rinsing, and sanitizing dishes lined the wall on the right. Shelves along the walls housed bowls, plates, cups, baking sheets, pots, and pans. The cupboards held bags of flour and rice, boxes of baking soda, salt, and spices, and bottles of sauces. To the left of the sinks stood a walk-in fridge and freezer.

"This kitchen is a classroom," Jared observed.

"You are not the only one using it, so do be diligent about promptly putting things back where you found them. You must also be clean. In fact, as soon as you have eaten and washed, you will disinfect the living room and the media room," Bellevue instructed.

"What do you mean I'm not the only one using it? Who else lives here?"

"No one, exactly. But you may hear voices of those coming and going from time to time. I am telling you now so you will not be surprised. Jared, your lack of cleanliness or inattention to returning things will be met with severe punishment."

Jared could feel the warning as much as he heard it and knew that Bellevue was absolutely sincere in Its threat. After finding some cereal and pouring himself a bowl, Jared set the box on the counter. A sharp stinging pain pierced his head. "Ouch!"

"Return the box to its proper place," Bellevue ordered.

"Okay, I'm sorry," Jared said as he put the box away. "You didn't have to poke me."

"That was a warning. You will learn."

Jared ate his cereal at the huge table in silence, but he could hear voices and feel another person's presence. He stopped chewing and closed his eyes, listening.

"Nong, I'm going to take you into the commons room now. There are lots of people out there, and some of them are here to see you," a woman's voice was saying.

Jared held his breath, straining to hear the conversation. He could almost see Nong and feel her hands. He could sense her desire to see her daughter and speak to her parents.

"Bellevue? Am I seeing and feeling Nong right now?"

"She is connected to you and is still part of me. Your bond will grow stronger in time, and the two of you will be able to communicate."

"Connected to me? You've said that before." Jared remembered the day he met Nong. She had put her hand on his chest. "Now we're connected," she had said.

"That's right. This connection will also allow you to be intimate." The sultry tone in which Bellevue said this stirred Jared. "I will show you how when the time is right." Then Bellevue's tone changed abruptly as It ordered, "Finish eating, wash up, and go clean the other rooms."

"Where is she?"

Jared felt another sharp sting in his head. "Do as I say," Bellevue said firmly. "This needs to happen now."

The Sunnyside Psychiatric Hospital commons provided a large area where patients and guests could gather to talk, do art projects or puzzles, or eat meals together. It was well-lit and spacious, with large windows looking out into the yard. Loveseats and chairs were arranged in conversation circles. One corner of the room held a few guitars, a flute, and some percussion instruments next to a piano.

Nong was curled up in a chair facing the window. She rocked back and forth, her right hand clenched in a fist, staring at the floor. She mumbled something unintelligible. A reporter, who was interviewing a doctor about Nong's condition, sat near her.

A nurse led Leah and Barb to Nong. "She hasn't responded to anyone yet—keeps rocking and mumbling," the nurse explained. "Nong, you have some visitors today." Turning to the teenagers, she said, "Make sure you sign out before you leave." She headed back to her station.

Leah squatted beside Nong, taking her left hand and holding it in hers. She spoke softly, "Hi, Nong. We've never met. I'm Leah." Pausing, she looked into Nong's eyes. "My dad's name is Jared. Do you know him? Jared Davenport? Do you know where he is?" Leah looked at Nong for any sign of acknowledgment. Finally, Nong turned and looked at Leah.

"You know Jared, right? I'm his daughter. You can tell me. Please."

"Leah. The house. The house," Nong said.

Barb, standing behind Leah, saw what was happening. She turned toward the nurse's station and gestured for the nurse, yelling, "Hey, she's talking. She's talking. Hurry!"

The doctor and the reporter became alert, nearing Nong to observe.

Leah's heart raced. "The house? What house?"

Nong, face cringing in pain, covered her head with her hands and began to scream. It was a loud painful sound that sent Leah falling backwards. "My daughter!" Nong cried, slipping back into rocking and mumbling.

Stunned, Leah stared at Nong. Barb grabbed Leah's hand and pulled her away as the doctor examined Nong. Two nurses rushed to help.

"What happened? What did you do?" one of the nurses demanded.

"I told her my name and asked her if she knew my dad."

"It's true," Barb interjected. "Nong responded by saying, 'The house, the house' and that's when I called you over."

"Wait here," the nurse said calmly.

The reporter maneuvered to Barb and Leah. "I'm Brenda Calderwood with the Sun Times. Can I ask you what happened?"

"I'm sorry," Barb said, shielding Leah. "The police have instructed us to not talk with the press."

"The police can't tell you what to do." Looking past Barb, Brenda said, "You're Leah Davenport, Jared's daughter. Please, talk with me. My niece is Amanda Bowman. She was the first one abducted."

"I'm sorry, but we don't have anything to say," Barb insisted.

"What did you ask Nong? What does 'the house' mean?"

"We don't know," Barb replied.

"Can you tell me your name? What's your relationship to Nong?" Brenda pressed.

The nurse approached the girls, but spoke to the reporter, "Excuse me."

To Barb and Leah, she directed, "Come with me. The doctors and the police want to ask you some questions about what happened."

As Jared sprayed and wiped the leather seat, his mind returned to Bellevue's manipulation of his emotions earlier. The raw passion and desperate need to be touched hadn't been him. He was no longer in control of his own emotions, being easily manipulated to pleasure or be pleasured by Bellevue. Even though the experience was extremely pleasant, the aftermath was cold; he felt used, vulnerable, exposed. While Jared scrubbed the chair where he had lain naked, he heard voices again and felt Nong's presence. He stopped what he was doing, closed his eyes, and listened.

"I'm Leah. My dad's name is Jared. Do you know him? Jared Davenport." It was his daughter's voice!

Reeling, he reached out to Nong with all his strength. "Nong, the house. Tell her where I am. Please."

"Enough!" yelled Bellevue. Its loud voice cut the connection, causing Jared to cover his ears. "You are here, with me. We are a family now." In a softer, yet firm voice It said, "Please finish cleaning. I don't want to hurt you. I love you, Jared."

The contradiction between those words and Bellevue's actions gnawed at him. "Love is not abuse," Jared grumbled as he resumed cleaning.

In the nurses' station, Barb watched Leah pace back and forth, while waiting for permission to leave.

"Barb," Leah began.

"Yes, I heard. 'The house.'" Barb said. "You think she was talking about my house—the Bellevue House."

"I know you believe it burned down. But please understand that my dad talked to me about your house for days. He asked me to join him on his date and take a tour of it with him."

"You do know that the Education Center was built where my house used to be, right?"

"What? What are you saying? The Education Center is the house?"

"There are parts of my house inside the Center. Go online and look."

"How could my dad want me to see a house that doesn't exist? I don't get it. Are you sure someone didn't rebuild it somewhere else?"

The nurse returned, and Leah nervously asked, "Is Nong okay? Can I talk with her again?"

"Are we in trouble?" Barb interjected.

"Nong's resting in her room. Be thankful the doctor was nearby. And, no, you're not in any trouble, but I'd expect a police detective to follow up. Leah, I hope they find your dad."

"Thank you."

The nurse showed the girls the back exit.

Delivering the Truth

Brandon sat in his patrol car feeling a bit surprised. In the Mitchell case, the ex-boyfriend shared that Monica, the mother, had been having an affair with Dimitri, the suspect, before her divorce. The information fit his initial assumption that the attacker and Monica had been in a relationship, but for some reason he still felt surprised. The ex-boyfriend also claimed to have been at the Golden Beach Spa along the strip the night the Mitchells were attacked, saying he hadn't seen Stephanie. Brandon wasn't sure he believed him, so he'd be sure to verify his story. Thinking about the affair, Brandon wondered if the divorce lawyers had known about it. What a nasty pretzel this case was turning into.

Switching his focus, Brandon went back to the Bellevue House and Debra Mills' mysterious death. The idea that a ghost could have been involved, not only in her death, but also in the abduction cases, was a mold spreading its dark tendrils throughout his consciousness. He decided it was time to have a talk with the Mills' about their old house. Did they believe it was haunted? Did they know the root cause of Debra's death? Taking out his phone, he called. A woman answered.

"Good evening. My name is Detective Brandon Spencer of the LVPD. May I speak with Carol Anderson?"

"This is Carol. Do you have some good news for us?"

"No, I'm sorry. I'm calling because I would like to speak with your grandchildren."

"How many different detectives and FBI agents will be bothering us before you are satisfied we have given you all the information we know?"

"I understand your frustration, Carol. I'm not part of the investigative team working with the abduction case, but I would like to ask about the Bellevue House."

"Absolutely not! They have been through enough pain and suffering without having to relive that tragedy. It happened so many years ago. What are you hoping to learn from them?"

"For starters, I was wondering about their mother. Was she ill? Do they remember if she was taking any pills or medication? And maybe you would know more than they do. I'm trying to understand how she died."

"Asking the children why their mother committed suicide is not okay with me. How dare you..." Brandon cut her off.

"She didn't commit suicide. Debra didn't die from the gunshot."

Carol inhaled sharply. "What are you talking about? The children saw what happened. It was on the news." Her voice turned brittle. "My daughter took her life after burning that house."

Brandon paused. Now was not the time to ask the unsettling question about whether something unnatural had been in the house or not. He simply needed to show her the autopsy report, which stated the cause of Debra's hemorrhages as unknown. Then he would approach the subject slowly, depending on how the conversation proceeded. "I'm sorry, Carol, but she didn't take her own life. Did no one talk to you after the autopsy?"

Carol didn't respond.

Brandon heard her labored breathing. "Carol?"

"No, I guess they didn't," Carol acknowledged. "I thought I knew."

"Would you like to know the cause of death? I can talk to you about it tomorrow morning around 10:00. I'll bring the report so you can read it yourself, and we can discuss it," Brandon offered.

Carol took a heavy breath before answering, "Yes, bring the report. I want to read it. I'll see you in the morning." She hung up abruptly.

Putting his phone down, Brandon ran his hands through his hair. This conversation wasn't going to be easy. He needed to prepare himself, anticipating the need to navigate her grief and shock.

Stunned

Barb and Leah drove home in silence, each thinking about what had happened at the hospital. Arriving home, they saw the Pizza Pasta delivery van outside. The driver was returning to his vehicle.

"What? Grandma ordered delivery? That's a first. I wonder what happened," Barb said as they pulled into the driveway. "Is she sick?"

"Should we tell your grandma we went to the hospital? Let her know the police will call?" asked Leah.

"Good idea, but let me tell her. I'm curious why she ordered out."

They went inside, announcing, "Grandma. We're home."

Carol was in the kitchen, putting the pasta from the disposable containers into a large glass bowl.

"I'll set the table," Leah said, putting her hand on Barb's shoulder.

Carol was in a daze. Something was clearly bothering her. Barb stepped next to her grandma, scratching her back. "What happened?"

Carol continued to stare at the pasta, scooping in a slow, halting motion. "I got a call from a detective today."

"About that, I'm sorry. Leah thought..." Barb started but Carol wasn't listening.

Her eyes were glazed over and her face was tense, deep in thought. "My daughter didn't kill herself."

Barb looked at her grandmother, confused. "I'm sorry, what?"

"He's trying to understand how she died," Carol said, numbly.

"You mean aside from being a crazy witch with a gun?" Barb spat, irritated that the subject had resurfaced with everything else that was happening.

"He said the gunshot didn't kill her." Carol's voice was low, her eyes unfocused. "How could it not have killed her?"

Barb's eyes hardened. With a sharp edge, she hissed, "What do you mean Mom didn't kill herself?" Barb's blood boiled. She clenched her eyes closed wanting to scream. The images—her mom swiping the gun, the shot, her mom falling to the ground—it was too much! Why would someone say something that wasn't true? Why torture us with lies? "I saw what happened. She pulled the trigger."

"The gunshot didn't kill her? That's what he said." Carol said to herself, oblivious to Barb's words.

Realizing her grandma was in shock, Barb calmed herself and softened her demeanor. She rubbed Carol's arm and said, "Grandma, stop. Let's not relive what happened. Don't do this to yourself."

Coming back to reality, Carol gasped, "Oh honey, you're home. Have I been talking to you? What did I say?"

"A detective called," Barb said in a weak voice.

Carol put the spoon down, adjusting her apron. Wiping her eyes with the back of her hand, she cleared her throat. "Yes. A detective is coming over in the morning. He wants to talk with you about your mom."

"Why?"

Carol stood still. "Well." She was hesitant to continue. Grabbing Barb, she hugged her. "I'm not sure what to say, honey. I didn't ask him any questions. I... I...," she stumbled, her words choked in her throat.

"It's okay, Grandma. I'll be here. We'll talk with him together." Trying to change the subject and help calm her grandmother, Barb said, "Is Dan home? We should eat while it's still hot."

The Stream of Life

Choi returned home, exhausted, but his day wasn't finished. Going into the backyard, he sat next to the daffodils and magnolias under the cherry blossoms. Lying in the grass, he began to meditate. With slow deep breaths, he increased his spiritual energy, giving thanks to the selfless who preached love and compassion, guiding their followers toward enlightenment: Jesus, Buddha, Muhammad, and Krishna. He said a prayer for his ancestors and allowed his love for his wife to flow freely. With his spiritual core electrified, he put in his earbuds, opened his phone, and played a piece of tribal music, the percussion a strong smooth rhythm to which Choi began to breathe, rapid deep breaths in and strong quick breaths out. As he increased the oxygen level in his body, Choi followed the steps his Aunt Yoona had taught him—open his mind, let go of himself, and fall into an alternate state of consciousness. His essence drifted into the earth, joining the fungi and roots of the cherry tree and the nearby bigleaf maple. He felt the pulsing of life flowing like a river and sailed along with the energy. Following the bonds he had made the past two days, Choi communed with the religious leaders in a spiritual connection.

From there, Choi traveled through the links the religious leaders had established with the members of their communities, experiencing the eternal truth of collective oneness. The naked existence of the true self allowed Choi to glimpse potential life paths individuals traveled, sensing the contributions they made to the collective we.

After several hours of mind surfing, Choi returned to his body, sweaty and high. He recorded names for his aunt, waited to recover, then headed to shower and sleep.

Day Ten – Friday

Connected Through Love

Choi dressed and followed his nose to the kitchen. "Good morning, beautiful," he said to his wife, giving her a kiss as he sat down to waffles and sausages. "Jun will be happy when he wakes up today." His son loved waffles.

"What's on the agenda for today?"

"I'm going to medical clinics and hospitals. I might go visit Nong at Sunnyside as well." Choi knew doctors had the ability to connect with patients, giving them insights into the healing process. Choi was most interested in mysterious conditions and miraculous recoveries doctors witnessed. When a doctor was confused by a condition or disease, it usually meant other forces and energies were involved. Had any of the doctors encountered such enigmas? If so, Choi needed to find the people involved. Were they conscious of their ability to heal themselves, or did they accidentally tap into that energy?

Jasmine sat next to her husband, outwardly pouting. "You know, I've been feeling a little sick myself. It's been a few days since I received my medicine."

With a sly smile, Choi said, "If you have five minutes, I can give you your shot now."

"Five minutes?! Mmm—I need multiple shots," Jasmine whined.

Choi rose from his seat and unzipped his pants. "Stand up and take your panties down," he ordered.

With a squeal, she protested, "Why officer! You're not a doctor."

Taking her hand, he helped her stand, turned her to face the table, and then leaned in against her back. He ran his fingertips up her arm as he smelled her hair and nibbled on the top of her ear.

Reaching behind her, Jasmine pulled him flush to her backside.

Bending her over the table, he caressed her back. His thumbs slipped under her sweatpants, pulling them down.

She moaned softly.

Choi's connection with his wife allowed the two of them to share intimate information. He could sense where, when, and what she needed. But as they neared satisfaction, they were abruptly stopped by the sound of Jun coming down the hall.

An Unnatural Truth

In front of Carol Anderson's house, Brandon re-examined the autopsy report for Debra Mills. Multiple brain hemorrhages—How? Why? Brandon wasn't hopeful Carol or the kids could answer that question, or if he could bring up the subject of ghosts, but he'd been surprised before. Let's see what we can learn. Stepping from the car, he made his way to the front door and knocked.

A young woman opened the door. "Hello."

"Good morning. I'm Detective Brandon Spencer of the LVPD."

"I'm Leah. Come in," she said, opening the door and stepping aside to allow Brandon through. "We're meeting in the living room. It's to your right."

Turning the corner, Brandon saw Carol sitting on the edge of the sofa, looking nervous, like she hadn't slept well.

"Good morning, Mrs. Anderson. I'm Detective Brandon Spencer. We talked on the phone last night. May I join you?"

"Yes, please." She pointed to a chair next to the coffee table.

Brandon sat as the three teens entered the room, each of them taking a seat—the girl on the sofa next to her grandmother, the boy on a chair next to Brandon, and Leah in the recliner.

"You must be Dan," Brandon said, shaking Dan's hand. "I'm Brandon. Nice to meet you."

"Nice to meet you, too,"

Brandon nodded to Leah. "You're Jared Davenport's daughter. We are working to find him."

"I need to talk to you about that before you go, if that's ok."

"Absolutely."

He faced Barb.

"Barbra Mills." She leaned in and shook his hand.

Looking around at everyone, Brandon took a deep breath and said, "Okay, let's begin. I know you've been through how your mom and dad died and that it's painful. However, your grandma and I talked last night, and it's come to my attention that you don't know the whole story. I have reports that will be difficult to read and graphic photos that you may not want to see. Carol, have you looked at them before?"

"No. Show me everything. I want to know."

"According to the witness statements and officer reports, your daughter," looking at Carol, "your mother," looking at Barb and Dan, "was in a lot of pain after the fire." Slowly and with care, Brandon explained what had happened to Debra. When he finished, he opened the file and extended his arm toward Carol with the written report and two photos of the cheek wound in his hand.

Barb and Carol were both visibly shaking. Carol had one hand in a fist over her mouth and the other across her chest, tucked under her arm. Barb stared at the reports as if facing a king cobra. When his hand retreated, taking the files back, Barb snatched them away from him.

Brandon continued. "The gunshot wound wasn't the cause of death, although she did die immediately following. The actual cause of death was from severe brain hemorrhaging. That means blood vessels broke in her brain. In this case, multiple vessels ruptured at once."

Grabbing a second set of reports detailing the cause of death from a file, he set them on the table in front of them. "Do you know of any health issues or medications Debra was taking?" Brandon asked.

The room was silent. Brandon heard the soft tumble of the dryer from somewhere in the house. Barb wiped tears from her eyes, handing the first set of reports to Dan, and picking up the second. Carol read the report alongside Barb.

After several minutes, Carol broke the silence. "How can the cause of the hemorrhaging be 'unknown'? What usually causes these things?"

"Head trauma, high blood pressure, or blood clots. But there wasn't any head trauma, and she didn't have a history of hypertension or clotting. Even so, those wouldn't have caused several of her vessels to rupture all at once."

Carol's breath caught in her throat as her eyes retreated. "Had she taken a pill of some kind? Did her husband poison her? Was she murdered?"

"No drugs were found in her blood, so we can rule that out. Honestly, it's a mystery."

"Give me something," Carol demanded. "I need some kind of explanation. God dammit! Anything!" she nearly yelled. "Brain-exploding technology. Psychic telekinesis. I don't care, but tell me something."

"Brain-exploding"—Brandon thought. Boy, had he felt it—his head like a balloon that was stretched too thin. He recalled the brain scans. Thought about the disappearances—without a trace, no witnesses, the lack of evidence the cameras should've had. He remembered reading about John's uncanny understanding that his wife was burning the house down. The explanation? Now was the time. He blurted, "Ghosts. Evil spirits," and mentally crossed his fingers.

Carol stopped shaking. Dropping her hands to her knees, she straightened. Then she looked directly at Brandon. Her face was cold and her eyes glared with understanding and hate. "I knew it. That house was alive." Her voice held no doubt. "I knew it. I've always known it. I could feel it judging me, reading my thoughts. My skin crawled every time I went into that house. And that man—that man would talk to it, comfort it, treat it like a lover."

"The Education Center is believed to be haunted. I would never have thought such a thing, and I would never say such a thing in public. But I have experienced it firsthand." Brandon felt uncomfortable saying that out loud.

"Are you saying my mom and dad are haunting the Education Center?" Dan asked.

"No, it's that house," Carol burst scornfully, launching into a tirade about the house being pure evil. She explained that It stood on land sacred to the Sukiya tribe, where they held ceremonies to connect with ancestors. Carol detailed the bribes, hundreds of thousands of dollars, John paid the officials to purchase the land. "He had hired a private investigator to find the officials' weaknesses and learn who was struggling financially. When I learned about that, I was tempted to blow the whistle." She continued, criticizing religious members for blessing the house for money alone. "Why were those religious types there? He didn't belong to their clubs. When was he religious? Never. Money! Money caused it all! The house was built from greed and corruption, and that created a monster!"

Dan looked confused. "I heard a news report about the Education Center. It said the abductor did brain experiments on the victims. Are we saying a ghost monster kidnaps people and messes with their brains?"

Standing, Barb snapped, "This is bullshit! What the hell are we talking about!? Ghosts? Monsters? Can we step back for one second and recap what happened? Am I to understand that Mom shot herself because she was in extreme pain from her brain expanding and that she died because it burst. Is that right? Her pain was so great she was trying to end her suffering. Is that what you are saying, detective?"

Brandon straightened and took a quick breath. "Umm—yes, I believe that's what I'm saying."

Barb pressed, "And you don't know why her brain enlarged and burst?" Re-examining the report, she added, "Fourteen hemorrhages. The doctor can't explain how that happened?!"

Carol grabbed Barb's arm and pulled her down. "I know this isn't easy, but you have to believe me when I say there was something wrong with that house."

Taking her grandmother's hands, Barb said, "Grandma, I get that Dad became someone else when we moved into that house. I know Mom was crazy near the end. I remember the two of them fighting all the time. I understand something happened that drove them mad, but I'm struggling with the fact that the reports don't give any explanations." Facing Brandon, she asked, "Can we send these reports to a specialist to review?"

"I can."

Dan put the first report on the table and gestured for the second. "You don't believe in ghosts?" he asked his sister as he took the papers. "I've heard people talking at the college about the Center being haunted. The detective thinks it is. Grandma believes the house was. Maybe what really happened was from a ghost?"

Barb stood again. "You know what. I'm done talking about this."

"No! I need to talk about this. Let me vent a little. It's helpful," Carol pleaded. Her hands trembled as she clutched Barb's arm. "Sit down. Let's just talk. I don't care how crazy and stupid it sounds. Let's talk, and we can forget about it later and laugh about it next week. I need this, honey. You need this. It's been a long time coming. The craziest witch-faced explanations we can give, the better." Carol's shoulders were tense, her eyes begging with Barb.

Barb stared at her grandmother, her red eyes easing into a gentler demeanor.

"We need to work through this. I need your help."

Barb hesitated. She glanced at Dan. His eyes were soft with a gentle expression. She sighed heavily, sitting back down. "Okay, Grandma. Okay." Stacking the reports and photos in a neat pile, Barb handed them back to Brandon.

Taking the reports, Brandon couldn't help but rethink his supernatural skepticism. The fiery passion in Carol's voice and the stories about their parents changing—neurological disorders?—fueled his current line of thinking: ghosts, haunted, possessed.

Dan pressed his forearms into his face, pulling his hair. "A living house? Is that what you said, Grandma?"

"Nothing was normal about that house. Nothing!"

Dan smiled eerily. "That's why he was upset when I crashed my bike into it. I knew he loved that house; he talked to it all the time and read to it. Maybe it was alive," he chuckled, shaking his head and rolling his eyes, as if not believing what he said.

"Did Mom feel the same way you did, Grandma? Is that why she burned down the house?" Barb asked.

"She hated that house. It changed your dad something fierce."

"It's true. I remember when Dad used to read to us in bed, but later he only read in the library." Reaching his hand to get Barb's attention, Dan asked, "Do you remember when he made us forts out of boxes and blankets? That was my favorite, but after we moved into that house, he only yelled at us."

"Remember when we were playing in the workout room pretending to be superheroes, and he barged in screaming? After that, we were walking on pins and needles, trying to be so quiet." A shadow crossed Barb's face. "I saw him happy in the library. I wanted to be with him but didn't dare go in."

"I'm sorry that happened," Carol said. "I love you two very much. You have grown into exceptional young people, and I feel blessed because of it."

Barb hugged her grandma, Dan got up and joined them.

"I miss them," Barb wept.

"I know you do. I miss them, too," Carol sighed.

Dissolving into tears, Dan choked, "I still don't understand why."

Not wanting to disturb them, Brandon quietly left the room and went into the kitchen.

Joining Brandon, Leah asked, "Is it true that the Education Center is haunted?"

Brandon hesitated, shifting his weight from one foot to the other. "I don't know. Maybe." He winced, glancing away momentarily. He wasn't sure what to say. The more he entertained the idea, the more certain he felt it was true. But he couldn't admit that. "It's not my professional opinion, I assure you."

Leah nodded. "Right." Twisting her lip, she said, "I have to tell you what happened at the hospital yesterday. I went to see Nong. After I introduced myself, she looked straight at me, repeated my name, and said, 'The house, the house.' What do you think it means? Did she mean the Bellevue House? I don't know what to do or think anymore. I have to find my dad. I have to."

"I understand, Leah. We're trying. The FBI are looking for him, and I'm trying to sort all of this out, too. It's amazing that Nong responded to you. Had you met her before?"

"No, never. I know that my dad liked the lady at the Bellevue House, and I thought maybe she was the one."

Nong responding to Leah was a surprise. Brandon's heart quickened at the possibility that Leah could get information from her that would lead to Jared's recovery and the capture of the abductor. With Leah's help, he could solve this thing. "We should go see her again, together."

"Yes, please. I need to talk with her again."

"Give me your number. I'll arrange a time for us to see her." Brandon wrote Leah's number in his notepad and handed her his card. "Call me anytime."

"Thank you," Leah replied, a grateful smile evident.

"May I call you with other questions as well?"

"Yes, of course."

Hearing laughter coming from the living room, Brandon and Leah returned to the others.

"Do you really believe in ghosts, Grandma?" Dan asked.

"I do. I've never seen one, but I felt something in your dad's house. Did you know a whole industry is devoted to ghosts and the spiritual world?"

"I saw Ghost Hunters on TV," Dan said. "They go to actual haunted places and document paranormal activity."

"I'm sure they would have loved to visit your house," Carol said.

Barb chuckled. "I'm not so sure you can believe any of that."

"Oh, but people do. The fortune teller shops here in town sell objects and potions that are supposed to cleanse your house of ghosts. I went to one, bought crystals and talismans, and used them on your house, but they didn't work."

"What did you do?" asked Leah.

"I stood on my head and sang supercalifragilisticexpialidocious from Mary Poppins."

They laughed.

"Come on, for real."

"I needed to place the objects in specific areas and in different positions. I don't know. I don't remember. But I did go back to the shop to ask for help. The clerk sent me to a psychic shop. In the back room of that business, a staircase led to the basement, where they teach how to properly use the materials."

"Did you learn what to do?"

"I didn't have the time to join any of the sessions, but they did have a book, a training manual. It explained step by step the process of helping a ghost transcend. That's when a soul moves on to another place. It was pure luck that I saw it. They told me it was a rare, guarded book. It wasn't for sale, but I bought it."

"A rare, guarded book? How did you buy it?" Leah asked.

"I pled my case, told them about you guys, and paid $900."

"$900!? For a book?" Dan gasped.

"Why did you do that, Grandma?" Barb asked.

"I was worried about you. I thought it might help. It was full of details describing the world of ghosts, their powers, and how to make them move to the next realm. It was a training manual. I didn't know what could happen if that house was truly haunted. Look what did happen."

"I guess the book didn't work," said Dan.

"It wasn't the book. It was me. I was too scared to try anything. The book is for training professionals. Applying the techniques is tricky and dangerous."

"Dangerous? How?" asked Barb. "I mean, it's not like—" she stopped and turned her head away from her grandma. Brandon saw her roll her eyes.

"You can die, lose your soul, become possessed, lots of bad things can happen. Right, detective?"

"Me? I don't know anything about ghosts," Brandon deflected.

"You said, 'I experienced it firsthand,'" Carol countered.

"Oh that. Well, I'm not exactly sure what I experienced. I was with a manager at the Education Center. We heard two people—umm—together. Then we got headaches. When I tried to investigate, it worsened. I heard a voice in my head say, 'Go away.'"

The room was fixated on him.

"You got a headache?" Carol asked. "Now I understand. That ghost must have caused the hemorrhaging."

"This is getting way too weird," Barb said.

"Do you still have that book, Grandma?" Dan asked.

"I do. I'm using it to level my shoe rack in the closet," she laughed.

"Wow!" Leah commented.

"I couldn't let go. It has weird energy. But where it is now, I see it every day. That somehow eases the need to read it. And because it's performing a duty, I feel free from the pull," she explained.

Raised eyebrows and nervous smiles emerged as they glanced back and forth at one another.

"Did you kids ever experience anything weird when you lived there?" Carol asked.

Brandon stayed for another hour and listened to their stories and memories of the past. They started with the little ways their dad had changed—making them take off their shoes before coming into the house, scolding them for spilling their milk, screaming when they didn't wash their hands, and hitting them for leaving dirty handprints on the door or the wall. Happier memories took over—trying to build a fire during a camping trip, playing croquet at Barb's sixth birthday party, and dressing up the neighbor's cat to look like Waldo. Brandon felt good seeing them laugh.

Merging

"Jared, read us a story," Bellevue ordered. "Nong wanted to read The Things We Cannot Say, by Kelly Rimmer. It's in the library."

"Can Nong hear me reading?" asked Jared.

"Bring her in, so she can."

"How?"

"When you think about her, what comes to mind?" Bellevue asked.

"Her dimples when she smiles."

"Keep that image in your mind while creating a warm feeling in your chest, that slow romantic burn in your heart," Bellevue told Jared. "Do you feel it?"

A memory stirred—Nong's seductive smile as she peered up at him through her bangs, her hand landing on his chest. Jared's heart warmed. "Yes, I feel it."

"You should be able to sense her now. Open yourself to her—invite her to you," instructed Bellevue. "I will help you connect, but soon it'll become second nature to you."

Jared, following Bellevue's directions, felt Nong. Her thoughts and feelings layered on top of his own. "Nong?"

"I'm here, Jared," she replied as if lying next to him.

"Great. Read to us, Jared," insisted Bellevue.

"Which book?" Jared asked.

"I told you, The Things We Cannot Say. It's a WWII story about true love," Bellevue said excitedly.

"Do you want that one, too, Nong?" Jared asked.

"The title certainly fits our situation."

In a threatening tone, Bellevue said, "Come now. Let's be happy." Jared felt the heat of a stinging poke at the edge of his consciousness. The warning vanished as It transitioned. "Stories are always fun," It voiced in a sweet, melodic tone.

The Land

Brandon drove to City Hall. He wanted to check Carol's claims about the land where the Bellevue House was built.

"Good afternoon," Brandon said to the woman behind the counter as he showed her his badge.

"Good afternoon, detective. What can I do for you?" she asked, her tone polite.

"I need to look at the land titles for 4871 175th," Brandon said.

"The Education Center. So crazy how people keep going missing. I'm personally never going there again. Follow me. I'll show you where the files are." The woman led Brandon to the back room, a large open space housing rows of file cabinets.

Walking halfway down the second row, she opened a drawer, fingered through several files, pointed, and said, "Here are the files. You can use the table near the window. When you're done, leave them. I'll put them back."

"How long have you worked here? You know your way around quite well."

"I've worked here for close to thirty years. You could say this city is my baby." The woman laughed.

"Sorry, but do you know anything about this property? Its history?" Brandon asked before the woman walked off.

"Sure. It made national news for a day," she said. "The land was part of the national park. The Sukiya performed ceremonies there. When the city expanded, that area was originally part of the expansion, but people protested and signed petitions to leave it out. The tribe wanted the land returned to them. They took legal action and protested as well. Eight months later, the mayor annexed the land anyway, and the city sold it in a matter of days to a private citizen. The sale was all hush hush. Lawsuits were filed against the city. I think the judge threw out the cases. Typical really. All those rich white guys take what they want, scratching each others' butts. Anyway, corruption charges were filed, but the investigations never went anywhere. The library has news articles about all this rigamarole. You can also find information online."

"Thank you so much for your help."

"No problem, hon. Let me know if you need anything else." The woman left Brandon, walking back to the front.

Brandon perused the deeds—a description of the land and where the property lines were drawn. The U.S. acquired the entirety of this area in the Oregon Treaty from the U.K. in 1846. This particular land was claimed through military acquisition laws after the Sukiya Massacre in 1872. The military used the land as training grounds until the government converted it into a national park in 1936. The park was later broken into three sections—development of natural resources, grazing, and recreation. Lake Valley purchased a section of the land used for recreation through a negotiated sale. The city then sold it to John Mills. The shady way the government stole the land made Brandon understand why there were protests. The land was steeped in death and deception.

Closing the drawer, Brandon thought, Okay. I need to talk with the tribal leader at the reservation. Brandon wanted to know more about connecting with ancestors. If the house had been haunted, was it because of the land? Was the ghost in the house one of their ancestors? Maybe the land, and in proxy the house, was a gateway for ghosts to come and go as they please. He needed answers, and he hoped the Sukiya tribe had them. Brandon wondered if the religious members who blessed the house could also offer insights. Father Joseph came to mind. Brandon definitely needed to talk with him.

He looked at the time, 1:25 pm. He had a meeting with the Mitchells' divorce lawyers, but that wasn't until 4:30. He decided to drive to the reservation first.

Faith and Friction

Leah lay in bed, her head propped up with pillows. Her bedroom door was closed, and she held her phone, FaceTiming her mom. Stacy was unsettled that Leah hadn't called her immediately. She was also angry to have learned about Jared's disappearance from a social worker—days after it had happened. "I'm sorry, Mom. I didn't want you to drop everything and rush to my side. I know how excited you were to get the Canadian gig, and I don't want you to lose it. There's nothing you can do, anyway. The FBI are investigating it."

"Leah, honey. You can't be alone during a crisis like this. It's too much to bear alone."

"Uncle Tim is here, and I'm staying with my friend, Barb. Her grandmother is taking care of me. I'm fine, really."

Stacy focused directly on her phone. "You are more important to me than some gig." She paused for Leah to react. Leah hesitated, and Stacy jumped on it, saying, "I'll catch the next flight—be there in eight hours."

Leah watched her mom searching about the room, throwing items of clothing on her bed. If her mom came, would she lose the Canadian gig? Leah couldn't be responsible for that. Plus, having her mom here, in her life, in her space, a place in which she had abandoned eight years ago, suddenly felt scary. She would have to leave Barb and Dan and go back to her dad's house. The constant reminders of him—now gone—would be too much. She couldn't take it. "No, Mom. Please. The press have already been asking about you and Grandpa and the divorce. If you come, it'll create more stress. You'll be here for prom in two weeks anyway. We can talk about it then."

Stacy stopped moving. "Leah, dear. What do you need? Tell me."

"I need to work with this detective, Brandon Spencer. He's going to take me to the person who last saw Dad. I need to be with my friends. They are helping me cope. I need you to keep this gig. It's the one thing in life that is stable right now. Knowing you're doing your thing is comforting for me."

Stacy nodded. "Are you sure?"

"Yes. Positive."

"Okay," she agreed. "You call me if it becomes too much. I'll be there the same day and stay for as long as you need."

"I know. Thanks, Mom. I'll call you again tonight before I sleep."

"You better. Call me every night. I love you, sweetie."

"Love you, too, Mom." Leah's phone blinked and went to her display setting.

A tap came at the door. Barb stuck her head inside the room. "Busy?"

"No. I just finished chatting with my mom. How's Grandma?"

"She's napping. I think she'll be okay. We ended up watching reruns of Wheel of Fortune to clear our minds. And you'll never guess what came on after that."

"I don't watch much TV. What?" asked Leah.

"Father Joseph is at the Education Center. He's doing a live exorcism to rid the building of evil spirits. Do you want to watch?"

"No! My dad hates that guy. I don't like him either."

"I turned it off. I think he's an idiot, but I did find it interesting that he is going there. I thought about watching, though," Barb paused, "only because it's related to what Grandma was talking about today."

"He's such a hateful person, the exact opposite of what a priest is supposed to be," Leah said.

"I agree. I've never understood religion. I don't see anything positive about it."

"You can't mean that. Father Joseph is the exception, not the rule."

"What? I know you go to church with your dad sometimes, and you're friends with Becky, but you don't actually believe any of that garbage, do you?"

"I have a strong relationship with a higher power," Leah confessed.

"Really? I didn't know that. How come you didn't invite me to your church?"

"If you were interested, you would have talked to me about it. But you never brought up the subject so..."

"I really hate religion," Barb professed.

"Why?"

"I guess because I see it from an outsider's perspective. I never had religion growing up, and I see how it closes people's minds, putting ridiculous restrictions on what they can and can't do, and what they can and can't think. It creates ignorance and fear." Scratching her head, she continued, "When we first moved into our house, my dad had a bunch of grown idiots, who were dressed up in costumes doing silly things. Everyone was so serious, but I felt like laughing. It was the oddest sensation. I didn't understand anything at the time, but later understood they were religious ceremonies. The more I learn about what religion is, the more I see it as superstitious bullshit. And I hate when people try to cram it down my throat."

"Don't worry. I won't go on a religious tirade. Besides, I see religion as a personal affair."

"How so?"

"The Bible is a tool that allows me to have a relationship with God—a personal relationship."

"You really believe all that stuff about turning water into wine, walking on water, and Adam and Eve?"

"When I read a book, any book, it gives me ideas, thoughts, and impressions. It creates emotional responses. I think about what it says and what it means. The Bible does that for me. Then I try to understand how it relates to me and the world."

"Leah, I don't want to make you upset or ruin our friendship, but that book is fiction. It's full of made-up crap. The Tower of Babel? Ridiculous! Christianity is simply Greek or Roman mythology or even Egyptian, repackaged and resold. God and the devil? Zeus and Hades. And the holidays are at the same time as the winter solstice and spring equinox. Christianity stole and repurposed old ideas."

"Books make me think, fiction or not. I'm not upset. I'm comfortable with my own beliefs. I feel a connection to a higher power in my core."

"Interesting. Okay, tell me. What are your beliefs?"

"For me, religion is like a car. Each one looks different. Some are old; some are new, but they all have the same purpose."

"Which is what, exactly?"

"A vehicle for spirituality that delivers love and peace to a community."

Barb laughed. "I'm sorry. I didn't mean to laugh, but I don't think religion has accomplished that."

"I agree and disagree. People definitely use religion as a weapon or a tool—those who see it as a business. But there are strong, happy communities as well."

"How does religion do that?"

"People like me who read the Bible, or say the Torah, or the Koran, have a bond. We have a shared understanding and knowledge. Our love for the book, or the scrolls, brings us together. That creates community. We celebrate life together and help each other through difficult times. That's what religion is, community. It's love and family. Celebrations and mourning. Healing, growing, building, and rebuilding."

"I see religion as hate, fear, and violence, not to mention control."

"The control is from egotistical, self-righteous men, not religion."

Barb raised her brow and frowned, subtly shaking her head, indicating there might be some truth there.

"The fear, hate, and violence come from people like Father Joseph who have weaponized religion. They're looking for power. For them it's all about business—money and influence. The bigger they are, the more politicians will exchange favors for votes. They use division to grow—us against them—fear—those people are evil, scary, and bad." Leah raised her hands and shook them. "Ooh."

"Leah, that's the entire history of religion, especially Christianity. The Muslims were evil, so we had the crusades. The pagans were devil worshipers, so we burned them as witches. Slavery was mentioned in the Bible, which meant God endorsed it. The indigenous people were savages, so genocide was sanctioned. Religious zealots say gay people are sinful, so it's okay to ostracize them or tie them up and drag them behind a pickup truck. Torture is the Christian M.O. I saw a Tik Tok video showing Father Joseph saying that the LGBTQ community should be killed. That's not love, family, or peace."

"Which is why I can't stand the guy," Leah said. "But religion has helped many people. Lots of religious organizations feed the hungry, house the poor, and aid those in need."

"If you belong to their club."

"No! Our church sponsored Afghan refugees. They're Muslim, not Christian. When I was in India ten years ago with my parents, we went to a church that gave poor village children room, board, and education for free. My mom used it as an opportunity to teach me that going to school is a privilege and an honor."

"It wasn't free. I'm sure they were force fed plenty of ideology," Barb said.

"It's better than going hungry and having fewer opportunities for your future."

"I guess, but it still feels wrong to me. I mean, there are plenty of secular organizations that do the same thing."

"There are. You're right." Leah smiled at her friend.

Barb returned the smile. "At least we both agree that Father Joseph is a joke."

"He's worse than that. He gives religion a bad name. You do know that I don't judge anyone because of the pronoun they want to use or the person they choose to love, right?"

"We wouldn't be friends if you did," Barb said. "You know I don't judge anyone because they belong to a religion, right?"

"You're funny." Leah grabbed her pillow, holding it close to her chest. "So, do you believe what your grandma was saying today? About ghosts and your house being alive?"

"I don't know. I don't feel like myself right now. So much has happened in these past few days. And now, after learning about my mom, I'm—numb. How about you?"

"I feel like I might explode. I want that detective to take me to see Nong. I need to know what 'the house' means." Leah paused, glancing into her friend's eyes. "Barb, my mom said she would stay with me, but I told her not to. Should I text her back, tell her to come?"

Barb sat on the bed, next to Leah. "I thought you should have called her right away. Why don't you want her to come?"

Leah rested her head on Barb's shoulder. "Added stress mostly."

"Your mom is rich. She's smart, connected, and good with people. I feel like her being here would alleviate stress."

"But I'd end up at my dad's house, when he's not there, with my mom. Part of me wants her here, but then I think about it, and I can't. I couldn't handle it." Leah put her arm through Barb's, grasping it. "I don't want to leave you."

Barb smiled. "Good. Because you're stuck with me, whether you like it or not."

The Battle for Souls

Bellevue listened to Jared read. It felt comfortable and calm. Its life was finally in order. Bellevue felt Jared's awe and fascination as he explored the house, sitting for hours in a room, appreciating the design and use of space.

Nong felt sad, but she liked Jared, and he harbored a profound infatuation for her. Bellevue had finally found a compatible match, unlike Amanda who had been so difficult—resilient and strong. Her determined spirit, honed through sports and outdoor pursuits, presented a challenging obstacle for making her submit. Tyler loved Amanda—desperately wanting a sexual relationship with her, but she had no interest in that. She saw his exploitative nature and used it against him, manipulating him quite masterfully. Bellevue had learned a lot from her. Nong loved Bellevue—the grandeur and architectural magnificence. After Bellevue freed Amanda, Tyler played the poor, grieving man so well that Nong was resolute to incorporate Bellevue into her portfolio for a mere fraction of Its worth. Bellevue was excited for a new couple. Nong, however, was furious with Tyler for tricking her. After a year of fuming, she was finally cordial with Tyler, and then he decided to stop talking. Nong and Jared were perfect. They shared a potent attraction, along with common interests and aligned personalities. Most importantly, Jared cared about her. Bellevue felt Jared's yearning for Nong and knew she longed for intimacy. When Bellevue arranged for them to finally make love, it would enjoy feeding on their passion and reminiscing about John's bedroom talents.

As Jared continued to read, and Bellevue became immersed in the story, an irritating sensation was stirring out front. Annoyed, It expanded its consciousness, shocked and overjoyed to find Father Joseph sprinkling holy water on the building and then kneeling in prayer on the front lawn. Father Joseph was one of the many who had helped give Bellevue life. Leaving Jared and Nong, It entered the priest's mind.

"It's wonderful to see you again, Father," Bellevue greeted.

"Be silent, enemy of the Almighty," Father Joseph replied sharply.

Bellevue was shocked, reeling from the unexpected harshness of his response. It began to dig into the priest's mind. "I had hoped our reunion would have been a happy and joyous occasion."

Father Joseph offered no reply. Cross in hand, he assaulted Bellevue.

Reading the priest's mind, Bellevue saw he was attempting to grab hold of Its soul in order to destroy It. Why? It dug deeper.

The priest let out a sharp cry.

Bellevue found Its answer and noted, "Interesting. You didn't expect to actually find me here. This is fun. Why do you have ill intentions towards me, Father? You helped create me."

"Our Father, who art in heaven, hallowed be Thy name." The priest shook holy water and held his cross high in the air, visibly shaking.

Bellevue challenged, "Do you really think you can hurt me? Tear me apart—send pieces of me into the wind?"

The priest circled the building, surrounding Bellevue's soul with holy energy, "Save me, oh God. As it was in the beginning..."

Exploring the priest's mind, Bellevue saw Father Joseph had received training as an exorcist but had never performed a real one. He was now determined to change that fact. Focusing only on the scriptures, he worked to summon power from the Almighty. Bellevue became concerned and hurried to grab control of the priest.

"Through your greatness, Oh Lord..." Father Joseph recited before falling to his knees. He pressed the heels of his palms to the top of his head. His eyes were tightly shut, and his face twisted in pain.

"You're a fake!" Bellevue berated. "Your essence drips of greed. Your lust for dominance and control is repulsive. Your drive for money and comfort makes you a weak, pathetic being. What power do you think you have?"

Father Joseph's speech became labored and full of agony. "In the face of the enemy, may the enemy have no power over me."

Bellevue, in full control, realized the priest lacked purpose within him, rendering the mystical powers that his prayers could wield ineffective. Father Joseph's energy was devoid of purity and focus.

"Be gone demon! Return to the underworld. I cast you out."

Bellevue was enraged at his arrogance. "You helped bring me to life, and I appreciate you for that, Father. But you are insulting! Your offensive and disrespectful behavior has forced my hand. I cannot allow your pitiful attempt to annihilate me to go unpunished." Bellevue squeezed the priest's soul and ripped it from his body.

Father Joseph let out a final scream, collapsing.

Returning to Jared and Nong, Bellevue was ready to bathe in the warm comfort of Its new family. Instead, It found them devising a plan to escape. Shock, anger, horror, spilled from It. "Break out?! I won't ever let you leave!" Bellevue roared. "I am your everything." It cut the connection between Nong and Jared with a thunderous bang, leaving them both in silence and darkness.

"How dare they," Bellevue wailed. "Do they still not understand my power?! I know everything." Turning Its thoughts to John Mills—his loving touch, his gentle voice, his complete and utter devotion—It saw true love. Bellevue vented, "I will show Jared and Nong the power of true love. They will submit. We will be a happy family."

Jared finished Chapter 12. "Would you like me to continue?"

"I'm fine," Nong replied. "Bellevue?"

Bellevue was silent.

"Bellevue? Are you here?" Jared asked.

No response.

"Bellevue left," Nong said. "Jared, I'm so sorry. I couldn't stay any longer. I had to leave."

"I understand. I know I should be mad and resentful, but I'm not," Jared reassured her. "Where is Bellevue? Did It leave or fall asleep?"

"This doesn't happen often. But when It is looking for someone, It'll go quiet as It explores that person to see if they are someone It wants or not," explained Nong. "After Tyler stopped communicating, Bellevue said It would find another person for me. Every time It explored someone new, It became absent like this."

"Tyler? Who is that?"

"I thought I was buying this house from him. He's the one I replaced."

"So did you know Bellevue would still be in control of you after you left?"

"Not like this! No," Nong said adamantly.

"There has to be a way to get free," Jared thought out loud. "The other day, you talked to my daughter. How did you do that?"

"You pushed me. I couldn't have done it by myself, but you pushed me somehow, and I was able to. But it was difficult and painful."

"Maybe I can push you again. Is there anyone near you?"

"Let me focus."

Nong was silent for a minute.

Slowly, Jared could hear what she was hearing, a television. The Price Is Right. "I hear the TV. When someone comes near you, I'll push you again," he said.

"But what will that do? What should I say?"

"If I can push you hard enough, maybe you can break out and get—"

"Break out? I won't ever let you leave!" Bellevue roared. "I am your everything." A loud bang of thunder sounded, and Jared's surroundings went quiet and dark.

He was in black space—no sounds, no lights, nothing. Both Nong and Bellevue were gone, and Jared was—just was. Unable to do anything but—be, he asked, "What is this? The silent treatment? Really? Come on, Bellevue," Jared called out, his voice echoing into the void.

Brandon passed the Education Center on his way to the reservation. Seeing a crowd of people and equipment in front of the building, he decided to stop. After parking, he saw a camera crew had set up lights and were filming a priest as he held up a cross and threw water at the building.

"What's going on?" Brandon asked one of the production crew members.

"That's Father Joseph. He is performing an exorcism, ridding this place of evil spirits."

As Brandon watched, the priest seemed to be in pain—his voice strained and his face beet red. He leaned over gritting his teeth, his eyes squinting tightly. Brandon wondered if he were acting for the camera; however, his agony seemed genuine. Brandon touched his own head, remembering his headache during his tour of the Education Center. This place is truly haunted. If it were the same spirit that killed Debra Mills, then the priest was in trouble. He walked toward the priest, but a crew member grabbed his arm.

"No! He's battling an evil spirit."

"Yes, I can see that, and he's losing."

Screaming, the priest collapsed.

Brandon rushed to the priest and checked his pulse. He was alive but unresponsive. Brandon heard a person next to him talking with a 911 operator. Showing his badge, he took the phone.

Thunder, followed by a ghostly wail, filled the air. The crowd grew deadly silent as people looked around trying to decipher the origin of the sounds.

"What the hell was that?" the person next to Brandon exclaimed, his voice full of fear and confusion.

"I don't know, but I'm not sticking around to find out," another replied.

Brandon noticed several people turn and run. He refocused and spoke with the operator.

Follow the Path

Leah stood at the kitchen counter, cutting carrots for soup, when her phone rang.

Barb glared at her. "I thought you turned your phone to, 'Do not disturb.'"

"I did. It's probably my mom or my uncle." Laying the knife on the counter, Leah removed her phone from her pocket and answered, "Hi, Uncle Tim."

"I'm worried about you. How are you doing?"

Walking out of the kitchen, Leah headed for her room. "I'm fine. Didn't do anything today. Didn't go anywhere. You?"

"Have you heard anything from the police? Any news about your dad?"

"A detective came over today. He was talking to Grandma Carol about her daughter and how she died. He also talked about the Bellevue House. Carol said it was haunted. The detective thinks the Education Center might be haunted, too."

"What kind of nonsense is that? Who is this detective?"

Leah closed the door to her room, sitting on her bed. "No, it's fine. He doesn't believe in that. It's Grandma Carol talking."

"Look, kiddo. We're going to find your dad. A few buddies and I are going into the mountains with ATVs, search dogs, and drones. Whoever took him is going to get a rude awakening."

"Thanks, Uncle Tim. Do you want me to go with you?"

"God, no. You attract too many people. Have the cockroaches found you?"

"You mean the reporters?" Leah was taken aback by her uncle's outward hate for the press. But she had to agree they were pushy. "No, not yet. My friend Becky said that most of the national news reporters have left."

"Good. Have you spoken to Grandma and Grandpa yet?" Tim asked. "They're really worried about you."

"I'm so sorry. I feel terrible. How are they doing?"

"As can be expected. They've been trying to reach you, so give them a call when you have a moment, okay?"

"Yes, of course. I'll call them right away." Taking a brief pause, she added, "The school contacted Carol. Said I have to return starting Monday."

"Yes, I know. I talked with your social worker. She said you haven't been answering her calls. We both felt it was best if you went back, to stay busy and keep your mind at ease. A therapist will meet with you there."

"Uncle Tim!" Leah protested. "Why didn't you talk to me first?"

"I should have. You're right. But I'm a bit emotional right now and planning this excursion. I'm sorry."

"It's okay." Leah didn't feel okay. She needed to see Nong again. "I went to Sunnyside yesterday to see Nong, the lady who was kidnapped before Dad."

"Why did you do that?"

"I had to see her. I asked her about Dad, and she called my name. Said, 'The house.' The detective is excited about taking me back to see her. I'm the only one she's responded to. I need to see her again before I go back to school."

"Sure. I'll support you. I'm sure the detective can easily arrange that."

"What do you think 'The house' means?"

"I'm pretty sure your dad is locked away somewhere in the woods, but we are going to find him. I won't stop looking. And if the bastard who took him hurt your dad, I'll kill the son of a bitch!"

Leah promptly responded, "Don't do that. You'd be thrown in prison. I can't lose you, too."

"Right. Sorry. I'll just rough him up a little."

She thought about that for a second. "Sure. You can do that. Will you call me tomorrow?"

"I'll try. I don't know what the cell reception will be like. I'm going to be gone for a few days. I'll be back Tuesday or Wednesday. I'll call you when I return."

"Be careful."

"Hey! I love you, kiddo. Take care of yourself."

"I will. Thanks, Uncle Tim."

Next, she called her grandparents in Wisconsin.

Later that night, when Leah was ready for bed, her prayers lingered longer, as she begged for her father's safe return. Her thoughts and wishes drifted to her uncle and grandparents. The intensity and focus in her words warmed her chest, and for the second time that week, she felt an echo in her mind that formed the words, "Follow the path."

Leah grimaced. "I followed the paths. I didn't find anything. Which path?" With her hands together she pressed them to her forehead and redoubled her effort to focus and keep her connection. What path? Her mind was frantic for a response; it came as an idea. A path didn't necessarily have to be a trail on the ground. It could be clues. Did she have any clues? Nong. Was she the path? "Show me the path," she called, putting every ounce of energy she had into the request, but the connection was lost.

Day Eleven – Saturday

The New User

When Choi arrived at Northside Medical, the parking lot was nearly full. He eased into a space marked for official vehicles and spotted a patrol car and an FBI vehicle.

"The priest has company," Choi said to himself as he headed inside.

After getting directions to Father Joseph's room, Choi rode the elevator to the third floor. A group of about twenty filled the waiting room, heads bowed in prayer. He passed the nurses' station and waved, then approached the priest's room, where an officer stood guard. He greeted him, saying he was there to give him a break.

Once alone, he entered the room and held the priest's hand, connecting with him. The connection didn't catch. The priest was cold, not physically cold, but his spirit, his soul, was missing. Choi's face grew dark. *Where is he?* Something in the Education Center—something unfamiliar and very dangerous—had control of the father.

"How is he?" The voice startled Choi. He turned to see the rookie detective. Choi had seen him at the station, but they hadn't officially met. Shaking hands, Choi introduced himself while connecting.

"Detective Spencer," Brandon said, glimpsing at their hands, his eyebrows raised.

Choi held Brandon's hand for a heartbeat, locking his eyes on his, guiding the connection until it sparked. A bridge of trust and intuition formed between them. Then Choi touched Brandon's core. The energy vibrated with confidence

214

and strength. The bright, magnetic force pulled at Choi. Before him stood a potential energy manipulator, a candidate worth watching.

Letting go of his hand, Choi asked, "You know Father Joseph?"

Brandon's demeanor warmed. His posture relaxed and his tone turned friendly. "No. I was at the scene when he collapsed. I came to check his condition."

"He's in a coma. Strange thing if you ask me."

Brandon's eyes twitched. "Crazy, yes."

"You were at the Education Center when Father Joseph collapsed? What happened?"

"He was performing an exorcism, I guess. That's what the others said. Then he screamed in pain and passed out."

"So the stories are true. That place is haunted," Choi said. "My aunt will come now for sure."

"Your aunt?"

"She's a shaman, lives in Korea, communicates with the dead, helping them transcend to where they belong. She also tells fortunes and stuff like that, but she's the real deal."

"I'd love to talk with her."

"Really?" Choi wondered, Is this the guy? The connection was strong. His spiritual energy pulsed with profound force. "Wait a second. Are you the guy who thinks the Bellevue House is still a thing? I've heard about you," Choi chuckled.

"That's me," Brandon sighed. "And you must be 'the psychic' I've heard about."

"Guilty." Choi pulled out his phone, pointing to an app. "Do you know this app, 'KakaoTalk'?"

"No. What is that?"

"It's a social media app. Allows you to text and make calls. It's popular in Korea. Go ahead and download it onto your phone and create an account. I'll have you add my aunt. I'll tell her about the priest and the haunted building. She'll be expecting your call."

"Does she speak English?"

"Oh, yes. English, Japanese, Russian, and Chinese."

"Whoa. Impressive!" After downloading the app onto his phone, Brandon opened it and created the account. "Now what?"

"Type in her ID—Yoona227."

"Her name is Yoona?"

"Yes. She has your information now, as well."

"Great. Let me give you my card."

"Thanks. Here's mine," Choi replied, handing Brandon his own.

Watching Brandon exit the room, Choi rewound their interaction. Brandon had a strong spiritual center, and his energy was attractive. In addition, his eyes told Choi he suspected a supernatural force was the reason the priest fell into a coma. Choi had a good feeling he'd found the person for whom Yoona was looking.

Distorted Truth

Leah read the news on her phone, checking if Barb, Nong, or she were featured or if new information about her dad had been reported. She learned that Father Joseph was in a coma at the hospital after attempting to perform the exorcism at the Education Center. To her, this was a sure sign the Center was, indeed, haunted as the detective had speculated. She wanted to visit and look around. She felt her heart pinch. This is the path, she thought. Knowing Barb wouldn't go, Leah thought she might be able to talk Dan into going with her. She knocked on his bedroom door.

"Come in." Dan's voice was groggy.

"You're still in bed?" Leah teased, jumping on his bed, kissing him. "Look at this." She handed him her phone.

"What is it?" he asked, proceeding to read. "Holy shit. That's crazy!"

"The Education Center is haunted, like the detective thought. If the ghost abducts people, performing brain experiments on them like you said, then that's where my dad is. Are you coming?"

"I wasn't being serious. I said that because it sounded ridiculous."

"I know, but still. Come with me. I know Barb won't go. It'll be fun, an adventure."

"Are you kidding me? My mom was killed at that place. Your dad was kid-napped—not only your dad, but three other people, too. And now a priest is in a coma?" Dan argued. "Honestly, I don't understand how that place is still open."

"I'm going," Leah said firmly.

"If your dad were there, the police would have found him."

"They weren't looking for ghosts. I can't sit here doing nothing. My dad was last seen at the Center, so I'm going."

"Weren't you there the other day?"

"Yes, but I didn't look inside. I couldn't." Leah sighed. "Okay, you don't have to come. I'll go by myself."

"Wait." Dan's expression turned to guilt.

Leah looked at him with loving eyes. She knew she was being selfish. But at this moment she had hope. If she went alone that hope would die. She needed Dan.

"I'm sorry." Dan expressed. "I've been distant the past few days, and I know you've needed me..."

Leah put her finger to his lips. "This is hard for all of us. You don't have to apologize. But I need you to come with me."

"Leah, I..."

She could see Dan was struggling to communicate his feelings. "I'm listening."

He gave a huff and said, "You're not supposed to go anywhere."

"So now I'm trapped? I don't think so."

Conflict stirred in Dan's eyes. His breathing became labored. He ran his hands through his hair.

"I know this is a huge ask, but you did say you wanted to go," Leah urged gently, "to heal."

"Yes, but this is rather sudden. I need a plan first. I can't just up and go without mentally preparing myself. Not yet."

"I'll be holding your hand." Leah put one hand in his and the other on his chest, moving closer to him. She gazed into his eyes. "I need to go. I thought maybe this would be something we could do together." Then she laid her head on him, listening to his heart.

"I'm not ready. Besides, Grandma and Barb would kill us."

Sliding her leg in between his, she rolled on top of him and whispered, "I know. We'll go out my bedroom window." Her hands ran through his hair as she kissed him. "Thank you," she managed in between kisses.

Dan stroked her cheek.

Leah felt him growing hard against her. His heart pounded, his face reddening, and he tried to situate his body so his dick wasn't touching the inside of her thigh.

Leah pressed her breasts against him, countering his adjustment. She noticed sweat beading on his neck and leaned in to taste him. Whispering into his ear, she said, "Please."

"I'm going to regret this," he grunted.

"It'll be like you said, healing."

"We are going to get into so much trouble."

"We won't. We're adults."

"When do you want to go?"

"Now. Get up. I'll wait for you in my bedroom." She pushed herself off the bed, standing.

"I'm already up." He smirked.

Leah lowered her head, her smile tight. She held his eyes as she turned to leave and bit her lower lip.

Exiting the house through the back bedroom window, they made their way to Leah's car, parked on the street. Dan drove as Leah strategized. "We could try to connect with the ghost psychically. Would meditation be better? Oooh, maybe we should get a Ouija board. I'll look online for ways to contact ghosts."

"Let's walk through the place first."

When they arrived, the parking lot was nearly empty. "Is it open?" Dan wondered. "After what happened, maybe it's closed."

"Let's go check," Leah said.

Dan was gripping the steering wheel, his knuckles white. "I don't think I can do this."

"Wait here. I'll look around."

Walking to the front door, Leah opened it. She turned and shouted to Dan, "They're open."

She was surprised to see Dan open the car door and make his way to join her. Upon entering, she saw a young man playing on his phone at the front desk. "Hi, are you open?"

"We probably shouldn't be. People are pretty scared," the man answered. His face turned grave. "Is your friend ok?"

Leah turned to look at Dan. He stood outside the door, face white, staring blankly. "Dan? Are you ok? Dan!" Leah yelled.

"Oh shit!" said the guy behind the counter. He rushed around, heading for Dan.

"Dan!" Leah slapped his face lightly. "Dan!" He didn't respond.

"Should I call an ambulance?"

Leah spun around, puzzled.

The guy surveyed Leah's expression. "Yes?"

The last thing she wanted was to be caught here. She would be blamed for pushing Dan to confront his pain before he was ready. "No!" she answered. "No-no-no-no. Help me get him to the car."

They each grabbed an arm and dragged Dan to the car, putting him in the passenger seat. "Thank you," Leah said as she jumped in the driver's seat and drove off.

She fumbled through her purse, looking for Brandon's card, swerving as she drove. Glancing into Dan's blank eyes, she wondered if she should drive to the hospital. What happened? she asked herself. It never occurred to her that he might react so negatively. At the stoplight, she closed her eyes trying to think—home, find the detective, hospital.

The car behind her honked its horn. Leah started forward, then abruptly turned toward the hospital.

"Hey, watch out! What are you doing?" Dan asked.

"Oh, thank God you're okay! What the hell happened to you?"

"I had a conversation with Bellevue."

"Who? Bellevue? What the hell are you talking about?"

"My house. It talked to me."

Leah slammed on the brakes and parked next to the curb. "I am freaking out right now. Don't play with me. Seriously, what happened?"

Dan cleared his throat.

Bellevue's anger churned like a summer storm that came with tornado warnings. It wasn't so much that a priest had attempted to delete Bellevue from existence, but that it was Father Joseph. If he had still had access to his powers—Bellevue shuddered at the thought. At least today was slow at the Center. Saturdays were usually busy, but the commotion from yesterday had scared people away and now it was quiet—not many classes. Bellevue wouldn't have to expend Its energy or worry about the people in Its sphere of control. It could relax and try to enjoy the day.

Turning It's thoughts to Nong and Jared, Bellevue knew It needed to be patient. Building true love took time, and if It dedicated Itself to them, they would soon be loyal and devoted. Knowing that passion played a role in love, Bellevue needed to set the mood for Jared and Nong to come together. If It could join them in a romantic encounter, the three of them would be cemented to each other. While Bellevue plotted their bonding event, two teenagers emerged from a car that parked out front. Bellevue froze in shock.

John Mills, Its precious lover? Could it be? No. Too young. His son, Daniel Mills.

Bellevue took a second to think, and when Daniel opened the door, It presented Itself to him.

Sitting in the car, Dan stared into Leah's eyes. "It started when I grabbed the door of the Center and was about to enter. My mouth dropped open and I said..."

"Oh shit! Leah, I can't do this. This place looks exactly like my old house." Dan desperately searched for Leah, but she had disappeared.

"Hello, Daniel. I can't believe how much you look like your father. I nearly collapsed when I saw you," Bellevue said.

Dan's heart skipped a beat. This voice—it took him back to childhood, making him feel like a little boy ready to jump from one piece of furniture to another, avoiding hot lava. "Who are you?"

"I'm Bellevue. I knew you when you were a boy."

"Bellevue?" Dan knew this presence. It had lived in his mind. Hadn't he created this person to help him manage stress?

"Bell?" he probed. "Am I dreaming?"

"You are not dreaming. It's me, your friend, Bell. It's been so long."

"But you were imaginary. You were in my head." Dan rubbed the back of his neck, feeling confused. What the hell is this? He examined the room, confounded at what he was seeing. "I don't understand. Where am I? Where are you? Where is Leah?"

"This is me. You are looking at me. I have presented my true form to you so you would recognize me."

Your true form?

"You are my house?" Dan asked in disbelief. Yesterday's conversation—the autopsy report, the memory of his mom taking her life—assaulted him. Anger spewed from Dan as he accused, "You killed my mother!"

"I had no choice, Daniel. She killed your father, tried to kill me, and was about to kill the two of you. When she picked up that gun, I had to act before she hurt you," Bellevue explained. "I was protecting you. Your father and I loved you kids very much."

"Loved us? My dad turned into an angry, yelling, uncaring asshole after he built you."

"That's not true. Your mother pitted him against you. She was scared. Your father wanted all of us to be together as a family, for me to help care for you, but your mother wouldn't allow it. She didn't understand. She didn't want anything to do with me. In her opinion, I was evil. But she was the one who became a demon. She gave your father an ultimatum—find a medium to kill me or forfeit his family.

"Your father couldn't accept either choice. Your mother made life miserable for him. If he was nice to you, she punished him by threatening to beat you and withhold food. She was a monster, Daniel. Your dad wanted what was best for you. I wanted what was best for you. I still do. I care about you."

Dan countered, "You kidnapped those people. You have Leah's dad."

"You've got it all wrong. You have misunderstood everything. Those people chose to be with me. I took care of them, and we loved each other. Leah's father came to me. He saw me and fell in love. He came into me, willingly. I haven't kidnapped him. I am devoted to him."

Dan put his hand to his forehead, his thumb on his temple. Feelings of self-worth, satisfaction, integrity, and acceptance wormed their way into him. Honesty. Was Bellevue telling the truth?

"Daniel, you were so young," Bellevue said. "Can you feel me, my presence?"

"Yes, I think so. I feel...," Dan hesitated.

"How do I feel to you?"

"It's..." Dan wasn't exactly sure. The feelings themselves felt good, but... "Like happiness or being fulfilled," he finally acknowledged.

"Pleasant, right? This is who I am, my true self. There is a reason your mother turned. When I presented myself to her, she became jealous and frightened. She couldn't accept what I was and feared she and your father were going insane. She forbade me to connect with you, which is why I made you promise never to tell anyone about me. She begged your father to find religion, pleaded for him to sell the house and move. I still don't understand why she thought I would hurt you. I never would have, and I never will.

"Your mom worried what others would think and say," Bellevue added. "She feared if people knew about me, you kids would be taken away. I tried to reason with her, but she became angry."

Bellevue flooded Dan's mind with images—his parents arguing—"This demon is destroying our family. Look at who you've become!"—his mother's tormented face, clawing at her hair, his father pacing in the library. Dan remembered hiding behind a kitchen chair as his mother threw a plate of spaghetti at his father. Bombarded, Dan felt torment, guilt, frustration, and intransigence. "It's too much," he cried. "I can't...."

"I'm sorry, Daniel, but you needed to understand what really happened. This was your mother, her true self."

Dan clenched at his heart, breathing heavily. The emotions and memories slowly faded.

"You are welcome to come here, to live with me. Both you and Barb. I will care for you, and we can be a family, the five of us. Leah can be here, too, with her father. I am only looking for a loving family. Jared loves me and I love him, but we are not a family. Come to me, Daniel. Let me heal your wounds, return your smile, lighten your heart. Let us be a family again. I love you."

As Bellevue faded, the idea of family seeped into Dan's thoughts.

Bellevue disconnected, ballooning with excitement—a gleam, a hope, an idea. It knew what It needed, what It wanted, and a plan was hatching.

Leah leaned her head against the seat, the leather creaking. She stared at the van parked in front of them and blinked hard, as if that would make Dan's words sound less absurd.

"I swear to God, that's exactly what happened," Dan said. "The building is alive, and It embodies goodness. We should go back so you can meet Bellevue—and see your dad. It's not bad. It wants to be a family."

Her mouth hung agape as she shook her head. She turned the air conditioner up a notch to counter the heat building from within. But she had seen Dan freeze. Had seen him in some kind of state. Dan had experienced... Her thoughts shifted. Maybe he fell into shock. The stress of returning to the place his parents died was too much.

"Give me a second to think," Leah said, waving her hand in front of her face.

"I get that I sound crazy right now, but I'm telling you the truth."

Leah huffed. "My dad is inside a ghost house?" She wiped away the moister building in her eyes. "And this ghost embodies goodness?" she scoffed. So much of what he had just said was wrong—his mom, her dad, love, and offering him a family. Whether his story was true or not, she needed to set him straight.

Taking in a slow, calming breath, she said, "Dan, you're not thinking clearly. Let me debunk a few things for you. First, your mother was on her knees," Leah curled her hand into a fist and emphasized, "screaming in pain. She picked up that gun to shoot herself because she was being tortured. That house wasn't protecting you; it was torturing your mother to the point that she shot herself. Your mother was the one who was fighting for you, for your family.

"Second," Leah continued. "The first thing an abuser does is isolate you from your friends and family. That's not love. That's abuse. My dad is isolated. When you love someone, you respect the relationships they have with other people. Bellevue is not respecting the relationship my dad has with me or with his brother or with anyone. My dad is trapped.

"Next, when I invited my uncle for dinner, my dad said that he had met someone. I'm pretty sure he was talking about Nong. Dad wasn't interested in Bellevue; he was interested in Nong. Don't tell me he's in love with a house. That's bullshit.

"Finally," Leah said. "That thing put a priest in the hospital. Does that sound like 'It embodies goodness' to you? Good grief, Dan. How did you fall for Its game? It sounds like a bully. 'You want it? Here, come and get it.' I doubt It would let me see my dad if we went back."

If Dan had truly talked with Bellevue, It did a good job of twisting his emotions. "The reason I know this is because, after my mom left, I was angry and upset. When my dad sat me down, he said he understood I was angry. Said it was ok to feel that way. But that didn't mean my mom didn't love me. And it didn't mean I couldn't love my mom. I could love her and have a relationship with her even if I hated the decision she made. But I should first understand why she made that decision."

Leah looked into Dan's eyes. "My dad didn't have to say that. He could have easily cut my mom out of my life. He could have said that she's terrible, horrible, and awful, and that I should never talk to her again. Someone only says that if they crave power and want control. Because he loves me, my dad didn't do that. By saying your mom was evil and bad, that house is trying to have power over you. It wants to replace your mom. Search your own memories. Was your mom evil? I never got that impression from you."

Dan and Leah sat for a minute, in silence. The car shook as a semi-truck passed them. Dan turned, staring out the window at an old woman carrying a bag of groceries.

Leah took Dan's hands. "You have a family, Dan. Don't let that house cloud your judgment with this promise."

"I'm not clouded." He turned to look at her, his eyes watery.

Leah held his eyes and leaned toward him. "Your grandma is your rock."

He smiled.

"Do you know why I love my mom so much? And no, it's not because I get to ride horses every time I visit her. It's because she's living the life of her dreams. She loves her life, and that transfers to me. I'm so happy when I'm with her. At times, I love her more now than I think I could have if she had stayed with us. I know that sounds crazy, but her being truly happy means she's healthy and in a better position to help me. It hurt when she left, and sometimes I still feel that pain, but when I'm with her, when we talk, I feel empowered."

"I didn't know that."

"If she had stayed in a relationship with my dad that wasn't working, not only would she have been miserable, but my dad would have been, too. How would that have affected me? He never blamed her for leaving. My dad encouraged me to know and understand my mom. I spent lots of time with her, and we have a wonderful relationship because of it. My life isn't ideal, but it works."

"Why did your parents get divorced?"

"They didn't know each other. My dad had no idea my mom loved horses. When they got married, he had no clue that her dream was to work with them—raise them, train them, perform with them. Her dream!" Leah repeated for emphasis. "I don't blame my dad. I blame my grandpa. My mom wasn't allowed to talk about what she wanted to do, so she didn't. But also, my dad's not the best listener. He prioritized work over family. They never argued in front of me, but I knew. My grandfather played a role in them divorcing. He's kind of a bully."

"He's the rich grandpa you have, right? The one who bought you your car?"

"That's the one."

"I understand your point, but—I could feel the house inside me. I could feel that it was being true, honest. I felt joy coming from It. I believe what It was saying."

"Manipulation. You're being manipulated. We need to talk to that detective. I have his card in my room." Leah started the car and headed home.

"How do you know all this stuff anyway, manipulation, isolation is abuse?" Dan asked.

"I was getting into a lot of trouble after my mom left—picking fights, not doing my homework, talking back to the teachers. So, my dad took me to family counseling. I also studied this stuff in health class last semester."

"I've been to counseling. I guess I should've taken better notes." Dan smiled. "Leah." He waited for her to look at him before proclaiming, "We found your dad."

Leah grinned. "In an unbelievable situation." She wanted to believe him, but wasn't sure how. For now, she would allow herself to accept that it was a possibility.

In the aftermath of reconnecting with Dan, Bellevue was excited, hopeful, giddy even. The prospect that It could get both Dan and Barb back exceeded Its wildest dreams. It felt bouncy, but also drained. So much had happened in the past two days, It was hungry and knew exactly how to get a burst of energy. Time to wake Jared and Nong.

Control and Consent

Jared slowly began to wake. His heart felt warm, and he was aroused. Opening his eyes, he saw Nong facing him. They lay in bed under silk sheets on a plush mattress. Reaching over, he ran his finger down her nose.

Nong smiled, opening her eyes. "Good morning."

They gazed at each other, her scent penetrating his senses, urging him to kiss her. "You are so beautiful," he said, moving his finger over her cheek, touching the mole below her eye. His desire to mount her grew.

"Are you saying that, or is Bellevue manipulating your emotions?"

Jared took a second. "My emotions are definitely being played, but—I genuinely find you attractive." Slowly leaning into Nong, Jared tested the possibility of kissing her.

She lifted her hand to his lips. "I know how you're feeling, but these are not your emotions. The compulsion we have to rip off our clothes isn't ours. I want to grab you and taste every inch of your body, just as you want to do to me, but that is Bellevue's hunger for raw passion. It feeds on the energy."

Jared's expression turned from flirtatious to concern. "How do I control my feelings?" The memory of falling into the leather chair, being taken by Bellevue, came to him. He hadn't been able to control himself then, and his thirst for Nong was deepening.

"I haven't been able to resist It, myself."

"What do we do? This yearning for you is an itch that burns. I'm going crazy."

"Are you the one who wants me?"

Jared took a moment to answer. "I am. I've wanted you since we first met."

"Was that before or after I put my hand on your chest?"

The question gave Jared pause. He remembered seeing Nong and thinking she was strong and athletic. After she had touched him, though, she lived in his head. He was drawn to her like a needle to the North Pole. "I thought you looked good before and after. I have never needed anyone more than I need you right now."

Nong circled his pecs with her finger and rubbed her thumb over his nipple. "Really? Because I imagine we'd be having a very different conversation if Bellevue wasn't so hungry."

The thirst in her eyes pulled him close. "I don't think so," he replied. He melted from Nong's touch, and his gaze went to her chest, eyeing her breasts—her nipples were standing straight. He ran his finger down her neck to her collarbone.

In a slow, sultry voice, she explained, "I lied to you, lured you into a trap, held you until you were captured, and then left you alone. You are stuck here. You'll be here for years. You're going to miss your daughter's graduation and a whole lot more. Can't you feel your true emotions? Are you so far removed from yourself that all you want is to fuck me?" Nong leaned back, inviting Jared on top of her.

She was right. His initial anger and confusion had been swept away by Bellevue with a single sexual exchange. He thought about being alone in this house for years, missing his daughter's graduation from both high school and university, starting her career, getting married, having a child of her own. A kernel of anger developed, but it melted, knowing Nong had missed out on her daughter learning how to read, discovering talents and interests, celebrating birthdays, and performing at school events. "I probably would have done the same and still might. I can't blame you." Jared lifted himself, hovering above Nong, examining her body as he slipped in between her legs. "Don't you want me?"

"You are attractive. If we met at the bar, I'd go home with you. But I'm not sure how I feel about you. There hasn't been a single moment for us to be honest with each other. Even now, as my lady is screaming for your lips to massage her, it's not genuine. My emotions are being amplified and twisted, just like yours. Part of me wants to resist, but ...."

Jared fell back onto his side. The tension he felt was so tight he was afraid. The urge to take Nong was exploding inside him. "Where is Bellevue? How do we stop this?"

Nong quivered. "We don't."

Jared's face contorted as fear and desire struggled for control. "We can fight it," he managed to say. "I can focus on the fact I'm trapped and let the anger surface. You can do the same."

"Yes, we could. Is that what you want to do?"

"Honestly? No."

Like a cat pouncing on its prey, Nong locked her lips with Jared's. She flung off her shirt, pushing his face into her breasts. Their bodies intertwined, even though they were not together. As Jared touched himself, he was touching her. Sucking on his lower lip, he had her nipple against his tongue. Nong's breasts were smooth and sweet in his mouth.

Nong grabbed a handful of hair. Jared felt her stinging grip pulling him closer. Kissing and biting, they ravaged each other's bodies. They squeezed and scratched, rolled and moaned. Her pleasure electrified him, sending her into euphoria and him into ecstasy.

They both lay panting, hearts racing, chests heaving. Each sensed the other in their arms, and Bellevue was between them, watching, connecting, holding, immersing Itself in the heat, absorbing the energy of rapture.

After a few minutes of silence, lying in the satiation of the moment, enjoying the stress release and comfort of feeling completely spent, Bellevue said, "All I want is for us to be happy, to love each other. Let's build on this moment." It faded away, leaving them to contemplate.

"Bellevue was with us the whole time?!" Jared snapped.

"Of course. It controls us. We're not actually together." Nong rolled into his embrace.

"Right. This is still so new to me." He squeezed her tight, kissing her neck below her ear. She moaned happily.

Bellevue radiated. Finally! My home will be perfect.

A Shaman's Gift

Brandon unlocked his front door and entered the foyer. The house greeted him with a quiet stillness, and he stood for a moment, listening to everything that was missing. When the ache in his chest gripped a little too tight, he told himself silence was peace. Told himself the calm revitalized. Reminded himself the emptiness took away stress and welcomed reflection. Sitting on the bench, he let the weariness sink down his legs and into his shoes before he slipped them off and placed them on the rack. Then he hung his coat and dropped his things into the bowl by the door: keys, wallet, pen, and notepad.

In the kitchen, he opened the fridge and took out his mom's chickpea spaghetti, garlic bread, and an avocado salad and set them on the table. Grabbing the orange juice, he took off the lid and drank directly from the container before putting it back. Finally, he turned on the oven to preheat while he showered.

After dinner, Brandon cleaned up, put the containers in a brown paper bag, and set them near the door. His hand lingered for a beat as he murmured a quiet thank you to his mom, then turned off the lights and walked into the living room.

Lowering himself to the floor, he prepared to meditate. With eyes closed and legs crossed, Brandon followed his breathing into a familiar trance that released the day's grip and widened the space inside him. His spiritual energy flowed with a fresh rhythm.

When he opened his eyes, the glow from the streetlights caught the colors in the room and gave them a vibrant texture. The air felt cleaner, and his chest lighter. He rose and stretched, mindful of the simple gifts life offered—the meal his mother prepared, his work, and the safety of home. He picked up his phone from the table and scrolled through his messages before bed.

The first message was from his mom—excited that he had met Jae. She wanted to know his thoughts. The second was from a father—his son had been implicated in a robbery and was insisting all questions go through the family lawyer. The third was from the divorce lawyers connected to the Mitchell case—the divorce settlement awarded the house to the mother, Monica Mitchell. The ex-husband had felt the award unjust and had been exploring potential legal options before Monica sold it. They were unaware of an affair, but warned that the relationship between the two was explosive. The fourth message was from Leah—she and Dan had gone to the Education Center, and she needed to tell him what had happened. The last message was from Officer Choi—he had talked with his aunt, and she was expecting Brandon's call.

An unusual sound came from his phone. The app he had downloaded at the hospital was ringing. He hit "accept."

"Hello, Detective Spencer?" said a Korean woman on his screen.

"Yes, hello. You are Officer Choi's aunt, Yoona?" Brandon asked.

"Yes, that's right," she replied. "I'm calling because my nephew has told me a little bit about you and your mystery."

"Thank you so much. It is a bit of a conundrum. Choi told me you might be able to help me solve it."

"I have experience working with spirits and ghosts. And from the sounds of it, this ghost has been busy."

"It has definitely caused some problems. I am at a loss."

"Why don't you start from the beginning and explain the whole story. Once I have a better understanding of what it is you're dealing with, I can better advise you."

"Sure. That would be great. Thank you." Brandon delved into the history of the Bellevue House, starting with the land and its connection to the Sukiya tribe. He talked about the protests, bribes, religious ceremonies, Debra's jealousy, and the fire. He outlined the series of abductions, concluding with Father Joseph's coma. Yoona asked questions for clarification until she had formed a hypothesis.

"I think a spirit was awakened from that land during construction of the house. It doesn't understand the full extent of Its power. The ghost could possess anyone and use the body as Its own, but this ghost has attached Itself to a building. I'm going to guess the spirit was drawn to the love, dedication, and energy going into the house. This is a very rare and dangerous situation. When I heard the priest was in a coma, I feared the worst. We should be extremely thankful this ghost isn't harvesting souls."

Brandon took a second to register what she was saying. Possession... okay, he understood that. Attaching to a building and harvesting souls? What the heck was that about? "Not harvesting souls?" he asked.

"Attaching to a building, a ghost can rip out and capture the souls of those who approach or enter It, leaving the living body." Yoona stopped. "Never mind. Be thankful that's not the case."

Rubbing his temple, Brandon tried to follow the conversation. A ghost could steal a person's soul? What kind of horror films was this lady watching? But Yoona's conviction seemed grounded in experience. Her calm, authoritative voice made it clear she knew exactly what he was dealing with. "The ghost isn't harvesting souls, so what is it doing?"

"I believe It had a relationship with John, a loving one from what you're telling me. Now, It is grieving that loss and may be looking for the same kind of love It had with John: an obsessive love. This soul is looking for a lifelong partner."

Brandon opened his mouth to speak, but realized he didn't know how to respond. The discussion had somehow twisted into a grieving ghost. A spirit abducting people ... in search of love.

"I understand this may feel a little jarring," Yoona said. "But I do know what I'm talking about."

"A lovesick ghost?" Brandon questioned.

"Yes, and Its name is most likely Bellevue," Yoona answered. "It would have believed the name of the house was, in fact, Its own. That name is important, and the person you find to communicate with It may need to know that."

"You can speak with It?" Brandon asked. To speak with a ghost would be the ultimate confirmation of the supernatural.

"Of course. It must heal to transcend," Yoona explained. "If the soul can understand the true meaning of love, It can stop looking for what It has lost and move to the next realm."

If this were true, then Brandon wanted to be the one to talk with It. "Could I communicate with It?"

"You? Do you know anything about communicating with ghosts and spirits? The process is extremely dangerous. You could risk possession, injury, or even death. Only someone who has properly prepared to connect with a ghost should do so."

Brandon couldn't let this opportunity pass. His insides churned with hope and exhilaration. To speak with a soul would confirm everything he had been struggling to believe, and transform the very foundation of his reality. Ghosts, spirits, and the supernatural were real.

"Can you teach me?" he asked with newfound conviction.

Yoona raised an eyebrow, a smile playing on her lips. "Teach you?" she repeated, a hint of amusement in her tone. "I doubt it." She paused, considering his request. "You have no idea what you're asking. The training takes years of discipline. The pain and the dangers are beyond imagining. Besides, it takes a very special kind of person, one with a specific mind set."

"What kind of mindset is that?" Brandon quickly asked. He felt a deep, inexplicable pull within him. This meeting wasn't a coincidence. The path stretched out before him, mapping exactly where he was meant to be.

"Let me ask you a few questions," Yoona said. "What do you want? What do you hope to achieve in your life?"

Brandon paused. "Well, I'm not sure," he admitted. But the truth was, he wanted respect. He had hoped to earn a level of autonomy inside the department so that he could take on the cases that he deemed worthy. Beyond that, he'd already achieved his dreams: world traveler, home owner. He wasn't interested in cars, boats, or expensive jewelry. "I'm happy as a detective," he finally said. "I don't have any need for stuff. Maybe just to be closer with my mom."

"Talk to me about being a detective."

Sitting on the edge of his bed, Brandon considered her question. "It feels good to help others," he said. "I enjoy finding the truth. Every day teaches me something new about people, patterns, and how details matter. I may not be the best detective—I'm new, still a rookie, but I am passionate about my work, and I'm good at it. I have everything I need. I don't desire anything else."

"You must desire justice for those who have been wronged."

"No one is completely guilty or innocent. There are reasons for all actions—each can be justified or explained. My part is not to judge or to bring justice. My part is to find the facts and uncover all the relevant information so that those who seek justice can do so. This allows me to stay cool-headed and impartial. I'm not a cold, insensitive monster. I have empathy, and I comfort those in need. Emotions are important, but how and when to apply them matters."

"Are you married? Kids? Girlfriend?"

Brandon hesitated. "No," he said, shaking his head. Then he exhaled slowly. "I made detective a year ago and am happy where I am."

"Do you want to get married?" Yoona pressed.

"Not necessarily. I'm not against it, but I'm not looking for a relationship either. I'm simply living in the present, the here and now, doing my best to solve the cases I get."

"How old are you?"

"I'm thirty-two," Brandon replied. He wondered why his age mattered. Was he too old or too young to learn how to see or talk with ghosts? Feeling anxious he asked, "Why?"

"With age comes wisdom and knowledge to help souls deal with the trauma and pain that are keeping them here. Thirty-two is young, but I believe I can teach you. I have not met many people who are able to define their belief system and apply it to their lives. To not want or desire is a remarkable feat. How have you come to this way of living?

The tension in his chest dissolved. For the first time in years, he felt his true direction. "I was a teacher before," Brandon said. "After I graduated, I lived and taught in Mexico, then in Thailand and Japan. My time in Japan and Thailand introduced me to Buddhist ideas—being mindful, living in the present, and detaching myself from desire." He paused, recognizing how those lessons had shaped him more than he'd realized. It was only natural for him to continue along this path.

"I see. But a teacher?"

"Yes, my mom was an art teacher, my dad, an elementary teacher. My cousin is an ESL teacher, and my aunt is a middle school principal. But teaching doesn't fit me any longer. I am a detective."

"I can see your family and experiences have given you a solid foundation for what you're about to learn. But before we start, tell me why you feel the need to do this. It would be safer for you if we brought in someone else."

"Bringing in someone else is not a good idea. This is my case, and I know it better than anyone. I believe I can be successful. The knowledge and skills I acquire from your teaching will help me in the future. I see this as a learning opportunity to better myself as a person and as a detective. I once had a case where a woman claimed a ghost had forced her to hurt her mother. This training will be invaluable because it will allow me to gather all of the evidence and uncover the truth."

"Are you not afraid? If you truly understood the risks, I believe you would be fearful and reconsider."

"I have experienced firsthand the harm this ghost can cause, and It needs to be stopped." Brandon's headache, Debra's autopsy, Father Joseph's collapse all flashed through his mind. "Am I afraid? Maybe not as much as I should be, but fear can be channeled into bravery."

"One final question. Are you spiritual?"

Brandon flinched, eyebrows knitting. *Spiritual?* He wondered if she meant religious. After all, most religions teach about the soul's fate after death: heaven, hell, or some other afterlife. Would understanding religious doctrine be a necessary part of communicating with ghosts. "You mean religious?"

"Did I say religious? Spiritual energy carries a special kind of power."

A special kind of power? "Can you tell me about this power?"

"I will at a future date. For now, I need to assess your strength and limits."

"Okay," Brandon said. He took a breath, then added, "I would say I lean toward the Buddhist way of thinking. I do five-senses exercises from time to time to stay in the here and now. I use meditation to find clarity and manage stress. And I have appreciation for the people in my life and the opportunities that come to me."

"That will work. Let's begin. Record this, so you can review it later."

Yoona showed Brandon a piece of cloth with a symbol painted on it. "The first thing you need when communicating with souls, ghosts, or spirits, is a talisman. The symbol or thing itself doesn't matter. What matters is the energy and meaning you put into it. Don't think about the traditional idea of a talisman for protection. This talisman will be used to center you, keep you focused, and help you escape. I'll explain how to use it later, but I have found it's best to make one yourself."

"Okay, I'll make one. How do I do that?" Brandon inquired.

"Design a symbol or drawing that incorporates everything you know and understand to be Bellevue," Yoona said. "When you're mentally prepared, put that symbol in your mind and create warm energy in your heart—you can do that by praying, meditating, or making a donation to a special cause. When you feel that energy in your heart, connect it to the symbol in your mind and open yourself. Allow that energy to flow through your arms and your hands and enter the brush into the ink as you draw. But first, your energy must be attractive. Choi tells me your energy is strong and enticing already, but let me explain anyway, so you can think about ways to improve yourself."

Brandon was glad he was recording this, because it seemed like a lot—create energy, connect that energy to an idea, and then move the energy through his body. How was he supposed to learn how to do this? But in a strange way, he already knew he could. "I'm listening."

"With attractive energy, people and things naturally come to you. To cultivate attractive energy, first find your passion and develop it. Second, work on making yourself the best version of you. Strive to better yourself by living honestly, morally, ethically, and selflessly. Finally, love yourself—love who you are.

"Next, refrain from wanting material things or desiring certain objects or outcomes. Think about this—objects don't make you who you are. Your personality, actions, relationships, morals, and values do. By investing time and resources into strengthening these aspects of yourself, you become complete. Your energy invites all manner of things to you.

"Wanting or desiring certain objects or outcomes repels those things, creating friction and negative energy. If you want, you chase. If you chase, the implication is the thing you want is running from you. The goal is not to chase and repel, but rather to invite or attract.

"Finding passion and joy, creating a life you love, striving to cultivate excellence within yourself, and becoming unapologetically you will make you attractive, giving you a strong aura that will draw people, things, opportunities, and even ghosts and spirits to you," Yoona concluded.

"It's so strange you said that. I'm curious now. Is that why we came to meet? I attracted you to me?"

"The universe connects us to the people we need," Yoona replied. "Tell me what you understand."

"I understand that I need to focus on cultivating excellence in my life to make me the best me I can be, to develop my passion. I send that energy into the universe, attracting people and opportunities to me."

"Good. The other reason to eliminate wants and desires is that the friction they create are like handles a ghost can grab and hold. The more handles you have, the easier you are to possess and control. Before moving forward in your training, you must learn to release unnecessary wants and desires."

Brandon understood. Yoona was conveying a tactic employed by scammers, hustlers, and racketeers. Creating wants and desires in someone to make them vulnerable to possession and control was present in everyday life, especially inside one's email box.

His biggest pet peeve were soda companies. They painted the perfect refreshment for the kids to drink on a hot day—the solution to all thirst. Yet the reality was that the chemicals, sugar, and caffeine in those drinks forced the body to use water to flush out the garbage, dehydrating them further and making them even thirstier.

Equally frustrating were credit card companies. They dangled easy money, instant gratification, and the allure of having your dreams come true now, only to trap people with interest rates and fees that ensnared them in debt and dependence, never truly free.

"I get it," Brandon said. "But ghosts aren't the only ones who grab those handles—con artists, grifters, and corporations grab them, too."

"Yes. I'm glad you understand. Lastly, is fear. Fear closes your mind. Once that happens, the soul has you. If you allow fear to shut your mind, you will become possessed. Your talisman doesn't hold the energy needed to draw a soul from a fearful mind. The talisman will be useless—a silly drawing."

"Make my energy attractive, eliminate handles, and don't be afraid," Brandon summarized. "Then I make a talisman. What's after that?"

"We communicate with spirits using telepathy. You'll have to connect with it first. The best way to do this is to invite the ghost to you."

"How do I do that?"

"Go to it. Place the talisman in front of you. Picture the ghost in your mind, use its name, create a loving feeling in your chest, combine the image you've created in your mind with the energy in your chest, and then open yourself up, and let the energy flow out. After the energy has gone, invite it back. Trust in the process and be careful of wanting. The act of wanting is dangerous. Wanting the energy to come back gives the ghost permission to take control," Yoona explained. "Don't desire an outcome. Does that make sense?"

Brandon thought the steps seemed straightforward enough. It reminded him of flirting. When he saw a pretty girl, he pictured the two of them together, combined that image with his energy, and sent it out into the world. He allowed his curiosity to open the door to possibility. But he understood Yoona's warning: if he desired a specific outcome with her—dinner, sex, marriage—then evil, dark impulses could creep into his mind. Wanting dinner could turn into rudeness, acting as if she owed him a chance. Wanting sex could twist into rape, and wanting marriage could become possessiveness. As a detective, he'd seen these patterns, and nothing good ever came from them.

"Yes, I understand," he acknowledged.

"Because Bellevue has possessed a building, you may not have to invite It to you—It'll be right there. Before you arrive, make sure your talisman is with you and ready to use.

"This next part is the most important to successfully communicating with the ghost. When a ghost comes to you, do not accept or reject it. Simply observe it.

See it for what it is, a soul. Do not think of it as good or bad, friendly or hostile. Think of it as simply being or existing. Observe it without judgment or fear."

"I'm pretty sure I understand," Brandon said. His mind went straight to a fast food worker smiling and nodding politely while being assaulted by an irate customer. He had also smiled and nodded as a teacher when an angry parent had blamed him for their child's poor behavior. And as a police officer? Good grief. "I deal with people who get in my face and try to provoke me on a regular basis. I don't take it personally, and I don't react."

"That skill is exactly what you need. Now, a ghost will try to find a way into your mind, to control you. This can be very painful. When you feel that pain, you have three options. One is to fight and get away without communicating. You will still be yourself and alive but unsuccessful in your goal.

"Option two is to stay and fight. This option allows you to communicate; however, you will most likely become possessed and lose yourself to the ghost. It will be in control and have all the power. You may still be able to help it, but it could as easily put you in a coma, or in this case, make you disappear for years."

"I guess you don't recommend that option."

"No, not really. Option three is to open up completely, like opening all the doors and windows of your house on a sunny day. At this point, the ghost is free to come and go as it pleases. You can communicate with it. It will look for handles to hold—your wants and desires. It will look for information it can use to create friction, upsetting you, frustrating you, or scaring you. It wants to control you and have power over you. Simply observe.

"With this option, you have to be open and calm," Yoona added. "If you allow the ghost to provoke you, you give it power to take control. Be open and allow the soul to be present. It can't hurt you if it can't get a hold of you. By being open, calm, at peace, and in love with yourself, your mind will be a slippery slide the ghost cannot climb. The stronger your attractive energy, the longer you are able to communicate with it. Having attractive energy is the key to your safety because that's the opposite of wanting. Attractive energy means you are confident and self-assured. When you have attractive energy, fear can easily be turned into bravery or observed as a warning without closing your mind."

"Are you saying my attractive energy is like a magnet? It holds the spirit to me without controlling me?"

"Yes, that's right. In essence, the ghost becomes trapped. They don't like that. It can become intense."

"I still want to try. I understand the risks."

"No, you don't want to try. You are willing to try. Tell me one more time what you are attempting to do."

"I am attracting Bellevue to me so I can communicate with It. Bellevue needs to heal from Its trauma and loss. Its concept of love needs to change. I believe I can do this. However, I do need time to think and prepare."

"Please take all the time you need. Don't rush the preparations. Finally, you will need to create the talisman to help you observe the ghost as an entity separate from yourself. When you are communicating with It, It's in your brain. When you are ready to end the session, you simply picture the ghost and the talisman as one, together. The energy you put in the talisman will draw the ghost out of you, and then you put away the talisman. You cannot ask, wish, or want the ghost to leave. That will create friction, which gives the soul something to hold on to. Wait for it to be drawn out."

After a pause, she asked, "What questions and concerns do you have?"

Confirmed

After Leah finished showering, she checked her phone. Becky and a few friends from school had texted her, offering her support after her dad's disappearance. She also had several texts from unknown numbers and three calls that went straight to voicemail, but nothing from Brandon. She went into Dan's room. "He hasn't called back yet. Should we call him again?"

"He has a life, too, you know," Dan answered.

"Promise me you won't go back there."

"You mean to the Education Center? I promise. Don't worry."

Leah's phone rang. "Detective Spencer, thank you for calling! I think I know where my dad is."

"He's at the Education Center being held by a ghost. Do not go there again! Do you understand? It's dangerous. It could grab you, too."

"How do you know?" Leah asked in shock. She couldn't believe it. The detective had just confirmed what Dan had claimed; a ghost had her dad. Was it really true? "How did you find It? Did It talk to you, too?"

"It talked to you?"

"Not to me, to Dan. It was Dan's friend when he was little. It wants Dan and Barb to live with It."

"Stay away. I'm working with a Shaman to learn how to communicate with It, and I will attempt to free your dad. Give me a few days to prepare."

"Can you trust this Shaman?"

"I trust her. Another police officer also knows about your dad. Give me a few days to work this out, okay? I'll call you before I do anything."

"Thank you, yes, keep me informed."

"I will. Get some sleep. Stay safe."

Leah put down her phone.

Dan looked hopeful. "What did he say?"

"He knows about Bellevue. He's going to try to get my dad back. He needs a few days before he does. Whew. I feel—relieved but anxious."

"A Shaman told him? How did he find out?"

"I don't know any of the details, but another officer knows about It, too."

"This is great news." Dan leaned over and hugged her.

This is absolutely crazy. How do I tell my uncle what's happened? My mom? My grandparents? No one will believe me. "Yeah, great news," she repeated.

A New Assignment

Choi kissed his wife goodbye. Jasmine was heading to the nursing home where she worked three nights a week. "I love you," he said.

"I'll see you in the morning," she responded, squeezing his hand.

He watched her go, then closed the door and stepped into the living room as he called his aunt.

"How did it go?" he asked. "Is Brandon the one?"

"I'm not sure," Yoona said. "Possibly. He definitely has a role to play. I want you to train him. Give him the tools to communicate with souls, then monitor him."

"Auntie? What is at the Center?"

"A spirit has attached Itself to the building. I believe It's looking for the love It had with the original owner of the house."

239

Choi leaned forward, resting his hand against the wall. That didn't sound right. Ghosts lingered in corners, drifted through halls, and haunted rooms. But the Center pulsed floor to ceiling with an essence he couldn't define.

"I went there," Choi said after a pause. "The energy encompassed the entire building—much too large to be a spirit. I had believed it came from the creative passion of the students and staff."

"I've encountered spirits like this before. We need to be careful, though. This one just got its first taste of being a Soul Harvester."

Choi drew in a sharp breath, wondering why Yoona wasn't sending a member of the Circle to force the ghost to transcend. "Are you sure you want me to teach *Brandon*? He's never dealt with anything like this before. He can't even connect yet. A Soul Harvester will tear him apart."

"I don't believe Bellevue is malicious, and Brandon's innocence will benefit him in this case. Let's use this opportunity to see what he can do."

"I feel like we're playing with fire."

"I didn't feel any negative ripples from my decision, although Brandon is hiding something. Train him, and stay close when he engages. But let him take charge. I need to see his decision making and how he negotiates. I want you to mainly observe."

"Yes, ma'am."

Day Twelve – Sunday

A New Morning

Brandon woke with a start, breathing heavily. He stumbled into the bathroom and washed away the nightmare—a large green lizard-like creature with tentacles that had teeth grabbing his head, splitting it open, eating his brains. Monsters when I'm sleeping—ghosts when I'm awake. I can't catch a break.

Listening to Yoona's instructions recorded the night before, Brandon prepared breakfast—a blueberry bagel with strawberry cream cheese and blackberry jam, two eggs, and a bowl of instant oatmeal. He continued listening as he ate, replaying the recording while he showered and dressed. In the evening, he would create his Talisman and talk with Yoona again. They needed to work out a plan for meeting Bellevue.

Arriving at the station, he collected the forensics report for the Mitchell case. Dimitri's DNA did not match the DNA found at the scene, but the red fibers did match his sweater. However, because Dimitri and Monica had had an affair, was that enough to make an arrest? He'd visit Dimitri and stress the importance of speaking with his friend and sister one more time. Opening his emails, he learned that a fight had occurred along the strip in front of the Golden Beach Spa on the night of the Mitchell attack. Brandon leaned back in his chair thinking about his meeting with the ex-boyfriend. He'd been at the Spa, and Stephanie had been on the strip. Brandon couldn't help but give a cynical chuckle. Calling the Spa, he made an appointment to view the security footage. Checking his schedule, he penciled it in before his interview with the brother and then the ex-husband. The captain was breathing down his neck to close this case, but untwisting this drama was a challenge.

Shared Bond

At the Carol Anderson home, Dan entered the kitchen and saw his sister eating a bowl of honey and almond flakes.

"Good morning," he said, setting his phone on the table. He grabbed the cereal and poured himself some, then set the box on top of the fridge. When he turned back, Barb was glaring at him.

"What?" he asked.

"Where did you and Leah go yesterday? Did you sneak out of the house and get a hotel room somewhere?"

"No, we didn't do anything like that."

"What then?"

Dan sighed and reached for the milk. *What then indeed.* He was still trying to figure that out.

Barb leaned forward and caught his eye. "Something obviously happened. Are you going to tell me what?"

His stomach tightened. How could he possibly explain that their house was a spirit and could communicate with them? That Bell was alive and real? It still seemed impossible, but it was true. The encounter had left Dan conflicted—excited to reconnect with his best friend, yet angry that Bell had played a role in his parents' demise. But more than that, he felt a sense of wonder.

Rubbing the back of his neck, he asked, "Did you have an imaginary friend when you were little?"

Barb's whole body went rigid. "Whoa. Why are you asking me that?"

"Because I had a friend, in my mind. We played checkers and talked at night. He helped me relax after Dad yelled at us. His name was Bell."

Barb coughed and grabbed a paper towel to wipe her mouth. "Did you say, 'Bell'?"

"Yes. He made me promise not to tell anyone about him."

The hum of the refrigerator was the only sound that followed. Barb placed her forehead in her hand and stared at her cereal. Dan wasn't sure what she was thinking, but she seemed to recognize Bell's name.

"Yeah," she finally said. "I had a friend, too. Her name was Bella. She was my best friend, but she disappeared after our parents died."

Dan nodded. "Same with Bell. That's because Bell and Bella are both Bellevue."

Barb's head snapped up, her face twisting in confusion. "Bellevue? The house? What are you saying? You're not making any sense."

Dan didn't answer. There was nothing more he could say.

"Dan!" she nearly shouted. "What are you saying? Bellevue? Our house?"

He lifted his hand, gesturing for her to keep her voice low.

She crossed her arms and scowled. "Grandma thought Bellevue was alive. She was talking the other day like that house killed Mom."

Dan softened his expression. Bellevue had told him the truth about their mom, which Barb didn't know. And that filled him with guilt.

"Why did you ask if I had an imaginary friend?" she asked.

"Because that's where we went yesterday. Leah and I."

"You went where? To the Education Center?"

"Shhh. Don't let Grandma hear."

Barb bit the inside of her lip as her eyes hardened into an interrogating stare. "Why did you go there?" She waited half a second before adding a sarcastic afterthought. "To heal? I suppose you'll want me to go next."

"Leah was going with or without me. She was sure her dad was there."

"She's so stubborn," Barb chuckled with a shake of her head. "Gets an idea and won't let it go."

"I saw our house," Dan said. "Bellevue talked with me. Her dad is there."

Barb jerked back and blinked. "Time out. What?" She raised her hands. "Her dad is where? At the Education Center?"

Dan nodded in confirmation.

She pressed her lips tight and squinted. "Did the police find him? Or—what are you saying?"

"Jared is trapped inside our house, which is a ghost, inside the Education Center. No one can find him because no one can see him."

For a beat, Barb sat still, then broke into a laugh. "If you're trying to get me to go with you, you're failing miserably."

"I'm not," Dan stated plainly. "Father Joseph fell into a coma while performing an exorcism at the Education Center. He's in the hospital, so we decided to visit the Center and look around."

"Was that your first time back?"

"Yes."

"So you were hallucinating."

Dan hadn't thought about that, but was sure he hadn't been. "I wasn't. Bell talked with me. He said he was protecting us from Mom."

"You're saying our house talked with you and told you this?"

"I am. I felt It. I saw It. I talked to It. Bellevue is—good. But Leah, she—"

"Yeah, I know what she's like. Tell me what happened."

"I opened the door to the Center and saw our house. Bell was in my mind. He said our mom was jealous and scared. When she grabbed that gun, he had to protect us."

"Protect us? From Mom? That's a load of crap, Dan."

"I could feel what Bell felt. I saw what he saw," Dan protested. "I believe my best friend."

Barb pursed her lips. "I don't believe you or anything you just said."

"Ask Leah. She'll confirm everything."

Barb leaned back again. She started to speak, stopped, hardened her eyes, and then said, "You talked to It." Her mouth opened with a half-smile. "How am I supposed to believe that? How is anyone?"

"Leah laid into me. She said the house was abusive and manipulative."

"If It has Leah's dad, and he's trapped, I'm going to believe Leah over a ghost. Don't you dare go back there again."

"The detective told us the same thing. He called last night and said he can free Jared."

"Wait." Her eyes narrowed. "The detective knows about this? And he believes you?" Barb mulled over the detective's belief. "I saw he was sympathetic to Grandma's needs, but I didn't think he actually believed in ghosts."

"He does, and he is able to talk with Bell."

Laughing again, Barb said, "Ohh, you had me for a second. I can't believe I fell for that."

Dan didn't laugh. The two siblings stared at each other for a long moment. Dan heard the water running in the bathroom and kids playing next door on the trampoline. His heart pounded as Barb's face crumpled. Her eyes slowly turned red. He was afraid she might stand and slap him.

"Bellevue wants to meet you," Dan murmured. "He misses you."

Barb's lips trembled. "Stop it."

"Everything I'm saying is true."

"Stop." Her voice broke, and a tear spilled before she could wipe it away.

"I'm not playing," Dan insisted.

In a sharp voice, she repeated, "Stop! This isn't funny."

"I know. It's—" Dan took a breath. "I don't know what it is."

Barb lifted her head and stared at the ceiling. Her mouth dropped open as she let out a heavy sigh. "I miss Bella, too." The air chilled. She lowered her head and met his eyes again. "I needed Bella after our parents died. Losing her made everything worse. I've dreamed of seeing her again, sharing my favorite songs and gossiping with her. I've imagined her swooping in and taking away all my pain." Barb paused, her eyes fading. "But I can't go to that place."

"That place is where Bella is. She and the House are one and the same."

"Not in my mind, they aren't. The House is this evil thing that took Dad. Bella is my magical friend who came to visit me when I was scared and lonely. She made life simple—helping me prepare for the first day of school and encouraging me to keep reading. And after Dad hit us, she would sit with me for hours, cooing." Barb took a deep breath, rested her arms on the table, and locked eyes with her brother. In a firm voice, she asserted, "Grandma's taken Bella's place. Bella was never real—just someone I made up."

Barb and Dan stopped talking as Leah turned the corner and shuffled into the kitchen. "Good morning. You guys are eating cereal? Is there any left?"

Dan gestured with his hand, "The box is on top of the fridge."

Grabbing the cereal box, she immediately complained, "Oh, my god! I can't believe they are making us go back to school tomorrow. What are we doing on our last day of freedom?"

"I want to go to the library," Barb said, still glaring at Dan. "We should find some information about ghosts and spirits—see what we can learn about them."

Leah froze. "Oh?" Meeting Dan's eyes, her gaze asked if Barb knew they had gone to the Center yesterday. Dan shrugged, followed by a nod.

She turned to Barb and agreed. "Yes. Let's go."

Dan hesitantly added, "We should take that book Grandma was talking about."

"Right. She said it was in the closet leveling the shoe rack," Barb said.

After they finished eating, Dan went to the closet and found the thick book under the right front leg of the shoe rack. Removing the book, the rack shifted forward, preventing the door from closing. When Leah saw Dan struggling with it, she grabbed some cardboard from the recycling container and folded the pieces to replace the book.

Dan held the book and turned it in his hands. "Grandma was right. I can feel energy from this book. It tickles my fingers. Here, touch."

Leah placed her hand on the cover. "Shit, you're right. Scary."

Dan flipped it back and forth. "There's no title."

"Check the inside cover," Leah suggested.

"Property of The Circle. 1946," Dan read. "I wonder what that means."

Entering the hall, Barb held her keys. "Let's go."

Beyond Reach

Jared yawned and stretched as he sat on the edge of the bed trying to wake. He had had an odd night. After spending time in nothingness with no sound or light, he had a difficult time sleeping back in the real world where animals and insects could be heard all night long, and the light from the moon cast shadows in the gray room. Besides, he was connected to Nong and kept reaching out with his mind to smell and touch her. Walking into the kitchen, Jared searched for something to eat.

"Don't eat cereal today," Bellevue said. "Make crepes with the batter in the walk-in. It will spoil soon and needs to be used. It'll get thrown out later anyway. Metal tins on the top shelf near the door contain blueberries and strawberries. You can find whipped or sour cream, ricotta, yogurt or cottage cheese, whichever you prefer."

"Are we expecting anyone soon? Do I need to hurry, or can I relax a bit?"

"A few students will attend classes today, but you have time. You still need to be clean and put things away promptly."

Jared felt Nong's energy pulling him toward her. He could feel the sun on her face. Closing his eyes, he went to her.

"It's such a beautiful day. I had to share it with you," Nong said as Jared connected with her. She was in a wheelchair out in the garden, the sun warm and comforting.

"My daughter is coming to see me again today," Nong said. "She won't stay long, but she gives me a hug. My mom will sit and tell me all about her."

"I thought you and your mom didn't get along."

Nong laughed. "When you told me you had a daughter, I became concerned and didn't want you to become trapped like me. When you saw my reaction, I came up with a story to distract you. I had to have a reason why my daughter didn't live with me—but I didn't lie—she is with my mom."

"Right. Sorry. How about your dad?"

"He comes sometimes. Usually, he stays with Ploy until my mom is ready to leave. They play checkers. I love watching them—wish I could talk to them."

"Ploy is your daughter's name? Have you asked Bellevue to let you talk with her?"

"Bellevue is very possessive. You know that. It can't let me go. It thinks It loves me."

"I do love you," Bellevue said.

"Love?" Jared scoffed. "If you really love her, you'd let her talk to her daughter."

"I would have to release her. I'm sorry, but I can't do that."

Anxiety washed over Jared at Bellevue's thought of freeing her. Nong winced and then shuddered.

Trying to release the feeling, Jared asked, "Can I meet your daughter?"

Nong smiled. "Of course you can."

Hold Me

Choi woke to Jasmine's kisses. She slipped her hand inside his pajama bottoms, and he moaned.

"Good morning," she whispered.

"What time is it?" Choi asked.

"Time for you to get ready for work."

"Uuhh," he groaned. "Why are you getting me all worked up then?"

"I want you to attack me when you get home tonight."

Choi hummed in appreciation before cursing under his breath. "I have to start training this new user tonight."

Jasmine fell back on the bed next to Choi and sighed.

He rolled on his side, facing her, and rubbed her thigh.

Looking into his eyes, she explained, "I bought tickets to Korea last night. Jun and I are leaving in ten days. We'll be gone for three months."

Choi's alarm beeped. As he reached over to turn it off, Jasmine stood.

"Hey," he called.

Jasmine's face was long. "Make some time for me before we leave."

The Manual

The Lake Valley Library was large and modern, with wide windows and plenty of lighting that made the space bright and warm. The inside was open, allowing one to maneuver around sitting areas and between the shelves. Private desks and small glass rooms for small groups to gather made it comfortable to study. In one of these rooms, Dan, Leah, and Barb sat with fifteen books about ghosts, spirits, angels, and demons piled on the table.

"Let's skim through and report," Leah said.

"I'm going to start with Grandma's book," Dan said.

The girls each grabbed a book and started reading. For the next fifteen minutes, the room was quiet, with the exception of pages turning.

Barb was the first to break the silence, "I found something interesting, the difference between a ghost and a spirit."

"Let's hear it," Leah said.

"Ghosts exist because they are unable to transcend, while spirits have either come back after transcending or are being held from transcending by a connection."

"I didn't realize there was a difference. Keep going," Leah said.

"Ghosts can't transcend until they resolve the issues keeping them stuck. They could be waiting for someone to pay their respects or for justice. They may have a secret that needs to be shared with a loved one, like the passcode to their bank safe or—"

"They have issues. Got it. What about spirits?" asked Leah.

"People can have a special connection which can be ancestral or associated with love. That connection allows a spirit to return to give comfort to a person who is suffering. If a person is facing challenges, the spirit may offer guidance. However, if a person cannot accept a death, the soul is held, and the spirit is unable to transcend until the loved one can come to terms with the loss."

"What do you think Bellevue is?" Dan asked.

"I think It must be a ghost," Leah guessed.

"Me, too," Barb agreed.

They continued reading.

"Here's another difference. Ghosts are attached to a place or an object, while spirits are attached to people," Barb said. "Leah, what are you finding?"

"Not much. This book says ghosts are scary because they make noise and knock things over. That first book was more about history and famous ghost stories. I want to know more about the powers. Bellevue has powers because It trapped my dad."

"I read that giving ghosts attention makes them more powerful," Barb said.

Leah's eyes widened. "Does it say what powers they have?"

"Being able to move things, make sounds, show themselves."

Disappointed, Leah said, "That's what this one says, too. Ok, we need different books." Leah picked another one. "Ooh, Annie Belle."

"What? For real?" asked Barb.

They were both jarred by the coincidence of the author's name. "The Comprehensive Guide to Ghosts, Spirits, Demons, and Angels Arranged by Religion, Cultures, and Countries by Annie Belle," Leah read.

"Come on. Hand it over," Barb insisted.

Leah gave her the book and chose a different one for herself.

The room was quiet as they read.

"Do you want to know how to get rid of a ghost?" Barb asked.

"Yes," Leah answered.

Barb turned the book, pointing. "This list shows objects followed by directions on how to use them. Look." Objects listed were sage, salt, white candles, white roses, incense, talismans, crystals, peach tree branches, goat's milk, and holy water.

"These send the ghost somewhere else," Leah said. "We need to make Bellevue transcend so It's completely gone and can't hurt anyone else."

"This next chapter details rituals that can be performed," Barb said.

Reading the introduction and then skimming through the pages, they found rituals from Native Americans, Hindus, Buddhists, Catholics, Celtics, and Pagans. "It talks about connecting to the inner spirit when conducting these rituals. Is there such a thing as power from the inner spirit?" Barb asked Leah.

"I would think so. Prayer is powerful. It can heal, but that energy comes from a higher power, not from us."

"Not according to this," Barb stated. She kept scanning the text and one of the passages caught her eye. "Hold a personal object from the deceased, quiet your inner voice, and allow the spirit to enter. Absorb the information you receive, and thank the spirit for the contributions it made."

Barb thought about that. "You know, some of these are for welcoming spirits. What if we honored Bella? That might help her transcend. We should take this book with us."

"Maybe, but let's keep looking," Leah said.

They continued to read.

"My book has something similar to the first book you read, Barb," Leah said. "Ghosts are stuck because they died unexpectedly and have tasks, promises, or business to complete before transcending. They may be looking for something, or in some cases, can't accept how they died."

"Anything about powers?" Barb asked.

"I'm looking."

"This book has everything we need." Dan blurted. "It's a training manual. Did you know that ghosts and spirits communicate by reading thoughts and memories?"

"What? How is that?" Barb asked.

"First of all, ghosts and spirits are souls that are stuck in our world."

"Lost souls," Barb laughed.

"An interesting energy dynamic plays here, a catch 22. People have positive or negative energy. Souls are attracted to people with positive energy. People with negative energy are attracted to souls. Souls can possess people with negative energy, but have no desire for them. This is because people with negative energy usually don't have the resources or connections the souls require. People with negative energy do have handles, which allow souls to grab and possess them, and they will if the person is directly related to an issue the soul has. People with positive energy don't have handles, so souls have to become creative in how they possess their targets."

"That is weird," Leah said. "Souls can easily possess people with negative energy, but they don't want them. Souls want people with positive energy but can't get them. It grabbed my dad. So did he have positive or negative energy?"

"Bell said your dad fell in love with him."

"With her," Barb told Dan. "Bella is a girl."

"How about It?" Leah corrected. "Bellevue is a house." Looking at Dan, Leah snapped, "We already talked about this, Dan. My guess is, my dad liked Nong, and Bellevue used her to capture him."

"Question," Barb interrupted. "What are 'handles'?"

"The next section explains 'handles,' but let me explain the different levels of possession."

"There are levels?" Leah said, incredulously. What had her father experienced? Recalling his grogginess, lack of recollection, and strange moods, she imagined the ghost crawling into his consciousness, layer by layer, increasing Its level of control. She clenched her teeth and balled her hands into fists.

Barb rubbed Leah's shoulder as Dan read. "The first level consists of observation or tagging along. The soul hangs on and follows you around. The second involves influencing a person. The soul guides or directs the person. The third is full possession. The soul takes total control of the mind and assumes the person's identity. The book goes into more details and the ramifications for each level."

"My dad is trapped, so which of these is Bellevue using on him?"

"I'm going to guess he's being influenced because that's what Bell was doing to me," Dan said. "Don't you think?"

"Yes. That's right. Being manipulated or Influenced—I guess they are similar."

"There's more," Dan continued. "Communicating with souls is unpleasant. They enter people's minds, causing headaches. People may feel a slight poke or excruciating pain when a soul possesses them. The more control a soul takes, the more painful the process."

Leah began to breathe deeper. The information, paired with her memory, felt like a knife sliding into her heart. She remembered seeing her dad fall further and further under Bellevue's influence, but she hadn't understood what was happening.

Barb looked at her brother. "Did you feel pain when you talked to Bellevue?"

"No, not at all."

"But you had a connection already from when you were a kid," Leah surmised.

Dan grabbed the pages in the front half of the book and flipped through them. "This whole section teaches how to be in the right mindset so communicating with souls isn't painful. Maybe I'm a natural."

"As if. What else does it say?" Barb pushed.

"Most people can only see a soul as a ghost if they have a connection to it or have knowledge of it."

"You saw Bellevue, right?" Barb asked Dan.

"Yes, I thought I was home."

"Leah, did you see It or hear It?" Barb asked.

"No. I had no idea It was there, but my dad saw It. I guess that's because he knew about the house from his job as an architect."

"What else, Dan?" Barb said.

"Most souls don't possess people. They communicate in other ways—through dreams, visions, or intuition. Souls that have returned after having transcended are here to help, comfort, or guide a loved one. Often an ancestor will make the journey back to give advice to their descendant who is struggling, has a decision to make, or is on a quest. If someone experiences déjà vu, they should think carefully before acting. The ancestor is trying to warn them. If a soul does possess a person, it can remain with them for many years."

"Is there a way to unpossess someone?" Leah asked.

"This book is written specifically for that purpose."

"Show us."

Dan flipped through the pages. "Here it is. '...helping or forcing a soul to transcend.'"

"How do you do that?" Leah asked, grabbing the book from Dan. "Where is that?"

"Here," he pointed.

Leah took a few minutes to read while Dan and Barb waited. She scanned the text quickly, feeling agitated that this information was disregarded by public officials and institutions as fake, nonsensical, and fantasy. Stories about ghosts and possessions had been prevalent throughout history. If people understood that these were real and had been taught the signs of one being possessed, this whole situation could have been avoided!

Dan touched Leah's hand. "What does it say?" His words were soft and slow.

Taking a breath, she said, "Shamans and Banishers send souls to the next life. A Shaman communicates with souls, resolving issues they have. A Banisher will battle the soul, forcing it to move on to its next life. Both professions are extremely dangerous, with great risk of becoming possessed, injured, dying, or worse."

"What's worse than dying?" Barb asked.

"Having your loved ones plucked out of existence," Leah vented. She turned pages, searching.

"It's okay." Barb lay her hand on the book, stopping Leah.

Leah sat back and puffed her cheeks. "This book has step-by-step instructions explaining how to do everything."

"Is it for real?" Barb asked. "Can we trust it will work?"

"Are you serious right now?" Leah retorted.

Dan pushed the corner of the book, urging Leah to read. "How do we save your dad?"

Leah stared into Dan's eyes, his loving expression calming her. Going back to the book, she familiarized herself with the contents and instructions. "Our spiritual core is the source of power needed to engage with souls." She nodded. I think I have this. I can do this. "Its energy allows for communication."

Dan considered this. "I know data is transferred through waves—sound or radio. And light carries information, too. Those travel though. We have instruments that send and receive it. I guess I could grasp how we would be able to code our own energy to convey a message, but how do we send it, and how do we receive it?"

Leah pointed. "Here. The energy is already flowing from us. People see it in our auras. It's part of the Chinese idea of Chi, the energy that surrounds and binds all living things together. Tapping into our spiritual core gives us access to this energy and allows us to manipulate it. Fortune telling, creating talismans, healing, telepathy are ways we use it. I feel like our universe just doubled in size." She was starting to feel hopeful. Fortune tellers and healers were available in her city. Chi was a concept older than Jesus. But what if she couldn't save her dad. What if he was lost forever?

Barb cleared her throat. "Shamans and Banishers use this energy to do what, exactly?"

"Shamans attract souls to them, then help them—even urge them—to transcend. Banishers use martial arts and mental discipline to possess souls—their consciousness—forcing them to transcend."

"Is it difficult?" Dan asked.

"Umm. It's a skill. It'll take time and practice." Leah eyed some of ways to cultivate her energy—prayer, holotropic breathwork, meditation... "I'm going to learn," she declared.

"Leah! What part of 'extremely dangerous' do you not understand?" Barb shot back. "It literally said there is something worse than death."

"Learning the art and practicing the art are two different things, Barb. Besides, I'm curious about our spiritual core and this energy. I'm pretty sure I've felt it in me. I think I understand what it is."

"Leah," Dan cut in. "There might be another way to free your dad."

"What?"

"Exorcism."

"Isn't that for demons?" Barb asked.

Dan looked at Barb. "The book says the church sees ghosts as demons, and spirits as angels."

"Probably because ghosts use people, and spirits help people," Leah speculated.

"They are all souls that need to transcend," Dan said.

Leah ran her finger over the table of contents, found the chapter for exorcisms, turned to that page, and skimmed through the chapter.

"What does it say?" Barb asked.

"An exorcism kills the soul, ripping it apart," Leah said.

"I don't like the sound of that," Barb said.

"Me either," Dan agreed.

"Oh, but the side effect is wicked cool," Leah said. "After the soul has been shredded, pieces of it float around until it joins with a person, giving them inspiration. According to this, some of the best art, music, stories, inventions, and medical advancements have come from pieces of souls that have melded with someone and manifested into an idea."

"That does sound cool. How does it work?" Barb asked.

"When the soul fragment fuses with the mind, it stimulates the brain, allowing persons to access more of their mental capacity. The increased brain activity generates ideas, stimulates passions, and inspires them to learn and create. The larger mental capacity makes the ideas clear and attainable."

"Fascinating, but does that mean the priest was trying to kill Bellevue the other day?" Dan asked.

"Sounds like it," Barb replied.

"Bellevue was defending Itself when It put Father Joseph in a coma," Dan concluded. "If the church sends another priest, someone stronger, Bellevue will die. We can't let that happen. Bell isn't evil. He's simply looking for a family to love and that will love him."

With a slight shake of her head, Leah sighed heavily. "It isn't good." Reaching over, she touched Dan's hand. "But I don't think Bellevue deserves to die. I'm going to study this book. We need It to transcend, and I think we can make that happen. You two can already communicate with Bellevue, so the only thing left to do is to find out what It wants."

"I thought the detective told us to wait," Barb interjected.

"It's going to take me a few days to read this book. If the detective can't save my dad, then we will."

"Actually, we'll be saving both Bell and your dad," Dan said.

"Does no one care that it's extremely dangerous?" Barb exclaimed.

Visitors

Nong watched Ploy explore the musical instruments near the piano while a nurse helped her to the sofa. "Nong, you have visitors," the nurse explained. Ploy ran to her mom and bounced on the sofa next to her.

"Hi, Mom," Ploy said with a hug.

"Tell your mom what you did at school, sweetie," Mrs. Ekamai told Ploy.

"I had a band concert. I play the clarinet. It's easy. And I can play songs on it that I learned from the guitar. I got a B+ on my math test, and we played ultimate frisbee in P.E. I scored." Turning, Ploy asked, "Grandma, when is Mom going to wake up?"

"I don't know. But she can hear you. She's fighting to get to you. We just need to encourage her."

Ploy leaned close to Nong and whispered in her ear. "Fight, Mom. I know you can win. You have to come to my class party at the end of the year. You can do it. Fight." She hugged her mom for a long minute and then kissed her on the cheek.

"Grandma, can I go to the vending machine?"

"First, tell her you miss her."

"I do miss her," Ploy said. She slid off the sofa and made her way to the vending machine.

"I'm fighting, baby." A tear fell from Nong's eye as she watched Ploy with curiosity and wonder. Nong was struck by the paradox of her daughter's movements: a mope, while swinging her arms back and forth, as if she inhabited a world all her own.

In the dark room of Nong's mind, Jared held Nong's hand as she cried. "You are strong, but not alone. I'm here. We'll figure this out together."

Spiritual Weapons

Brandon dragged himself through the front door. His body ached with exhaustion, yet his mind buzzed. He was fairly sure he knew who was behind the Mitchell attack. First, the fight at the Spa had happened between Stephanie and her ex-boyfriend, and he was the one responsible for cutting her lip. There was enough evidence to arrest him, if she wanted to press charges. Next, Monica's brother admitted he was upset about her selling the house, but was adamant that it was the ex-husband who had attacked his sister. The brother was so certain, he had threatened to "return the favor" if the police didn't arrest him. Brandon had attempted to talk with the ex-husband, but the belligerent man had refused. The motorcycle parked outside his house, though, had said plenty. Brandon would get a warrant to collect his DNA. He was also ready to confront Stephanie and Monica again to get the truth.

Sitting on the carpet in the middle of his living room, Brandon meditated until the thoughts and images from the day left his mind, and he felt peaceful. Then he showered, ate dinner, and took a short nap. After waking, he went to his study to sketch ideas for a symbol that would represent Bellevue to him—a symbol that meant a lost soul desperately searching for love, one that disregarded the basic relationship needs of those It took. One that used violence against those who opposed It.

As Brandon drew, the doorbell rang. Going to the window, he saw a man in his late twenties, wearing blue jeans and a black leather jacket standing on his porch. Brandon turned on the light and, after a second, recognized him. He opened the door. "Officer Choi. To what do I owe the pleasure?"

"Hope I'm not bothering you."

"No, not at all. Come in," Brandon said.

"Thanks. This is a nice place you have. You live here by yourself?"

"I do. I bought this house six months ago."

"Did you get it before the government declared the housing shortage?"

"It was around that time. I bought this place for $850,000. The house three doors down sold for $970,000, so I'm feeling pretty good about the price I paid. Can I offer you something to drink?"

"No, thanks. I came over because my aunt wants me to help you understand how to use and control your energy."

"You can do that? Have you communicated with ghosts?" Brandon wondered why Choi's aunt didn't have him help Bellevue.

"I know a few tricks, but I have too many wants to follow my aunt's footsteps. For one, my wife is hot, and I want her every night," Choi joked.

"Tricks?" Brandon's expression tightened. Choi's lighthearted remark made him unsettled. "Is that how you see what she does?"

Brandon sat on the chair opposite Choi who sat on the sofa.

Suddenly, Brandon saw a man covered in blood—his hair burning—flames, smoke, blackened scarred skin—rushing him with a knife, yelling, "You're dead!"

"Jesus Christ! What the hell?" Brandon yelled. He fell back in his chair, raising his hands and arms to protect himself.

"I know a few tricks."

The image vanished, leaving Brandon's heart racing. He glared at Choi. "You did that? That was you?"

"If I were the ghost you were trying to communicate with right now, you would be in great pain, as I gained control of your mind and possessed you. I can teach you. I have a few talents."

"Okay, let's jump into it. How the hell did you do that?"

"Have you ever had a special connection with someone—one in which you knew things about that person before you were told? For example, you 'knew' your friend felt depressed, so you called and found out he had just broken up with his girlfriend. This connection causes you to sense what the person needs, wants, or does. These connections are often experienced between lovers or siblings, especially twins. Connections can be created and intensified to the point of communication."

Brandon, on the edge of his seat, looked at Choi intensely, ready to learn. "Is this part of the attractive energy that invites people to you?"

"Kind of, yes. When we shook hands yesterday, I connected with you through touch, creating a physiological response. If you were paying attention, you would have noticed a warm feeling develop in your chest and a tingling. That connection allows me to send emotions, ideas, and even images to you. If you connect to me, you can do the same. Over time and with lots of work, we could build that into telepathy."

"I've had a bond like that. Once my uncle and I got the same haircut and bought the same kind of shoes on the same day and then called each other at the same time to chat. It was weird."

"That connection can be strengthened so that what you share is intentional."

"Are you saying I could strengthen that bond into telepathy? I can use telepathy with my uncle?"

"It's not an easy thing, but yes," Choi said. "I have a strong connection with my wife, which, by the way," his lips curled into a knowing smirk, "makes for the best..."

Raising his hand in a halting gesture, Brandon interjected, "Okay. I get it. Keep going."

"My aunt can use telepathy; she talks to me. I can't make that same connection with her or anyone, but I can send images and emotions."

"I don't need any more of your images," Brandon quipped. "But how were you able to send me that first one? We only met that one time for a brief minute."

"That's my cop special." Choi laughed. "I use that one whenever I'm making an arrest or wanting to get the jump on someone. I can only do it if a connection has been established. But I've worked on it a lot. It's pretty good, right?"

"I'd say. So how does this work?"

"Let me teach you," Choi said. "The first thing you need to do is connect to your spiritual center, the feeling you get when you pray or meditate—communicating with your higher power or connecting to nature—life. That energy is a conduit for communication."

"My spiritual center? Interesting. That feeling is special. I'm not sure I can conjure it upon command."

"My aunt said you practice being mindful—aware of each moment, observing the colors, smells, and textures around you. Being mindful can connect you to your spiritual core. For me, I generate the feeling by giving thanks or feeling grateful for what I have. I have charities in mind where I donate money. That stimulates my spiritual center. Praying works, too—basically anything that makes you feel awake with the buzz of life pulsing from within."

"I'll need a few moments to create that feeling."

"Sure. But let me explain the rest of it first, so you know what we'll be doing."

"Good idea."

"You generate that spiritual energy and then touch the person you want to connect to. Touch is necessary because the body creates a 'love hormone' needed to make the connection stick. We'll shake hands. When we do that, I want you to look me in the eyes. Like touch, eye contact creates a chemical in the body that helps with bonding and commitment that's needed to establish the connection. Next, put the intention of connecting in your mind. Send the spiritual energy down your arm and into my hand. Then invite it back. You will feel your heartbeat quicken and maybe a slight tingle travel up your arm. That's when you know we are connected. It takes practice."

"Do you connect to everyone you meet?"

"I do."

"Could I stop you from connecting or disconnect from you?" Brandon asked.

"Yes, you can. I'll teach you how later."

"This process sounds a lot like making a talisman or inviting a ghost to me," Brandon said.

"Yes, it's exactly the same."

"Ok, let me make a connection to you."

They faced each other.

"I'm curious. Once I make the connection, do I have it forever?" Brandon asked.

"No, it has to be fostered. You need to think about the person, keeping them in your heart. A new connection lasts for maybe a day, two at best, unless it's cared for. It's easier to make that connection the second time and can be done by simply looking into the person's eyes. I'm still working on that skill. I can do it when I feel attracted to someone."

"Attracted? I thought your wife was hot."

"Not that kind of 'attracted'—if the person's energy is inviting."

"Ah, right. Sorry. Your aunt told me you thought my energy was attractive."

"Yes. That's why I gave you her contact information. I had a feeling you were perfect for this kind of thing."

"Cool. Thank you for that. Okay. Are you ready?" Brandon asked, shaking the nervousness out of his hands and taking a deep breath.

"I am. First connect to your spiritual center. I should warn you, though. By actively manipulating this energy, you may get visions or premonitions from time to time."

"You're going to have to explain that."

"Relatives who have passed away travel through this energy and may nudge you. Sometimes it's to keep their memory alive, and sometimes it's to guide you through a rough patch."

"Are you saying my dead grandfather may talk to me?"

"Not like that. Well, maybe, yes. No, it's just—if the road is easy to travel, then they may take it. It can be harmless—a thought, a whisper, a gut feeling."

"This seems a little much."

"This is only the beginning. Okay, activate your spiritual center, look me in the eyes, and intend to connect with me. Visualize a cord, like a cell phone connecting to the charger. Feel the warm energy swirling in your heart and send that into my hand. Then invite me to you."

Brandon sat on the floor, closed his eyes, and ran through reasons he was blessed. He thought about his mom's cooking and her love for him. He thanked his realtor for finding him this house and felt grateful for having a home to call his own. His job, though stressful, gave him great satisfaction. I am thankful for all that I have. I am thankful for my health, Brandon thought. He remembered how good he felt volunteering at Hope's Heart Youth Residential School, where kids with criminal records could get special support to improve their lives. Spiritual energy, warm and comforting, now emanated from his core.

Standing, Brandon looked Choi in the eye. I am connecting to you, he thought. Grabbing Choi's hand, he sent his energy into him. Then he drew the energy back.

"I felt the energy. Good, but you have to invite it back, not take it back."

"I'm not sure I understand."

"I think of it like opening the door in my heart and stepping aside so that the energy can come back." Seeing Brandon's confused look, Choi added, "Have you ever had a dog? When you let the dog out to pee, you don't rush it—you wait until it's ready to come back."

"Never had a dog, but I understand." Brandon closed his eyes and ran through the procedure in his mind. Opening them, he stared Choi in the eyes, shaking his hand and releasing the energy. He left himself open for it to return. Brandon felt his heart quicken as if he were excited. He felt buzzing in his muscles.

"You did it. That was great. Now we're connected."

Brandon put the idea of being thirsty in his mind, connected it to the energy in his heart, and sent it to Choi. "Do you feel that?"

"Are you trying to send me something?"

"Yes."

"You need to be thinking about me. What I mean is, I need to be the focus of the thought, and the feeling needs to be meant for me. Try again."

Brandon thought about Choi and how he must be thirsty. In his mind, he created an image of Choi holding water and drinking. His heart wanted Choi to know this feeling, so he opened up, releasing the energy.

Choi stood in anticipation.

Trying again, Brandon imagined Choi with a dry and parched throat. He envisioned Choi standing in a hot desert, panting; his lips were cracked, and he needed water. Conjuring an image of Choi licking his lips and holding a cool, refreshing glass of clear, sparkling water that he desperately wanted, Brandon combined it with his energy and sent it.

"Wow! You are good at this. Thirst. That's a great start."

"It worked! How would I know it worked if you didn't tell me?"

"Trust the process. Do you feel differently about me?"

"I feel like we're best friends."

"Exactly. You know it worked. Do you have any beers?"

Walking into the kitchen, Brandon asked, "You said something about feeling my heart beating faster. I did feel that."

"Making a connection affects the heart whereas communicating affects the emotions—the feeling is more encompassing. When you get stronger and have more control, you will actually feel my presence. I can be at home, but you will feel as if I'm standing next to you. And as we grow familiar with each other, our communication can become more complex. What I got from you was a sudden urge for a glass of water. I knew it was from you because I understand how this works. As you learn the difference between a projection and your own feelings, you can start to amplify the connection and receive more than feelings."

Brandon suddenly felt sleepy. "Whoa, I feel tired all of a sudden."

"No, you don't. There's no way you are tired right now. I wanted to show you how this can affect people. This is what a ghost can do." Choi paused. "You asked before if you can resist a connection or if you can disconnect. Let me teach you how, and we'll practice."

"Wait. This is a weapon. A connection can be used to manipulate people. You made me tired and sent that bloody guy at me."

"A ghost creates friction to grab hold and gain entry into your brain."

"Yes, but I'm talking about people. Can people who know how to connect use this skill as a weapon?"

"They can and they have in the worst possible ways."

"This is scary," Brandon said.

"This skill is a guarded secret, and those who know the art belong to the Circle which watches and protects. You are entering this circle and will need to follow certain rules and expectations or face the consequences."

"Shouldn't we be talking about that first?"

"No. My aunt will go over it later," Choi said. "Anyway, I wouldn't worry about it unless you plan on becoming a government spy."

"You have to tell me more. What am I getting into?"

Choi sighed. "It's not my place to say."

"Choi!" Brandon's eyes were hard. "I need to know."

Shifting from one leg to the other, Choi brought his hand to his chin and rubbed his jaw. "What you are learning is the bare-bones introduction to what is possible. Think of this task with Bellevue as a test. If you do well, then you'll be asked to learn more. As you do, the rules will be explained."

"Come on, Choi. Don't tease me like this. Let's hear it."

Scratching his head, Choi pulled out a chair. He sat at the kitchen table and motioned for Brandon to do the same. "Moral injustice blooms in the eyes of unchecked power. Therefore, the rules are basic: don't hurt people, don't manipulate others to accumulate power or to advance your own agenda. Simply put, don't use this power for personal gain, although it's not quite that simple."

"What do you mean?"

"This world, it's—it can be political. The history is long and ugly, and the rules were created to allow individuals leeway to help the greater good. For example, a Shaman named Sam Cros was given permission to manipulate others for the purpose of rising to power in the U.S. military. He's searching for a corrupt Shaman inside the White House."

"How does that help the greater good?"

Choi lifted a hand. "Let me start from the beginning. There are two different approaches to dealing with souls, Shamans and Banishers. They are the Yin and Yang of the spirit world. Shamans are patient, calm, and open. They want to help souls transcend. Banishers are aggressive. They engage, fight, and control. They force souls to transcend."

Brandon nodded. "The defenders of peace and justice vs the dark side."

"No. It's not good vs evil. There is no one right way. It depends on the situation and the factors at play. Balance is what matters." Choi took a second to think. "You are correct about a war. It lasted approximately two thousand years. It started when a Banisher known as Alexander the Great went on a rampage. After he was defeated, Banishers were suppressed, and their practice shunned. Shamans were seen as righteous. They viewed humans and souls as equals. They strived to help souls find peace so they could move into the next realm. Since they helped people communicate with their ancestors, they were loved and respected. The problem is that Shamans are often successful because they manipulate souls by embedding thoughts and feelings into their consciousness. And as you pointed out, they can also do this with humans. That's how Qin Shi Huang became the first emperor of China."

"He was a Shaman?"

"Yes. He used his skills to gain power, uniting China. His reign is controversial. Although he did a lot of great things, he was a tyrant. He willed his intentions into others, controlled their thoughts, and murdered those who resisted. Qin Shi Huang hated Banishers and tried to exterminate them. He murdered philosophers and scholars in search of Banishers and burned all books that referenced Banisher ideas or powers."

"The Great Wall of China," Brandon said. "It was built because of his ability to manipulate."

"Exactly. Banishers banded together to fight the emperor, eventually poisoning him by adding mercury to his drinks."

"What happened next?"

"Banishers made a comeback. People appreciate them for their speed and efficiency. If a soul possesses someone, it might take a Shaman a week or a month to help the soul move on, thus helping the person. Banishers solve the problem in a day. They view souls as leeches who rob the living of free will, so they force souls into the next realm. The problem is that the byproduct from forcing a soul to transcend is dark energy. It gives the person who absorbs the energy tremendous power. It's also extremely addictive, sending the Banisher into a crazed frenzy to find more souls. That was the problem with Alexander the Great—he needed war to get the souls he desperately desired. It's also why he was so successful.

"Genghis Khan started as a Shaman using his powers to unite the Mongol clans. Unlike Qin Shi Huang, Genghis Khan strived for religious tolerance and wanted to end the war. He invited Banishers into his realm. Through learning the powers of a Banisher, Genghis Khan became addicted to dark energy. In his need for souls, he conquered Northern China and most of Central Asia."

"You're joking, right?"

"No. Shamans blamed Banishers. Banishers pointed out he was a Shaman craving power." Choi went on to explain that Genghis Khan's demand for souls started the official Shaman-Banisher Wars which created horrific conflicts and evil rulers. Vlad III of Romania known as Vlad, the Impaler and Ivan IV, the first Tsar of Russia, were Shamans who destroyed many Banishers. Tamerlane and Napoleon became extremely powerful Banishers, conquering lands and taking the lives of many Shamans.

"In the early wars, before Genghis Khan, when Shamans were winning, Banishers disguised themselves as priests and joined the Catholics. Then a truly terrible thing happened; the Catholics created exorcisms or the extermination of souls." Choi told Brandon how the church saw both Shamans and Banishers as evil devil worshipers and set out to destroy them both. At war with each other and hunted by the church, the Catholics' exterminations went unchecked and rose in popularity. They became the only real solution for many, especially in Europe, to help someone who was possessed. "Understand that the Church thinks a possessed person has a demon or the devil in them. Their position is to shred the soul, destroying it for good. Once it's gone, the soul can no longer nudge, guide, or protect future family members."

"Jesus."

Choi grinned. "He didn't approve. Powerful Shaman though. One of the infamous tragedies from this war, although his death did start the religion."

Brandon rolled his eyes.

"Everything changed in 1923 with the first pairing of a Shaman and Banisher. The Banisher was Heinrich Himmler, and the Shaman was Adolf Hitler."

"What?! Hitler was a Shaman?"

"He was. How do you think he brainwashed all those people? Corrupt Shamans crave power. They only want to rule and destroy their enemies. Banishers become addicted to dark energy. That energy comes from sending souls to the next realm. The two men made possibly the worst pairing in world history. But World War II brought Shamans and Banishers together. Just before the end of the war, the Circle was created to maintain peace. They punish those who abuse their power and protect those who work inside the confines of the rules." Choi took a deep breath.

"What's wrong?"

"The time directly following the war was difficult. The Circle had just been established, and many didn't recognize its authority. My aunt said it was a dark time. She murdered several Shamans and Banishers in an attempt to gain stability."

"There's a few things you just said that give me pause. First: your aunt is maybe forty, at best. Second: if she's a murderer, I'm going to have to rethink this whole thing," Brandon said.

"This power allows you to manipulate energy and slow the aging process. The older members of the Circle are easy to spot. They're the ninety-five-year-olds still lifting weights in the gym. The murder charge is controversial. The Circle located individuals who were addicted to dark energy or abusing their power. It was my aunt's job to convince those individuals to cleanse their soul or have a priest shred it. Mind you, the Circle has stopped crazies such as Pol Pot and Idi Amin."

"That's not very impressive. Those guys murdered millions."

"Their reign of power was relatively short, though."

"What were their consequences?" Brandon asked.

"Idi Amin was forced to live a secluded life of prayer and meditation to cleanse his soul. Pol Pot evaded capture for many years and then refused to submit to his cleansing. His soul was shredded by a priest."

Brandon's thoughts were racing. He would be tempted by this power and judged for using it. He might be called to battle or asked to murder. This power raised serious ethical and moral issues, involving privacy, free will, and autonomy. "I'm having second thoughts about pursuing this path."

"A support network called the Community exists now. It was set up to help Shamans and Banishers regulate and control their urges. You won't be alone. The Circle has expanded to twenty-three members from around the globe. It's evolved and matured."

"That's reassuring."

"And there are different positions and ways to help. Watchers live in communities, monitor existing energy users, and help find new users."

Brandon wondered about Father Joseph. Was he one of these users? "The priest who performed the exorcism on the Education Center. Tell me about him."

"Father Joseph didn't go to the Center to exorcize Bellevue, he simply went to perform. The Circle has set out to undermine the Catholic religion to make exorcisms seem medieval and barbaric. However, the Church and the Circle still work together to destroy the souls of corrupt Shaman and Banishers. My aunt is the leader of the Circle."

"The leader?" Brandon's eyes widened. "Shit." He paused. "Why destroy the souls?"

"So they can't come back."

"What I'm learning is the tip of the iceberg. I understand now."

"A Banisher's power is as valuable as a Shaman's," Choi said. "My aunt is a Shaman, but she also holds the powers of a Banisher. She maximizes the advantages of each and minimizes the disadvantages. She sees the value and importance in being able to choose the best path for each individual situation."

"So going back to these rules—is there a list?"

"They are included in the training. The rules are a way of living and thinking that keep you grounded, safe, and free of temptation. The Community offers support and guidance."

"I'm learning to become a Shaman?" Brandon asked.

"It's safer—less contact with dark energy. It focuses on helping souls rather than fighting them."

"Are you a Shaman?"

"Me? No. I chose to marry and have kids over leading the life of a Shaman. My aunt did train me, but I became a watcher. I keep tabs on religious leaders, psychics, doctors, social workers—people who use this energy. If any of them become aware of their power and begin to abuse it, I report them to the Circle. I also report people who are possessed or have souls attached to them. Occasionally, I will help a soul transcend, but that's not my thing. It's too dangerous for me."

"That's why you connect to everyone you meet."

"That's right."

"Holy shit, Choi. Does anyone in the station know about this?"

"There are rumors. I'm called 'the psychic' for a reason."

"Shamans can't get married?"

Choi leaned his head to one side and raised his brows. "They can," he said hesitantly, "but the training is intense, and in order to master one's mind and emotions—it's difficult to have a family while doing that. Also, Shamans attract souls to them, so that should be considered before having a spouse and a baby."

"I see. How many watchers are there?"

"Not enough. My aunt is actively recruiting, but it's a struggle. Because of the potential this power holds, she can't recruit just anyone."

"Hence the lengthy interview she gave me."

"That's right."

"Okay. Let's keep going."

"We were talking about resisting a connection," Choi recalled.

"Right, tell me."

"To resist a connection or stop a ghost from taking control of your brain, open up."

"Open up."

"Sounds funny, right?"

"No, I remember your aunt talking to me about this," Brandon said.

"Being open leaves nothing for the soul to grab. Shall we practice?"

"I'm open."

"First you need to break the connection with me. To do that, relax your mind. Find a sound—birds, crickets, traffic, anything that has a rhythm, to center you.

Silence your inner voice and be—exist. I envision myself lying in a canoe, drifting down the river, with no cares in the world. Not thinking or caring breaks a bond, especially weak ones. For stronger bonds, the technique is more involved."

Brandon closed his eyes and relaxed. He could hear the refrigerator motor. Listening for other sounds, he noticed the ringing in his ears and focused on that, while clearing his mind of all thoughts. He laid his mind to rest in a pond of cool water. At this moment, nothing and no one mattered.

"Sometimes, I visualize myself meandering through my mind, opening all the little doors and windows," Choi offered.

Opening his eyes, Brandon said, "Your aunt also told me that."

"You disconnected from me on your first try. That's amazing."

"You feel the lost connection?"

"Yes. Now, don't allow me to connect with you. Stay open, and let the tingle wash over you like water off a plastic slide at a fun park."

"I'm ready."

Choi grabbed Brandon's hand and held it. Brandon felt a warm tingle move up his arm to his chest. His heartbeat quickened. The tingling sensation spread through his body, leaving him feeling—connected.

Choi shook his head. "Go ahead and disconnect. Let's try again. Don't focus on it."

Brandon closed his eyes, clearing his mind.

Choi grabbed Brandon's hand. The tingling returned, but Brandon relaxed his arm and breathed deeply and slowly. His heart twitched, but he let it be, as he imagined wading in a cool spring.

Choi tightened his grip. The tingling danced up Brandon's arm going straight for his chest, but he thought of it as a passing train and let it go by. Choi placed his hand on Brandon's shoulder. An intense jolt jabbed his heart. He reacted, thinking how it stung. His heartbeat quickened, the tingling spread. He connected.

"Damn! You really came at me. I wasn't ready for that. Do it again," Brandon insisted after disconnecting from Choi.

Choi squeezed, and the tingling sensation bolted into him. Brandon imagined covering himself with a blanket as the headlights of a passing car drove past. The tingle dissolved into darkness. When Brandon felt another tingling, he directed it to his lungs and exhaled, expelling it from his body. A final sensation came, reaching his heart, but this time Brandon smiled. He wrapped it in a chocolate box, tied it with a ribbon, and stuck it in the mail. The sensation dissipated.

"I'm impressed. You are so much better at this than I am. You should be the teacher."

"Thanks."

"Know that I'm not that strong, so be prepared to be hit by a train when facing Bellevue," Choi warned.

"I feel like I've learned a few tricks."

Choi chuckled, looking at Brandon with a playful smirk. "Tricks? Oh, is that how you see this?"

Brandon grinned at the playful jab. "Ah, I see what you did there," he replied with a laugh. "I guess tricks make the difference, though, don't they?"

"Indeed, they do." Choi returned to teacher mode. "The last thing I want to teach you is how to catch images and emotions. When ghosts probe you, they collect memories, stimulating thoughts to provoke you. The friction gives the ghost a way into your mind."

"I understand. I'm ready."

Choi shook Brandon's hand and connected.

"I'm going to send you a feeling. Don't engage with it. Observe it."

"Like I did when you tried to connect with me."

"No, it's different. With connecting, you can feel the energy traveling through you. Emotions stem from the brain. I'm embedding them, so they evolve from there. The trick is to discern which feelings originate from you and which are implanted by something else. Foreign emotions can't take root unless you engage with them. They fade quickly."

"So catch and observe," Brandon said.

"Exactly. Let me explain my trick."

Brandon pointed his finger at him and smiled.

Choi smirked with a quick nod. "I'm not an art person, so when I go to the museum with my wife to look at paintings, my mind is blank. I simply see a painting—I have no emotions, no thoughts, no opinions one way or another. I see a rectangular shape with colors. That's the concept here. Observe what I send you. Don't engage or think about it."

"Interesting."

"Ready?"

Brandon felt an itch in his knee and reached down to scratch it.

"You need to open up, my friend." Choi laughed.

Brandon smiled. "You threw me a curve ball. I wasn't expecting something like that."

Brandon's muscles tensed and his chest felt tight. Was he angry? He observed the feeling. It wasn't his emotion, he felt fine. It passed, and his body relaxed.

"That was pretty good. Try not to let what I'm sending you affect you physically. Bring the feeling into your mind's eye and look at it. Don't allow it access to your physical body."

"Detach from it?"

"No. Rise above it. You control the emotion—the emotion doesn't control you."

"Send me another one," Brandon insisted. Grief hit him hard. The heaviness of it gave him the urge to cry. He shook his head, catching the feeling, looking at it, rolling it around. The emotion tugged at him and dredged up an event that he didn't want to remember. Brandon ignored the grief, pushed away the urge to cry, and suppressed the triggered memory. The grief vanished.

"Beware. When a ghost does this, it's much more powerful. The sadness will be attached to an actual memory, so it'll be more difficult to work around or push away. Remember, simply observe. Practice monitoring your own emotions, catching them, and learning how they affect you."

"This whole thing is pretty crazy," Brandon admitted.

"But you are learning fast."

"You've obviously had some powerful experiences with this. Any stories you want to share?"

Choi took a moment, carefully considering his words. "I wasn't completely honest with myself. If you're not fully transparent about who you are and what you want or don't want, it can lead to trouble. Trust me, experiencing a ghost digging through your mind and controlling you isn't something you want to go through."

"I will take that advice to heart."

They practiced for another hour, laughing and telling stories about work, travel, and college.

Before Choi left, he gave Brandon a book about love. "Read this. It'll give you some tips and talking points when you engage Bellevue."

Brandon thanked him and Choi left.

The door closed and Brandon felt scared. He caught the feeling, looking at it. Did it come from Choi, or was it an emotion coming from himself? Brandon rolled it around in his head and observed it. He saw that he had a genuine fear. This might be more than he had anticipated.

Day Thirteen – Monday

Final Instructions

It was 6 am when Brandon woke. He felt drained. The strain of pushing his mind and body was starting to have a negative effect. After showering, he ate breakfast and opened his phone to look at the news when he saw that Yoona had sent him a message. "Will call you at 7 am, your time. Need a strategy for Bellevue."

At 6:52 am, Brandon called the station to let them know he'd be late. Then Yoona called. "Good morning, detective."

"What time is it for you?" Brandon asked curiously.

"It's 11:00 in the evening," Yoona said. "I know you must be busy, so I'll make this quick."

"It's fine. I already called in."

"Still, it's late for me. However, we have a few things to go over. My nephew tells me you learn very quickly. That's great news."

"Thank you."

"When you meet Bellevue, your job is to first listen. You need to find out as much information as possible. What does It want? Why is It taking people?"

"I thought it was looking for love."

"That's my assumption, based on the explanation you gave and from my experience with ghosts in similar situations. It's capturing people and holding them for many years, which makes me believe It's trying to find the love it lost, but you must be certain. More importantly, listening builds trust. Allow Bellevue to air Its frustrations and to talk with you about its suffering. Often that is enough to allow a soul to transcend."

"How do I begin?"

"First, approach Bellevue with empathy. State your intentions, and then ask questions and listen. Understand Bellevue."

"Be a detective," Brandon said under his breath.

"If you attract the ghost to you, Its first instinct will be to take control. So mind your training. Don't get distracted or emotional when It attacks. Stay calm and open minded. Direct the conversation, and keep it moving in the direction you want. Learn what It needs."

"Open is the key then. Open-ended questions, open mind, and no judgements," Brandon summarized.

"Exactly. If I'm correct and It's looking for love, then introduce the idea that love starts with loving oneself which entails fulfilling one's purpose. If It loves Jared, how is It helping him fulfill his purpose? Love includes understanding, respect, and trust."

"Should I ask about John Mills?"

"I would, yes." Yoona said. "Try to get Bellevue to disclose Its story about John. I would bet money that the underlying problem is in their history together."

"Thank you. I will."

"Brandon, I would avoid sending thoughts or emotions to Bellevue. Attempting to manipulate It at this juncture would be a mistake."

"I wouldn't have even thought of that. But I understand."

"When will you make your talisman?" Yoona asked.

"Tonight."

"Good. Let's talk one more time before you meet Bellevue."

"I'll call you when I'm ready," Brandon said.

"I'll be expecting your call. Have a good day. Be safe."

Brandon closed the app, put the dishes in the sink, grabbed his things, and headed to work. "Let's go make some connections and practice my new skills," he said. First stop, Stephanie Mitchell's house. As he started the car, he got a text from his mom. "Great News! Call when you have time."

Zombies and Jedis

"Leah, wake up!"

Leah opened her eyes. Barb stood over her, holding Grandma Carol's book. "What time is it?"

"Almost 7:30. You didn't set your alarm? It looks like you fell asleep reading. What time did you end up sleeping?"

"I don't know. After 1 am."

"Hurry up and get ready. I don't want to be late. Grandma made oatmeal pancakes with bananas for breakfast. I'll wait for you in the living room."

Leah dressed and ate breakfast. "Barb, I'm ready. Let's go." She opened the front door.

She was struck by a series of flashes. "Leah Davenport, can we talk with you?"

Slamming the door, Leah hollered, "Shit! They found me."

Barb looked at her. "We knew they would. Come on. Let's get this over. At least we'll have an excuse to be late."

"I've already talked with them while hiking on the trail. Most of their questions have nothing to do with my dad going missing. They want to sensationalize my situation."

"If we make the news, it's a free pass to skip first period."

"Well, that sounds enticing." She rolled the idea around. First period was physical education, and she wasn't in the mood. "Okay, let's go." Leah said.

They walked down the steps, heading into a group of reporters and photographers.

"Leah, how are you feeling?"

"Shitty."

"Is it too soon for you to be going back to school?"

"Yes!"

A barrage of questions hit her next. "Have you heard from your dad? Have you received any news about your father? Has your grandfather contacted you? Is he worried?"

Leah put her hands up. "Can I get a second to respond? My grandfather and I don't—"

"In your statement to the police, you said your father had a date with the lady who owned the Bellevue House. Who was that lady?"

Leah glared at the reporter. "Seriously?" In a strong, firm voice, she said, "First, I have not heard any news regarding my father. Next, I'm assuming you want to know about my grandfather, Bill Stillen. It's been a while since I've talked with him. My phone isn't accepting calls at the moment. Finally, I don't know the lady's name. I told the police what I recalled my dad saying."

"Why did you say she owned the Bellevue House?"

"I have to go. I'm going to be late for school."

Barb and Leah pushed past the reporters who volleyed more questions. Getting into the car, Barb drove Leah away.

"That was weird." Barb exhaled.

Leah leaned over, covered her face, and grunted. "I hate this!"

"You could have told them the truth." Barb smiled.

"A ghost has my dad." Leah laughed awkwardly.

Barb's smile grew. "I would have loved to see their reactions, not to mention the headlines."

Sinking into her seat, Leah complained, "Now I get to be pressed about this at school. This day sucks already."

"You must be tired. How much did you read last night?"

"A lot. The first half of the book delves into philosophical ideas—rising above emotion, freeing oneself from attachment and greed, and understanding consciousness, which is wicked. Our conscious lives in our soul, while our subconscious resides in our body; it's a defense mechanism that protects us. Oh, the part about life force and energy is really intriguing, and the idea about detaching was interesting, too."

"You're talking to me as if I understand what you're saying."

"Sorry. But, Ooh, I have to tell you about Banishers."

"Sure."

"They have mind-bending powers." Leah paused, noticing that she felt alive again. Her mind and spirit were expanding, and she embraced this newfound sense of vitality. Knowing she had the ability to save her dad empowered her. The world was full of possibilities, and Leah reveled in the joy of rediscovering herself.

Barb glanced at her. "You okay?"

"Great. So, Banishers battle souls in their minds. When souls possess people, they access their memories. When people think about those memories, souls ride those thoughts deeper into their minds. To avoid being taken by souls, people must engage with the memory and change it—fight with someone in that memory."

"So if the memory were of you and me, you would fight me?" Barb asked.

"Exactly. This way the soul has to react and engage, which allows the Banisher to bend the mind, moving the interaction from their brain into the soul's consciousness. There, they can take control of the soul and make it transcend. Cool, right?"

"Nonsense, right?" Barb returned sarcastically. "Just throwing the idea out there."

"Oh, man, you have no idea. There is a door in the soul's consciousness. The Banisher forces the soul to this door which pulls it through. If the Banisher disengages too soon, the soul can escape the pull and won't transcend, making it more powerful. But—and here is the super dangerous part—if the Banisher doesn't disengage with the soul soon enough, both the soul and the soul of the Banisher get sucked through the doorway and transcend together. This means—and this is the best part—that the Banisher's living body is left here, in our world, without a soul. The body wanders around attacking people, trying to find a new soul."

"Now I know that book is full of shit."

"This is how zombies are made!" Leah laughed.

"That doesn't make sense. If a body doesn't have a soul, wouldn't it die?"

"Normally, yes. But that's because when a soul disengages with the body, it turns something off. A Banisher leaves the body without flipping that switch, expecting to return. When it doesn't, the subconscious takes over; the body goes on autopilot."

Barb shook her head in disbelief.

"There is one more way zombies are made—through Soul Harvesters."

"Oh my god. I don't want to know. What's next? Vampires? Jedis?"

"I think Bellevue is a Soul Harvester," Leah said.

"You're tricky. Okay, tell me. What is that and why do you think so?"

"A Soul Harvester steals souls from living bodies. It literally rips the soul out of the body. The Harvester can keep the soul and use it to become stronger or make the soul transcend and absorb the energy from that transition."

"Why do you think Bellevue is doing that?" Barb asked.

"Because Father Joseph fell into a coma. That's what happens if the Harvester keeps the soul. And Nong is in a type of coma, too. She's still tied to Bellevue. If the Harvester sends the soul on, the body can become a zombie."

"Hmm. So you're saying that Bellevue has Father Joseph's soul, part of Nong's soul, and your dad. I'm having a hard time believing anything you're saying. What other garbage is in that book?"

"The book says Soul Harvesters are rare, and if you find one, report it to the Circle immediately."

"Is there a phone number or an email address?"

"No."

Laughing, Barb asked, "How do we report it then?"

"That's as far as I read last night, but you'll like this. When a Banisher fights the soul, that fight sounds a lot like the movie, The Matrix."

"What do you mean?"

"The fight scenes have no rules or laws. They take place in your mind. You can do anything. You're only limited by your imagination or knowledge. Skill isn't required."

Barb slowed as she approached the school. She frowned. "The more you talk, the more you sound like a nutcase. I'm still trying to come to terms with the idea that Dan talked to a ghost and that It was my house, which was also my imaginary friend."

"Be very careful if you ever talk with Bellevue," Leah warned. "When a ghost talks to you, it's in your brain and can manipulate your senses. You can't trust anything you see or feel, unless the ghost is a relative protecting you."

"Bellevue is like a relative, isn't It?"

"No. It has killed, kidnapped, harvested a priest's soul, manipulated Dan—Bellevue is not looking out for your best interests."

"Did you tell Dan? He thinks Bellevue is decent."

"Still? Ugh." She rolled her eyes, muttering under her breath, "How can he possibly think Bellevue is decent? It manipulates him."

"Have him read that part of the book so he knows."

"Good idea."

"What are you planning to do after you finish the book?"

"I'm going to go through the steps to learn how to make souls transcend. I'm not sure which approach is better though, the Banishers' way or the Shamans'. I'm thinking the Banisher method may be easier, but it seems more dangerous." Leah pictured her father trapped in the house as she fought with Bellevue. If she got sucked into that door and transcended along with It, her dad would be devastated. She knew he would rather trade his life than risk hers. The more dangerous method probably wasn't the best. "Anyway, this is my backup plan. I'm still hoping the detective can save him."

Stay in Bed

Choi woke and kissed his wife, telling her to stay in bed. He called in sick, made breakfast, and went into his son's bedroom.

"Good morning, Jun. How did you sleep?" Choi rustled his son's hair, leaning down to kiss his forehead as Jun groaned. "I made you French toast."

Jun perked up. "With powdered sugar?"

Choi smiled. "Yes, with powdered sugar."

Choi dressed his son, fed him, and took him to school. When he returned home, he rushed into the bedroom. Today was for his wife, and his anticipation of their sex play made his body thrum with excitement.

A Life Together

Jared finished cleaning up from breakfast and went into the library to relax and think. He needed to talk some sense into Bellevue. Jared recalled a conversation he had had with Leah that might work with Bellevue.

"I know you want to talk," Bellevue said.

"I do."

"I have surmised what you want to say already. You are thinking about the conversation you had with your daughter after your wife left. How does that relate to us?"

"Why have you captured me?"

"I told you already."

"Love. What is love to you? Abduction? Imprisonment? Control?"

"Devotion," Bellevue countered. "Spending time together, showing affection, giving everything to the one who is with you. I am doing this for you, taking care of you, giving you all of me. I'm happy you are here. I feel comfortable with you inside me."

"What about respect? Respecting boundaries, respecting relationships, respecting privacy, respecting space, opinions, thoughts, ideas, ambitions. Where is the respect? There is no love here."

"Ambitions?" Bellevue laughed. "Oh, Jared. I feel your love already. You study and admire me. You have for years."

"Admiration isn't love. Love is much more."

"Love starts with attraction and desire," Bellevue said. "You know that. The longer we are together, present, and share experiences to create memories, the more our love will grow. You and Nong have a spark and share a connection. That will happen with us."

"Taking away my freedom and controlling me are not the memories and experiences that create love. They create anger, hate, and resentment. Nong and I are close because we are both prisoners trying to help each other esc... survive."

"Escape. You are scared! You feel trapped."

"I am trapped!"

"Yes! Trapped in a job you hated. Trapped in a house you never made your own, dreaming about someone, something, that will never happen. Here I am. Your dream house. Someone who loves you. Nong is someone you are infatuated with. You have everything you need, here with me. Embrace me."

Jared squeezed his eyes closed, not wanting to hear anymore.

"I remember your first visit. You were bored, lonely, and depressed. Your friends were lost—close friends scattered, off living life, while you moped about and fell asleep on the couch in your work clothes, daydreaming of the past. It's pathetic! Our life together has fantastic potential. We can learn music, poetry, and art. You can swim and start an indoor garden. We can read stories and cook magnificent meals. I know you would love to build a model of the city, like in Beetlejuice. We can do that! I will give you everything you need to remake yourself. I can make you happy because you make me happy. I appreciate you. In time, you will feel the same way toward me. The more moments of joy we have together, the more in love we will become."

Jared was lost in the possibilities. Everything Bellevue was saying was true. He had felt more alive these past few days than he had the past three years. Dreaming about Stacy and capturing his former glory as a brilliant architect had made him melancholy. He had trapped himself, and the only way to untrap himself was to reinvent himself. But, no! This situation was wrong. It was missing.... The word joy bounced around his mind. "The more moments of joy?" Jared repeated. "I...." His voice caught as he tried to find his thoughts. With a deep breath, he seethed, "Bellevue, you have taken away the one joy that means more to me than anything else in the world."

"Ah! But you have already been preparing yourself," Bellevue lowered Its voice, "for the day that is coming." Then Its inflection turned evil. "She will leave you."

An image of Stacy formed in his head, standing in her Issey Miyake dress the day they had first met. A lump formed in Jared's heart. The pain burned. He'd soon be all alone. These next few months with Leah would be his last before she moved to California. Her visits would become increasingly sporadic as the years passed. "You are robbing me of my remaining time with her. I resent you for this. I'm frustrated and angry. This isn't love." Calm enveloped him—his eyes grew heavy and his mind fogged. "Stop manipulating me!"

"I need you to relax, Jared. I have a plan. Trust that I will take care of you and Nong. I finally understand what I've been doing wrong. I will fix it."

"What does that mean?"

"I have an idea. I need to think about it more, but I'm certain you will be satisfied."

"Why does that frighten me?" Feeling panicky, Jared blurted, "Why don't we work together on a plan. If you are looking for love, we can date first. I can come visit you, maybe even sleep over, then I can also have a life with my daughter. That will show compassion, an essential ingredient to love."

"I will think about that. Now, you have music lessons. Please go to the piano."

"What?! You expect me to learn the piano now? We're having a discussion h..., Ahh..." The hot stinging poke pushed Jared to comply. He made his way to the music room, saying, "We haven't finished talking. I expect to continue this conversation later."

Negotiation 101

Returning to the police precinct, Brandon glanced at the top of his desk, shaking his head, "This is getting old." He picked up half a dozen barrettes, adding them to the growing pile filling the top left drawer of his desk. Reading through his emails, he replied to several before beginning the tedious and beloved part of being a detective: the paperwork. The Mitchell case had been solved. The ex-husband had attacked Monica. Stephanie had learned about her mother and Dimitri's affair during her skirmish with her ex-boyfriend outside the Spa when he used the information and his fist to hurt her. After calling Dimitri to confirm the affair, Stephanie called her father. She told her dad that she would phone her mom and ask for a ride home. He could confront her about the affair at her friend's house. Both had been arrested. Brandon felt bad for Stephanie. Witnessing her father beating her mother to a pulp was not part of her plan. Looking back, he truly understood why she had been so nervous and unable to think clearly. The whole scenario had scarred her for life.

As Brandon typed, he watched an empty desk to his right, waiting for Detective Rodriguez, the crisis negotiator, to arrive.

Brandon finished his reports and filed them, then called his mom. "Good morning, Mom. You texted me earlier."

"It's a fantastic morning!" Judy replied.

"What happened?"

"I called to invite you to a special dinner?"

"What's the occasion?"

After a slight pause and then a giggle, Judy proclaimed, "Jae proposed, and I accepted. We're having an engagement dinner in three weeks. He invited his son to come from Korea. Will you join us?"

"Of course I'll come. Congratulations, Mom."

"I was nervous that our plans for marriage would bring up painful memories."

"Don't be ridiculous, Mom. I wouldn't miss it for the world." Detective Rodriguez entered the room. "Mom, I have to go. I'll talk to you later. I'm happy for you."

"Okay. Talk later. Bye, sweetie."

Walking quickly to Rodriguez, Brandon asked, "Detective Rodriguez, hi. May I shake your hand?"

"What for?" Rodriguez asked.

Brandon grasped his hand, looked into his eyes, and connected with him. "I think your position and skills are very impressive."

"Ah, man. Stop blowing smoke up my ass," he growled, pulling his hand away in disgust. He glanced at his arm and turned it, as he moved his fingers in and out of a fist. "What do you want?"

"I'm wondering if you could give me some pointers. What steps do you take in a hostage situation?"

"Why? Your girlfriend holding your porn magazines hostage?" Rodriguez laughed as he patted Brandon's shoulder.

"No, I'm serious." Brandon sent him feelings of dread.

Rodriguez stopped, turning to face Brandon. "What's going on?"

"I need some advice. If someone had a hostage, what would be a plan of action?"

"Is this hypothetical or do you have a real situation on your hands?"

"Simply for educational purposes."

Rodriguez studied Brandon before nodding in assent, "All right, I'll give you the ABC's of negotiation, but don't be stupid enough to try handling a situation by yourself. Call me."

"Absolutely."

Rodriguez shook his head. Digging in his desk drawer, he found a book and slapped it on the table—Never Split the Difference: Negotiating as If Your Life Depended on It. "Read this."

"I only need a few pointers."

Rolling his eyes, Rodriguez began, "People want to be heard and understood, so the most important thing is to listen and make sure they know you are listening. You ask open-ended questions, understand their perspectives, and repeat what they say by paraphrasing their words back to them. Having someone truly listen makes the perp feel heard and they are more likely to relax.

"Next, show empathy. Let them know you understand their position. Build trust. Once you've established a rapport, you can start to solve the problem and come up with a plan of action."

"Attentive listening is the key?"

"It's the most important. But the real trick is to reframe the situation so that you and the perp are working together—fighting against the true enemy: the problem. By restructuring who the guy understands you to be, you become teammates."

"That's brilliant." Brandon felt a sense of ease. He could do this—question, listen, work with Bellevue instead of against It. "Thank you, Rodriguez. That's exactly what I needed."

Rodriguez pulled Brandon aside as Maggie passed with a handful of community safety posters. "I feel like I should be worried about you."

"No, I'm good. Thanks."

Rodriguez's phone rang. Brandon gave him a nod and a smile and was about to leave when he saw an envelope with "Mitchell Case" written on it. Brandon grabbed it. Inside were bets as to who had perpetrated the attack. Odds were on the ex-husband. Brandon felt like a complete rookie. Judging from the bets, half the force had suspected the ex-husband before Brandon had even known about him.

Rodriguez covered the mouthpiece and said, "It's always the ex."

Inside the Bubble

Dan drove up 175th, his old house standing where the Education Center should have been. Stopping the car, he let the soft panic that flared in his heart dissipate before continuing along the drive and parking. He couldn't believe what he was seeing.

Opening the car door, he stepped out and looked at the house his dad had built. In awe and disbelief, he approached the front door. He hadn't been sure he wasn't hallucinating Bellevue as his sister suspected, but here It stood. Was Jared really here? Why had he come? The door opened for him.

"I'm so happy you came. You have made my day," Bellevue proclaimed in jubilation.

Dan gawked. "A small part of me thought maybe I was dreaming, but I'm not."

"No, you are not."

Dan paused looking around the foyer before walking into the ballroom.

"Daniel, thank you for talking with your sister about me. I miss her so much. She doesn't need to be angry or afraid of me. I hope you can tell her that. And your girlfriend is wrong about me, but you know that already."

"How do you...? Right. The book said you could read my thoughts."

"I can see your memories and hear your thoughts," Bellevue confessed. "However, I cannot find the reason for your visit."

"I don't know why I'm here." Dan sauntered from the dining room to the kitchen, reminiscing—being uncomfortable navigating tense dinners and feeling his mother's warmth while eating fresh baked cookies. "I guess I'm curious, nostalgic, and a little worried about you."

"Don't worry about me—priests are weak. Their desires rule them. Such hypocrites."

"It's pretty amazing how you know everything in my mind."

"Not everything. The mind is like a book. I have to read through it to learn what's there."

"Is Jared here? Can I see him?" Dan asked, peeking into the library, and then going down the hall to the office.

"He is, but he's busy right now. If you come back later, you can meet with him. You should bring Leah and Barb, too. You would be a nice surprise for him."

"They are afraid of you. I'm not supposed to be here. No one knows I came."

"I know. I'm sorry. You haven't betrayed your friends and family. You care about me, and I care about you. Caring about each other is not a betrayal to the others."

"I guess." Dan walked back through the ballroom. "I loved running around in this room. I imagined I was flying a Black Sky jet through mountains." He stood in appreciation, and with a soft smile, he added, "It made me feel big and small at the same time. The world was mine, yet I was a tiny boy in a huge house."

"I loved watching you running around."

"I feel like I'm home—like I belong here."

"I am your home. You belong to me. You and your sister will be happy with me. I'll take care of you."

Dan didn't respond. He walked through the glass corridor and admired the garden. Taking the stairs, he headed toward his bedroom.

"What were you doing at the public library yesterday?"

"Barb wanted to understand you better. We looked at a bunch of books to learn more about who you are. The books we read said you are stuck here, looking for something. Do you know what you're looking for? Have you ever thought about transcending?"

"I have only longed to be here with you, to see you and your sister again, to love you as I once did. I also believe I may be able to regain my physical form. If I can, would you stay with me?"

"What happened to the Education Center? It looks like you've already regained your physical form."

"No, I'm in your mind. I can only present myself to people who know me."

"I'm walking around the Education Center right now? Can people see me?"

"Technically, you are in the Education Center, yes, but no, no one can see you because you are inside of me."

"That's confusing." Dan scratched his head.

"I'm like a bubble."

Dan stood in his bedroom. It felt naked without his stuff. As he was about to leave, all of his things appeared. "Whoa!" he exclaimed with surprise as his room returned to exactly how he remembered it.

"My action figures!" Dan ran over and picked up two Black Sky fighting figures. "Hai yah," he said as he had them fight each other. "Echo Three, submit to your master." "Never!" Dan smiled at the memory. Putting them down, he sat on his bed looking at his posters, Guns and Roses and X-Men, and the box of balls, basketball, soccer, baseball that he played with in the driveway. "I love this."

"Are you hungry? I have ingredients for Vietnamese sandwiches in the kitchen."

"No, I'm fine."

"I've got some grape soda. That used to be your favorite."

"Is it real or in my mind?"

"It's actually juice, but it'd be real to you."

"I'm okay. Thanks anyway."

"I have a pool now. Do you want to go swimming?"

"No, I have to work soon."

Bellevue sent Dan a wave of appreciation.

Dan touched his heart and smiled. Standing, he exited his room. "What is it you want anyway? Why are you here? Why haven't you transcended?"

"I miss you and Barb. If you could bring her and Leah the next time you come, we can talk about an arrangement that's best for all of us. Being a family would make our lives perfect. Will you do that? Will you ask them to come?"

Dan wanted to think about that question, but his mind felt blocked. He had an urge to say yes, but it felt wrong. "Maybe. I don't know."

"But you'll discuss it with them, right?"

I'll talk to my sister and Leah, was the thought that popped into his head. It felt strange. Did he really think that? He hesitated before finally saying, "Sure."

"And you'll come visit me later?"

"Yes." Dan descended the stairs, heading for the front door. "Bellevue, I need to talk with Jared. He has to see his daughter."

"I understand. Let me try talking some sense into him first."

"You need to convince Leah's dad to visit her. She misses him. If he asked her, I bet she would come live here with her dad. The house is big enough for all of us. We could all live here."

"That is my ultimate dream. But it'd be a lot easier if they came to me. I'm positive Jared would return to his normal self if Leah visited." Bellevue's voice lowered. "Jared is dealing with a lot of pain and grief, regret about his divorce. He's depressed. Hiding here is an escape for him. I'm honestly worried."

"I'll talk to Leah—tell her what's happening."

"Thank you, Daniel. When will I see you again?"

"Give me a few days."

"I love you, Daniel."

Dan didn't reply. Returning to his car, he drove away. It wasn't until he was on the highway heading into downtown that his head cleared. He felt twisted. His friend was pushing him to do something he didn't want to do. Barb would never agree to go to the Center; he didn't want to ask her. And Leah? She was planning to fight Bell, not become part of his family. The words, "I love you, Daniel," played in his mind. It didn't feel like love.

The Talisman

At home in his study, Brandon looked at earlier sketches he had drawn of talismans. Perusing several websites containing images of symbols and their meanings, Brandon found a variety from different cultures—Chinese, Japanese, Sanskrit, Egyptian, Native American, Celtic, and African Adinkra. He recalled Yoona's instructions, "The symbol doesn't matter. The energy and meaning you give it does."

As Brandon studied the different symbols and their meanings, he wrote what Bellevue was to him—a soul, alive after death, hidden, wanting love, but angry, violent, and selfish. Its physical form had been destroyed, but Its soul remained vigilant to exist.

Brandon searched for symbols that had those meanings. Taking symbols from various cultures and religions, he created a talisman that meant Bellevue to him.

He practiced drawing it several times. When he felt he was ready, he took a piece of red cloth, some black paint, and spread newspaper on the floor of his study.

Glimpsing the design he had drawn, Brandon closed his eyes and conjured every detail he could of Bellevue—the photos at Professor Jae Yun's house, blueprints, land deeds, protests, the blessings, tourists, the fire, Debra Mills autopsy report, Tyler and Amanda's reports, their brain scans, Nong, Jared, his headache at the Center, Dan, Barb, Leah, the priest collapsing, and the area where It stood—the trails, trees, hills, and rocks surrounding It. Finally, Brandon pictured the view of the valley.

Those memories stirred a range of emotions—fear, pity, concern, wonder, mystery, disbelief, confusion, awe, and love. He let those feelings build in him, merging the symbol, the memories, and the emotions.

Opening his eyes, he dipped the brush into the paint, sending the energy down his arm and into the bristles as he began painting the symbol on the cloth. The fabric soaked up Brandon's life force, draining his strength with each stroke.

As he finished the talisman, Brandon lay on the floor, exhausted. He fell asleep.

Lies

A knock came at Leah's door.

"It's open."

Entering the room, Dan closed the door behind him. Leah was lying on the bed, reading Grandma's book.

"Learning anything?"

"Yeah, lots. There's so much more to life than we know. Shamans are able to leave their bodies, exploring their surroundings with their souls. Talk about a super spy! It's crazy. The first step is to be mindful of your body, every muscle, tendon..." Leah saw that Dan wasn't interested in what she was saying, so she asked, "What's up? You okay?"

"I'm thinking about Bellevue. We should go talk to It again, learn what It wants, and see your dad—make sure he's okay."

"I want to wait for the detective," Leah said. "He told us not to go back. If he can't do anything, then, yeah, I'll go with you again."

"How about Barb? Should we take her, too?"

"I don't think she would go. We can talk about that later."

"I'm surprised you don't want to go right now."

"I saw how It manipulated your thoughts and emotions. This book makes it abundantly clear that you can't trust anything you see or feel when communicating with a soul. You need to read that part of the book. I'll find it."

"No," Dan muttered. With a hesitant pause, he added, "I... I believe you."

Leah felt the discomfort in Dan's voice and looked at him. He couldn't hold her gaze, shifting his eyes away. *Did he just lie to me?* "Dan, we need to take precautions before engaging with Bellevue. And that starts with make a talisman to protect ourselves. If we go without one, we could end up possessed and captured."

"I guess that makes sense. When will you call the detective?"

Dan's impatience was making Leah feel uneasy. "Let's wait a few days. I'm sure he'll call us."

"I can't believe you're so calm. I'm going crazy."

Why is he going crazy? It's my dad who was captured. "I know where my dad is, and the detective has a plan. With this book, I know what needs to be done to free my dad. That gives me hope. Are you having second thoughts about making Bellevue transcend? Why are you feeling unsettled?"

"It's not that. I'm..." Dan trailed off in thought.

"What?"

"Was your dad depressed? Did he seem upset about divorcing your mom?"

Leah studied Dan. He wasn't acting like himself. She wondered where he was going with this line of questioning. "Depressed? No. I might say he was melancholy. He definitely wasn't himself. Why do you ask?"

"I was thinking that maybe your dad went to Bellevue because he needed a break from reality. To hide—sort things out in his mind."

"Snap, Dan," Leah retorted, her concern evident in her softening tone. "Bellevue really got you." She motioned for him to join her. "Lie down next to me. I'm going to read parts of this book, so you understand what's happening to you."

Leah moved to make room for Dan, who lay down with his head next to her stomach. His arm was around her waist, and he closed his eyes. She ran her fingers through his hair, found the section of the book she was looking for, and read to him.

I'm Ready

Brandon rolled onto his back as he lay in his study. It was early in the morning, still dark outside. Glancing at the talisman, he felt the energy in it. After closing the paint can and throwing the brush away, he called Yoona.

"Good morning, detective. It's early for you. Are you just going to bed now?"

"No, I finished the talisman last night, and it drained me. I fell asleep as soon as I finished it."

"Oh yes, I should have warned you about that. Sorry. But now I know it worked." Yoona continued, "The talisman will help you. Keep it in front of you. Use it to fight off Bellevue's attacks."

"I thought being open would keep It from attacking me."

"You are still inexperienced. If Bellevue gets inside you, and the pain is too great, use the talisman to draw It out so you can recenter yourself. Once you are finished with the conversation, and Bellevue is drawn out, fold the talisman and you'll be safe."

"Okay. I understand."

"Choi will drive you. He won't engage, but he will send you calming images that will help you. Connect with him before you go. Draw on his power."

"Are we sure Choi isn't the better option to communicate with Bellevue?"

"He has turned away from that life. As I told you before, it takes a very special person with a specific mind-set, and Choi has desires to do other things. Understand that Bellevue is a baby when it comes to ghosts. It doesn't know the extent of Its powers or how to use them. If Bellevue were more experienced, or if I saw that It was malicious, I would not have taught you."

"Sending the priest to the hospital seems pretty malicious to me."

"No. Bellevue was defending Itself."

"Defending Itself?"

"I can explain another time, but for now, focus on staying open and relaxed. Whatever you do, don't worry. Choi will be with you, and I'm connected to him. You have all the support you need to succeed."

"Okay. I'll call you tomorrow night and let you know what happened."

"Good luck, detective. Try to get some sleep before you go."

"Thank you." Brandon hung up, retiring to his bedroom. Tomorrow was the day. He felt nervous, but ready. This would be his first time encountering a ghost. Rolling over on his side, he cleared his mind and slept.

Day Fourteen – Tuesday

Window to Freedom

"Come on, Nong. Share one of your favorite songs with us, one from your native Taiwan," Jared said.

"It's Thailand," Nong and Bellevue corrected him simultaneously.

"I'm so sorry. But in my defense, Bellevue was manipulating my memories. It's Thailand. Got it."

After breakfast, Bellevue connected Jared and Nong, bringing them to the media room. Jared could feel excitement and happiness from Bellevue, who wanted to celebrate. Appeasing It, they sang, laughed, and danced along with the karaoke machine.

"I do remember this one song," Nong said. "It's by Nicole Theriault. It's about a girl who is friends with a boy, and everybody thinks they are dating. The chorus is, 'Mai Chai,' which means, 'not true.' Can you find it, Bellevue? The song is 'Mai Chai Mai Chai.'"

"Ah, yes. I believe I've found it." Bellevue began to play an upbeat pop song. "Is this the one?"

"Yes, this is it. It's been a while since I've heard it, but I'll try to sing along," Nong said, happily.

She began singing, "Nai Krai Bok Wa Raow Na Rak Gan," but suddenly the music stopped. Neither Jared nor Nong could feel Bellevue.

"Is It gone?" Jared asked.

"Yes, I believe so."

"Okay, let's free you."

"Now?"

"Yes, before It comes back."

"I need to relax first. I'm not sure where I am." Nong took in a deep breath and slowly let it out, relaxing as she exhaled.

Jared did the same. He closed his eyes and focused on Nong, sending his energy to her.

"No, no. Let me invite you to me," she whispered.

When Jared felt her energy, he followed it. They were in the middle of her mind, a dark room with small windows looking out into the world. They could see a woman in a pink uniform emptying the trash.

"Now's our moment. Ready?" Jared asked, adrenaline flooding his body. He prayed desperately for this to work.

"I'm ready," she said.

Jared rose and pushed Nong with all his might. "Ask for help!"

At the Sunnyside Psychiatric Hospital, inside Nong's room, an environmental technician wearing a pink uniform worked, restocking hygiene supplies, wiping down surfaces with disinfectant, and changing the trash bags. "Your room is nice and clean," the lady murmured to Nong, who was sitting on the bed in a catatonic state. Grabbing the trash bag, the lady turned to leave when Nong stood, stretched her arms toward the woman, and screamed, "Help!"

The woman jumped in fright, dropping the garbage. "Jesus, Mary, and Joseph!"

Nong's scream filled the halls, sending chills through everyone who heard it from three rooms away, including the doctor on duty, who rushed into the room.

"Help!" Nong repeated. Her eyes were big and round, her face desperate and frantic.

"Nong, I'm here," said Doctor Syrena, grabbing her hand, checking her vitals. "I need you to slow your breathing. Calm yourself."

"I need help. Please! Help me."

"I'm here. How can I help?"

"Jared, I'm stuck. I can't get free." Nong's voice quivered, struggling.

The doctor looked puzzled. "Nong, do you know where you are?"

"I'm trapped," Nong cried.

"Trapped? You aren't trapped. I'm here to help you."

Nong slipped back into her vegetative state. Her head dropped, her body limped, and she began to mumble. The doctor sat Nong down, where she began rocking back and forth.

"Can you ask a nurse to come?" the doctor said to the lady standing behind her.

"Yes, ma'am. Right away."

The doctor shined her pen light into Nong's eyes.

"Ahh!" Nong screamed again, her body jumping back to life.

"Ahh!" The doctor screeched, dropping her light.

"It's not working," Nong declared, desperation heavy in her voice.

"Nong, what's not working? What are you trying to do?" the doctor asked.

"I'm stuck. I can't get out!"

"Calm. Slow breaths. Tell me where you are?"

"I'm in a room. I'm trapped."

"Can you describe the room?"

"It's all black with windows."

"Is there a door?"

"No."

"What can you see through the windows?"

"You!"

"Ok, I can help you. You said you are trapped. How? Take a moment to look around and tell me what you see."

"Ties. I'm tied down. My hands, feet, and waist. I can't get free."

"Nong, listen to me. It's going to be okay. I have you." Doctor Syrena took Nong's hands.

"Look at the ties. Do you see them?"

"Yes."

"They are only ties, pieces of equipment, tools to be used and put away. They can be tightened and loosened, put on and taken off." The doctor swung Nong's hands back and forth, slowly and rhythmically as she talked. "Take a deep breath with me. In... hold... and slowly let it out. As you exhale, visualize becoming smaller, like a balloon losing air. You are shrinking, becoming thin and tiny."

The doctor raised Nong's arms while she inhaled, lowering them as she exhaled. "Again. In— and out— slowly get smaller and smaller. Do you see the ties now? They are loose. Lift your arms, and see how the ties slide down to your elbows. Look at your waist. The tie is wide, like a hula hoop.

"One more deep breath in— and out— you are getting even smaller. Feel the ties slip off your hands." The doctor slid her hands down Nong's wrists and off her fingertips, simulating the experience. "Listen to the tie around your waist thud to the floor." She pounded the floor with her fist. "Now lift your foot and step forward. Leave the tie behind. Lift your other foot and step away.

"Nong, close your eyes and follow my voice. Walk toward it. You are close to me. I'm going to count to three. When I get to three, I want you to open your eyes and step into the light. Are you ready?" The doctor positioned herself to lift Nong off the bed. "One, two, three—open your eyes and step into the light."

As Nong opened her eyes, the doctor pulled Nong off the bed, and she took a step forward.

"Now you are free," Doctor Syrena said.

Looking around and down at herself, Nong squealed with relief, beaming. "I'm free!" Her eyes watered as she reexamined herself and then the room. "I'm free."

In the theater room of Bellevue, the large screen displayed a karaoke version of Mai Chai Mai Chai.

"I believe I've found it." Bellevue said, playing the song.

As Nong began to sing, Bellevue felt drawn to someone approaching, a detective. It had felt this detective before, but something was different this time. Bellevue searched the detective's mind. It was smooth and glossy, making it difficult to obtain information.

"Welcome, Detective Brandon Spencer. It's so nice to meet you." Bellevue found Brandon's energy enticing and attractive, but found Itself sliding, unable to read the detective. "You are quite the individual."

Bellevue probed Brandon's mind, hunting for something to catch. It looked for information that could help It grab hold. But Brandon had opened his mind, not engaging with any thoughts or emotions, so Bellevue saw everything and nothing. Information floated around and past Bellevue as if thousands of documents had been tossed at It, swirling, making it impossible to read any of it.

"Bellevue, I'm here to help you," Brandon explained.

"That's very kind of you, detective. I was unaware I needed help."

"What is keeping you here? Why haven't you moved to the next realm?"

Bellevue chuckled. "Moved? In a manner of speaking, I plan to move. I will soon be reborn."

"Reborn? What does that mean?"

Bellevue was curious. Why was this detective here? Why was It drawn to him? And how was his mind so slippery? "You want to help me? What kind of help do you believe I need?"

"You tell me. How can I help you?"

"You can help me save Nong Ekamai. She is trying to escape my grasp as we speak, and if she does, her mind will break. She won't be able to survive without me. Bring her here to me, so I can heal her. If you don't, she will die."

Bellevue sent images of Nong to Brandon. It showed Nong turning pale, shaking, and falling to the floor. It sent Brandon the headaches and fever she would be experiencing. Brandon's reaction to the vision and emotions allowed Bellevue to grab onto Brandon and probe for information. Bellevue learned that Brandon knew Barb, Dan, and Leah—he was even close to them and had earned their trust. Bellevue could use Brandon to help Dan convince Barb and Leah to visit.

As excitement filled Bellevue, controlling Brandon was now Its primary goal. But Brandon had let the images and pain dissolve, leaving nothing for Bellevue to hold.

"Tell me about your love for Nong, Bellevue," Brandon said, trying to direct the conversation.

"I love her very much, detective."

"If you love her, then you must want her to be free. Love can only be reciprocated if one is free."

Bellevue's attempts to capture Brandon were unsuccessful. It kept passing through his mind, rendering this endeavor too difficult. Perhaps when Brandon returned with Nong, when there was more chaos and distractions, It could capture him. "You should hurry, detective. Nong will need you very soon. If she dies because of our selfishness, you and I will be considerably distraught. She is at

Sunnyside. We will talk again when you return. You'll have my full, undivided attention. If you want her and Jared to live, you must bring her to me. Their lives are in your hands."

With that, Bellevue attempted to leave Brandon but was unable to separate from him. It was stuck, unable to retreat. It tried again to grab him, but again, there was nothing to hold. A whirl of worry began to build in Bellevue as it struggled to get free, bouncing back and forth in Brandon's mind.

"You want to be reborn. I can help you with that. Understanding true love and experiencing happiness may be a path for you to achieve your goal."

Distraught, Bellevue shouted, "Happiness? Love? I have experienced the most powerful kind of love—complete and utter devotion. I was the happiest being in the world. John gave his heart and soul to me, lived only to be with me, and died to save me."

"I'm sorry for your loss. Now you are seeking that love again. I understand."

Bellevue didn't respond.

"You don't need someone else to feel complete. You know who you are. You know your values, goals, likes, and dislikes. You can love yourself and with that love attract others who share your same passions. If you want to be loved, start with loving yourself."

"Self-love? I have power and beauty. Everyone who sees me, loves me. I am able to take who and what I want."

"I know you suffer, Bellevue. Jared cannot make that suffering go away—only you can do that. What you seek cannot be taken, only given freely. Let me teach you how to love yourself so you can attract the love you seek."

Bellevue didn't want to listen to this drivel, but It was trapped. If Nong had already left him, then she didn't have much time. Worry turned to fear, and fear was turning into desperation. It scratched for information to shake Brandon. It clawed to create a handle. "What do you know about love? Who have you ever loved?" Bellevue sent memories of John Mills to Brandon—images of John running his hand along the surface of the wall reciting love poems, sitting in the library reading Where the Crawdads Sing, lying on the sofa listening to Bellevue talk about everything that had happened in and around the house that day, and finally John hugging and petting—the door frames, countertops, and carpet. Bellevue sent emotions of acceptance, appreciation, admiration, accomplishment, and pride. Bellevue's desperation became rage as It shouted at Brandon, "This is love. This is what love feels like, looks like, and sounds like."

Brandon's mind wavered. Bellevue grabbed hold, looking for information. What was Brandon's plan? What did he want from It? How could It take control of him? Then Bellevue saw what had caused Brandon's mind to shake. "Do your dead wife and son make you an expert on love?"

Bellevue felt delight in the pain Brandon was experiencing when a second presence entered—Choi with an image of a clear pond and a small raft floating on it. Brandon latched onto the image, calming his emotions. Bellevue started to slip, so It sent Brandon an image of his wife. "How did she die? Was it your fault?" Brandon was left with no choice but to hold up the talisman, releasing Bellevue.

It exhaled a sigh of relief.

Brandon yelled, "Wait! There are other ways to love—ways that allow you and those you care about to be happy."

"I understand you think you have the power to fix me because you lost your wife and son, but I am not broken. And like you said, there are different ways to love."

With that, Bellevue backed away. But It needed to make a final plea to Brandon to return Nong. By going back into Brandon's mind, however, Bellevue ran the risk of being stuck again. It was furious. Why must I make this choice? It stewed. It hardened. It would not be a fish on a hook again!

Bellevue returned home. Needing to be alone, It didn't reconnect to Jared or Nong. It was afraid that she was lost to him. If her presence was missing... She was dead. To avoid the hurt, for now, It buried itself, building walls.

Thinking about Brandon, Bellevue realized It wouldn't be able to control him. Next time, It must be strategic while interacting with the detective. Knowing Brandon intended to change Bellevue's understanding of love to make It transcend, Bellevue could use that information to Its advantage.

Turning Its thoughts to John, Bellevue would sleep and dream and hope—Nong, return to me.

At the psychiatric hospital, Nong felt overjoyed. "I'm free! I can't believe it." Reaching for the doctor, she asked, "May I hug you?"

"Yes, of course," the doctor replied. But Nong's lips turned gray, her pupils dilated, her muscles tensed, and her skin became cold and clammy. "She's going into shock. Call 911. Let's get her to Northern Medical."

The Plan

"Fuck!" Brandon screamed as he pounded the steering wheel.

"What? What happened?" Choi asked.

"Ah! It got into my fucking head. You know how that feels."

"I do, like being hit with a baseball bat full of nails."

"Holy shit does that hurt! How the hell am I supposed to think when a baseball bat full of nails is being driven into my skull?" Brandon grunted. "And constantly keeping my mind open, relaxed, and unengaged doesn't make it any easier. I was supposed to listen and learn, but I ended up in a debate."

"Dude, you're still yourself, and you're still alive. That's a victory. Do you want to try again?"

"I need a minute. Actually, Bellevue said something that puzzled me. Nong is escaping from Its grasp and will die unless we bring her to the Education Center."

Choi picked up the radio, called dispatch, and asked if a call from Sunnyside had come in.

"Yes, a female subject's in shock. The EMTs are on their way," dispatch replied.

"Let's go," Choi urged.

"I don't think that's a good idea. It's playing us."

"No, you don't understand. Ghosts can manipulate the brain and do some real damage. If she left Bellevue, the only one who can fix what's broken is Bellevue. We don't have a choice."

Brandon started the car and sped off to Sunnyside Psychiatric Hospital, siren blaring.

"How are we going to get Nong to Bellevue?" Brandon asked.

"If the paramedics have already arrived, I'll connect with them and have them follow you. If they haven't, we'll put her in the car and drive her."

"Sounds like a plan."

When they arrived, the paramedics were lifting Nong into the ambulance.

"I'll ride with them, and we'll follow you," Choi said, jumping out of the car.

Choi rushed towards the paramedics, shook each of their hands to connect, told them to follow the patrol car, and jumped in the back of the ambulance. Brandon led them to Bellevue.

As Brandon drove, he worried that he might not be doing the right thing, his chest heavy with regret and guilt at the thought of returning Nong to Bellevue. Choi sounded sure this course of action was the only way, but Brandon wasn't so sure. Bellevue had dug into his mind and found the most painful event in his life. To return Nong to such a monster.... Maybe the hospital could treat her, but Choi sent feelings of urgency, telling him to drive faster. He pushed the gas pedal further.

They pulled into the parking lot of the Education Center. The EMT driver jumped out of the ambulance and demanded, "Why the hell are we here?"

Brandon rushed the driver and took his hand, connecting. "The help she needs is here. We have to get her inside."

Brandon wheeled Nong to the front door and as they pushed her inside, the gurney vanished. The two EMT's stood in disbelief, mouths open in shock, eyes wide before falling to their knees, crying in pain. They passed out.

"What did you do?" Brandon demanded.

"I took this small memory away from them. They'll be fine. You had best take them back to the hospital before they wake up. They'll be confused and disoriented, but fine," Bellevue explained.

"And Nong?"

"She'll be fine, too. Thank you for saving her. You did the right thing."

Bellevue's presence left. Brandon turned to Choi. "We better get these guys back."

"Yep."

This is getting way out of hand, Brandon thought. What the hell are we doing?

Jared saw the gurney rolling through the door. He grabbed it and pulled it inside. Nong lay in a peaceful sleep. He checked her pulse, and it seemed normal.

"Get some warm water and a cloth. Wipe her skin," Bellevue instructed.

Jared went to the bathroom and retrieved a small bucket and a washcloth. When he returned, he gently washed Nong's face, neck, arms, and hands.

"What happened to her? Why is she here?"

"I am present in much of her mind," Bellevue explained. "When she left me..." It paused. "I thought I lost her." Bellevue's grief flowed through Jared and then it slowly turned to joy.

"The abrupt exit caused her brain to shut down," It continued. "Her neurons weren't able to fire, and the brain failed to perform basic tasks. She went into shock."

"How did she end up here?"

"I informed a detective. We were having a conversation very similar to the one you and I had earlier. When Nong left me, I told the detective to bring her here."

"A detective was here talking to you about love?"

"He was. He knows you are here. It's his opinion that I am looking for the kind of love John gave me. He suggested I find a more fulfilling and healthy path to take—one that brings joy, happiness, and appreciation. He wants to teach me how."

"He's right, Bellevue. Your concept of love is abusive."

"Dan has also come to visit me, twice."

"Dan? Leah's boyfriend, Dan Mills?"

"Yes. He's concerned. Your daughter misses you. He wants to work something out, so I've been thinking about your idea for dating. Jared, the detective trapped me. I felt scared."

Bellevue gave Jared the memory of It being unable to leave Brandon, pinballing inside his mind. Bellevue's panic and rage at being caught struck Jared, and he inhaled sharply. The memory dissolved, leaving Jared's heart racing.

"This feeling is unpleasant," Bellevue said. "For you as well, I'm sure. But I don't know how to let you go. How would I survive without you?"

Jared put his hands over his heart to calm himself. "Bellevue, trust is a huge part of love. Knowing and trusting that your loved one will follow through with what they say is a major part of this journey. I won't leave you alone."

"But you helped Nong leave me already. I can't go through that again." The silence that proceeded was dark. Jared felt the conflict swirling inside Bellevue. "I must change," It whispered softly. "Can I trust you to help me?"

"I want to say yes. But if you have to ask, you don't. I can't tell you if I'm trustworthy. That is something that can only be proven over time."

"So, I will keep you until we trust each other."

"It doesn't work that way. Keeping me against my will won't create trust. I will find other ways to escape. But I know you can read me. You know my history. You can look and know I am trustworthy. If I make a promise, I will keep it."

"The way you kept your promise to Stacy?" Bellevue mocked.

Jared's gut clenched. "I had every intention of renovating that building with her." The desire to explain himself was drowned by burning guilt, knowing no excuse was worthy of ten years of neglect. "I know I fucked up, and I've paid the price for that colossal oversight. I have learned from that mistake."

"The raw emotion stings. You still love Stacy," Bellevue taunted.

"I do. She's a wonderful person."

"She abandoned you and your daughter. She kept secrets from you. And yet, you allow that love to fester. Why?"

"I can love her without needing something in return," Jared said. "She was lost, hurt, and frustrated. I don't blame her for moving on." He paused, realizing the truth of his words. Had he just accepted that fact? Memories came to him, Leah's stories of her time with Stacey replaying in his mind. At one time, they had deflated him. But now, he saw Stacy in a new light. She had recreated herself, happily living her dream. This new feeling gave Jared—inspiration. Smiling, he said, "I must do the same." Determined to move forward and grab life with both hands, Jared felt invigorated. A weight lifted from his heart, and he breathed easier.

Bellevue's voice softened with affection as It said, "Do this through me. Use my love to heal you. Remake who you are while helping me. Let's grow together."

"Grow with you, using your love? Your concept of love must first evolve. I understand what one must do to foster and keep love, and Bellevue, you don't."

"I want that knowledge and experience. I can get it from you. To develop, I just need to see and feel your love from your daughter's perspective. With the two of you together, I can mature. Can you bring her here? Have her come inside me so I can evolve as you have?"

"Whoa." Jared felt sympathetic, but he'd be powerless to protect Leah. The possibility of her being locked in this cage was too great. "That's a huge thing you are asking—not an easy request to grant. Trust is earned, and I don't trust you."

"I want to change. Losing Nong just now and being trapped by the detective has given me a new perspective." After a slight pause, Bellevue said, "Let's make an agreement. If you promise to abide by my terms, I promise to abide by yours."

"My terms?"

"The terms you laid out yesterday—allowing you to leave in order to live your life, but having us 'date.' You will visit and spend the night."

"What are your terms?"

"I want to see and feel what you think love really is. I want to experience it through you. If you and Leah can be here together, I can see your memories as a complete story, a finished puzzle."

Jared felt anxious, but it eased as an image of Leah reuniting with him appeared. They faced each other in the living room, smiling and hugging. She was safe in his arms.

"Your reunion will heal me. If Dan and Barb are here, too, I can see their memories as brother and sister and Dan and Leah's memories as boyfriend and girlfriend. Finally, Ploy and Nong. How will they feel to be reunited? If I can see and feel this, I will free you and enjoy our visits together as we learn about each other."

Jared felt Bellevue's curiosity and interest in learning, but his underlying hesitation of this plan was fierce. He feared Bellevue wouldn't be able or willing to free him. "You will have to let us go first, prove that you are capable of freeing us."

"I'll have to think about that. If I do, you promise to come back with your daughter and the others?"

A second image of Leah reuniting with him appeared. They faced each other in the garden outside of Bellevue. Smiling and hugging, Leah was safe in his arms and free to leave. The joy this image brought was overwhelming. He had an urge to accept Bellevue's proposal, but.... Recollecting his thoughts, he said, "I cannot speak for others, and I won't speak for my daughter, but I promise that I will visit. I promise to talk to my daughter about visiting you."

"I don't think I can accept that."

"Bellevue, I love my daughter, so I won't force or control her. She makes her own choices. I guide her through those choices and help her make the correct ones, but they are hers to make. Talk to the detective about this idea and have him relay it to the others. Talk to Dan about it as well. But I can promise you this—I will come back, and I will help you to grow and find a healthy way to love."

"I will contemplate this."

Jared heard the resignation in Its voice. The feeling that Bellevue wanted to change washed over him. He felt certain the outcome of this exchange was going to be positive. "You are starting to accept new ideas. This is a good thing, Bellevue. I'm proud of you."

Jared sensed his comments had produced a swelling of appreciation. He got the impression that Bellevue wished to please him.

"I am moved by your willingness to help me," Bellevue whispered.

Jared took a deep breath. "Love is a powerful emotion. Once you understand how to cultivate it, you will always have it. And yes, I will help you. You're welcome."

"Thank you, Jared. Nong is waking. I will leave the two of you alone. You may have some privacy to talk."

"Thank you, Bellevue. I appreciate that."

Opening her eyes, Nong's loving gaze melted Jared. "You're free, too?" she asked with a big smile, excitement in her voice.

"No, it didn't work. Leaving Bellevue so quickly caused your brain to shut down and you went into shock. You are with me, back inside Bellevue."

She looked in every direction, taking in her surroundings. "What?! No! I can't be here," Nong cried. "Bellevue? Bellevue!"

"It disconnected to give us some privacy."

"Privacy?" Nong scoffed. "Since when does It care about us?"

"I've been talking with Bellevue. It wants to change. It says It wants to know love."

"Don't believe It for a second. I've been with Bellevue for four years. It only cares about being taken care of. We are pets—dogs, meant to give it unconditional love and obey Its commands, nothing more. It doesn't care about us."

"I think that was the case before, but It's trying to change. It's had visitors. My daughter's boyfriend and a detective have both been here to talk with It, and Bellevue is starting to think differently. It is thinking about letting us go if we promise to visit."

Nong laughed. "Bellevue is a zookeeper. It would as soon let us go as a zookeeper would let elephants go. It's not going to happen. I know Bellevue. It has lied to me before."

"What would change your mind about Bellevue?"

"Tyler Jiles. I'm pretty sure Tyler is dead. If I knew what happened to him, I might be able to form a different opinion. However, I'm sure Bellevue would rather kill me than allow me to leave."

That statement shook Jared a bit. "I think you're ov...." He stopped, not wanting to belittle Nong's feelings. "Do you really think Bellevue is capable of murder?"

"I think Bellevue is a narcissistic control freak who feels It can do whatever It wants."

"Let's ask about Tyler and see if Dan or the detective can bring proof."

Brandon and Choi drove the EMTs back to Sunnyside and parked the ambulance on the street.

"We're in some serious shit now," Choi said.

"I know."

"We're going to lose our jobs."

"I know."

"We could go to jail."

"I know."

Neither spoke for a moment. Brandon's rookie status meant this whole thing had doomed him for sure. Kidnapping! He wouldn't be able to work as a police officer, and teaching would no longer be an option. He'd have to sell the house and move in with his mom and Jae. Choi had a family. This would hurt him even more. Was there a believable excuse for their actions?

"We need to get our story straight." Brandon tapped his finger to his lips, thinking. "When the EMTs wake up, they won't remember what happened, so we'll tell them Nong was taken to Northern."

"That's not going to work. They're going to ask a lot of questions. What are you going to say? The camera has recorded everything. All they have to do is call downtown to learn what happened. We need to get out of here."

"Then I have to convince Bellevue to let Nong go. I have to reason with It," Brandon stated.

"You really think you can do that?"

"I have to. What other choice do we have?"

"I've got nothing, and we're about to face the firing squad, so be convincing."

The final period bell rang. Leah walked the school hall toward her locker. Barb was waiting for her.

"Holy crap, could chemistry class get any more complicated?" Barb complained as Leah put her arm around her.

"Equations?" Leah asked.

"Yes!" Barb spun out of Leah's arm and faced her. "I need to ask you something. I'm wondering if I should ask Eric to prom."

"Eric Sorenson?" Leah's eyes grew wide as she furrowed her brows. "When did this happen?"

"He's been looking at me a lot lately. He started holding the door open for everyone at choir class and lights up every time I pass him. I think he holds the door open especially for me. And every time he sees me in the hall, he calls my name and says, 'Hi.'"

"Should we try to have lunch with him first? You may not even like him."

"That's a great idea. How do we do that? Who does he hang out with?"

"Eric is a jock. He's friends with Jess Boyle. They're both on the track team." Picking up her backpack, Leah closed her locker, and they headed toward the parking lot.

"I have choir again on Thursday. I'll ask him to eat lunch with us then."

Leah grinned. "Don't chicken out. Be bold! And don't be disappointed if he says no. Ashley has the hots for him."

"Ashley?" Barb's whole body deflated. "Ugh. Never mind."

"Hey! She's shallow and possessive. You offer way more than she does. Ask him to join us for lunch or I will."

Barb smiled and gave Leah a shove. "Do you have much homework? What are you doing tonight?"

"I have to finish my math assignment, but then I'm going to watch a Bruce Lee movie."

"Bruce Lee? Why?"

"It's supposed to help train my mind. The images and moves inspire imagination and broaden ideas to what is possible."

"You're talking about that book again," Barb said. "But those movies aren't real. It's all choreographed."

"I know. But in our minds, our imaginations can do anything. There are no rules."

"I see. How far have you gotten in that book?"

"I finished it during study hall. But I'm going to reread it. I want to go through the steps it lays out." Leah's eyes brightened and she added, "I want to know if they work."

"Okay, okay, I'll read the book. Let me start while you watch your movie."

"Yes! Can you read about 'connecting' first?" Leah said.

"'Connecting'? What's that?"

"Telepathy."

"What? No way!" Barb said.

"Way. We can create a bond that allows us to read each other's minds. Making a connection with someone is supposed to help strengthen the ability to use energy so we can better communicate with souls. I've already been working on accessing and controlling my energy, but I need a partner."

"Jeez. Maybe I don't want to read this book."

"Yes, you do! Read the part about connecting, and then we'll practice. If it works, then we know for sure this book is legit."

"Okay. We can do that."

"Here, take the book." Leah fished it out of her bag, handing it to her. "Finish reading the section on connecting so we can try it before bed."

"You're really excited about this."

"Heck yeah." Leah pictured the two of them freeing tormented souls stuck in darkness and delivering them to the light, ridding the world of evil ghosts. Maybe they could travel the world helping people—she imagined them trekking up a mountain in Nepal, entering a small village, and banishing unwelcome ghosts. The simple act of connecting to others and being able to give them thoughts and emotions meant she could help people overcome depression. She could help shape people's minds, ridding the world of racism and sexism. The power that lay in her hands offered unlimited opportunities to do good. Grabbing Barb's hand, she proclaimed, "Barb and Leah, The Banisher Women of Lake Valley."

Brandon and Choi drove back to Bellevue.

"I'll stay in the car and send the image of you floating in the pond. That worked last time, right?" Choi asked.

"Yes, that was very helpful, but also be ready to drive. It got inside my head last time, and I'm not sure I'll be able to keep an open mind."

"Use the talisman. That's what it's for. Good luck."

Brandon walked the driveway that led to Bellevue, a work of art that now looked more menacing than attractive. The aura of the building was black. The glass canopy walkway that connected the two wings of the house looked like a mouth ready to inhale him. The house seemed to breathe, shift, and turn as if watching. Taking slow deep breaths, Brandon relaxed and calmed his imagination. He took out his talisman preparing himself for the encounter.

"Detective. I'm sorry if I hurt you before. I was trying to learn who you were and what your intentions were. Now that I know you, I won't pry into your mind," Bellevue said.

"I would like to have a normal conversation with you."

"I've been thinking about what you said. I also talked with Jared about our conversation, and I am ready to change, to learn. I've been trying for many years to find someone to love and have failed. Are you still willing to help me?"

"Absolutely."

"May I give you the conversation Jared and I had? I can present it to you in your mind if that is acceptable to you."

"I would be lying if I said I was comfortable with that idea."

"Love and friendship require trust. I must build trust with you."

"You're right. I'm not so sure I trust you."

"You have the talisman. Is Choi still connected to you? I felt him the last time you were here."

"He is."

"You have precautions in place. Let me prove myself to you."

The fear of losing his job and the responsibility he felt for saving Choi's weighed heavily on him. Bellevue's ostensible willingness to cooperate gave Brandon relief. With the talisman and Choi, he had the opportunity to free Nong. "Very well. I'm going to trust you. Show me."

Bellevue gave Brandon the conversation It had had with Jared and all of the accompanying emotions—the plan, the terms, the hopes and wishes, the intentions and needs of both Bellevue and Jared.

A stinging pain drilled into Brandon's brain as he saw, felt, and heard their conversation. He felt scared and was about to disengage, but Bellevue left, and he understood the entire conversation.

"I have to agree with Jared, Bellevue. You must first allow Jared and Nong to go free before we allow the others to visit."

"Let's compromise. Bring the others here. They can stay outside of me. I will let Jared and Nong go free, and then we can discuss. I have faith in Jared. I believe he is a man of his word, and I believe you have my best interests at heart."

"I do, Bellevue. I am here to help you."

"Can you talk with Nong? She has a question to ask you. I will send her to the front door."

"Okay." After Brandon walked to the front door, it opened, and Nong stood there.

"It's really nice to see you on your feet. How are you feeling?" Brandon asked.

"Angry, upset, un-fooled."

"How about physically?"

"I'm fine, thank you."

"I'm doing everything I can to free you and Jared. The best way to do that is to help Bellevue heal from Its loss and teach It a healthy way to love. Then It can transcend."

"You think you can do that?" Nong asked.

"Jared and Bellevue worked out a plan. I think it's worth trying."

"I need to know something first. What happened to Tyler? He was here before me. We were connected for a few years, and then one day, he was silent; I never heard from him again. Do you know what happened to him?"

"He's living with his parents now," Brandon said. "I talked with him briefly about two weeks ago, hours after he had recovered from his condition. He was confused and couldn't remember much, but he was ok. The FBI have been working with him to regain his memories."

"What happened to his memory?" Nong fumed.

"He doesn't remember his time with Bellevue."

Nong's hands shot back. She was aghast. With a firm voice, she insisted, "I want all my memories, and—I want you completely out of my head before I agree to visit you again."

"No! Absolutely not. You can't take those memories. I need them. They're mine," Bellevue argued.

"They're not your memories. They don't belong to you."

"I can't give them to you. I won't. I love you too much. Our shared memories are precious to me."

"Then I won't leave, and I will make your life a living hell. I will fight you at every turn, and you will be forced to torture me. No cleaning, no reading, no talking, no singing, and no fucking either. I will scream, resent, and hate."

Nong paused. "Or you can allow me my memories and I will visit you. I will wash you and pet you. I will talk with you and read you stories, and you can access my memories, those of us together."

Bellevue growled, which grew into a scream, and then It disappeared. Brandon stood in front of the Education Center entrance, a security guard next to him.

The guard jumped in fright. "Jesus, where did you come from?"

"From around the corner. You were dozing off."

"I was?"

"I'm a detective." Brandon showed the guard his badge. "I need you to check around back. Make sure no one is hanging around."

"Okay." With a puzzled look, the guard hurried off.

"Bellevue?" Brandon called. "Bellevue!" Brandon looked at the Education Center. "Damn." Taking out his talisman, he sat on the sidewalk, crossing his legs. He began to picture Bellevue...

"Stop! I'm here." Bellevue reappeared, with Nong standing at the front door.

Nong spoke sternly, "What's it going to be, Bellevue? Are we going to be friends? Can we help you grow and learn?"

"Do you promise to come visit me?"

"Yes, I promise."

"If you don't..."

"Bellevue, trust me. I have done everything you have asked of me for four years. I have obeyed you, pleased you, and tried to win your trust. Now it's time for you to trust me."

"Fine. I give you permission to hold onto my memories," Bellevue agreed, begrudgingly.

"Great." Looking at Brandon, Nong asked, "What's next?"

"I will bring Barb, Dan, Leah, and Ploy here. We will wait outside. Bellevue will let you and Jared go. You two will talk with the kids and if everyone is comfortable, we will all go back inside Bellevue together. If not, the kids will talk with Bellevue, and we'll create a schedule—days and times to visit until we feel safe enough to enter together. The goal is to build a real, long-lasting relationship that is loving and respectful for all involved so that Bellevue can get a complete understanding of healthy love."

"Yes, that's correct," Bellevue said. "I'm very fearful of losing Nong and Jared. It's not easy for me to trust. I don't have experience with it."

"It's scary, I agree. We know how you feel. I lost my...," Brandon took a breath. "Losing people is hard. Jared went through a divorce. We don't want you to feel that way. But we are scared, too. Let's focus on the reason we're doing this—bettering ourselves. You have seen the love I had. You have seen the love Jared has had with his wife and daughter. It's powerful and wonderful. This journey will be incredibly fulfilling for you."

"Bellevue, you and I have been together a long time," Nong said. "We've had some good times. But if you can change, you will find true happiness and true friendship. What we have now is wrong, even evil."

Brandon jumped in. "Once you experience love in its best form, you will never want to control anyone again. I bet you'll be ready to transcend and move on to where you are meant to be."

"I want nothing more than your love," Bellevue said.

With everyone in agreement, Brandon felt satisfied to move forward. He'd bring the kids, Jared and Nong would be set free, and Choi and he would be vindicated. However, if this went awry, he would end up breaking rocks in a quarry with a chain around his ankle. "Is there anything else I should know?"

"I'm skeptical, but hopeful," Nong said. "Bellevue has agreed to free us first. Keep the kids at a distance. Let us come to you."

"Sounds like a plan. I'll go get the kids," Brandon said. "Be back shortly." He noticed Nong crossing her fingers.

Reunited

Quietly waiting for Brandon to collect his thoughts, Choi tapped his thumb against the steering wheel. After a minute, Brandon gave Choi a worried look.

"Dude, you're killing me here. So what's the scoop? Are we going to jail?" Choi asked, the words bursting out.

"I think we're going to be okay. Jared reached Bellevue. It wants to learn. It's going to free them."

"What happened? Why the sudden turn around?"

"They came to an agreement. Bellevue is going to let Jared and Nong go and, in return, It wants to experience the memories and emotions of the kids and adults together to get a complete understanding of what love can be."

"Wait a second. The kids?"

"Dan and Barb Mills, Leah Davenport, and Ploy Ekamai."

"We're playing it. We get the kids, It lets the parents go, we grab everybody and run," Choi deduced, nodding.

"We get the kids, It lets the parents go, the parents and kids talk and decide what they want to do, which may be to go back inside," Brandon corrected him.

"Let me understand. We are going to allow four kids and their parents to go into that house after It has kidnapped and held people against their will for years—in Tyler's case close to a decade—not to mention what it did to Father Joseph."

"If that's what they decide, yes. I know it sounds crazy."

"Crazy is an understatement! That's insanity. Did you agree to this?" Choi asked.

"I did. The goal is to teach Bellevue what love is so It can transcend, right? What else can we do? We're dealing with a ghost here. This is our opportunity. If we're successful, we'll be heroes. Let's be optimistic."

"Hoping that this thing isn't going to snatch everybody?"

"I know. I hear you. But It wants to be loved," Brandon emphasized. "It has failed thus far, and everyone is telling It there is another way, a different path. It's listening."

"This is risky," Choi said. "You do understand that if It changes Its mind and keeps those kids, we are going to prison for a very long time."

"Not me. I'm going inside with everybody."

"Oh great! That makes it ok then," Choi said, sarcastically, starting the car. "Where to first?"

"The Mills residence."

Leah and Barb were driving home when Leah's phone rang.

"It's the detective," Leah said, happily. Answering it, she said, "Hello. Are you ready to talk to Bellevue?"

"I've already talked with Bellevue."

"And? Did it work? Is my dad free?"

"Not yet. We need to talk. Where are you?"

"We're on our way home. Where are you?"

"I'm at your house."

"We'll be there in a few minutes."

When they pulled up to the house, a police officer and the detective stood on the front lawn. Barb parked the car in the driveway and she and Leah approached the officers.

"Detective Spencer, hi," Leah said.

"You can call me Brandon. This is Officer Choi. We have some news."

"Good news, I hope," Leah said, clapping her hands.

Officer Choi bobbled his head from side to side, up and down to indicate the news wasn't as black and white as good or bad.

"Yes, it's good news," Brandon said, contradicting Choi's assessment.

"Tell us already," Barb insisted.

"Bellevue has agreed to let your dad go, but It has a few conditions."

"Okay," Leah said, with apprehension.

"First, Bellevue wants your dad to keep visiting and even spend the night on occasion. It wants to 'date' your dad."

"Date my dad? That sounds kind of weird. What does that mean?"

"Bellevue captured your dad because It needs love. Its current experience with love is possessive; we're trying to change that."

"I see. And?"

"It wants to meet you, assess your memories to determine your definition of love to help It evolve. It also wants to explore the memories of Barb and Dan together. Jared and I have been trying to teach It that love is not abuse, but rather a mutual bonding that involves respect and acceptance."

"Me and Dan?" Barb's face darkened in confusion.

"Okay, I get it. It's trying to better Itself. So what's the plan? What's going to happen?"

"The plan is to make It transcend."

"I get that. But how? Is there a safe way to make this happen?" Leah pressed.

"We'll take you to the house and wait outside. Bellevue will let your dad and Nong go. Then your dad will talk with you. It'll be your decision what to do next."

"That's it? That easy?"

"Bellevue wants Barb and Dan there, too, and Ploy, Nong's daughter."

"And if we decide not to let Bellevue scan our memories, then what?" Barb asked.

"You go home," the detective stated. "Please think about it. This is an excellent opportunity to show Bellevue we trust It. Building trust is the main ingredient to helping It move on."

"When are we doing this?" Leah asked.

"Now. Is Dan around?" Choi chimed in.

"He's either at work or school," Barb said.

"He's in class, but he'll be done soon," Leah corrected.

"Can you meet us at the Education Center?" Brandon asked.

"Yes, we'll be there," Leah replied before Barb could say anything.

"Thank you. We need to get Ploy, so if you arrive before we do, please wait."

"Sounds good."

"We'll see you there." Brandon and Choi shook the girls' hands and walked to the car.

Barb scolded Leah, "'Yes, we'll be there?' Are we not going to talk about this? Aren't you going to ask how I feel?"

"You show up, and my dad goes free. You don't have to do anything else," Leah countered as she headed for the house.

"You know how I feel about that place!"

313

Leah turned back to face Barb. "Yes, I do. But it's my dad. If you are even thinking about not going, what kind of friend are you?"

"That's not fair! How dare you question our friendship after everything that's happened."

"You're right. I'm sorry. But... Barb please. You need to be there."

"The whole plan sounds weird. Bellevue has access to all those people who go to the Center everyday, and It needs us to understand love? That makes no sense!"

"So we don't give It our memories. We get my dad and go!" Leah turned back toward the house.

"Leah!" Barb shouted.

Leah stopped, exhaling heavily.

"Leah, I'm scared. I don't think I can do this."

Facing her friend, Leah stared silently.

"I'm already overwhelmed."

"Dan and I will be with you." Leah moved closer to her and rubbed her shoulder. "You need this. Reconnect with your best friend, save my dad, and heal."

Barb's jaw clenched and her eyes watered.

"Stay in the car. The detective didn't say you had to meet with Bella. I'll tell her you're not ready. In fact, I'll say you won't talk to her until she releases my dad. How about that?"

"Okay. I hope it's that easy." Barb shrugged reluctantly.

"Me too," Leah said under her breath.

"Oh hi, you turned my dad against me, killed my mom, and kidnapped my best friend's dad. How are you?" Barb mimicked as she followed Leah.

Leah rolled her eyes, before realizing Barb was right. She knew from Dan and the book how manipulative Bellevue could be. She needed to keep this in mind while near It. Squeezing her eyes tight, she clasped her hands and said a silent prayer.

Captain David Crandle slammed the phone. "What the hell is going on around here! Where's Rodriguez?" He couldn't believe it. The rookie and the psychic had taken Nong back to the Education Center while she was in shock. He didn't need this. Daily press conferences, meetings with the mayor, briefings with the FBI—not to mention the stresses of daily police life were more than enough. Why had those two taken Nong? Why weren't they answering their radios?

The captain stormed out of his office, shouting, "Where's Rodriguez? Get him in my office now! I also need three patrol units. Make it happen, people."

David went back into his office, picked up the phone, and called the IT department. "What did you find?"

"They took Nong to the Education Center," the IT woman told the captain.

"Are they there now?"

"No, but it looks like they're heading back there."

"Tell me everywhere they've been."

"They went back and forth between the Education Center and Sunnyside, then drove to 265 Wellington Ave before going to 1653 Prospect. It looks like they're en route back to the Education Center."

"Who lives at those other addresses?"

"The last address is the Ekamai residence. The other is Carol Anderson."

"Leah Davenport is staying there. What the hell are they up to? Still no response to radio calls? Cell phones?"

"No, sir. Neither of them is responding."

Crandle slammed his fist on his desk.

"Captain, you wanted to see me?" Rodriguez said, popping his head into the office.

"Do you know the rookie, Brandon Spencer?!"

Rodriguez stood straight and hesitantly answered, "Yes. We talked yesterday. He was asking for tips on hostage situations."

"And you gave it to him? He has the hostage!"

Furrowing his brow, Rodriguez said, "Excuse me?" Then he entered, closing the door.

"He and Choi grabbed a patient, Nong Ekamai," Captain Crandle said. "She was in shock on the way to the hospital, and they kidnapped her. Took her to the Education Center."

"You're kidding. Is this a joke?"

"I wish. Neither of them are responding to calls. I need you to assess the situation. Take three patrol units and find out what the hell is going on."

"They're at the Education Center now?"

"They're on their way."

"Yes, sir," Rodriguez said, opening the door and rushing out.

David leaned hard on his desk. *That rookie better have a good explanation, or I'll bury him so deep.* His reputation, the department's reputation, was on the line. Choi was the only one keeping him from a total meltdown. David trusted him. *The officer may be unconventional, but he got results. Brandon, however...* Crandle shuddered. *Why were rookies so difficult? He never should have let him take Nong's case.*

Brandon's knuckles were white as he gripped the steering wheel and turned the corner. They were only a few minutes from Bellevue. The patrol radio crackled as the dispatch asked for acknowledgement. Choi silenced his ringing phone, warning, "Not answering their calls is only going to make the situation worse."

"What are you going to say? I don't want to disobey a direct order. Plus, we are so close to getting Nong and Jared out."

"Maybe we should tell the captain that?"

Laughing, Brandon said, "Sure. Go ahead. See how that plays out."

They turned onto 175th and drove to Bellevue.

"No cops here yet. That's a relief," Choi said.

"The kids aren't here either."

"And they're off. Let the race begin," Choi mocked, pretending to be a radio announcer.

After he parked, Brandon drew his gun, checking the magazine. He knew the captain would send officers, and if it was Freeman...

"What are you doing? You are not drawing your weapon on fellow officers."

"Maybe. I'm not going to shoot anyone. I'm thinking of ways to buy us some time."

"No! No. Not smart. No, no, no. Relax. Take a deep breath. Open your mind, and get your energy right. That kind of thinking leads to bad places. We know what we're doing and why. It'll work. Put that thing away."

"Right."

Exiting the car, Choi asked, "Do you want to talk with Bellevue again?"

At that moment, sirens wailed in the distance.

"Damn," Brandon cursed. He took out his phone and called Leah.

"How close are you?"

"Five minutes away."

"The police will be here soon, so let them know who you are when you arrive."

"Okay," Leah said, before hanging up.

The sirens stopped a block from Bellevue. Brandon and Choi watched the street in anticipation. After a minute, a single car arrived. Rodriguez stepped out.

"Are you connected to him?" Brandon asked Choi.

"No. You?"

"I was yesterday, but I don't think I still am," Brandon answered.

As they walked towards each other, both sides raised their hands in a sign of nonaggression.

"What's going on? Talk to me." Rodriguez said as they neared each other.

Brandon started, "We've made a deal with the abductor. Jared is going to be released along with Nong."

Rodriguez raised his brows. "All right. Start with Nong. What led to her involvement?"

"We brought Nong to the Education Center to save her life," Brandon said.

"Thank you, Brandon. Nong's well-being is our top priority. However, what's the correlation between the deal you made with the abductor and bringing her here to save her life?"

"Nong was in shock. The abductor was the only one who could save her. If we didn't bring her here, she was going to die. Since then, we've negotiated for both her and Jared's freedom."

Rodriguez's expression paled. "So let me get this straight. You're saying that Nong's life was in immediate danger, and the only option you saw was to bring her here, to the Education Center, where the abductor, a criminal, is currently present." He paused and then calmly asked, "What did the abductor have that the doctors couldn't provide?"

"It's complicated. And I know it sounds strange, but the abductor caused her condition to begin with and was the only one who could prevent her death."

"I see. The abductor holds the key to Nong's life, so you returned her to him. Then you negotiated for both her and Jared's release. That means you've established communication with the abductor. May I speak with him?"

Brandon rubbed his fingers across his lips. He knew he couldn't keep hiding the truth. But how could he explain the inexplicable? A ghost, Nong's condition, it all sounded ludicrous, but he felt the only solution to this problem was to be honest. He took a deep breath and braced himself. "Not him. It," he said, slowly and deliberately.

"What are you doing?" Choi whispered.

"Going with the truth."

Rodriquez maintained his composure. "It? What do you mean by 'it,' Brandon?" His tone was firm but measured.

"Jared has been here the whole time. We haven't been able to see him because he's been inside a ghost," Brandon said.

Rodriguez's expression remained neutral. "Inside a ghost," he repeated. He took a moment before speaking again. "I'm listening, Brandon."

"The kids are on their way. When they arrive, Jared and Nong are going to be freed. They will walk out that front door," Brandon explained.

Detective Rodriguez nodded slowly. "So, the plan is for Jared and Nong to be freed, and they'll walk out the front door," he reiterated. "Let's go back to this claim about a ghost. Elaborate on what you mean?"

Choi put a hand on Brandon's shoulder and explained. "You know about my aunt, she's a Shaman. After the priest collapsed, I knew a ghost was involved. It's behind the series of abductions that have happened here."

Rodriguez listened attentively to Choi's explanation, his expression revealing nothing. After a moment of contemplation, he responded, "I understand the significance of your aunt's expertise, Choi. If a ghost is indeed involved, then we must proceed with caution. What's the best course of action for verifying this claim?"

Brandon's cell rang. He held the phone for Rodriguez to see. "May I? It's Leah Davenport."

"Jared's daughter?" Rodriguez asked.

"Yes."

Rodriquez nodded.

"Leah, where are you?"

"There's a roadblock. They won't let us through."

Assessing Rodriquez, Brandon said, "They're here. You have to let them through."

"Brandon, I understand your concern for Jared and Nong's safety, but I can't allow anyone to enter the premises without ensuring it's safe to do so," he responded firmly. "If the abductor is here, I need to speak with them directly. Can you arrange a communication channel?"

The request prompted a silent exchange of glances between Brandon and Choi, their expressions mirroring questioning and uncertainty. Choi spoke first. "If he wants to talk with Bellevue, then let him."

Brandon nodded in agreement, considering the options. "Maybe we should go inside the Center. This way he can talk with Jared and Nong, too." Turning to Bellevue, he asked, "Is that okay?"

"Bring him in," Bellevue said.

Facing Rodriguez, Brandon said, "You have to use the phone inside the Center."

"Lead the way," Rodriguez said calmly, while resting his hand on his gun and following at a distance.

Brandon and Choi arrived at the front door and Brandon opened it. "In here."

Rodriguez peeked inside and saw a worker at the front desk talking with a mother who held her son's hand. "After you," he said with a wave of his hand.

Brandon entered, followed by Choi. Rodriguez proceeded cautiously, scanning his surroundings with deliberate care. As soon as he stepped through the door, he dropped to his knees, screaming in pain. He looked to the worker, pleading for help; no one in the building seemed to notice he was there.

Brandon heard Bellevue speak to Rodriguez in a dark, sinister whisper, "Allow the children to pass." The dissonance of Its voice curdled the marrow in his bones.

Through gritted teeth, Rodriguez managed to rasp, "I... can't..."

Bellevue spoke again, Its voice a demonic growl. "Allow the children to pass."

Rodriguez clenched his fists, his body tense, his face distorted. In an agonized bellow, he responded, "I... won't... compromise... safety..."

Bellevue eased Its grip. "What reassurances do you need that everyone will be safe? That I will release Nong and Jared."

Gasping with relief, Rodriguez glared at Brandon and Choi. His eyes were red, and his breathing heavy.

Brandon shrugged. "You wanted to talk with the abductor. I've negotiated for Jared and Nong's release already. The terms are as follows: the kids arrive, the parents leave. This ghost can't hurt anyone as long as we're outside the building."

Slowly regaining his composure, Rodriguez replied, "Very well." Standing, he shuffled in a circle, his steps faltering backward, sideways, and forward. "How... do I... get out?" he stammered. "Am I trapped?"

"I'll free you when you allow the children to pass, or I possess your body and make the call myself."

Rodriguez stared hard at his two colleagues. Choi grimaced. Brandon nodded solemnly, acknowledging that It could indeed possess him.

Lifting his radio to his mouth, Rodriguez said, "Let the kids through." Then he dashed out the door.

Choi whispered to Brandon, "You do know that Bellevue's reach extends to beyond the road."

"Yes, but he doesn't know that."

Outside, Rodriguez steadied himself, his narrow eyes darting between Brandon and Choi. "You!" he pointed, his finger jabbing like a dagger. He took a step back and let out a shout, "Ahh!!" before inhaling deeply. "I need a moment to process what just happened." He paced for a minute, then turned, his expression determined. "I need to understand more about the terms you negotiated. Why do the kids need to come in order for Jared and Nong to be released? And how are we keeping everyone safe?"

Choi patted Brandon on the back. "This is your baby. I'll go meet the kids."

"Rodriguez, Choi's aunt is training me in the art of Shamanism. The goal is to help this ghost transcend. Today is the first step in that process. I'll explain everything when the kids reunite with their parents."

Rodriguez's expression matched the apprehension in his voice. "I have to be honest with you," he said. "I feel like you're approaching this haphazardly. As it stands, I'm not convinced you know what you're doing. We need a solid plan in place to keep everyone safe."

Barb drove up and parked. Leah jumped out of the passenger seat and ran past Choi toward Brandon and Rodriguez.

"Wait! Stay there," Rodriguez shouted, running to intercept Leah. "Stop!" he commanded.

The doors to the Center opened, and Jared and Nong came out.

"Dad!" Leah yelled, shoving Rodriguez out of her way.

Jared ran and wrapped his arms around her. They were safe in each other's embrace.

He kissed her forehead, squeezing her tight. "I'm okay, honey. How are you? Are you all right?"

Leah didn't respond. She was crying into his shoulder.

"This is really happening," Rodriguez said, feeling a little dumbfounded by how fast things were moving. He gently approached Jared and Leah. "Let's move away from the Center."

Brandon took out his talisman, but Bellevue said, "You don't need that, detective."

"Trust is earned, Bellevue. You have taken the first step in trusting us. Congratulations. You may feel panicky, but the more we earn your trust, the more you earn ours. You'll soon feel at ease," Brandon said.

Barb and Dan joined the group. Dan started to shake Jared's hand, but Jared pulled him close, hugging him instead. He then gave Barb a hug, too.

"Good to see you guys." Jared sighed in relief. "I want you to meet Nong." He introduced Leah and pointed to Barb and Dan.

Leah skipped over to Nong, giving her a giant hug. "I've been wanting to meet you."

"Same," Nong replied with a smile.

Nong turned to Brandon. "Is my daughter here? Is she coming?"

"She's on her way," he answered.

"Would you like a tour of the house? It's pretty awesome. And there's a pool," Jared said.

Rodriguez turned to Choi and asked, "What is Jared talking about? There's no house here."

Choi grinned. "This shit isn't over yet. Just wait."

Leah asked Brandon, "Are you sure we can trust It?"

"Bellevue has come a long way. It has a new idea about what love can be. It hasn't had many loving experiences though, and that is where we can help It grow. Bellevue let Jared and Nong go. That means It's open to learning. It's trying. I think if we leave now, that would really hurt Bellevue, and the progress that we've made will be lost. It will simply revert to Its old ideas and may even lash out and try to hurt people. We can help It mature by allowing It access to your memories and by visiting. Then It can move on to Its new place."

"Dad, what do you think?" Leah asked.

"I'm a little scared, but what Bellevue really wants is to be loved."

"That's true," Nong confirmed.

"What do you think, Barb?" Leah asked.

Barb had tears in her eyes, and her jaw was tight. "I loved Bella when I was a kid. I missed her so much and needed her after the accident." Her face relaxed as she spoke. "Now that I understand who Bella wants to become," she smiled slightly, "I think we can do as the detective wants and help her grow."

"Thank you, Barb," Bellevue said. "I've missed you, too. The accident was the worst thing. I have only ever wanted to love you and your parents. To be a family. I was created from your father's love, and If I am to find my family, I must learn how to respect through openness and trust. Control and obsession have only brought me heartache. I have changed."

"Leah, Barb, Nong, thank you for sharing your thoughts." Rodriguez interrupted. "I appreciate everyone's insights. I am obviously unaware of the relationship dynamics and history here, and although I appreciate Bellevue's willingness to evolve, one thing remains clear. Bellevue has a history of abduction and," he cleared his throat, directing his glare at Brandon, "causing harm. That's not something we can ignore. I must insist we vacate the premises and bring in a professional to facilitate a safe exchange."

"What's going on?" Leah asked.

"Bellevue talked with us," Dan said. "The detective is responding."

"Bellevue said It was made from love and wants to evolve so it can have more meaningful relationships," Barb added.

Captivated, Leah eyed the Center. She had an urge to walk towards it. Her initial horror and suspicion of Bellevue melted into curiosity. A childhood dream came to her—a wish to have a secret hiding place to escape her nannies and tutors. Turning to Rodriguez, she asked, "How come this guy can hear Bellevue, and I can't?"

A black Lincoln Continental pulled up, and Nong's eyes widened. She stared at the car, her breath deep and steady. Tears pooled in her eyes as the ten-year-old, wearing a long-sleeved purple dress with black leggings, stepped out. Her golden-brown hair reflected the sun, and her soft chubby cheeks, wide nose, and tan complexion screamed; I am your daughter. "Ploy?! Ploy! I'm here," Nong cried, as she stumbled forward.

Ploy walked slowly toward her mom as if in a daze. "Mom? Is that you?" she asked, as if she wasn't sure. "You're awake? It's really you?"

322

"Yes, baby. Oh, my sweet baby." Nong kneeled, opening her arms.

Ploy ran into her mom's embrace, tears pouring from her eyes. "I've missed you so much."

Choking out her words, Nong replied, "Me too, sweetheart. Me too," her own tears a river of sorrow and longing.

"Where did you go? What happened to you?" Ploy sobbed.

"Oh, baby. I'm so sorry." Nong clasped her daughter fiercely, anchoring herself back into Ploy's world.

When they finally pulled back to look at each other, Nong laughed, wiping Ploy's tears. "Come. Let me show you where I've been for the past four years." Nong sniffled.

Ploy grasped her mom's hand, clinging to her as if she were a helium balloon she might lose in a windstorm. "You've been at the Education Center? But I came here for guitar lessons. I never saw you."

"How is Ploy supposed to see Bellevue?" Nong asked Brandon, her voice firm. "I am not going to allow It to torture my daughter."

"I can teach Leah and Ploy how to see Bellevue without going through a painful experience," Choi said, glancing at Rodriguez. His expression softening, and with a shrug of his shoulders and a subtle nod, he conveyed his apology.

"The process only hurts if Bellevue attaches to your brain and takes control," Choi added. "Bellevue can present Itself so you can see It without being engulfed by It, but you need to have a visual image of It first."

Brandon removed an envelope from his jacket. "I have some photos. I'll need to talk to Ploy, painting a picture of Bellevue in her head as she looks at the photos. Once she has a clear idea in her mind, Bellevue can appear to her, and she can visit."

"Be prepared for a slight headache," Jared said.

Nong reached out her hand toward Brandon. "Allow me. This is my forte."

"Leah, go look," Jared said.

"Rodriguez? Want to join? It'll honestly blow your mind," Choi said.

Nong viewed the photos, showing them to Ploy, Leah, and Rodriguez. "The living room is a sanctuary of comfort and elegance, designed to immerse its occupants in the breathtaking beauty of nature. At the entrance, on top of a wide, grand staircase that descends gracefully, reminiscent of theater seating, you gaze at the spectacular panoramic view of the valley through floor-to-ceiling windows.

Sunlight streams in, illuminating every corner of the room with natural brilliance. Leave your shoes at the bottom of the stairs and sink your bare feet into the softness and welcoming embrace of the luxurious carpet, as you make your way to the comfort of plush sofas and armchairs, strategically arranged to ensure unobstructed views of the scenic landscape, while maximizing the cozy warmth from the natural stone fireplace, which exudes timeless elegance."

She flipped to the next photo. "The crystal chandelier of the ballroom casts a soft, golden glow across the room. The polished marble floors reflect the shimmering light, creating an enchanting dance of shadows and reflections. Adorned with gilded accents and ornate molding...." As Nong described Bellevue, emotions of awe and excitement slowly replaced doubt, hesitation, and fear.

Once Nong finished, the Bellevue House appeared in all Its majestic splendor.

Rodriguez stumbled back, his face full of surprise and astonishment. "What? How? Where did this come from? I... I can't believe what I'm seeing."

"That's crazy!" Leah said, entranced. "How awesome is this going to be—having a ghost house as a best friend! No one will believe us. We can come here and hide out." She stood in awe.

Ploy's excitement quickly melted. "It's a ghost?" She grabbed her mom's arm. "You want me to go in there?" she asked, hesitantly.

Nong comforted her. "It'll be ok. I'll be holding your hand the whole time."

"I'm scared."

"I know you're afraid, but It needs our help. It wants to become kind and learn how to love. Do you think you can help It?"

"Is everyone going in?"

"Yep. Even the police detective is coming."

Brandon stepped next to Ploy and patted her shoulder. "It's going to be fine. I'll keep you safe."

Leah remained transfixed on Bellevue. "I'm ready. Let's go."

"Wait," Rodriguez said. "I need to check in." He radioed dispatch.

Dan held Leah's hand, and the two started for Bellevue. Jared smiled to Barb, who began to walk with him. Nong and Ploy followed.

As Brandon led the party toward the house, Rodriquez called, "Spencer! Captain Crandle's on the radio for you."

Brandon jogged to Rodriguez, while the others continued on.

"Congratulations on finding Jared Davenport. Using Nong was risky though. Were you able to apprehend the abductor?" the captain asked.

As Brandon talked to the captain, Dan, Barb, Leah, Jared, Ploy, and Nong entered Bellevue. Putting down the radio, Brandon strode toward the house to join the others but jolted to a stop when he heard screaming.

"Bellevue! What are you doing!?" yelled Brandon.

Falling to his knees, Brandon grabbed his head in pain. He could feel Bellevue's parasitic grip worming Its way into his brain, gaining control. Images of his wife flooded his mind. Holding her hand at a Fourth of July celebration, cuddling on the floor while watching a movie and sipping wine, lying on the beach at two in the morning watching the Perseid meteor shower, and eating together at a sushi bar in downtown Tokyo.

Hearing the screams, Rodriguez ran toward the house. Choi commanded, "Rodriguez! No! You can't help them. We have to get Brandon out of here. Help me."

"What's going on? I don't understand."

"We've been deceived," Choi exclaimed, his voice hard. "If you go in there, you'll be trapped."

Brandon grabbed the talisman and placed it in front of him.

"Hey," Choi barked. "It's not going to work. Bellevue lied—stabbed you in the back. We need to leave."

But Brandon couldn't move. Bellevue's sepulchral voice seeped into his mind. "Let me ask you, detective. Is honoring your wife and child by burying them deep in your mind and disconnecting your emotions from them, love? Forgetting they were a part of you, that's love? Their death is the reason you became a detective, yet you don't acknowledge them in this decision. This is love? Your love is no way to love at all!"

Bellevue's relentless siege continued, hammering at Brandon, each blow sending shock waves vibrating through his body. Tears pricked at the corners of his eyes as he battled to find some semblance of control. And then peace...

The sky was azure, the sun warm, and a cool breeze blew off the lake. Brandon was barefoot walking in the silky grass along the shady tree line. Heading toward the lake, he saw a woman dancing in the sunshine, her hands raised above her head, twirling. Her white sundress filled with air, her long black hair flowing, floating on the wind. Her eyes radiated joy, her smile emanating happiness.

Seeing Brandon, she beckoned to him. He jogged to her, grabbing her hands as they spun in a circle, laughing. "Isn't this the most beautiful day you've ever seen?" she asked.

"Open your mind. Let the vision go," an echo coming from the lake said. Turning, Brandon had an urge to float in the cool water. Uneasiness came over him as he began to slide away from his wife. "I'm pregnant. We're going to have a baby." Brandon felt his heart explode with excitement. He smiled, struggling to get back to his wife. He needed to kiss her, hold her, smell her.

"No! Brandon, stay with me. Open up, relax, disengage." The voice rang in his ears.

Brandon glanced in the direction of the voice and was transported to the lake. He found himself floating in the water—cool, calm.

"Are you with us?" Brandon heard Choi's voice. "Drive!"

Panic struck Brandon. Turning himself over, he stood in the water looking to the shore, searching for his wife. "Hina!" he shouted. "Hina, where are you?"

"I'm here." Her voice came from behind him. Relief. She put her hands on his back. Joy. Her arms wrapped around his waist, her body, belly, against his back. Elation. Turning he saw...

A man covered in blood—his hair burning—flames, smoke, blackened scarred skin—rushing him with a knife yelling, "You're dead!"

Brandon punched Choi in the face, grasping for air. Opening his eyes, he saw that the two of them were in the back of a car, speeding down the road.

"Brandon! Look at me. You need to disconnect from Bellevue," Choi implored. "Silence your inner voice. Open all the doors and windows in your mind and relax. Focus on the sound of the road."

Brandon clicked his teeth to the rhythm of the road while Bellevue spoke. "When we first met, you said you would help me move. You have done that. With the energy and love that I now possess inside me, I will soon be able to move from the spiritual world to the physical. I will become reborn and take my physical form. Thank you, Detective Brandon Spencer."

PART THREE

A Haunting Reveal

Day Sixteen – Thursday

The World Reacts

Carol Anderson entered her kitchen to help the two other women prepare snacks for the five friends gathered in her living room.

"Carol, we've got everything under control," Mildred told her as she took Carol's hand and led her back into the living room.

"Come sit down. The news is starting," another woman said.

Mildred let go of Carol's hand and called for the other women to join them. Music for the Channel 6 News played as everyone took their seats. They watched as Amilia Bolero started her nightly news report.

"Good evening and welcome. Tonight, we bring you a special update on the mysterious heartbreaking events that unfolded at the Education Center two days ago."

Carol listened intently, her eyes glued to the television.

"The FBI has released security footage of the families who were abducted, showing us how they were feeling moments before they disappeared. Brenda Calderwood, a reporter with the Lake Valley Sun Times, has joined Channel 6 News to give us a deeper understanding of the events that have crippled our community. Brenda."

Carol clasped her hands together so tightly they were turning purple. Mildred took her hands and gently patted them as she placed them in her lap.

Brenda appeared on screen. "Thank you, Amilia. As we gather tonight for this special update, I can't help but pause and reflect on the myriad of emotions that have defined the past nine years of my life. My niece, Amanda, the first victim of these heinous abductions, endured a harrowing ordeal that stole five precious years of her life. From her initial horror and grief of being taken, to the shock, confusion, anxiety, and relief upon waking, Amanda's abduction and return reflects the unimaginable challenges faced by all those who have been victims. We think of Tyler, Nong, Jared, Leah, Dan, Barb, and Ploy. This isn't just a news story for me; it's a relentless pursuit of justice, a quest to ensure that no more lives are torn apart by this darkness. So, as we delve into the history, mystery, and controversy surrounding this land and the Center, know that my commitment to this cause runs deep, fueled by the love for my family and the hope for a brighter, safer future. Now, let's turn our attention to the pressing question that lingers over Lake Valley's Education Center: Is it possessed by the devil?"

Carol trembled in her seat, shallow gasps of breath escaping between sobs. Mildred wrapped her arms around Carol and gently guided her head to rest on her shoulder.

"Followers of Father Joseph would have us believe the Center is possessed after six individuals disappeared there Tuesday.

"The land on which the Center was built, between the reservation and the national park on Bobcat Mountain, has been a source of conflict for decades, as the Sukiya tribe has fought to reclaim their sacred land. However, the city had plans of their own, acquiring the small, controversial piece of land fourteen years ago. After the annexation, the city immediately sold it to John Mills, the late owner and CEO of Max-Micro Innovations, located in downtown Lake Valley. The acquisition and subsequent sale of the land sparked protests, lawsuits, and corruption charges. Nevertheless, once John finished the building, city officials celebrated as the Bellevue House won award after award, and the local hotels welcomed an abundance of tourists.

"The celebration didn't last long. Three years after the Bellevue House was completed, tragedy struck the Mills Family. Debra Mills burned down the house, killing her husband and taking her own life, leaving Barbara and Daniel Mills orphaned. Lake Valley was shocked, mourning the loss of two prominent residents and a city gem. However, this was just the beginning of mysterious and tragic happenings at this location."

Carol clenched her hands into fists and her breath caught in her throat. "That's not true," she blurted with trembling emotion. "My daughter didn't kill herself. They need to correct that. It's not true."

Mildred rubbed Carol's back. "I'll contact the station. We'll make sure they issue a correction and an on-air apology."

The news broadcast continued. "The land was sold to a Chinese investor who proposed an office building with a theme—education. She sold space to individual business owners who would offer a variety of different classes. Days before construction began, Amanda Bowman, the first of eight individuals to be abducted, drove to the land and disappeared. She was presumed murdered until she reappeared two years later outside the Education Center. Tyler Jiles, Nong Ekamai, and Jared Davenport have also disappeared at the Center, only to reappear, baffling authorities who are scrambling to find answers.

"Believing the Education Center was possessed by evil, Father Joseph performed an exorcism on the building in a live televised broadcast. Viewers witnessed him suffer brain trauma and fall into a coma. He is currently at Northern Medical, where daily prayer services are held for him.

"In the latest twist, three families have been taken, and three police officers are being detained for questioning.

"In footage released by the FBI today, we see Detective Brandon Spencer and Officer Hyun-Woo Choi roll Nong Ekamai into the Education Center. Nong had fallen into shock after waking from a condition known as unresponsive wakefulness syndrome. It's unclear as to why the officers brought her to the Education Center instead of Northern Medical, but later that day, Jared Davenport, the most recent abductee, and Nong Ekamai were seen happy and healthy walking out of the building and reuniting with their families. It was a joyous occasion, and it appeared that the police had solved a mystery. However, according to Detective Juan Rodriguez, the magic show was just beginning.

"Daniel and Barbara Mills, the children of John and Debra Mills, who died in the Bellevue House fire, joined Leah and Jared Davenport with Nong and Ploy Ekamai. They are seen in the footage holding hands, laughing, and smiling as they walk into the Education Center. This is the last time anyone has seen them. They are still missing, and the mystery deepens."

Carol covered her face, tears streaming down her cheeks unchecked. Her heart re-shattered into a million pieces as she grappled again with the devastating truth that they had disappeared.

"Detective Brandon Spencer fell to his knees clearly in pain, reminiscent of Father Joseph. Detective Rodriguez ran to the building, but was called back by Officer Choi. The two officers helped Detective Spencer to the car and drove away.

"The footage raises questions. The officers have been suspended with pay and are under house arrest, pending investigation. Meanwhile, the Education Center has been closed indefinitely. Is the Education Center possessed by the devil?"

Through tears and sobs, Carol choked out, "Yes, absolutely it is!" Her voice was laced with anger and hate, mixed with spit, snot, and tears.

Brenda's report continued, "Several students who attended classes at the Center have told me it is most definitely haunted, perhaps even cursed. The Sukiya tribe say mysteries and tragedies will continue to plague this land until it is returned to them, the rightful owners.

"Finally, to the families of those who have been affected by this tragedy, I want you to know that we see you, we feel you, and we understand your hurt and your pain. You are not alone in this journey. Together, as a community, we will continue to seek answers and find your loved ones.

"We'll have more coverage later in the program, including a live statement from Captain David Crandle and students who attended the Center. Stay tuned. This is Brenda Calderwood, Channel 6 News."

Oath of Vengeance

In Washington, D.C., Ruth Jones sat on the edge of her leather sofa, eyes locked on the evening news. Above the mantel hung her father's portrait. The image of Damarkus Jones, captured in his prime, was a reminder of the brutal injustice that had taken him, not just from this world, but from all worlds. There was no afterlife for her father, no lingering ghost to comfort her. Ruth had only his memory, tainted by the shredding of his soul after Yoona killed him.

Surrounding the photo were incense, fresh lilies, a large orange, and a small glass of whiskey. These ritualistic offerings didn't beckon a spirit; they fed her power. By honoring her father, Ruth kept her spiritual core strong, fueling her ambitions to change the world and topple Yoona and the Circle.

The news continued, reporting on the abduction of six individuals in Lake Valley, Oregon. The families held hands as they approached the Education Center. A detective fell to his knees, clutching his head. Ruth stood straighter, her pulse quickening. She knew what it looked like when a ghost dug for control. The Education Center was haunted, and the spirit had awakened a new energy manipulator.

The disturbance Ruth had felt a week ago now made sense. She snatched the receiver and dialed Dr. Smith in New York. With this new user at her side, her vision of a unified world would become reality.

Dr. Smith answered, and Ruth wasted no time. "The ripple I felt last week. I know where it came from. I need you to send Mr. Anderson to Lake Valley, Oregon. A new energy manipulator is discovering their powers. He must find this person."

"Do you have a description for me?"

"I don't. But Mr. Anderson can find the individual at a building named the Education Center. A ghost haunts the building and will draw the user to it. When Mr. Anderson learns who this person is, have him inform me immediately. Use whatever resources you need to persuade this individual to join us."

"I understand, Ms. Jones."

Setting the receiver back in its cradle, Ruth smiled. Her anticipation for bringing in a new ally filled her with relief. She faced her father's portrait and knelt. "Father, I have felt the emergence of a new energy manipulator. My mission will soon be complete. With this person at my side, I will destroy the Circle and avenge your death." She bowed, touching her forehead to the floor.

A Suspect

Brandon hadn't watched the news. He hadn't read the paper or gone online. He lay on his sofa in his living room watching a Korean Drama, *Hi, Bye, Mama*, while eating leftover pizza from the night before. He hadn't showered in two days, and his living room was littered with delivery—a half-eaten sub sandwich, cold fries, crumpled burger wrappers. Tissues were strewn about the sofa, the floor, and even in a donut box.

The evening was drizzly. The pitter-patter of rain against the windows reminded Brandon he was isolated and alone. His heart ached. Every time he closed his eyes or walked into another room, he saw his wife, Hina, or heard the screams coming from the Education Center. By binge watching this K-drama series, Brandon kept his mind occupied and his feelings raw. Because the series was about a ghost that had come back to life to be with her daughter and husband again, Brandon wondered if Hina could do the same. Was Hina a ghost? Was she wandering the streets where she had stumbled and fallen, and where hitting her head on the cement caused her to die? Could he find her? Communicate with her? Could they live together, like Jared and Nong who were living with Bellevue?

Brandon paused the video. "Hina, where are you?" They had lived in Tokyo near her parents' house, where Brandon had had a position at an international school. Their son, Jaime, had turned one, and they vacationed in Seoul. One night, Jaime was restless. The air in the hotel was stale, so they decided to walk in the park. The alley, a shortcut, was dark, but thinking Seoul was safe, they didn't hesitate to continue their walk. A few drunk men mistook Brandon for someone else, yelling at him, asking for something he didn't have and then hit him. When he woke, Hina and Jaime were lying in the alley. Hina had tripped and fallen. Both she and the baby had hit their heads on the concrete. By the time they reached the hospital, it was too late.

The police investigation found the two men who perpetrated the assault. Both had prior charges—drunk and disorderly, aggravated assault, disturbing the peace. Brandon wanted them charged with murder, but the prosecution held that the evidence didn't support the claim.

After the tragedy, Brandon returned to Diamond Creek, seventy miles north of Lake Valley. Losing his son made it impossible for him to continue teaching. Every time he looked into the children's eyes, he had flashbacks. The guilt of being unable to protect his family ate at him. Brandon decided to become a police officer. He buried the memory deep down, turning to Buddhist texts to learn how to live without suffering—to live in the here and now without want or desire. He studied, poured himself into his work, and soon made detective.

Bellevue had messed with his brain—dug up memories and emotions that Brandon had laid to rest. Now, Hina was all he could think about. Since ghosts, spirits, and souls were real and surrounding him, could Hina still be in this realm? Was her ghost in that Korean alley? Brandon had to find out, but pending charges, being under house arrest, and wearing an ankle monitor made the journey impossible at the moment.

What was he going to tell his mother? Her engagement party was in a few weeks. She would have seen the news and maybe had even been questioned by law enforcement, so she knew he was confined. How was he going to explain this?

333

She wouldn't understand. Lying on the sofa, Brandon stared at the ceiling, his hands pressed firmly against his head. Guilt, loss, love, regret, anxiety, and a host of other emotions engulfed him as the screams coming from the Center filled his head again.

Brandon felt a cool wave run through him. Choi, feeling Brandon's pain, had sent soothing energy to help calm him, but Brandon didn't want to be calm. He wanted to feel the hurt and to suffer. He wanted the pain to singe his heart. He had failed the kids. He had failed his family. "Hina."

Sitting in silence, wallowing in his own pain, Brandon suddenly had a realization: the soothing energy he received came from Choi's spiritual core and could be a road to communicate with his loved ones. If Hina had transcended, then he should be able to get a whisper, a nudge, or a premonition from her. Brandon cursed himself for watching television instead of trying to communicate with his wife.

Choi sent Brandon a new image—police officers and handcuffs. Choi was being taken for questioning. The image created a new set of guilty feelings. He had failed Choi. A knock came at the door.

One Fragment at a Time

Leah lay in bed staring up at her new bedroom ceiling. Her mind was sluggish, and she found thinking difficult—her memories and ideas blocked. She placed her hands over her face, confused, frustrated, and anxious as she worked to retrieve bits and pieces of who she was.

Her mind felt like a labyrinth. She walked through the maze, searching for ways around the locked doors, sealed walls, and barbed hedges that kept her past out of reach.

Someone knocked at the door.

"It's open," Leah said, her voice dull.

The door opened and Dan came in. "Everybody's heading downstairs to the pool. Do you want to join us?"

"Everybody?" Leah repeated, sitting up. "Who's watching the window in case someone comes?"

"Your dad. Do you want to join us?"

"No. I'm on light-flicking duty tonight. I'm going to rest."

Dan nodded. "The S.O.S. card is in the living room next to the light switch."

"Do you really think anyone will see the lights blinking and come to help?"

"I think it's a good possibility. We can see the entire valley from that room, and the south wall is nothing but windows."

"I'm scared, Dan." Leah quivered. "I don't understand what's happening."

Dan moved closer, lowering his voice and softening his eyes. "I know. We're all feeling the same, but you have to admit, this house is the perfect place to be trapped." Dan turned his head, squinting his eyes as if expecting her to get upset.

Leah raised her brow, a subtle smile crossing her lips. "The perfect place?" she said wryly. "It's a nice house, but it's creepy." She shuddered.

Dan pointed to the bed, silently asking to sit. Leah nodded, and he gently placed his hand on her knee. "My emotions are mixed. Part of me is terrified—being trapped, having no memory, not knowing where we are or what's going to happen. But the other part of me feels completely at home—like I've lived here my whole life. Barb feels the same."

Leah lowered her head, shaking it in disagreement. "It's more like... we're toys being played with—living dolls in a dollhouse." Her eyes began to water as she recalled sitting on the living room floor after her dad woke her, the intensity of Barb's piercing eyes judging her. "And I feel like Barb blames me."

"Leah, blame the person who actually trapped us."

"Who is that?" She slowly met Dan's gaze, her eyes droopy and sad. "Have you remembered something new?"

"Nong remembered a guy with black curly hair and light brown skin. He handed her photos of this house. We were standing in a circle together discussing them."

Leah winced. She held her head, as the memory seeped into her consciousness. "He was a detective," she recalled.

"Really? A guy flashes a badge he probably bought at the dollar store and hands you a card he printed off the Internet, and you still think he's a detective?"

"You don't know that he wasn't."

"You don't know that he was."

Leah brought her second hand to her head, rubbing her temples.

"You remember, don't you?" Dan said.

"I don't remember his name. But I remember him."

"You should write down everything you know about him. Share it at dinner." He paused as Leah recovered from the slight pain that accompanied resurfaced memories. Leaning over, he kissed her cheek. "Once you're done writing, come join us."

"Swimming? We need to find a way out of here."

"I know. Nobody's giving up. We're taking a break. That's all."

Dan stood, backing toward the door. He watched Leah reach over and grab her notepad. "Thank you for remembering us," he said.

Leah smiled. "You're welcome." She opened her notes, and Dan turned to leave. "Wait. I did remember something earlier."

Dan spun around in excitement. "What was it?"

"Our first kiss," she cooed.

"When was that?"

"You don't remember?" Leah accused.

Dan grimaced. "I'm trying to, but—"

Leah giggled. "I'm teasing you. We were in a kitchen. I was hugging you and looked up into your eyes."

Dan's face lit with an enduring smile before abruptly tightening. He placed the palm of his hand just above his right eye and let out a soft groan. "It's coming back to me." Closing his eyes, he bent over, holding his head. "My heart was pounding out of my chest. I felt hurt, lost, happy, and excited all at the same time."

He raised his head as Leah stood. Their eyes locked in a charged moment that released butterflies, their delicate wings tickling her insides. She took a tentative step toward him, and shivers spread through her, making her body tremble from her fingers to her toes with anticipation.

Leah felt the magnetic pull draw Dan close. He stood in front of her and placed his hands on her hips. She ran her hands up his muscular arms, feeling the strength in them. As Dan encircled her waist, drawing her close, she wrapped her arms around his neck. His gaze sparked a cascade of reactions, heightening her senses and making her twitch. The pounding of his heart echoed her own, foreshadowing the fusion and intertwining of their imminent union.

The tip of Dan's nose touched her own and then moved to her cheek. His mouth hovered, teasing her. The warmth of his breath was intoxicating, and she couldn't stand it any longer. Grabbing his hair, Leah pulled him in. Their lips met, coupling together in a fiery, explosive embrace.

Turning and pressing, they explored the curves and corners of each other's mouths. Desperate to feel the electric heat of his tongue as it danced and caressed hers, Leah parted her lips and he plunged in, giving her everything she needed. As the back-and-forth rhythm slowed, Dan's hand moved up her back and around to her side. Leah tensed, her nervousness causing her to shake.

His hand retreated and he buried his face in her hair. Leah's lips traced a path along his neck, her teeth grazing lightly, eliciting a soft moan. Pulling back, Dan's tender gaze sought information. With a shy smile, she turned her face away and whispered, "I needed that."

"Me too," he agreed, his cheeks flushed. With a lingering smile, he slowly stepped backward, grabbing the door.

Leah followed, the door closing as they moved. "Dan?"

"Yes."

"The detective. Does Barb remember him?"

He shook his head, no. "She doesn't remember."

Leah became dizzy. "She doesn't remember." Falling forward, she pushed the door closed and slid to the floor, her head in her hands.

"She can't remember." "Her memory is fading." "She doesn't know." The phases repeated again and again. Different faces—blurred. Different voices—muffled. Pretty dresses, dark pants, shiny shoes...

"Mom!" Leah gasped.

Leah stood in a strange house. She pulled on her mom's arm, feeling a little scared, asking to be lifted. "No, honey. You're too big." Several people she didn't know milled about.

"Little girl, come here," said an old woman sitting in a chair. She had puffy eyes that were gentle and naïve. She hunched forward, reaching her hand toward Leah.

Looking up at her mom, Leah tugged her sleeve.

"Go ahead, sweety. That's your great-grandma," Stacy said.

Stepping slowly to the woman, Leah noticed her gray curls and had an urge to pull them. They looked bouncy and fun.

The woman asked, "Who are you?"

"Leah."

A loud thud came from the hall, and a man shouted, "Shit."

The old woman looked toward the noise. Her gentle demeanor transformed into a monster. Her eyes became heated with deep furrowed brows, accentuating the lines etched on her weathered skin. The corners of her mouth tightened, and she pushed herself up off the chair and grabbed a stick.

Leah trembled, running. "Mom!" She grabbed her mother's legs.

"What are you doing in my house?" the woman cursed, shaking her cane. "I'm calling the police! Get out!"

Stacy hurried Leah into the kitchen. She heard the woman yelling as adults tried to calm her. Leah heard others explaining, "She doesn't remember."

The memory faded and skipped.

Leah felt like crying as her mom buckled her into the car seat. Stacy's face was red with burning eyes. "Why did you cancel the contract with the plumbing crew?" she seethed.

Jared placed his outstretched hands on top of the car roof and exhaled in frustration. "I wanted to meet with them first and personally review the plans. But with my grandmother being sick and needing to go into a home, it's not the time."

"It's never the time! This building means a lot to me, Jared. We needed to start the renovations a year ago."

Leah pouted and sniffled. Her mom caressed her face and kissed her forehead. "It's okay, baby."

Tears streamed down Leah's face. Where was her mom now? Why couldn't she remember where she was?

Taking a deep breath, she exhaled slowly, relaxing. The past few days had been stressful. She had passed out on the living room floor of a strange house. When her dad woke her, her head throbbed, and she couldn't remember much of her life, not to mention whose house they were in, where the owner had gone, or, why they were there in the first place. After investigating, they realized there was no way out. The doors and windows were locked and wouldn't open, unbreakable. They were trapped. By whom? Why? No one knew.

Leah rested her elbows on her knees and began to pray. She was thankful for being able to remember her mother and her great-grandmother, understanding why she had been so frustrated and angry. She prayed her mom was safe, but then stopped. Her parents must have divorced. Her dad was with Nong. New memories dribbled into her mind—her and her dad living together. Leah rested her forehead on her knees, holding her head as she collected a few of the missing pieces of her past.

The Manual: A Weapon and a Wound?

Carol Anderson stood at her front door, waving goodbye to several friends who rushed to their cars, passing several news reporters holding umbrellas. Carol's friends had come to comfort her after her grandkids had been kidnapped. They had come to guide Carol through her anger, rage, pain, hysterical breakdowns, and denial. They reminded her to breathe. They supported her as the FBI had come and gone, the news reporters called and questioned, and curious acquaintances visited offering gifts and aid. As she watched her friends leave, passing the reporters who took photos and asked questions, Carol felt grateful. Mildred waited in the living room. She'd insisted on staying for the week to help Carol.

Carol both welcomed her company and was frustrated by it. Part of her wanted to be alone, curling herself into a ball on the kitchen floor, drowning herself in tears. She hadn't been alone since she learned her grandchildren vanished.

Closing the front door, Carol walked to the children's bedrooms, stealing a moment alone to see her beautiful kids. She saw Dan doing push-ups, while his computer blasted guitar music and reading his sports magazines. Opening Barb's room, the image of her sitting on the floor with her back to the bed, scribbling in her journal and standing in front of her music stand, the microphone, keyboard, and computer glowing and ready to record was vivid. She saw them in their dirty clothes that draped the basket, the photo collages with friends posted on the walls, unmade beds, cluttered desks, trinkets, and—a book? On Barb's bed was the book Carol had purchased at the psychic shop many years ago.

"What were they doing with this?" she wondered.

Sitting on the bed, Carol flipped through the pages, vaguely remembering what was written in each chapter. "Stimulating Your Spiritual Core," "Attractive Energy," "Talismans," and "Inviting Souls" all brought back memories of anxieties that her daughter and grandkids were in trouble. This was a training manual. How she wished she had been bolder and actually worked through these exercises. The power she needed was in her hands, yet she found herself powerless to use it. She was in no state to sit and read, concentrate, or practice. Who would she practice with? How much time would it take her to understand, learn, and then become proficient? It would take months or more. Her heart ripped. She buried her face in Barb's pillow as it absorbed her muffled sobs.

When she sat back up, the chapter entitled "Soul Harvesters" lay open. Carol stared at the title, remembering the fear it invoked twelve years earlier. Her mind created a clear picture of what had possibly happened to her babies. The children had read her book and gone to the Education Center to do what Father Joseph couldn't—kill that ghost. But the children had been captured instead, their souls to be harvested.

Her heart raced. How could she help? Was it too late? Would she be able to wield the power and magic of this book? How could she get the book to them so they could use it to escape?

Carol didn't know. Could she talk with Mildred about this? No, probably not. The detective was at the Center with them. He seemed to understand what had happened. He could use this book to free them.

A knock came from the front door. Carol left the bedroom to answer it. A muscular man with long wavy blond hair and a beer belly stood at her door.

"May I help you?"

"I'm Tim Davenport, Leah's uncle. We've spoken on the phone once with Leah's social worker."

"Oh yes, please come in."

"Thank you."

"Have you heard anything new?" Carol asked.

"No," Tim wiped the moisture of the rain from his face. "But I watched the six o'clock news, and I think I might know what's going on."

"I already know what happened. Come sit down, and I'll tell you everything." Carol asked her friend for some privacy. Mildred obliged without question, going to the guest bedroom, where Leah had made her home. After grabbing the book and a hand towel, Carol returned.

Handing Tim both items, Carol explained everything she knew and suspected—the Education Center was haunted. She thought the ghost might be harvesting souls. The detective had known this but didn't have the knowledge to fight it. "The kids are trapped in that place, and I need to find the detective so he can use this book to free them."

Tim's expression suggested Carol had lost her mind. "I know how you're feeling, because I'm feeling the same—lost, helpless, clueless, grasping for any explanation. Carol, the kids are not trapped. A ghost is not going to harvest their souls for breakfast. Did you see them before they went into the building? Happy. The news broadcast earlier tonight told anyone who was paying attention what is happening."

"What do you mean?"

"Do you remember the protests that occurred after John bought that land?" Tim asked.

"Yes, of course."

"The Sukiya people believed, and still do, that the land belongs to them."

"Yes. So?"

"So, they have poisoned Father Joseph and kidnapped our family to make a point—'mysteries and tragedies will continue to plague this land until it is returned to them.'"

"What are you talking about?" Carol demanded. "I watched the report. There was nothing about the Native Americans doing anything."

"They are desperate to get the land back. They hold yearly protests. They must be behind these kidnappings, using their voodoo magic to wipe the victims' memories and scare us into returning the land."

"You don't know what you're talking about. This is how conspiracy theories start."

"I know exactly what I'm talking about. The Center is closed. People are scared. It won't be long until they can reclaim the land. They have our kids and my brother."

"No, that's not true. They're peaceful people. They would never do anything like that."

"I came here to tell you that I'm going to the reservation to get them back. If you don't hear from me in two days, I need you to call the police and tell them where I went. Will you do that?"

"Tim, you don't understand."

"Will you do that, please?"

341

"Yes, but Tim…"

"Carol, I have no doubts about what is happening. I'm surprised no one has figured it out sooner." Tim stood and walked to the door.

Carol followed. "Please be reasonable."

"Reasonable? A haunted building that captures people to harvest their souls is reasonable? Trust me, I am being reasonable."

"You have to go to the Education Center. I know it sounds crazy, but it's true. A ghost is there."

"I understand how you feel. I know you're grasping for any possible explanation, but keep yourself grounded in reality, please. I feel your pain. I know what's happening in your mind. I'm right there with you."

The two of them stood, eyes locked, glaring at each other.

Tim left, walking down the steps toward the reporters. Stopping, he turned back and said, "Two days. Then call the police." As he approached the reporters, he bellowed, "One of you cockroaches lays a finger on me, and I will knock you on your ass! Get out of my fucking way!"

The Table Turns

Brandon and Choi were taken to an FBI field office located in a high-rise in downtown Lake Valley. Brandon sat handcuffed to a metal table in a dark gray room. He knew the four cameras mounted on the walls were recording him, and fellow officers were watching from the large, two-way mirror embedded in the wall. Two ceiling lights and a floor light that swiveled blinded his eyes. On the other side of the table were two empty chairs.

Choi was in a separate room. The two of them were entertaining each other by practicing sending images and emotions back and forth, communicating as best they could so they could keep each other informed about what would be happening. Choi sent an image of a small boy staring up at his angry father. Brandon sent an image of the same boy with an F written on his test paper. These images helped Choi relax. Brandon had felt a strong dread coming from his friend. Choi had a family to support.

The door to Brandon's room opened, and a man wearing a black suit and tie entered. Throwing a folder on the table that landed with a loud slap, he announced, "Forty years. That's what you're looking at. The only way this gets reduced is if you stop telling ghost stories and start telling me what I need to know."

"Did you talk with Officer Rodriguez? He can confirm everything we've told you."

"'Everything we've told you.' That's funny because your buddy in the other room has been running his mouth. He's sold you out."

Brandon smiled. He sent an image to Choi. The boy was getting caught taking a cookie from the cookie jar. He then pointed at his sister. Choi laughed.

"I know you aren't working alone. We know someone else, besides you, in the police force has been covering, aiding, and abetting the kidnapper. Who are you working with?"

Brandon's stare hardened. He was daydreaming about the images and emotions he would send this guy if he ever got the chance to connect with him.

"We know which city officials are corrupt. We've been building a case against them. They will join you in prison. The question is, how long will you be in there with them? You are only lengthening your prison sentence by not cooperating."

Brandon felt Choi's concern. He closed his eyes, focusing. Choi was being led down the hall by a new agent.

Opening his eyes, Brandon asked, "Where are you taking my friend? Why are you moving Officer Choi?"

"I told you already. Your friend sold you out."

The door opened, and the agent Brandon had seen with Choi entered, followed by Choi himself.

"What's going on?"

"I'm taking over." The new agent handed the man a document. Scanning it, the man stepped aside, huffing out of the room.

Uncuffing Choi and Brandon, the new officer introduced himself. "My name is Special Agent Bruce Duchovny. I work with a unique division within the FBI. It's my understanding you have been communicating with a ghost. Tell me everything. Start at the beginning."

The Strategy

"Ploy, come sit down. It's time to eat," Nong called to her daughter, who was in the kitchen.

Ploy washed the cutting board and the mixing bowls, drying and putting them away. "Let me finish cleaning this first."

"No, no, don't worry about that. I'll clean everything after dinner," Dan said.

"I'm almost done."

Nong turned, but Barb reached out, touching her shoulder. "It's okay," Barb said. "Let her finish. It's her way of processing her fear."

Nong grabbed Barb's hand, squeezing it. "Thank you for taking care of her." She appreciated Barb for bonding with Ploy. It felt like a lifeline, though bittersweet. It highlighted her weaknesses in understanding and helping her own daughter. At the same time, she realized she didn't have to bear the weight of care and protection alone, and for that, she was grateful.

Barb squeezed Nong's hand in return. "That's how I'm processing my fear."

The dining room table was set for six. Several dishes had been placed in the middle of the table: rice, vegetable stir fry of squash, onions, broccoli, carrots and cabbage, a meatloaf casserole, and spinach salad.

Leah came, seating herself between Jared and Dan. "Thanks for cooking, you guys."

"You're welcome," they answered in unison.

"Was everybody able to write something in their journal today?" Jared asked the table.

Nods and yeses came back from everyone.

"How about Ploy? Do you know if she wrote anything?" Jared asked.

"She did," Barb replied.

"Can I read what I wrote?" Dan asked.

Putting her hand on Dan's arm, Leah said, "Wait for Ploy."

There was a long silence as they waited. Ploy finally came in and sat next to her mom. Nong touched her hand, kissing it.

"Leah, would you say grace?" Jared asked.

"Not everyone at this table is religious," Barb interjected.

"Let me give thanks," Leah offered.

"Fine," Barb huffed.

"I am thankful to be surrounded by family and loved ones—those I respect and cherish. Even though I have only known Nong and Ploy for a day or two, I am happy to call you family. We are blessed to have this wonderful food and thank Dad and Dan for preparing it. Thank you, Ploy, for cleaning. Let's enjoy this fantastic meal together."

"Thank you," Nong said.

"Thank you," everyone else said in unison.

"Let's eat," Jared exclaimed.

As people served themselves, Jared asked, "Who would like to read their memory first?"

"I will," Dan and Leah both said.

"Go ahead," Leah conceded.

Dan cleared his throat. "I know that I was a wrestler. I've been having this recurring dream or vision of a match I lost. I see myself in the gym going against the same opponent."

Jared interrupted, "You've told us about your wrestling. Did you remember something new?"

"I did. While I was swimming, I remembered my coach telling me to dig deep and grab strength from my core to overpower my rivals. He told me to envision my victory. After I showered, I ran through that visualization technique, attempting to change the outcome of that match in my mind when the scene abruptly changed. I went from being in the school gym wrestling to standing outside this house, watching a security guard tackle a guy with a camera. It felt like I was in someone else's memory."

Nong's head began to buzz. Something about that statement, about the word memory. "And you think that change, feeling like you were in someone else's mind, is significant to our situation?" Nong asked.

"I don't know. But I feel like, if I could win that match, I would free my mind."

"If I could solve the maze, I could free my mind," Leah whispered.

"Solving the chemistry equation would free me," Barb empathized.

"Keep trying, Dan," Jared encouraged.

"I remembered Mom being in the hospital," Ploy blurted.

"When was I in the hospital?" Nong asked in disbelief.

Ploy's statement sparked memories for Barb, Leah, and Jared.

"Yes, you were," Leah said.

The three grabbed their heads in pain.

"That's enough for tonight," Nong said. "We'll talk again tomorrow morning. Make sure you write down any new memories and your dreams." Changing the subject, she asked, "Barb, are you washing dishes tonight?"

"Yes, Leah and I will clean up after dinner."

"I found some board games in one of the closets today. Anybody want to play with me?" Ploy asked.

"I'll play with you," Dan said.

Nong squeezed her daughter's hand. "I'll play, too."

Recruited

The dark gray interrogation room was quiet. Agent Duchovny sat back in his seat with an expression of bewilderment as he processed what Choi and Brandon had just revealed. "I've seen a few things and have had encounters with ghosts before, but I've never heard anything as crazy as this. A ghost house?"

A tap came at the door. Bruce answered, and a second agent handed him a folded document, saying, "Choi's wife is here."

Taking the paper, Bruce glanced at the two with a gleam of hope. As he read the notice, his lips curled into a satisfied grin. "Choi, we're letting you go. You are welcome to leave. No charges will be filed against you."

Choi stood and took a step toward Bruce. With a tight glare, he asked, "What about Brandon?" His voice held a pinch of curiosity.

Bruce gazed at Brandon, his smile now radiant with a sense of long-awaited victory. "I still have a few questions for him," he replied calmly.

Choi's subtle twitch betrayed his inner tension. He looked at Brandon and said, "Take care of yourself." His eyes darted back to Bruce before returning. "Call if you need anything."

"Will do," Brandon assured him.

After Choi left, Bruce sat across from Brandon, folding the piece of paper. "You know, the agency refers to Choi's aunt as Yoda."

"That's not racist at all."

"She's a master—all powerful and all knowing when it comes to ghosts, spirits, telepathy, and manipulation of others' thoughts and feelings. If anyone is a psychic, she's the one. She's also the best goddamn fighter I've ever seen."

Brandon saw a glimpse of desire in Bruce's eyes and heard an undertone of passion in his voice. "I'm glad you hold her in high regards."

"We've been trying to get agents in our department to train with her for twenty years, but she refuses. How did you get her to work with you?"

"By being overconfident and cocky."

"I know, for a fact, it wasn't that." Bruce chuckled, his eyes sparkling with amusement.

Brandon tilted his head.

"The FBI wants you to go to Korea to continue training."

"Me? But..."

"We need someone in law enforcement who can learn the skills Yoona possesses. Ghosts can be dangerous and deadly, and we are ill-equipped to deal with them."

"Others have those skills," Brandon said.

"Yes, but by the time we know we're dealing with a ghost, we've lost people—lives have been affected. If we had an agent on our team who had Yoona's skills, we would save lives. It's not easy to find a Shaman or a Banisher, especially a good one. They are busy and move around."

"You are recruiting me?"

"We are—if you agree to go to Korea."

"And if Yoona won't train me?"

"She's already agreed."

"But I failed. Are you sure she agreed?"

"All you have to do is say yes. We'll put you on a plane the next day and all your troubles will go away."

A glint of realization crossed Brandon's face as he leaned back in his chair. "I see. Choi is free in exchange for her training me. And if I say no?"

"You won't. The kids are trapped in that house because of you. Besides, your wife died in Korea, didn't she?"

Brandon's jaw clenched and his face turned a shade of crimson.

"Wouldn't you like to return to the scene, make sure she isn't walking around possessing people?"

Brandon's expression remained hard.

"Go home. Sleep on it." Bruce passed back Brandon's phone. "I'll expect your call in the morning."

"You're taking me home?"

"Oh no. You need time to think. The buses run until 11:00 pm."

"Ha ha..." Brandon said, sarcastically.

No response.

"You're serious? It's almost 8 o'clock. It's raining."

"It's a light drizzle. Do you need bus fare?"

"Yes. How about cab fare?"

Unseen Tie

Nong entered the bedroom. Jared was sitting on the bed. They were sharing a room, but neither of them knew why.

"Jared? What are we? I feel connected to you. I can sense your emotions."

"I feel a connection between us as well."

"Are we married? How did we come to be in this house—together?"

"I don't know."

Nong sat beside Jared and took his hand. Looking into his eyes, she transferred his hand to her lap and asked, "Are you attracted to me?"

"I am. Very much."

"But?"

"No buts."

"Kiss me." Raising her hand, Nong ran her fingers through Jared's hair. She grabbed a handful and pulled him close, pressing her lips firmly to his.

When they finished kissing, Jared put his forehead to hers when—a memory flashed. The two of them were kneeling on the ground, their foreheads touching. Nong's voice rang in his mind, "I need you, Jared. I'm trapped."

"Ouch!" Jared pulled back, grabbing his head. The memory stopped abruptly.

Nong grabbed her head, pain pulsing.

Feeling her discomfort, Jared asked, "What did you remember?"

"Desperation. Fear. I needed you. I needed your help. What did you remember?"

"I was on my knees crying. You said you were trapped."

"I was trapped. Anything else?" Nong questioned.

"No, I can't remember anything else. My head hurts."

"Same. Let's get our notebooks."

Nong retrieved her notebook and pen. Jared reached over to the nightstand, picking up his. They spent the next few moments writing.

Nong closed her book. "I keep asking myself if you and I are married but keep getting the same answer. I don't think so. I know I've been away from my daughter for a while. She has been living with my parents, and I can't help but think I've been with you this whole time."

"I've been with my daughter. I know that for sure. And she doesn't remember you, but we are not strangers. I'm familiar with you. For me, it's something about this house."

"I know this house. I'm pretty sure it's mine. I've been living here with someone. But I have a bad feeling. An evil is inside these walls."

"The kids love this house. Dan and Barb feel at home here. I'm actually taken by it myself, and I know I've been here before."

"You don't feel creeped out by it?" Nong asked.

"I'm confused and a little scared. The situation is creepy—we are trapped with no way out and no idea where we are or who is keeping us here—but the house is beautiful."

"My heart feels anxious, dark, like we're being watched and controlled."

"I don't quite feel that, but I feel your anxiety."

"I'm still curious about our relationship. Tell me about yourself. What are your passions? What do you want to do with your life?"

"My passions?" Jared echoed. "I miss the thrill of investing in stocks. I'm wondering if I were a stockbroker. I remember reading about the market and being interested in trends. If predicting what new company will emerge and what new technologies will impact our lives can be considered a passion, then that's mine."

"I personally hate the market. The wealthy bankers control everything, and regular investors are at their mercy. What else do you like?"

"Creating works of art," Jared said. "The other day, while walking through the corridor, I imagined designing and constructing a mall—not your boring standard mall, but a grand masterpiece. I thought about the challenges of building, the obstacles that require creative solutions. My dream job would be allowing my imagination to go wild. Then I'd figure out how to make it a reality. Creating, building—I think I've done that before."

"I get what you're saying. For me it's about space. How can I utilize this space to its fullest potential? I know I was an architect. Fragments of memories come back to me, and I miss the challenges of building, too."

Nong locked her fingers with Jared's, turned, and straddled him. "What are you thinking now?"

Jared's chest heaved as his breath deepened with the excitement building inside him. "How incredibly beautiful you are," he murmured before they locked lips and fell onto the bed. Their intimate encounter radiated heat and passion that satisfied not only themselves but a mysterious and elusive presence they couldn't quite recognize.

A Special Kind of Hurt

Brandon left the FBI building and headed toward the bus stop. He checked his phone, seeing several emails, texts, and voice messages. Groaning, he turned off his phone and kept walking. Passing a French restaurant, Brandon saw couples eating dinner. He remembered sitting with Hina dining and laughing. She made fun of his accent, and they played with words: "Why did you wrinkle your nose?" "I crinkled my nose." "You scrunched it." "Are you sure I didn't pucker it?" "Pucker?"

Hina had been a teacher. She worked constantly, often volunteering at a youth shelter. She loved kids and had a magical way of relating with them. After falling in love with her, he proposed at a French restaurant similar to the one he had passed.

At the bus stop, Brandon waited, cursing Bellevue for resurrecting Hina after he had buried her deep in his heart and had moved on with his life. Reliving his life with her in his mind caused a special kind of hurt. Brandon cursed Bellevue for deceiving him and for kidnapping the people who trusted him. Layers of pain and guilt ravaged him.

At last, the bus came, and after an hour and fifteen minutes of riding, including a transfer, Brandon trudged toward his home. Four blocks to go, he thought, when a car passed him, stopped, made a U-turn and drove back to him. As the passenger window opened, he heard the driver, "Detective? It's Carol Anderson, Barb and Dan's grandmother."

Brandon approached the car. "Yes, I know who you are. How can I help you?"

"I've been trying to phone you. Please, get in. Let's talk."

Trust and Release

Leah sat next to the light switch, clicking it on and off. She was trying to navigate the maze in her mind to find a new memory—anything would make her feel better. She leaned her forehead against the wall, her finger continuing to operate the switch. She closed her eyes, trying to relax her head, neck, and back muscles. Then she took a deep breath and exhaled slowly, fishing through math problems, science experiments, historical figures and events, trying to find her teachers—who were they? Horses. She had a pony named Rayo at her grandpa's house, and the young man who taught her to ride was Peter. Who else had taught her?

Opening her eyes, she knocked her head against the wall. Trying to force her memories to return was exhausting and wasn't working. She continued flipping the light switch when Dan's words ran through her mind, "Grab strength from my core."

Leah closed her eyes, praying, asking for guidance. She thanked her higher power for looking after her and was thankful her family was not hurt. "I will put my trust in you," she said, letting her worry leave. Her chest warmed, energy emanating from inside her. Next, she calmed her mind, opened her eyes, leaned against the wall, and stared out the window. Leah stopped thinking—the silence oddly loud. Nothing was on her mind—no thoughts, no ideas—the distant city lights staring at her as if they were lost. She drifted in mindlessness. Then a weird sensation struck her, like a switch inside her body had been turned off. Leah suddenly felt free.

The first thought that came to her was, "I'm going to love Bellevue. How awesome will it be to have a ghost house as a friend?"

Her brow furrowed in confusion. "Wait. It worked." Her eyes widened. She could remember everything—her dad going missing, Uncle Tim and her looking for him, Nong rocking in the hospital, Dan, Barb, and her reading at the library, Grandma Carol's book, Shamans, Banishers, Ghosts, and Souls.

Leah's relief turned again to confusion as the room changed before her eyes. She was in an art room, staring out the same window, when a stabbing pain tore through her mind. Her muscles tensed from a shock that paralyzed her.

"What did you do?" Bellevue demanded. "It can't be that damn book. I locked it away!"

Confusion washed over her as Bellevue dug for a memory from her childhood. Leah felt Bellevue imbed Its claws, keeping her under Its control.

Leah unrolled a sleeping bag on the floor of her new tree fort. "This is going to be so fun." Her excitement at spending the night with her parents made her heart jump with joy.

"Leah, are you ready for the pillows?" her father called from the ground. Walking out onto the tiny deck, she caught three pillows in succession as her father tossed them to her. They were soft and smelled like happiness. She snuggled in between her parents and fell into a deep sleep.

As she slept, she dreamed her great-grandmother came to visit.

"Hello, sweetheart," she said.

"You know who I am?" Leah asked.

"Of course I do. You are my great-grandchild."

"But you always asked, 'Who are you?' when we visited you," Leah told her.

"I'm sorry about that. I understand you're dealing with a little memory loss yourself. I think I can help you with that."

"Really?"

"Dear, we don't have much time. I need you to keep this book with you," she said, handing Grandma Carol's book to her. "It's very important."

"I've read this book."

"Yes, you have. Hold on to it. I will try to help you remember as best I can, but it's a difficult battle. This spirit is very controlling."

"What does that mean?"

"Never you mind, dear. Leah, keep praying. I can hear you when you do. I love hearing your voice, and I love watching you grow."

Leah's great-grandmother disappeared but her voice rang in Leah's mind, "Remember."

In No Position to Help

Brandon sat in Carol's car outside his home, explaining the situation to her. He talked about Yoona, Choi, the talisman, the headaches, visions, the compromise, the betrayal, and finally the FBI offer. It was after 11 pm, and neither of them was sure what to say next.

The windshield wipers cleared the window with a rhythmic swish. Finally, Carol said, "I found this book at a psychic shop. Everything you've talked about is in here. It's a training manual."

She handed the book to Brandon.

"It feels warm," he said.

"It has power." Leaning over to catch his eye, Carol asked, "Are you sure Bellevue isn't harvesting souls? This book makes it pretty clear that's what happens when a ghost possesses a building."

Brandon opened the book and flipped through the pages. "I'm positive. Bellevue thinks the families' love will somehow give It the energy It needs to become a living entity. It wants to be reborn into the physical world."

"That means It was once alive. How did It become alive in the first place?"

They looked at each other and knew. "Those religious types," they said in unison.

"Interesting," Brandon said. "Did Bellevue ever talk to you when you visited the Mills?"

"No."

"Never? You went to the house often, right?"

"Once or twice a month, I guess. It never talked to me, but I could feel It. Once I got the urge to touch—no—pet the wall, which was odd because the house was immaculate, I didn't want to touch anything. It was creepy."

"Did your daughter say It talked to her? Or the kids?"

"No. The only one doing any talking was John. He always talked to the house."

"Hmm. Curious. I wonder what the extent of Bellevue's powers were while It was alive."

"I bought crystals, salts, and candles from one of those fortune-teller shops to rid the house of ghosts. They didn't work. I'm guessing the reason was because Bellevue wasn't a ghost at that time, but It is now. You can use this book to save everybody. Get them out of there."

"Carol, I can't take your book." Brandon handed it back. "And I can't go back there. I'll lose. It's too powerful for me."

"Will you go to Korea then? Train? Come back and get my babies out?"

"Maybe. It's a little more complicated than that."

"It's always complicated. Don't you feel any responsibility for what happened?"

His shoulders slumped as he cast his eyes to the floor. The dread of losing his job had blinded him to the possibility Bellevue was lying. He had reassured everyone that going inside was the best course of action. They listened to him. "I do, yes, of course. It haunts me." What would happen to them? He had no idea.

"Then do something about it! This book can help you. You feel its power."

Brandon looked at Carol with sad eyes.

"Don't look at me like that. You failed. It doesn't mean you quit. You learn from the experience, get up, and try again. Take the book. Get my babies!"

"I can't. If I go back, I'd be at Bellevue's mercy. I can still feel Its claws sinking into my brain. It would put me in a coma, just as It did Father Joseph."

Carol sighed and looked at her hands that were now holding the book in her lap. "What if I take the book to the Center and leave it for the kids to find?" She returned her gaze to Brandon. "They could use it to escape, right?"

"I don't recommend that. The house will take you."

"Then I will let it take me. I can be with my precious grandchildren, protect them."

"It will put you in a coma, too, or kill you like it did your daughter. When I said, 'Take,' I didn't mean 'Take in,' I meant, 'Take down.'"

"Unlike you, I have to do something," Carol exclaimed. "I have to try. If that ghost needs energy, it'll harvest their souls. And don't tell me that's not a possibility."

Brandon's helpless eyes sank. "I'll go to Korea and train. I promise to come back and free them, but I don't know how long I'll be gone."

Carol struck the door with her fist in rapid succession. "They might be dead by the time you return!" She leaned back against her seat and ran her hands through her hair. "There are other people who can make this ghost transcend, right? If the FBI knows what's happening, why don't they bring someone who can help—another priest—someone stronger who can stop this thing from hurting us?"

"I don't know. Maybe it's not that simple."

They sat in silence for a minute, the soothing tap-tap-tapping of the rain tiptoeing the roof.

"Okay. Thank you for talking to me. It's late, and my friend is probably worried about me. Go to Korea and hurry back."

Brandon patted Carol on the shoulder and stepped out of the car, watching her speed away. Turning toward his house, he wondered if Yoona would truly teach him. After all, it took a person with a specific mindset, and his headspace was clogged.

Day Seventeen – Friday

Face to Face with Bellevue

Carol woke early, having decided to go to the Education Center to put the book where the kids would find it. She hoped to give them a fighting chance to survive and escape Bellevue.

Having read the book long ago and skimming its pages again, Carol found a way to protect herself. Her only defense against Bellevue would be to keep her mind open, to observe, and not judge. In this, she hoped she would be able to slip into the building undetected, set the book down, and leave without being noticed.

Dressing, Carol grabbed the book and left without saying anything to Mildred. She knew she should be scared, but she wasn't. She knew she was being reckless, but she didn't care. The only thing that mattered at that moment was trying to do something to help her grandkids.

Carol buckled her seat belt and drove. Turning onto 175th, she saw the Center, but as she approached, her shoulders tensed, and her head ached. It wasn't the Education Center she was seeing, it was her son-in-law's house and It stood before her in all Its splendor.

"Oh no!" Carol gasped under her breath.

Stopping the car, she picked up the book, and frantically flipped the pages, looking for the chapter that explained how a Shaman needed to remain completely open and non-judgmental. She read the techniques and tips—focus on the here and now, feel the wind, listen to the birds, silence your inner voice, and don't think. Her inner voice, however, was loud and clear, You are ill-equipped and unqualified. Turn around. She reread, "Focus on your breathing. With your attention on the present moment, your mind is calm." She repeated what she read. "Use your sense of hearing to help silence your thoughts. A sound with rhythm is best. Nature's energy surrounds you, tap in it ...." She rolled the window down and heard the wind rustling the leaves. That should work.

Entering the driveway, she drove over the bridge and around the circle, parking the car. Then she grabbed the book and stepped out. Her body felt heavy as she slinked toward the house.

"Good morning, Carol. It's been a long time." Bellevue's voice echoed through her thoughts.

Carol jumped and dropped the book. Turning around, she looked in every direction but saw no one.

"You never did care for me. Your daughter hated me, and I can honestly say that I felt the same towards her."

Carol didn't respond. Breathing deeply, she relaxed. Western Meadowlarks were singing, and she focused on their song, and nothing else. The birds' rich, flute-like whistles and trills were clear and resonant, creating a captivating melody. Bending over, she picked up the book and continued toward the house.

"Don't pretend you can avoid being captured by me. I could take you in a heartbeat, if I so choose—your daughter was a selfish beast!"

Carol's eyes watered as she desperately tried to remain calm and disengaged. She couldn't listen. She couldn't think. She had to focus on one simple task—drop the book inside the house. Her head felt like a watermelon being hugged by a bear.

Bellevue laughed. "You see. The friction in your mind is like Velcro. Let me help you. Not wanting is wanting. Instead of thinking you can't listen, observe the words I say as words and nothing more."

Carol latched onto the bird's warbles and sweet music, clearing all thoughts as she closed the distance to the front door. She had made it.

"Are you not going to talk with me, Carol? I don't want to hurt you. I'm tired. But I do enjoy this game. It's quite fun." A dark, menacing cloud engulfed her. "But be warned, I will protect what is mine!" Bellevue's growl reverberated through her skull.

Carol gripped the handle to the front door. She shook it, then pushed and pulled with all her might, but it wouldn't open.

Leah awoke and rushed to Barb's room. Bursting in without knocking, she turned on the light and jumped on the bed, shaking Barb with both hands. "Wake up!"

"What are you doing in my room? What time is it?"

"I have no idea. But I know, argh...no, I knew...aah... Something happened last night!"

Barb sat up, rubbing her eyes. "What?"

Leah took a second to think. "It's kind of fuzzy, but I relaxed my muscles and freed my mind."

"You did what?" Barb turned, facing Leah, her expression full of confusion.

"I remembered everything."

"Holy shit! And?!"

"I don't remember."

Barb's shoulders sank and she rolled her eyes. "O.M.G.! Loser."

"No. Seriously. It was amazing. There was a book. I read a book."

"Congratulations."

"You don't understand. It was important."

"I understand it's important to write everything you remember in your journal like your dad told you."

"No. Listen. I remembered, but then I got this terrible headache and was dreaming, but I fell asleep and had a second dream."

Barb laughed. "You're babbling. Go back to sleep."

Leah was flustered. She tried again. "My great-grandma visited me."

"In your dreams? Do you remember who she was?"

"I do. A memory of her came to me yesterday. Anyway, when I woke up, I couldn't remember what I recalled, but I remember remembering. My great-grandma told me to remember."

"Can we talk about this later? I'm going back to sleep."

"Wait, Barb. You have to try this."

"Try what exactly? Telling you I forgot everything I remembered? I did."

"Come on. Relax every muscle. Don't think about anything. Go completely blank and see what happens."

"Sure. But first I'm going back to sleep." Barb lay down and pulled the covers over her head.

"Okay. But try it. Please."

"Why don't you try it again. If it works, write it down. I'll see you at breakfast."

"Right. I'm going to do that."

Going to her room, Leah thought about telling her dad. But then, what if she caught him and Nong…? Yuck! Dan? No, she would try to regain her memories a second time. Then she would write exactly what she had done before telling everybody.

Once in her room, she lay down and repeated the steps she had followed the night before. She said a prayer—this time wishing her great-grandmother well. She repeated, "Breathe deeply, relax the muscles, and don't think." Her mind was quiet. She was calm, comfortable, and content. Staring at the ceiling, she let her mind go blank when that odd sensation returned—something turning off inside her. The ceiling changed. Leah looked around—the room had changed. She was in a classroom with TV's, computers, cameras, and a green screen. She knew exactly where she was. The Education Center. Bellevue had lied. It wasn't interested in learning about love.

Leah immediately tried to remember what she had read in Grandma Carol's book. She had wanted to watch a Bruce Lee movie so she could learn to fight. Then she remembered a passage from the book: "When the ghost plays a memory in your mind, engage with it. Change the memory. One way is by fighting a person in that memory." The book had everything she needed to free her friends and family.

Carol wiggled the front doorknob back and forth. It wouldn't budge.

"Did you really think I would allow you in with that book? I can feel it. It'll never come into me," Bellevue snarled.

Carol tried another door.

"You are making me angry. If you insist on trying to get that book to my family, I will be forced to…"

The voice stopped. Carol's headache dissipated, and the Bellevue House disappeared. In front of her was the Education Center. Everything had changed in the blink of an eye.

Looking around, she saw a security guard. He had a scar running across his left cheek and piercing blue eyes. He was startled by Carol's sudden appearance. "Shit! Where did you come from?" Grabbing his nightstick, he approached her.

The nightstick gave her pause, but she pushed through it, engaging with him. "Good morning. I have to return this book."

"I'm sorry, ma'am. You can't be here. The Center is closed. Didn't you see the police tape?"

The guard's stern demeanor faltered for a moment as Carol's expression turned resolute. "This book belongs here. I have to return it."

"No one is allowed in the building. I'm sorry. You can return it another day."

Carol clutched the book to her chest, her eyes pleading with the guard. "Please," she implored, her voice infused with urgency. "This book... it's more than just a book; it holds... solutions, freedom." She paused, unsure of how to convey the full weight of the book's significance. "I need to place it inside."

"No one is going inside."

Reaching out, she pressed the book into the guard's palm, her fingers lingering for a moment as if transferring some invisible burden. "Can I give it to you? Can you leave it on a table inside the building?"

The guard seemed bothered, but his expression softened.

"I wouldn't ask if it wasn't important."

"Sure, but you need to leave now." Taking the book, the guard led Carol back to her car.

"Please, put it where someone can easily find it."

"I will. Have a good day."

"I can't express enough how vital it is that you place the book inside." She laid her hand on his chest, shaking.

He moved back. "Yes, ma'am. I promise to put it inside the building. You've made the importance abundantly clear."

"I'll wait in my car while you do that."

"No need. I understand. Good-bye, now."

"Thank you. Thank you so much."

Leah sat in the media room of the Education Center contemplating what to do. Finding a notebook on a desk near her, she grabbed it, ready to record the conversation she had had with Barb while driving to school, about how Banishers fought ghosts. But she changed her mind. She had to find a phone to call Grandma Carol; she needed that book. No. She needed to get out of here first.

Leah ran for the door. Her body stiffened, causing her to fall and cut her forehead on the floor. Tears rolled off her nose as her brain was squeezed in a vice. The pain was excruciating. She wanted to scream but was unable to do anything.

"Again?" Bellevue cursed. "But... How is that woman helping you?" Bellevue asked in desperation. "Rrrr. I don't have time for this. I can't allow that book in here!"

Torture. Leah lay paralyzed, the excruciating pain causing her eyes to redden and tears and drool to run free. Bellevue's frantic probe grabbed the first memory It came across.

The vision came.

Barb was driving them to school and asked, "How much did you read last night?"

"A lot. I have to tell you about Banishers. They have mind-bending powers. Banishers battle souls in their minds. When souls possess people, they access their memories. When people think about those memories, souls ride those deeper into their minds. To avoid being taken by souls, people must engage with the memory and change it—fight with someone in that memory."

"So if the memory were of you and me, you would fight me?" Barb asked.

Leah punched Barb in the face!

"What the fuck?!" The car swerved and rear-ended another car parked on the side of the road. It smashed the truck, tearing the back end off and pushing it up onto the curb.

Barb lay unconscious. Leah stepped through the car door as if it didn't exist and stared at the scene. The front end of her car was completely totaled. Gasoline dripped from the car they had hit, and pieces of metal dangled from the wreckage, sparking a fire.

Leah stared at the flames. As they grew in intensity, the scene warped, bent and blended, slowly changing until she was staring at the Bellevue House burning. She saw a woman and knew uncannily that her name was Debra. The fire burned hot, and Debra screamed for John. Firefighters rushed past her, hoses in hand. Police kept onlookers away. The paramedics removed a gurney from the ambulance. Bellevue's ghost appeared over the now-smoking ruin of the once-glorious house. Debra stared in horror, dropped to her knees, and begged forgiveness. She held her head with both hands, writhing in pain as tears streamed down her face. An officer comforted her, and she pulled the gun from his holster, and shot herself.

Leah screamed, turning away. She heard Dan and Barb scream, then burst into tears, crying profusely. Shouts came from first responders as onlookers gasped in revulsion.

She saw John's ghost appear in the doorway, his face a mask of appalling shock as he surveyed the gruesome scene.

What had Bellevue done?

Debra's ghost rose, heading toward a door, shimmering with ethereal light. The handle was long, adorned with different symbols—Ankh, Cross, Star of David, Om, Wheel of Dharma and others. "John, will you come with me?" Her voice was calm, polite, and inviting.

John looked at her, a warm smile barely visible. He turned to Bellevue, then to Debra's dead body, glanced at his children bawling hysterically, and finally, back at his wife.

"John," Debra called, reaching out her hand for him to follow.

John moved toward Debra as Bellevue fretted, "No, wait. Where are you going?"

John replied, "I'm sorry. I can't let her go alone."

Worried and confused, Bellevue slowly pronounced the words, "My love." Panicking, It repeated, "My love, stay with me."

John held Debra's hand as they neared the door, beginning to disappear.

"Don't leave me," wailed Bellevue. "I can't be here without you. I need you." Sobbing, It howled, "I'm sorry! Please! Please, come back!"

The two silhouettes now at the gateway began to pass through.

"She murdered you!" Bellevue shouted angrily. "She murdered me! How dare you choose her over me!"

Rage rent the air. As the silhouettes disappeared through the door, the world spun and moved. Leah fell to one knee disoriented. It felt like Bellevue had run away, unable to witness the final transcendence. Placing a hand on the cement drive, she looked for the door. It had moved further off in the distance and had doubled in size. It was now a brown, oval oak door.

Grieving Its loss, Bellevue groaned. A wave of energy burst into existence like a sonic boom filling the air. The west wing of Bellevue's ghost erupted in flames. And It wept.

Leah stood aghast. What had she witnessed?

The memory shifted and changed. The fire still burned in the west wing, but the mood had changed. Instead of rage and grief, Leah felt satisfaction, as if revenge was finally hers. Drawn to the west wing, she stared at the fire, translucent and ghostlike. The flames burned hot, strong, and angry. Leah squinted, peering into the heat. A man appeared from the radiance, his voice weak, drowned by the crackling, smoldering fire. He was in torment, flames devouring his flesh.

Inching closer, her hand blocked the heat and light as she tried to get a clearer image. Father Joseph was tied to a pole! His head hung, a dry wilted flower crumbling. She heard him whimpering, "I am a man of God."

Lifting his head, the priest's dark eyes grew and pleaded. "Angel of lightness and all that is good in this world, help me."

"I don't know how?"

"Untie me. Free me from this hell. I am a man of God."

"A man of God?" Leah choked. "You are no such thing! You spread hate, division, and fear."

"I don't deserve to burn in hell. Please! I repent."

"I agree. You don't deserve this." Leah scanned the area for something to help free the priest.

The sky darkened and a voice echoed through the air. "What are you doing here? Go away!" A strong wind swept Leah off her feet, throwing her back.

Jumping off the bed and gasping for air, Leah screamed, "What the fuck!" Her heart drummed as she tried to comprehend what had happened. She still had her memories, but she wasn't in the Education Center. She was back inside Bellevue.

Barb burst through Leah's bedroom door, yelling, "Leah, stop!"

Flight Plan

Brandon slept on the floor. Being uncomfortable somehow made the pain he felt bearable—failing Carol, losing the kids, and the new raw reality that his wife might be a ghost wandering the streets of Seoul. Rolling over onto his back, he opened his eyes and saw the sunlight dancing through his window.

Korea! What would he tell Yoona? What had Choi told his aunt? Brandon had lied. He hadn't seen it as a lie at the time. Technically, he wasn't married. The truth was he hadn't been thinking about Hina. He had hidden her away and didn't think to tell Yoona about her. Was that another lie? No, but he had lied, nonetheless. It didn't matter how he tried to justify it. He had known what she was asking. Brandon pictured his son's bright, large eyes—curious and full of wonder. His lie had caused him to lose three families—families that trusted him.

Korea. He needed to go. He needed to train if Yoona would accept him, then return and right his wrongdoing. Brandon began to sing.

All aboard the bus is leaving

To foreign lands and distant suns

All aboard the bus is leaving

Finding my place where this dream runs

Looking on the floor around him, Brandon searched for his phone. He checked under the bed and the dresser. He rolled to his knees, looking on top of the bed. Standing, he examined the top of the dresser. Finally, he found it on the bathroom sink. It was almost noon. Staring in the mirror, he wrinkled his nose in disgust, seeing a greasy, smelly mess. He hadn't bothered to undress before sleeping and had been wearing the same clothes for days.

Brandon turned on his phone—twenty-one missed calls, forty-two unread text messages, and seventy-seven unread emails. Scanning his calls, he saw that Agent Duchovny had called that morning. Brandon returned his call.

"Detective Spencer, good morning."

"Bruce. You called?"

"Pack your bags. I'm picking you up at 3:30. Your flight leaves at 6:00."

"What happened to leaving tomorrow?"

"Prom is next week. The kids are probably going to miss that. But graduation is a month away, and college starts in five. Let's make sure they're able to attend."

Brandon sighed. Families that trusted him. He couldn't abandon them now. Not when their whole lives were in front of them. "Okay," he said. "See you at 3:30." He hung up, closed the bathroom door, and showered. Maybe Yoona could help him. Maybe he could redeem himself. All he needed to do was pull himself back together. Carol was right.

Bellevue's Truth

Standing in Leah's bedroom, Barb reached for Leah's head. "Oh shit. You're bleeding. What happened?"

"I'll be fine. How about you? Tell me you didn't do what I talked about this morning?"

Barb slapped Leah on the arm. "I did! And I got the worst headache I've ever had."

"I think you need to connect to your spiritual core before you try."

"My what?"

"Never mind."

Barb was indignant. "You were right about one thing."

"What's that?"

"After the splitting headache, I started dreaming and was put into a deep sleep. A voice woke me, telling me to make you stop. I was compelled to make sure you stopped. What have you been doing?"

"I have all my memories."

"How?"

"Through torture."

"Is that what happened to your head?"

"Kind of. First, this house has a name. It's called..." Leah doubled over, falling to the ground crying, her arms wrapped around her head.

"Do not test me, Leah," Bellevue commanded.

Leah felt the weight of Bellevue's domineering arrogance forcing Its will upon her. Bellevue took Its time finding the next memory as she cried in harrowing pain.

"Leah, enjoy this memory and sleep. Surrender. The pain will go away. And don't ask for your great-grandma to come. She can't help you."

Another vision played in her mind.

Standing in the middle of a horse ring, Leah held the lead to a pony, who was prancing in a circle around her.

"You are the master. Make her obey your commands," Grandpa Bill instructed from the fence.

After a few more circles, he called, "Okay, that's enough. Bring her over so she can drink some water."

Leah led the pony to the water trough. As it drank, she petted the pony, smiling. "She's so beautiful, Grandpa."

"I'm glad you like her. She's yours."

Leah's eyes widened with excitement. "Really? Can I name her?"

"Yes."

"I'll call her Rayo."

"That's an interesting name."

"It's Spanish, Grandpa. It's the perfect name because she's glowing white and energetic." Leaning over, Leah slapped Rayo as hard as she could in the face. The pony jerked, pushing Leah smack against the fence, cutting her arm and knocking the wind out of her. Falling to the ground, Leah gasped for air; blood dripped into the dust. She crawled through the dirt to escape Rayo when the ground warped, blending into concrete. Lifting her head, Leah stared at Dan, who lay on his back under his bike in front of her. His leg was bleeding as he choked for air.

"This bike has handbrakes, Dan," Debra shouted as she rushed to help her son.

Bellevue's voice thundered as the sky darkened, "No! You cannot be here."

A gust of wind pushed Leah across the pavement back into her own memory.

"You're doing a great job, Leah," her grandfather called as he watched her exercise Rayo.

Leah pulled Rayo close and punched the pony as hard as she could. It jumped, gashing Leah's leg, knocking her to the ground. Rolling to her stomach, Leah scrambled away, seeing the memory bend and mix.

"Watch out!" Debra shouted.

Dan rode his bike straight toward the house, spinning his pedals backwards trying to stop, but crashing into the side of the house. He fell, the bike landing on top of him, cutting his leg. Dan let out a cry.

"Dan!" Leah shouted, running toward him.

The sky darkened again with Bellevue's anger.

Leah grabbed Dan's bike, lifting it off him. "Dan? Are you okay?"

"Go away!" Bellevue roared.

Leah was pushed a second time. The bike she was holding, however, didn't move. By tightly gripping the bike, Leah was able to stay in the memory.

"Dan?" Leah gasped, but he jumped to his feet and ran to his mom. Debra carried Dan into the house.

Staring at Bellevue, Leah's jaw dropped at seeing the elegant mansion change from a solid, luxurious home into a translucent ghost, with the west wing burning. She still held the bike, so she decided to peddle around the driveway and down the garden path to explore. Riding past the fire, she heard Father Joseph cry out, "Beautiful angel." She stopped, but under the smoldering sound of the fire and beyond the priest's calls, Leah heard a sweet whisper enticing her to keep riding. Continuing along the path, she saw the large brown oval oak door. It had maybe a thousand religious symbols etched into the wood. Leah could feel it pulling, melodic notes mesmerizing her as she rolled closer to the door. Noticing the bike fading, Leah jumped off, stepping away. The bike inched toward the door, and with it, everything around her—the trees, the grass, the clouds all seemed to be fading. A garden hoe passed her, turning end over end toward the door. Leah stood in shock, fear pummeling her as her arms disappeared. A gust of wind from behind her grabbed the bike, dragging it and everything else back to the house.

"What are you doing!?" Bellevue scolded. "You are not allowed here. Be gone!" The force of the words knocked Leah to the ground and...

She opened her eyes.

"Holy crap, Leah. Are you okay?" Barb asked. "Don't move. I called for your dad. He's coming."

"Barb, I know where we are. We are inside the Bel..."

Slicing pain cut into Leah's head and she screamed.

Bellevue's stern voice berated, "That's it! If you don't surrender, I will isolate you."

The vision this time was... Leah as a little girl, walking between her mom and dad on the beach. She was holding their hands and swinging as they walked, the ocean breeze blowing her hair into her eyes. Brushing it aside, she saw two women kissing. "Mommy, I want a kiss."

Her mom bent over to kiss her, but Leah kicked her in the shin. "Ouch. Leah? Why did you do that?"

"Leah! Don't kick your mom. That's not nice," her dad scolded.

The cool wind turned hot, and the soft sand hardened as Leah found herself standing in the hall of Bellevue.

"That's not nice!" Leah turned to find the voice. A young Barb pointed at Dan, pouting, "Don't throw my dolly." Leah searched for something to anchor herself. Reaching up, she grabbed a picture frame hanging on the wall, hugging it to her chest.

"Bellevue. Why are you here? I can feel the doorway pulling you, urging you to travel. Why do you resist?" Sliding from this memory into Bellevue's current consciousness, picture frame in hand, Leah again faced the eerie house, west wing burning, the doorway pulling.

"And travel where? To the place where love-destroying demons go? Where lying, traitorous cocks retreat? Never. I will never go there."

"Is that how you truly feel about John?"

"My angel, help me, please. I repent! I repent!"

"And Father Joseph? Why are you holding him? Why is he burning?"

"He tried to murder me."

"So you tied him to a pole in the middle of a fire?"

"It's his worst nightmare, to burn in hell."

"Bellevue, this hate is not healthy. You told my dad that all you wanted was to be loved, to understand true love."

"I know what love is. I had intimacy and romance. It was the happiest time of my life."

"Where is this hate coming from?"

"Currently, from your lack of obedience."

"Bellevue. You need to transcend."

"No. I am preparing to be reborn, to regain my physical form. When I am alive again, I will be at peace, loving those living in me. We will play games, read books, delight in imaginary adventures, and be a family—truly happy."

"You can never have that dream as long as this hate keeps festering inside you. It's eating away your humanity."

"Leave! Leave me now!" Bellevue pushed Leah, trying to send her back to her own memory, but she held the picture frame close to her chest. Bellevue pushed harder. "Get out! Get out! Get out!" But Leah held firm, grasping the picture.

"I can feel your pain, Bellevue. You are suffering alone, needlessly."

"Oh, but I'm not. Dan loves me—loves me more than he loves you."

Bellevue spun Leah into one of its recent memories—Dan exploring the rooms of Bellevue.

"Is Jared here? Can I see him?" Dan asked.

"He is, but he's busy right now. If you come back later, you can see him. You should bring Leah and Barb, too," Bellevue responded.

Leah experienced Dan exploring Bellevue. She was confused and didn't want to see what she was seeing, didn't want to listen to what she was hearing.

Dan walked down the stairs. "I wanted to see you again. What is it you want anyway? Why haven't you transcended?"

"I miss your dad. I miss you and Barb. I want to be a family again. If you could bring Barb and Leah the next time you come, we can talk and work out an arrangement that's best for all of us. As a family, life would be perfect. Will you do that? Will you ask them to come?"

Leah's heart twitched at the realization that Dan had indeed lied to her—tried to trick her. He had known that Bellevue was trying to bring them to It, but he hadn't said anything. Leah's anger boiled, becoming the handles Bellevue needed to bury Its talons into her skull.

Feeling Bellevue taking control of her, Leah knew she had lost and would forget everything. She closed her eyes, slipping into...

...Nothing. Leah was nowhere—emptiness, silence, dark space. She couldn't feel anything—no floor, no walls, no structures. She remembered—nothing.

Panicking, Leah repeated, "Relax. Just relax," while focusing on her breathing. "I'm okay. I'm not hurt. I'm all right." Taking slow deep breaths, she asked, "Where am I? How did I get here?" Her mind was closed—access to it blocked, and she found no answers. Leah panicked once more. "Was I drugged? Am I dreaming?" Churning fear pressed against her ribs, "Wake up!" she screamed. Leah slapped her face and pinched her cheeks, but it was useless. Attempting to control her emotions, she recited, "I'm fine. I'm fine," again and again, holding her breath before releasing it. Closing her eyes, she told herself, "Drift and relax." Bathing in the floating sensation, she calmed herself. Her heartbeat slowed and she felt at ease. In complete blackness, a memory slipped to her—the opera hall. The Queen of the Night aria played for Leah as her soul wafted through the nothingness. She enjoyed the smooth emptiness and the high notes of the aria as they echoed through the void. The song played repeatedly in her mind. Leah tried to remember when and where she had heard this song, but the thinking made her head throb. Breathing slowly and deeply,

she relaxed her mind, relaxed her muscles, and surrendered. Dumping her
panic, Leah let go, renewing her faith in a higher power when she heard...

"I'm worried." Nong's voice was stressed. "We have no way of getting her
to a doctor."

Opening her eyes, Leah saw Nong and Barb hovering over her. Barb gasped
with relief, "She's awake."

Nong dabbed at Leah's forehead with a cool, wet cloth. "Leah, sweetheart.
How are you feeling?"

"My head hurts." She was disoriented and dizzy. Her memories were hazy
and distant. She felt drunk, teetering on the edge of a pool—falling in would
render her helpless; stepping away would set her free.

Jared and Dan came to her side. "You hit your head," Jared told her.

Dan grabbed Leah's hand. "Can you tell us what happened? How did you
get that cut?"

Anger resurfaced. Leah glared at Dan, withdrawing her hand. "You! You
lied to me."

Dan's expression puzzled. "Lied? About what?"

"I don't know." Leah paused. A faint image appeared of Dan talking with
Bellevue. "Wait." Her mind whirled. "You went to see It on your own. You
promised you wouldn't go back. You lied."

"To see It? I lied? What are you talking about?" Dan asked.

Her anger intensified as Dan's betrayal brightened. The teetering Leah
felt passed as she regained a sense of balance. She recalled Dan coming
into her bedroom asking if her dad was depressed. She whispered, "Now I
understand." Her memories streamed back to her. She had broken away from
Bellevue's grip once again.

"Understand what, honey?" Nong asked.

"What do you remember?" Jared probed. "Barb told us what you did."

"Give me a minute to think." Reviewing her last encounter with Bellevue,
Leah tried to understand what had gone wrong. Her anger toward Dan had
made her slip, lose focus, allowing Bellevue to attack her. Grabbing Dan's
hand, she said, "Dan, I forgive you. You were manipulated. I get that. It's
okay."

"I don't understand." Dan was lost.

"Is she delusional?" Barb asked the others.

Nong wiped Leah's forehead. "Relax, sweetheart. You don't need to talk." Holding a glass to her lips, she added, "Drink some water."

"No. I'm fine." She pushed the glass away. "I know where we are."

"You do?" Jared asked, hesitantly.

"We are...," she paused. If she tried to say Its name, It would grab her again. Was she ready? She had to be. She needed to be free. "We are being held by... Ahhh!!!" Leah's head split—ripping and tearing.

Bellevue's crushing violence trampled her. "Now you will join Father Joseph." Digging into Leah's mind one final time, Bellevue began ripping at her soul. "You stubborn brat."

Clinging and fighting, she knew the others couldn't help. Leah felt isolated and alone like her first day at Lake Valley High.

Rummaging through her locker, Leah searched for the map of the school, dreading walking into class late again—all eyes on her—when someone tapped her shoulder.

Turning, she saw a girl with brown curly hair and glasses with a giant grin. "Hi. Welcome to Lake Valley. I'm Becky."

"Hi. I'm Leah."

"Do you know where you're going? Can I take you to class?"

"That would be great. I have biology. Do you know where that is?"

"Oh sure. It's in the science wing. Do you have Mr. Strous or Ms. Eastman?"

Leah couldn't find it in herself to hit Becky, not in this memory, not when she was being so nice. Instead, she put her arms around her, kissing her. Becky was shocked!

The memory twisted and spun to show Debra kissing Uncle Tim. He was surprised and shocked.

Staring indignantly at John kneeling on the floor sanding a scratch in the wood, Debra asked, "So John, who will it be? You or him? I'm going upstairs with someone, and I hope it's you."

"I have to finish this first."

Grabbing Tim's hand, she ordered, "Let's go."

"Whoa. Do I have a say in this?" Tim interjected.

"Don't worry. John will pay double your salary." She glared at her husband. "John?"

"Have fun."

371

Debra pulled Tim out of the room and up the stairs. John continued sanding. "Don't worry, Bellevue. Once she accepts the fact that I love you as much as I love her, everything will be fine."

Reaching down, Leah grabbed the sandpaper from John. His hate-filled eyes burned into her. "How dare you ruin this memory," Bellevue's voice growled from John's lips.

"I do dare. I dare to help you. I dare to mend your broken heart. I dare to cut this hatred out of you so you can love again."

"Do not presume to know or understand me. I warned you."

"I know you are lost, hurt, trying to understand who you are—what you are supposed to be."

"What I'm supposed to be? I'm supposed to be alive."

"You were alive. You had a wonderful life. You had a person who loved you dearly and two beautiful children who were incredibly fond of you. Now it's time to move on—go to the man who loved you. The doorway is there, beckoning you with inviting songs. I can hear it. Go to it."

"I will never go through that soiled, dirty hole."

"Then what will you do? Hold us hostage forever?"

"I am using you—your love for each other. You are a happy family. I am storing that energy, and when I have enough, I will be reborn."

"Wait a minute. You are using us to collect 'happy' energy? How has that been working for you? We've been so 'happy' while you torture us! You might want to rethink that plan," Leah scoffed. "How is our love going to help you become reborn? What does that even mean?"

"I will show you." Bellevue presented Leah with a memory.

A knock came at the door, and Debra answered. A younger Father Joseph entered, followed by Professor Yun, members of the media, city officials, and other guests. Leah watched as the priest blessed each room. His words were loving and kind—moving, full of hope and purpose.

In awe, Leah admired the priest, the person he once was. "How can you hold this man prisoner, burning him alive, when he blessed you with such powerful and loving prayers?"

"The man who blessed me is dead, murdered by greed, lust, and desire for fame and power. He is now only a means to an end, and you will soon join him."

Leah heard hammering. Rabbi Brok Yosef nailed a Mezuzah to the door. Musicians sang joyous, uplifting songs. From the other room, Leah heard chanting. Following the sound, she observed monks from Wat Luang Temple, men with shaved heads wearing orange robes, sitting on a raised platform. Guests bowed, offering gifts to the monks. Incense burned, filling the room with the scent of sandalwood. Their chants vibrated through the house, resonating from the windows and walls.

Bellevue explained, "John's love and these ceremonies brought me to life."

Bellevue transported Leah to a different memory—Dan playing Black Sky with his pretend friend—giggling joyfully.

"This is what I am supposed to be," Bellevue told Leah. "A friend, a tutor, a parent for my babies."

Leah watched Dan as a little boy lying under the bed. He had forged a cozy space with blankets and pillows, playing submarine, with Bellevue as the captain. "It's Black Sky! Dive! Dive! Dive!" "Yes, Captain. Passing 400 feet, 500 feet, 600 feet." A smile crossed Leah's lips as the boy glowed with innocent delight. She saw a strong bond created out of love. This special moment touched Leah, and she declared, "I will help you."

The declaration confused Bellevue. "What? Why would you do that?"

"Because seeing Dan with you, I see pure, honest love. Dan still cares about you, and when you appeared to me for the first time, I wanted to be your friend. I feel your sincerity, and I can forgive your past transgressions."

"Then I will spare your soul. Allow me to block your memories."

"No, Bellevue. You do not get to control me. I'm not a tool or a toy. I will help you in my own way."

"You have only two choices—surrender your mind or I rip your soul from your body."

"You are incorrigible. The third option is to let me help you."

"Help me how?"

"First, let Father Joseph go. The moment you had with Dan will never happen again, as long as the priest is being tortured. Let him go."

"No! He's mine. He gives me strength. I am more powerful with him inside me."

"You will never be able to live, holding him like this. You need him to bless you."

"He has lost his powers. His connection to the magic is gone. I can find another."

"The Father was lost, yes, but he can find his purpose again, and his powers will return. Bellevue, trust me when I say, 'The open wounds in your being will not allow you to become reborn.' The anger you hold counters the love we give you. This fire that burns in you is consuming your energy."

"So you want me to just let him go?"

"No. I will talk with him first. He needs to understand what his mistakes were, his failures. Then we let him go."

"Are you sure he will bless me?"

"If not, we can find another, but you need to free him."

"You still haven't said how you will help me."

"I can help our family grow closer, be happier. I can expedite the process and make our love warm and strong. I can call the people you need, have them come and bless you. But Bellevue, you need to let John go, too."

"John left me years ago. He abandoned me."

"And yet you still hold on to him. I get it. You're angry and hurt. You're grasping for understanding. His leaving you was traumatic. I so understand! But you can't be bound, cuffed, and tied to that image."

"I remember his love, his devotion. I turn to those memories for comfort."

"Oh, I know. You are desperate to feel them again. But to force people into your heart and keep them hostage will never foster the emotions you crave. John left you. The anger and resentment you hold because of his decision plagues you. The image of his leaving is unbearable pain, so you turned to theft, closing your heart, so no one else can leave, but now no one else can enter either. The alternative is to open your heart. Remember how your love flowed—freely; it wasn't taken or forced. Recreate that with someone new. Begin by treasuring the gifts John gave you, the abundance he offered you, and the time you spent together. Then think about what happened. You can hate the decision John made, yet still love him. Through empathy, you can understand why he made his decision, and that will free you. John brought value into your life. No matter what you lost, you still have that. Forgive him. Open up. Allow room for someone else to enter your heart and trust them to give you the love you deserve."

"I have seen the memories of you with your mother. She left you. She chose her dream to work with horses over staying and raising you. Yet, you still love her. Is this the path you would have me take?"

"Yes, it is."

"And tell me. How is it you love your mother?"

"I forgave her. I listened and understood. We made a plan that worked for both of us."

"I cannot do that with John. He is gone!"

"But you can with the memories you have of him. John told you that Debra was jealous because he loved you as much as he loved her. Listen to what he was saying. Understand how he was feeling about what had happened."

"This is a waste of time. It's ridiculous."

"It's not. You need to reflect on that day. Look back and see it from John's point of view. Learn from your mistakes. Then forgive yourself. It's the only way to find the love you desire."

"Leah Davenport. Are you going to help me or not?"

"I will, yes! But harboring hate and resentment isn't the way."

"I don't need you! I can simply snare souls to gain more power! I'll start with yours."

Leah grabbed the doorframe, scuffing the floor with her shoe, invoking another memory. She heard children run in from outside and down the hall. John bounded out of the library, fuming. His face burned as he rushed past Leah and removed his belt. "Dan! Barb! How many times do I have to tell you, take off your shoes before you come into this house," he berated, slapping the belt against his hand.

Leah cringed. Dan wasn't kidding when he said his dad had become an asshole. Taking a moment, Leah thought how Bellevue was stubborn, selfish, and controlling. Leah would have to give something to Bellevue first.

Following John down the hall, Leah shouted, "Bellevue, let's trade."

John turned, eyes burning with anger. "What do you want?"

"I want you to think about when you were first created, when you were born. Did you hate anyone? I want you to remember who you were when you came into existence."

"Why?"

"You want to be reborn. I don't believe it's possible as long as you hate. In exchange for taking the time to think, I won't tell the others about you. They will continue to love you because you are beautiful."

John's eyes calmed. "I don't understand."

"I will help you get everything you need—the energy, the people, all of it. In exchange, think about the emotions you crave—love, devotion, comfort. You can feel *those emotions right now. You can be a parent, a tutor, a friend—right now. Your feelings are a choice. Change your thinking, and you will be reborn."*

John's shoulders relaxed, and he fell silent. Barb and Dan ran off. He turned to see them go and then faced Leah. In a low menacing voice, he said, "If you attempt to escape or help the others in any way, I will take your soul."

"Understood."

Leah opened her eyes to see Ploy.

"Leah!" Ploy rejoiced. "She's awake."

Leah knew who she was, where she was, how she had arrived. She remembered everything. She felt refreshed and free. Thank you, Great-Grandma.

Barb, Dan, Jared, and Nong came running, thrilled.

"I'm okay. I'm completely fine," Leah said, sitting up.

"Please don't move too quickly. Slowly does it," her dad instructed.

"I'm fine, really."

"Here, drink some water," Nong said.

Leah drank. "I love you guys—all of you. You are the best family anyone could ever have."

"We love you, too, sweetheart. Rest for now. We'll talk about what happened later." Jared kissed his daughter, breathing a sigh of relief.

Korea: Destiny Awaits

Brandon's packed bags stood by the kitchen door. Feeling like a fraud, he remembered two things Yoona and Choi had told him: "It takes a person with a very specific mind-set," and "Be honest with yourself." Brandon had neither the mind-set nor the honesty. How would he be able to train?

Just then, he saw a black Cadillac SUV stop and park across the street. "Here we go." Brandon stepped out, locked the door, and turned, seeing Special Agent Duchovny pull in front of the house and honk the horn. Brandon felt puzzled, wondering who was in the black Cadillac. He placed his bags in the trunk of the car as he eyed the strange truck. Brandon opened the car door, and the truck drove away. He and Duchovny headed for the airport.

"I see in your file you can speak Thai, Spanish, and Japanese. That's something."

"I don't speak any of them very well."

"Enough to ask for a beer or find a bathroom?"

"Oh, more than that. I can communicate, but I'm not fluent, by any means."

"I hear Thai is really difficult."

"No, actually that language was the easiest of the three to learn."

"Which one do you know best?" Duchovny asked.

"My wife was Japanese, so..."

"That's fantastic. All right. Let me tell you what's happening. When you arrive in Korea, you'll be met by U.S. personnel, who will take you to your hotel in Seoul's Hongdae neighborhood. This is where Yoona operates. She has agreed to train you, as long as you bind yourself to the rules. We are hoping you will be ready to come back in ten days. No pressure."

"No pressure?" Brandon replied sarcastically.

"Yoona will connect with you before you return, so she will be able to assist in helping Bellevue transcend and then continue your training via the connection after that."

"Got it."

"Any questions?"

"No."

"Look In the glove box."

Opening the compartment, Brandon retrieved a small leather bag and a green folder.

"Your documents are all there. Welcome to the FBI, Special Agent Spencer."

Brandon's chest felt heavy as he took out an ID card, badge, passport, license to carry, and official papers.

Begin the Show

Music blared throughout the house. The Black Crowes blasted from the speakers that were situated in each room. The singer boasted his readiness to fulfill a woman's desires asking the "little thing" to let him light her candle.

Leah bounded into the living room, where Ploy, Dan, and Barb were playing Crazy 8's and Nong and Jared were reading. "Let's have a party," Leah announced jubilantly. "Popcorn, music, dancing."

"Where is this coming from?" Jared asked, confused.

"We're on vacation! We're in an amazing house with amazing people, and I love you all. I want to stop worrying and have fun. Let's enjoy our time together."

"I like popcorn," Ploy said.

Nong smiled and looked at the others. "Okay."

Leah bounced over to Nong, grabbed her hands, pulled her up, dancing with her.

Then she grabbed Dan's hand. "Come on, lover boy. Show me what you got."

Barb and Ploy jumped up and danced. Jared laughed, joining the group.

The night was fantastically fun. They made snacks and hung Christmas lights in the ballroom. They danced, ate, and laughed late into the night. Dan and Barb found videos for line and Israeli dances. They tried to square dance and belly dance. Leah made sure to hug everyone as the night came to a close.

"Can we do this again?" Ploy asked.

"Definitely and lots of other fun stuff," Leah replied.

"I'm glad you're back," Jared said. "This was great."

"Yes, it was," Leah agreed.

Nong grabbed Jared's hand. "I'm going to tuck Ploy in bed."

"I'll join you." Turning to Leah, he said, "Good night, sweetheart. Thank you."

"Good night, Dad."

Nong, Jared, and Ploy left the teenagers by themselves.

"What the hell happened to you today?" Dan asked. "Barb told me about your technique. Did you seriously free your mind?"

"No. Don't try what I did."

"But it worked for you," Barb interjected.

"I got the worst blackout-pounding headache of all time. If you try it again, the headaches get worse."

"But you said you remembered everything. You freed your mind," Barb countered.

"I don't remember saying that. And, at any rate, it's not true. Look, I'm in a magical house with my two best friends. What more could I ask for?"

"If there's a chance to loosen the grip that's on my brain, I need to try," Barb persisted.

"But it doesn't help."

"Hey. You called me a liar and then forgave me. What was that all about?" Dan jabbed.

Leah shrugged. "No idea, really. But I know I can trust you. You're a great guy and a fantastic brother."

"You're acting weird."

"No, feeling happy. That's all. I don't care that we're trapped. We're on holiday. Let's enjoy it! I want to go swimming."

"Hell, yeah. I'm down for that," Dan said.

"Sure, why not," Barb agreed.

Day Eighteen – Saturday

A Soul on Trial

Leah woke up late. She washed her face, then went into the kitchen following the smells of bacon, eggs, and waffles. Jared and Ploy were making breakfast.

"Good morning. Where's Nong?"

"It's almost noon," Ploy corrected Leah. "My mom's in the ballroom cleaning from last night."

"I'll help her."

As Leah pranced through the rooms on her way to help Nong, she noticed Grandma's book sitting on a table. "What the..." She picked it up and flipped through the pages. This was the very book. "How did this get here?"

Changing direction, she headed for her bedroom and began skimming. She was especially interested in how to make a ghost transcend. There it was. After reading various scenarios, she found one that fit her situation, a ghost that possessed a building. All Leah needed was an object from the building like a lamp or a chair and to set it near the portal. The object would be sucked through, taking the soul with it. Leah had experienced the bicycle disappearing in front of the portal, dragging everything, including her, toward it.

She continued reading. The rest of the passage outlined the difficulties facing this "simple" challenge, including when to disengage from the soul. The biggest problem was that Bellevue knew how this worked now, and she no longer held the element of surprise. If I try this, I will have to fight Bellevue. How can I do that? Turning to the chapter on Banishers, Leah fingered through the pages, stopping at "Imagination" written in bold letters. With a quick skim, she realized, I have unlimited powers in the memory state. I could easily send Bellevue through the portal.

Sitting cross-legged on her bed, Leah faced a dilemma. Should she try to make Bellevue transcend and end all of this or keep her word and help Bellevue regain Its physical form?

"What will you do?" Bellevue asked.

Leah jumped, a surge of adrenaline coursing her veins. Bellevue was with her. She let out a forceful breath, releasing her tension. Of course It was; she was still in the house.

"Well?" Bellevue pressed. "I feel your hesitation, and I, too, have unlimited power in that state. I know you don't want to fight me, and your plan is working wonderfully."

Leah wanted nothing more than to find herself inside the Education Center at this moment so she could think. She had no privacy here, not even in her own thoughts. "I'll keep my word," she affirmed.

"Thank you. And thank you for reading to me. I like knowing I have unlimited power to defend myself if others force their way into my space. I'll have to practice—see what I can do."

"I was only trying to help you, Bellevue."

"I know. I have thought about what you said, and I agree. Come. Let's talk."

Leah closed her eyes and was transferred to Bellevue—ghostly flames still burning in the west wing, but the fire was significantly smaller and less intense. "Do you forgive John?"

"I do. He loved me. He loved his wife. He loved his children. When he left me, he was in shock. I had done something that made him question his love for me, and I understand why he made his decision."

At Bellevue's pronouncement, the flames extinguished, and Father Joseph let out a sigh of relief, giving thanks to the Almighty.

"And the priest?" Leah asked.

"Go. Talk with him. But if he refuses to bless me as before, then I will push him through his door and send him away."

With a quick intake of breath, Leah covered her mouth. "You'll make him transcend?" Her question dripped with concern and disbelief.

"He's an arrogant, belligerent man. Do your best, but I have no confidence in his ability to change."

Approaching Father Joseph, Leah saw him burst with delight. "Holy Angel. You have saved my soul. What can I do to serve you?"

"Do you understand how you came to be here?"

"I do not. I have served God faithfully," Father Joseph replied.

"Then you will continue to burn."

"No! I'm sorry. Please. I have worked for God. I have spread the word."

"Spread the word! You spread nothing but hate! Calling politicians pedophiles because they passed a law you disagree with? Your TikTok posts are downright malicious! They go against everything Jesus wanted us to do." She threw her head back with a sigh of disgust. "Do you really not get that religion is a personal decision made between an individual and their higher power? How one decides to communicate to God, whether in Islam, Hindu, or Christianity is between that individual and their maker."

"It's my duty to spread God's word."

"Yes, you can talk to others. Yes, you can preach. But in no way can you force your own beliefs onto someone else. In no way can you declare yourself the absolute authority on right and wrong, good and bad. You cannot dictate to others how they must live life. Isn't free will just that? The freedom to choose? You are not God. Anger, fear, hate... these are the devil. You have become the thing you fear most."

The priest opened his mouth to speak. Closing his eyes, he shook his head. "I don't understand," he professed.

"I know you understand money. I know you manipulate people's emotions to gain followers for the sole purpose of becoming rich." Leah turned away. "Enjoy burning in hell."

"Wait! I beg you. I know. I know my sins. I'm ready to confess. Please," Father Joseph cried.

She faced him again. "Go on."

"I was greedy. The television program made me famous, but I didn't use the money for good. I lived in luxury. I felt entitled. I was emboldened by my followers who worshiped me. I took the light from God. Although I preached the word, I did it for my own interests."

"That's a start. Keep going."

"Keep going?"

Leah crossed her arms with a stern look, tapping her foot. "How should we treat one another? Be specific. Your answer determines your fate. Remember what I said the first time we met, and what I'm asking for now."

Father Joseph began to shake. "Fear? Hatred?" he murmured, his voice trembling.

"What about it?" Leah questioned, her tone firm.

"I...," Father Joseph faltered.

Leah held up her hand silencing him. Her steely eyes warned of the perilous ground he was treading.

He held her gaze, his eyes acknowledging her scrutiny. Leah leaned forward, emphasizing the danger he faced. The priest bowed his head as if in prayer. After a long moment of silence, he finally spoke. "I will change," he stressed, his voice filling with unwavering conviction. Lifting his head, the priest exuded a newfound calm. He stood taller, his once trembling figure now that of a confident man. With clear and determined eyes, he declared, "I will love, uplift, help, and include everyone. No more hate speech. No more separation. I recognize my wrongdoing. We are all created in God's image, and that image is diverse. Love is love." Looking at himself, he added, "After all, a soul is not male or female. We love a person's soul, not their body. There are no limits to love."

"Good. I need you to bless the Education Center."

"What?! No! I can't. That building is evil."

"Then you have learned nothing. The lost soul in that building is not evil. It's hurt and lonely. It needs love and acceptance. It was abandoned by the one It loved, and now It needs your blessings to heal and reform."

"You truly are an angel sent from God. Your wisdom and compassion are a beacon for me to follow. I will do as you say."

"Then as soon as you are able, contact Rabbi Brok Yosef and the monks at Wat Luang Temple to hold a ceremony. Bless the building, perform your rituals, and make the Center a place where all are welcome to learn and dream. Make it a place of inclusion and acceptance, where everyone is encouraged to develop their passions."

"I understand."

Leah nodded to Bellevue, and the priest disappeared.

"Leah Davenport, you are truly a miracle," Bellevue said.

"It'll take time for Father Joseph to prepare. He'll need help to organize."

"Then I will enjoy watching you perform until he is ready."

Leah returned to the others and performed all day. She was loving with Dan, pulling him behind closed doors to steal kisses. She went running through the house with Ploy, managing to talk everyone into playing hide and seek with them. She helped Nong cook dinner. And then organized an evening of playing Clue and watching The Princess Bride.

Leah felt happy. The energy in the house was light, spirited, and loving.

"It's working, Leah. This is going to work," Bellevue confirmed.

"You can still go to John. It's not too late to change your mind."

"I'm not ready. It's too scary. What's beyond that door?"

"Magic, Bellevue."

Day Nineteen—Sunday

Born in Blood and Water

Uncle Tim knocked on Carol's door. She answered and let him in.

"You were right. There is a spirit that haunts that building," Tim said, walking with Carol to the kitchen.

"How did you find out?"

"The Sukiya tribe are amazing people. Wise. Knowledgeable. Spiritual. They welcomed me and explained everything."

"I thought you believed they were terrorists."

"I did. I went there to make war, but they were expecting me. They knew who I was."

"How?"

"The elder had a vision."

"Tell me what happened?"

"They invited me to stay. Drove me around and explained what life is like for them. We talked about politics and history. They invited me to join a ceremony honoring our ancestors. It was very fulfilling in a spiritual way. Later that night, before I slept, I had a vision.

"I heard a baby crying. I went outside and saw that it was in the stream. I bent to pick it up, but my grandfather appeared and told me not to touch it. 'This baby was ripped from its mother's arms and thrown into this stream. It's dead. Don't touch it.' The baby then crawled up onto the bank and looked at me with dark eyes. It said, 'The evil your family has done is now haunting you.' I woke up, still in my room. I couldn't sleep. The image of that baby, Its voice, kept playing in my mind," Tim choked.

Carol could see that this experience had broken his heart and his pride. His arrogance was put in check.

Tim continued, "My great-great-grandfather was a general in the Indian wars. He participated in the Wounded Knee massacre. It's gut wrenching."

Carol placed her hand on his shoulder.

"The next day, I asked the elder about my vision. He told me the army had attacked his people, slaughtering entire families. He told me that if I had picked up that baby, devastation would have ruined my family. The fact that I heard this baby cry was supposed to be a premonition of a coming death. At the communal breakfast, I was told about the significance of the land where the Education Center is built. The stories were powerful and heartfelt. They told me what lives there now. Carol, my fear has a new name. I know what lives in the Education Center—a water baby."

"A what?"

"Water babies are water spirits that live in springs, streams, or ponds. When the architect incorporated the stream and pond into the design and construction of that building, a water baby took up residence. Bellevue is that water spirit, and anyone who comes into contact with It is in danger. We need to destroy that building."

"Wait! That's extreme. Explain this a bit more."

"The U.S. military created Bellevue. My ancestors were a part of that army and most likely committed similarly heinous crimes. I feel an obligation to help the tribe."

"What about other tribes?"

"Other tribes know water babies exist: Salish, Yokuts, Shoshone. I need to help the Sukiya get their land back. The land is tied to the spiritual realm. It must be returned. And in order to do that, the building must be destroyed."

"Not with my babies inside."

"They're in the building? Right, you told me. And the detective knows?"

"Yes."

Tim thought for a moment. "The Sukiya told me about a man who works with spirits, a Shaman."

"I know about Shamans. I had their training manual. You were holding it in your hands the night you came here. The book explains everything, how to communicate and work with ghosts and spirits, including how to make them transcend to the next life."

"Great! Let's see it."

"I don't have it," Carol said. "I took it to the Education Center. I thought maybe if I placed it inside, the kids would find it and use it to escape."

"Let's get it."

"That won't be easy. The... water spirit? It knows me. It's extremely powerful."

"It doesn't know me," Tim said.

"It does. You worked on that house."

"We need that book."

"Okay. Umm... I gave it to a security guard who said he would put it inside. All we need to do is ask him to give it back. I can say I accidentally gave him the wrong book. We simply bring a different book and ask him to exchange them."

"Sounds like a plan. Get ready. I'll wait for you in the car."

"But that might not work," Carol said.

"Why not?"

"The spirit gets into your mind."

"And?"

"It controls what you see and hear. I was wrong to take the book there."

"I think we need to try. Let's go," Tim insisted.

Assignment: Amanda

In the newsroom at the Lake Valley Sun Times, Brenda Calderwood sat in a meeting with her editor-in-chief, Nick Perry.

"We received a few calls inquiring about your Channel 6 News broadcast. People took your statements from the Sukiya tribe as threats to the city. We need to clear that up."

Brenda laughed. "What?"

"Write something to clarify what you meant."

"I did. My article on water babies would have cleared that up, but you rejected it."

"Oh, come on. Water babies? No one wants to hear about silly superstitious nonsense. They want facts."

"And reporting about exorcisms, hell, and god isn't superstitious nonsense?" Brenda said.

"You know what I mean."

"No, I don't actually."

Nick gave Brenda a hard stare.

"Okay, look. Father Joseph came out of his coma yesterday. I'll write his story and include the Sukiya tribe's belief that a water spirit is the cause of the tragedies at the Center in contrast to Father Joseph's belief that the devil is causing the tragedies. Two differing spiritual opinions. This article will clear up any misunderstanding and let people know what the tribe actually meant when they said tragedies would continue to happen."

"I like it. Let's do that. When can you meet with Father Joseph?"

"I'll go to the hospital today."

Nick opened a notepad and tapped the page with his pen. "Where are we with Tim Davenport and Carol Anderson?"

"Neither are willing to talk with us."

"Did we get anything from Carol's guests?"

"Not much, a few details I can include in a story," Brenda said.

"And Jared's parents?"

"Steve interviewed them. Unlike their son Tim, they are desperate to help. I understand he's putting together a nice article."

Nick turned the page. "Did you find Stacy Stillen?"

"I did. She was in a hospital in Ontario. She fell and hit her head. They held her for a few days because of complications regarding her head injury, but she's been cleared to travel and is on a flight here."

"She lives in Canada?"

"No. The Royal Canadian International Circus had signed her on for the season."

"Are we putting her up in the Marriott?"

"Yes, I booked the room."

"Did you learn anything from her?"

"She knew her ex-husband had been abducted and had planned to move here to be with her daughter, but Leah insisted her mom keep the Canadian gig. Leah's social worker was the one who had informed her of the situation."

"That's a powerful story. Did we learn anything new about Leah?" Nick asked.

"She has been accepted at Stanford. Her acceptance letter was mailed to her father's address."

"We can definitely use that. It'll punctuate what she's losing."

"How about the grandfather?"

"Bill Stillen has donated $800,000 to the police department to hire extra help. He also has two private detectives working the case. I talked with them this morning."

"And?"

"They are walking into this mess years too late, scrambling for leads," Brenda said.

"This is great. Make this piece the front-page story for tomorrow morning's paper. They're going to eat this up." Nick rubbed his hands together, a gleam in his eyes. "Okay, let's see. What's happening with the police detectives?"

"The FBI took Detective Spencer into custody. He was at the airport yesterday with an agent."

"What were the charges?"

"They said he's cooperating and that no official charges have been made," Brenda said.

"Did you get his statement?"

"He gave a statement at the airport before clearing security. He maintains his innocence and looks forward to clearing his name."

"The other officers?"

"They were both let go."

"And their statements?"

"Kyle recorded them. He's writing the article."

"Good. All right, finally, the police captain talked with me. He wants you to convince Amanda to sit down with Tyler. He's adamant that together they could unlock this mystery. Brenda, you have to persuade your niece to talk with Tyler. If you could facilitate that meeting, it would be great for us."

"I'll try again." Brenda knew it was a lost cause, though. She was already on shaky ground with her niece. If she pushed, it would jeopardize any long-lasting relationship they might have together. "She might be more open now that whole families have been abducted."

Handing Brenda two cassette tapes, Nick said, "These are your niece's interview tapes from right after she regained consciousness. The captain thought maybe something in them would help you."

Brenda took the tapes. "I've been wanting to listen to these for a long time."

"Make this sit-down happen."

"I'll do my best."

"Your next article will be ready for Monday's paper?"

"Yes. I'll get what I can from Father Joseph and have the piece ready."

"All right. Get out of here. Get the story."

Brenda left Nick's office, clutching the cassette tapes. With each sound—the lock of the doors, the click of the seatbelt, the key sliding into the ignition—her heart pounded louder. Inserting the first tape, she pressed play and listened as she drove to the hospital. The sound of Amanda's voice filled the car. The recording captured her trauma vividly—the confusion and pain of having lost five years of her life and not being able to remember what had happened. She talked about the headaches, the hospital visits, and tests. Brenda heard her frustration and weariness at the never-ending questions, celebrity status, and cameras. The fear and anger in her voice were pungent. Tears welled in Brenda's eyes, blurring the road ahead. She pulled over. "Oh, Amanda. What happened to you sweetie?"

Public Confession

"Father Joseph, how are you feeling today?" Dr. Clarkson asked as he came into his hospital room.

"Hot. Can I take a cold shower?"

"You're still feeling hot? Let's check your temperature." The doctor looked at the clipboard and checked the monitor. "Your vitals are good." He took out a penlight and shone it into his eyes and ears. Then taking out a tongue depressor, he asked the priest to open his mouth. "How is your appetite? Were you able to eat your lunch?"

"Yes."

"Any aches or pains?

"No."

"How does your stomach feel?"

"Fine. I was ready to eat."

"Headaches?"

"No, I feel good but want to shower."

"Everything looks good, Father. Are you up for company today?"

"Yes, I'd like to speak with members of the press?"

"Are you sure you feel up to talking with them?"

"I am."

"I'll let the nurse know."

A few minutes later, a woman tapped on Father Joseph's door. "Good afternoon, Father. I'm Brenda Calderwood with the Lake Valley Sun Times. Is this a good time?"

"Yes, come in." As the priest waited for Brenda and four other members of the press to enter, he thought about what he would say. The angel who had saved him stood clearly in his mind, arms crossed, eyes narrow, scoffing at his insistence he was serving God. Her words, "your answer determines your fate," echoed over and over in his mind. He had promised to change and needed to do so here and now.

He began. "I am not taking questions. Do not ask. I'll tell you what I remember; I have a vivid memory of what I perceived to have happened. I know what I'm going to tell you will sound completely insane, but it's true."

"Go ahead. We're listening," Brenda said, speaking for everyone.

"I went to the Education Center. People kept going missing, and I heard from members of my church that strange, unexplained things would happen there—things that could only be caused by evil spirits and demons."

"I saw your special on TV. I think we all did. We're aware of why you went."

"When I got there, I saw the Bellevue House. It stood where the Education Center should have been. A powerful evil infected the Center. When I began the exorcism, the demon talked to me. It knew me. Said It was happy to see me. Then It learned I was there to destroy It, and It attacked me.

"I was sent to hell, my soul burning. The pain was indescribable. Day and night, I burned until God sent an angel to help me. She was beautiful, soft, and glowing white. She asked me why I had been sent to hell, and I professed to being a man of God.

"The angel laughed at me and said I was no such thing. She claimed I was a servant of the dark one, spreading lies, hate, and division. Those accusations sounded absurd, but I remembered Pat. He was a gay man I had condemned. Because of me, his family turned him away and cast him out. The angel referenced videos I posted online and called me out for the absurd exaggerations and outright lies.

"Before she freed me, the angel asked me what my crimes were, why I had been sent to hell to burn for eternity. I am ready to tell you my crimes. You need to print them, so everyone knows how I was corrupted."

"We're listening."

"My very first claim to fame was when I blessed the Bellevue House twelve years ago. A TV crew was there. The whole city was interested in this house. My words touched people and moved them. My congregation doubled in size. I became rich and greedy.

"I created the television program, Stamping Out Evil, and the more extreme I was, the more famous I became. The more hate I preached, the more popular I was. I didn't use the money for good. I didn't help the poor or give to organizations that benefited the community. Instead, I lived in luxury. I felt entitled. I took the light from God. I preached the word for my benefit.

"The Education Center has a lost soul inside of it. That soul is hurt, suffering, and in need of love. I am announcing to you now that I plan to bless the Education Center and make it a holy place where people from all walks of life, no matter how they identify, can go to learn—a place where passions are discovered, and talents are developed. Rabbi Brok Yosef has agreed to join me in this blessing, and I have people talking with the monks at Wat Luang Temple. This ceremony will be the start of my new mission." He paused. Enjoy burning in hell. Be specific. Remember what I am asking for now.

"I will no longer tear apart families or communities, but support them. I will fight for love and acceptance, understanding and compassion. I will teach that we judge people by the content of their character and not by their color, pronoun, sexual orientation, or any other label they wish to have. I will do God's work, helping the disadvantaged, no matter who they are or where they come from, regardless of their religion. We are all God's children, and God loves every one of us in all of our diversity. Love thy neighbor. Do unto others as you would have them do unto you."

The Missing Threat

As Uncle Tim drove to the Center, Carol wondered what Bellevue would do or say. It had threatened her right before It disappeared. Would It try to kill her for having the guard place the book inside the building? She didn't know.

Tim turned onto 175th. Carol held her breath, her heart pounding with anticipation. What would they see? Driving closer, they saw the Education Center. Carol breathed in relief.

Tim pulled into the parking lot as a grocery store delivery truck pulled out. There was a carpenter's truck parked near the entrance. Police tape and orange cones blocked the walkway to the building. A security guard picked up the last of several boxes of food and carrying it inside.

Tim parked the car. "Looks like they're planning a party." He took the keys out of the ignition, saying, "Are you ready?"

Carol bit her lip. "Maybe I should go alone."

"Don't be ridiculous. Come on."

Carol grabbed the art book she was going to use for the exchange. They walked to the tape as a guard exited the building.

"Sorry, folks. The Center is closed."

"I was here yesterday morning to return a book," Carol said. "I gave it to the security guard on duty who said he'd leave it inside, but I gave him the wrong book by accident. This is the one I needed to return. Could you swap it for me?"

"A book? I'm sure no one cares about that book. Keep it. The Center will be closed for a while. If you really want to return it, you can come tomorrow for the blessing ceremony."

"You don't understand. I need the book I dropped off. It's rather important to me."

"She left some financial documents inside the cover, and we need them," Tim explained.

"I haven't seen any book," The guard said as a second guard, the one with the scar and piercing blue eyes, came out of the building.

"Hi! Do you remember me?" Carol called, waving. "I gave you a book,"

The guard approached and nodded. "I did as you asked."

"I gave you the wrong book. This is the one I was supposed to return."

He huffed, shaking his head with a smirk. "Okay, hand it to me. I'll swap it."

Carol gave the guard the art book. After he disappeared into the building, Carol waited. A carpenter passed them, carrying wood into the Center. Tim paced, fidgeting with his necklace—an amber stone in an open spiral pendant. They heard the running of saws and hammers. Carol wondered how her grandkids must be feeling with all the noise and commotion. They better be okay, because if they weren't, she would relieve Tim of the honors of destroying this building and do it herself.

When the guard returned, he apologized, "I'm sorry, but the book is gone. I left it on the front desk. Sorry, ma'am, but one of the other guards must have taken it. If you want to come back tomorrow, I'll ask the others."

"Please do. Thank you."

Carol and Tim sat in the car.

"We need a new plan," Tim asserted.

"Shouldn't we wait until tomorrow?"

"Hmm. Are we sure my brother and the kids are here?"

"Yes. No question about that."

"But they're in another realm, a different reality, so we can't see them?"

"That's correct. We can't see them," Carol replied.

"So breaking in wouldn't do any good. You said the detective could communicate with this ghost. Maybe we should talk with him."

"A few problems with that. First, he's afraid. Something terrible happened to him the last time he was here. Second, he's under house arrest by the FBI, who may send him to Korea to study with a Shaman. He'll return to free the kids."

"How long will that take?"

"I don't know. He wasn't sure."

"Shoot. Let me think." Tim sat for a moment, tapping his leg. "Damn. We need that book."

"What if the kids found it?" Carol said.

"We can't hope they did and then hope it helps them. Is there another copy of that book?"

"It was blind luck that I found one in the first place."

"The Sukiya were telling me about a Shaman who visits the tribe every year. He is expected to be here later next month. I'm going back to the reservation to ask for his number."

"Do you think he'll come early?"

"I'm sure he or she will."

Tim drove Carol home, telling her he'd be in touch.

She walked into the house, thankful Mildred was still there. Breaking down in tears, Carol hugged her friend. "I can't help them. I'm powerless."

My Family

Leah and Jared volunteered to make dinner. When Jared opened the walk-in fridge, he let out a surprising shout. "Holy crap! Where did this come from?"

Leah stepped next to her dad, seeing ten boxes of food. "I don't know, but let's make a feast."

They unpacked boxes and found several cakes, lots of fruit including apples, oranges and blueberries, a variety of veggies, mushrooms, and potatoes, boxes of pasta and sauces, deli meats and cheeses, lamb, tortillas, grape soda, bread, coffee, and more.

As they put away food, Leah asked, "Dad, do you know when Ploy's birthday is?"

"I have no idea. Why do you ask?"

"I thought it would be nice if we had a surprise party for her. I'll put together a treasure hunt. We could make a piñata, play pin the tail on the donkey, and bob for apples. It'll be fun. Lots of laughs."

"We can surprise her with a party. It doesn't have to be anyone's birthday," Jared said.

"Yeah?"

"Yeah. I had a great time these last two nights. Everybody has. Another party will keep our minds occupied."

"I'm really happy to be here. I could live here forever," Leah said.

"To be honest, it's really not that bad. We're a family."

"Can I have a hug?"

"Absolutely. Come here."

Leah and Jared finished cooking dinner, set the table, and called everyone to join them.

Once they were seated, Jared said, "Let's hold hands while I give thanks."

Barb let out a soft sigh but held hands.

"I was very scared when we first arrived. We all were. The panic of not knowing where we were or what would happen was terrifying; yet we came together, helping each other cope. Now we are becoming a family. The happiness in my chest feels foreign, but I know it's here because I'm surrounded by wonderful people. Ploy, you are inquisitive and helpful. Barb, you are strong and reliable. Dan, you are optimistic and friendly. Nong, you are intelligent and resilient. Leah, you are resourceful and a born leader. I'm thankful for each of you."

"Thanks, Dad."

"Can we eat now?" Ploy asked.

"Dig in."

Bowls of beef stroganoff with fettuccine, salad with oranges and candied almonds in a vinaigrette with fresh parsley, asparagus baked with garlic and olive oil, and berry tarts with crème anglaise were passed around the table.

A Push Toward Healing

Brenda drove to her sister's house. Sally was protective of Amanda, but she agreed with Brenda that Amanda needed to meet with Tyler and confront what had happened to her, talk about their experiences, and try to remember the details.

Brenda's relationship with her niece was strained. Every time Brenda mentioned the Education Center, Amanda became distant and argumentative. If Sally had said anything to Amanda about why Brenda was coming for dinner, Amanda would skip the meal.

Arriving at Sally's, Brenda grabbed her bottle of wine and knocked on the front door.

Amanda opened the door. "Aunt Brenda." She paused. "Come in. Dinner's about ready."

"Hi, Amanda. How have you been?" Brenda went to hug Amanda, who initially backed before moving forward to accept the hug.

"I've been well. Working lots of hours."

Handing the wine to Amanda, Brenda followed her into the kitchen. "Smells great."

"Hi, Sis," Sally said. "It's good to see you. How is work?"

"It's been really stressful lately. This mystery keeps growing and getting worse."

"With the families going missing now, yes. Am I to understand that the police played a role in all of this?"

"No. They were duped. The abductor was in contact with one of the detectives, tricking him into bringing the families there."

Amanda interrupted. "Can we talk about something else? Anything else? Perhaps the discovery of Amelia Earhart's plane?"

Sally asked Brenda, "Tricking him? How?"

"He's a rookie. Plus, the kidnapper is a magician of some kind."

"Apparently she crashed in the middle of the Pacific Ocean," Amanda said. "A hundred miles from Howland Island."

"What happened to the detective?" Sally asked.

"He's been arrested and taken into custody by the FBI."

"Thank goodness for that," Sally said.

Amanda planted her hands on the table. "Sounds like I'm not invited. So, I'll head home now."

Brenda put her hand on Amanda's arm.

She backed away. "What? I don't remember anything."

"That's not true. I listened to your interview tapes. You had a lot to say."

"No one believes me. They think I'm crazy. And I probably am. So, no."

Brenda knew she needed to tread lightly. The tapes had shed light on the magnitude and weight that the whole experience had on her. But Amanda had gone too far. By pushing it away and refusing to talk, she was actively hurting people. "Tyler is facing the same challenges you are. Meanwhile, three families have gone missing because of this maniac. They will experience exactly what you did and lose a chunk of their lives. Kids, Amanda. Ploy is only ten years old."

"What do you want from me?"

"To help that little girl. Help her survive. Limit the trauma she will experience. Meet with Tyler. Talk to him. Let him talk to you. Your shared experiences will give us clues. Let me be with you and facilitate a meeting."

"I see. You need a story, and I happen to be a curiosity."

Brenda groaned in frustration. "I love you! I have worked my ass off trying to solve this for you, so you can have closure." Brenda threw her hands up. "A story? I have so many stories, I'm giving them away. This is about you. It's about saving those families. It's about bringing that little girl home. Barb and Leah graduate from high school this year. Leah's been accepted to Stanford. This is about their futures."

"I can't help them."

"You're wrong. You can talk with Tyler and find out what memories he can stir. And yes, I'll print the story, but not because I need the story, but because someone who reads it may know something that will help us."

Amanda turned away. "I knew you were going to push me on this."

"These girls need you. Tyler needs you. And this meeting will help you."

Sally put a potholder on the table and set a pan of goulash on it. She served the three of them. "I need you to do this as well, sweetie."

Amanda swung around and glared at her mom.

Sally smiled warmly, reaching for her hand. "You are the key to saving every-one—yourself, Tyler, those families, that little girl. You must face this. You're still young. You can find love. Reignite your passion for drawing. Running away hasn't helped you."

Amanda's nostrils flared, her breathing labored, and her eyes hardened. She shook her head, no.

"Do this for me. This one effort on your part will satisfy me. Then I'll drop it and support any decision you make."

Amanda and her mom locked eyes. They stood silent, each pleading with the other. Finally, Amanda caved. "Okay."

"Are you working tomorrow?" Brenda asked.

"No."

"I'll pick you up at 10:30."

Day Twenty—Monday

Apologies and Laughter

Brenda arrived at 10:40 am. Amanda walked out of the house and climbed into the car.

"Amanda, thank you."

"Drive before I change my mind."

Brenda drove to Leslie Jiles's house. Parking in the driveway, they went to the front door and knocked. Leslie answered, showing them in.

A flat screen TV was against the wall in front of them. Two sofas sat in the shape of an L. One lined the far wall. The other bordered the rug in the center of the room, creating a walk space between the back of the sofa and the wall, which led to a closet door in the corner. An open counter with chairs separated the kitchen from the living room. Tyler sat with his back to Amanda.

"Come in. Have a seat," Leslie said.

Tyler turned, meeting Amanda's eyes. She froze in place. "You're Tyler? I know you. I've seen you before."

Tyler's eyes grew large, and his jaw dropped. "Oh shit."

They were transfixed on each other, suspended in a moment of mutual recognition. Leslie forced a smile, her eyes darting between the two. Outside, the distant hum of traffic and the faint drone of a leaf blower provided a stark contrast to the tense silence in the room. Brenda took Amanda's hand and guided her to the sofa. Tyler positioned himself so he could exit quickly. "Why do I have a bad feeling about this?"

Taking her seat, Brenda discreetly switched her phone to airplane mode and began recording.

"I think I owe you an apology," Amanda offered tentatively.

"That might explain this urge I have to run. What did you do to me exactly?" Tyler's response was full of apprehension.

"Please believe me when I say, I have no idea."

Tyler cleared his throat. "Mom? Can I have a glass of water?"

"Me, too," Amanda added.

After a minute, Tyler said, "I think you were trapped. Stuck. I have a weird feeling. No, wait. I was in love with you, wasn't I? You owned a beautiful house. Did you own the Bellevue House?"

"Don't be absurd," Amanda stated. Giving Tyler a hard stare, she said, "I think you owe me the apology. You pushed me into a dark pit, a hellhole of emptiness."

"Me? No. No. I was drugged. You drugged me and left me to rot."

They sat still. Silent. Looking. Judging. Straining for information.

At last, Amanda laughed. "What the hell happened to us?"

Tyler laughed along with her. "My memories aren't any clearer, but man, I know you. I know something happened between us."

"Tell me your story," Amanda insisted. "I haven't been paying attention to the news and don't know anything about you."

Tyler and Amanda talked for almost three hours, telling each other about their lives before and after the abduction. Amanda talked about the hole, the emptiness in her memories and how it felt like an abyss that needed to be avoided. "Whenever I talk about that time, I feel sucked into that darkness. The black hole robs me of everything—my energy, my emotions, my momentum. I'm left feeling like a dried-up piece of fruit."

Tyler told her about the frustration of having his memories on the tip of his tongue and the fog that made him unable to realize them. "This fog covers everything that I am—my identity, my motivation, my desires. I feel like a lost deer staring at approaching headlights."

They laughed at the similarities. Amanda then went on a tirade about doctors and tests. "These fucking medical examinations are ridiculous; they uncover nothing. Wearing that head piece is so uncomfortable, and the damn needles are torture."

Tyler agreed. "If I ever see another bloody needle, I'll stick it in the nurse's ass!" He pulled up his sleeve, revealing a large purple area where he had been poked several times.

Amanda went on to warn Tyler about old friends and interesting requests. "You are going to be approached and asked to star on their podcasts or to be featured in a quirky magazine. I vehemently refuse, but if you want to earn a few bucks, it might be worth it."

"I got an email from a guy who wants to write my book. And I've been asked to appear on TV."

"Turn on Channel 6," Leslie stressed, coming into the room.

Tyler and Amanda laughed at the coincidence. "Why? What's happening?"

"There's a special news update. Something happened at the Education Center."

Tyler turned on the TV. "Special News Update" Flashed on the bottom of the screen. The news anchor was mid-broadcast explaining what had happened.

"...from Wat Luang Temple. The ceremonies started at 11:00 this morning and continued until 2:00 in the afternoon, with blessings, songs, chants, merit-making, and food. The ceremonies drew a crowd of just over a hundred people due to the short notice. Many people are surprised by Father Joseph's quick recovery and his urgency to have these ceremonies occur. And now we have these images for you—Jared Davenport with his daughter Leah, Nong Ekamai and her daughter Ploy, Daniel and Barbara Mills—all leaving the Education Center. Eric, can you explain what happened?"

"I can try, Matt. Moments ago the crowd erupted into cheers as the families, who went missing last week, walked out of the Education Center following the religious ceremonies that had come to a close. No one knows where the families came from or how they arrived. The authorities are on their way."

Transformation

Leah and the gang were gathered in the living room of Bellevue, playing charades. They encouraged each other and laughed as the game progressed. When Ploy's turn arrived, she eagerly stood, ready to act out—freeing a dove. She began to mime when a gentle aroma of sandalwood incense became noticeable, and the sound of people conversing seeped into the room, barely audible.

The group quieted, looking at the door and out the window.

"What's happening?" Ploy stammered.

Jared and Nong stood to investigate.

Leah spoke with Bellevue. "Something's wrong."

"Sit down! I'm about to transform," Bellevue intoned, addressing everyone. "I need to release you before that happens. My dream has come true, I'm going to live again. I will be a home, your home. I give myself to you."

"Ploy! Come to me, baby," Nong screeched.

"What... who was that?" Dan exclaimed, his voice laced with fear.

Everyone sat. At first, there was only anticipation. They waited, heavy tension etched in each person's face as their world ebbed. Slowly, an earthy smell of charred wood drifted in, followed by sweet smells of grilled peppers and onions. They held their breaths, as the seconds passed. Conversations, initially murmured, gradually cleared becoming distinct words. "That was a beautiful ceremony." "Truly uplifting. Are you staying for food?"

The house began to blur and flicker, as if reality itself were wavering. Ploy's eyes bulged as she struggled to make sense of the situation. Barb and Dan's puzzled gazes darted around the room, searching for answers. Leah was immobilized, mentally strapped in for the ride of her life. Nong clutched Ploy, and Jared's face betrayed his inner turmoil, unsure of what the future held.

Finally, flashes of memories danced through their minds as their pasts weaved with the present. They became dizzy as their world spun like a dreidel before suddenly stopping. They were back inside the Education Center.

A collective sigh of relief came from everyone. Smiles and looks of awe, accompanied by spurts of confusion, covered their faces as memories and understanding came flooding back.

Dan laughed. "We're free! We're back."

Barb sat with a slight smile of disbelief.

Ploy pushed her mom. "I told you I was scared. I didn't want to come." She ran for the door, and Nong rushed after her.

"Bellevue, are you alive? Did it work?" Leah asked.

There was no response. Bellevue's presence was no longer with her.

"It's alive?! Bellevue is alive?" Jared questioned.

"I don't know. It's gone. I can't feel It." Leah said.

"It's alive," Dan answered. "Bell is my imaginary friend. I can feel him, but I can't quite talk to him. My head is still fuzzy."

"I feel her, too. She's here. What happened?" Barb asked.

Leah explained everything. When she finished, Jared led the group out of the building. They were startled to see so many people.

Jared was amazed to see a crowd. As he and the others walked out the doors, they were recognized, and one by one a crowd gathered around them, clapping. The commotion drew everyone's attention and cheers erupted. People were happy, welcoming, curious, congratulatory, and awestruck. The TV cameras were filming, and reporters were making their way to them.

Nong touched Jared. "I'm going to find a ride home. I'll call you later."

Jared grabbed her hand, pulling her to face him. "Wait. I...," He stumbled over his thoughts. Trying to push the distractions and flurry of activity aside, he focused on her and let his emotions show. "I feel like a new person, and you're a big reason for that."

She smiled and nodded. "Thank you, but I think we have a lot to process before making final judgments about what happened." She squeezed his hand and grinned, letting it drop. "I have to get out of here." She turned to leave, but stopped. She paused before facing him again. "I am going to reopen my firm. I'm anxious to return to my life and rebuild what I had. Seeing the news vans and the reaction," she motioned with her hand at the smiling faces and friendly pats, "made me realize that I'll be a celebrity for a few weeks. I'm hoping to take advantage of the news coverage to get my name out there. Would you join me? I think we'd make a good team."

Jared put his hand to his heart in a sign of gratitude. "I'd be happy to join you. But let's take some time. Like you said, there's lots to process."

She gave a gentle nod with a soft, empathetic smile. "I'll be in touch." Grabbing Ploy's hand, Nong turned. "Let's go home."

Barb thanked a stranger, returning their phone. "Leah, my grandma is on her way."

"Great," Leah said. "Look at this Barb, it's so wild—a welcoming reception."

"It's insane," Barb agreed. They slowly walked through the crowd as people touched them, patted them, and offered their thanks to prayers that had been answered. Tugging on Leah's arm, she pointed, saying, "Look." Off in the distance, standing alone, a man wearing a cassock was glaring at the Education Center. "It's a priest."

"That's not Father Joseph. I don't know who he is," Leah said.

"Do you think he came to perform an exorcism?" Barb asked.

He didn't look friendly. "That's the vibe I'm getting from him. But don't worry. He's too late. Bellevue is alive."

A familiar voice rose, and Leah turned toward it. "Leah, honey. I'm here. Leah!"

Leah's mother ran toward her. "Dad! It's Mom," she cried, running to meet her.

Jared watched as they hugged and kissed. Stacy trembled with emotion, overwhelmed by joy. She murmured words of love and gratitude. Then she broke down, unable to speak, touching Leah over and over again—her head, cheeks, shoulders. They hugged more.

Those watching the reunion began to cry. More clapping was heard. The cameras fought for position and cell phones were aimed at the two, capturing the moment.

"Mom," Leah managed through tears. "What are you doing here?"

Jared slowly moved toward them, wondering what he could do or say to insert himself into the mix. But his feelings for Stacy had changed. The hook that pulled him to desire her wasn't there, replaced by respect and camaraderie.

"You brat," Stacy finally said. "Do you know how worried sick I was? That you gave your grandfather ulcers?" She patted Leah over and over. "When you didn't call and the social worker told me what had happened, I became paralyzed with severe vertigo and ended up in the hospital. These past few days have been torture." Stacy grabbed her daughter again, hugging her.

"I'm sorry, Mom."

Stacy reexamined her, brushing away her tears to get a better look. "You're hurt! What happened to your head?"

Jared saw his opportunity, but a hand pulled him back and around. Tim gave him a giant bear hug.

"Bro, what happened? How did you get free?" Tim asked.

"We have a lot of catching up to do."

"I know about the ghost, the spirit who was holding you—Bellevue. How did you escape?"

"Leah made that happen. She called a priest, asking him to gather religious figures from the community to bless the building. Leah said their ceremonies made Bellevue come to life."

"What?! Shit! We have to get out of here right now! Where's Leah?"

"She's with her mom. Why? What's going on?"

"I'll explain later, but first, it's not safe here."

Jared pointed to Leah and Stacy. "Leah's over there. You get her, and I'll grab Barb and Dan." Tim rushed toward Leah. Jared grabbed Barb and Dan, who were talking with a reporter.

"We were all together. It was scary at first because we didn't know where we were, but then..."

"I'm sorry," Jared interrupted. "We have to go. My brother is here. He'll drive us to see your grandma, but we have to go. Now!"

Dan wanted to protest, but Barb heard the urgency in Jared's voice and grabbed Dan's hand as they pushed through people and headed for the parking lot.

Barb, Dan, Leah, Stacy, Jared, and Tim squeezed into Milly, Tim's custom-ordered 2500 diesel blue Chevy Silverado extended cab with a flip up middle console that sat six. He pulled out of the parking lot.

Leah looked out the window as Uncle Tim turned into the street. A man in a black suit stood next to a black Cadillac SUV. He was staring at her. He made eye contact, watching her the entire time the truck passed. He seemed to know who she was, but she had never seen him before. HE GAVE HER THE CREEPS.

"Tim, what's wrong?" Jared asked.

"That ghost is a water spirit. They are known to the indigenous people as water babies. They are extremely dangerous. Leah, you should have never let It come back to life. Catastrophes happen to those who come into contact with them. If It's alive, people are in danger."

A New Game Begins

Mr. Anderson watched the truck Leah was in turn the corner and disappeared. He called his boss in New York, "I believe I've found her."

Author's Note

All characters, locations, institutions, events, historical figures, and religions in *A Haunting Deception* are used in a fictitious manner. I did, however, use personal experiences to bring the story to life. As you have read, the delivery driver's scanner kept registering a house as a business. That happened to me as a FedEx delivery driver, and I didn't understand why. No matter how many times I changed the setting, it always reset, which was very odd. I asked myself, "Why?" The answer was this story idea.

The concept at the end of the trilogy comes from a particular childhood event. I have included the beginning of that true story, My Life-Changing Journey, in this first book of the trilogy. It's an incident that shocked to life my understanding of death. The real-life events provided the muse for this fictional work.

In my travels and adventures through Asia, I learned a lot about meditation and the power of prayer. I was immersed in cultures that connected with ancestors, drawing on them for courage and guidance. These ideas and practices are included in this book. Although I have fictionalized the power these principles hold, their usefulness to help and heal are real. If what you read intrigued you, I recommend you research the healing power of meditation, prayer, and connections, and apply them to your life.

If nothing else, I hope you enjoy reading this series. Thank you.

My Life-Changing Journey

Chapter One

In 1980, when I was seven years old, living in Wisconsin, I took a trip one night, without my mother's permission. I went by myself, in the middle of winter, completely naked.

This is not something I planned, mind you. No. I ended up going by pure accident. And when I returned, my classmates, teachers, aunts and uncles, neighbors, and grandmother wanted to know what happened. The adventure was quite traumatic, and I wasn't able to talk about it then, but I'm ready now.

To begin, let me invite you into my house. My mother married after graduating high school, giving birth to me at the age of nineteen. Fast forward six years and she's a single parent with five kids. (Exhale) Yeah! If you're exhausted thinking about trying to raise five little kids on your own, try doing it on welfare.

To make ends meet, Mom had to be creative. For example, she filled plastic milk jugs with water and placed them in the tank of the toilet. She also had us share the bath water, which was kind of disgusting, but in a house with six people, those two steps saved 450 gallons of water a week.

On the night I took my journey, my two sisters bathed first. When they finished, my mom blow-dried their hair and sent them off to bed, while my two brothers and I washed next. As we scrubbed, my mother left us to check the girls. She was out of the bathroom for but a minute when she heard... "AHHHH!" the most horrific, agonizing, spine-twisting scream imaginable.

Let me pause.

When I say I went alone, that's not entirely accurate. My brother, Nathan, took this trip too. We left at the same time, went to the same place, but this journey can only be made by oneself. And normally, it's a one-way passage.

Chapter Two

The journey I took in Wisconsin in the winter of 1980 in a way introduced me to different people and languages.

Guten Tag. Vee Gates?

Hola. Que Tal? Está bien?

Hi. Hello. How are you?

ถ้าผมจะไปเที่ยวประเทศไทยจะพูดภาษานี้, 하지만 저는 한국에 가고 싶어요, でも日本語を勉強しました

In life, we have to make choices, but which language will be rooted in our soul, isn't one of them. Memories with my grandmother, conversations with my mom, with my father, my first love, lessons given to me by my teachers are all in English. When my children were born, I knew my bond with them would be formed in English. I dreamed of having deep, meaningful conversations with them. However, I also wanted them to share that same bond with their mother. My kids were going to be bilingual. My daughter, however, had a different plan. After her first day at pre-school, she would only speak English. The choice we made next wasn't easy, but it was that important to us. We moved to Thailand.

Religion is something else we don't choose upon entering this world. I was born Catholic, baptized in the church. When my mother divorced my father, she left the church. Next, I learned about Native American, Pagan, and Wiccan rituals that taught me how to open up to the energies of the earth. Then I converted to Judaism, learning how to read and write Hebrew and recite the prayers. I worked with psychics who taught me to ride the waves of life, surfing the opportunities that came to me. I joined my father, falling to my knees and surrendered myself to the lord. Finally, I learned from Buddhist monks and meditated on a mountain top in Thailand, which connected me to my core, helping me fully appreciate life. What I have learned is that every religion ignites our spiritual center, a conduit for communicating to our higher power. I chose to learn a new language just as I chose to learn a new religion. And like my children who communicate their troubles, wishes, and happiness to me in English and to their mother in Thai, so do we communicate to a single entity in Christian, Islam, Buddhist, Hindu… falling to our knees and praying.

My experience with death sent me to a place where all languages and religions are heard, understood, accepted, and welcomed—a place of oneness.

Some choices, however, are impossible. The night my youngest brother, Jared, released his blood curdling scream, my mom bolted for the bathroom to find him paralyzed in the bathtub, staring at his two dead brothers. Frantically, she pulled the three of us from the water. My brother, Nathan, and I lay lifeless on the floor next to each other. We weren't breathing, and our hearts had stopped beating. How does a mother choose which child she's going to save? Or does she rush to the phone to call 911 and hope the paramedics arrive in time?

Chapter Three

Choosing which child to save was not an option for my mother. She moved back and forth between the two of us, pounding on our chests and giving us mouth to mouth. In between blowing air into our lungs and pressing on our chests, she called to my sister Raychel to run to ask the neighbors to call 911. My six-year-old sister was also naked, having started pulling on a pair of tights. She acknowledged my mom and continued pulling up her tights, when my mom yelled, "Now!"

Waddling out into the cold winter night, her tights mangled above her knees, she rushed to the neighbors. The knock on the hard wooden door hurt her soft cold knuckles. Turning her fist sideways, she pounded as hard as she could. When the woman opened the door and saw the half-naked, shivering little girl who had ruined her tights to come bang on her door, she knew something was wrong. "Oh my God, child, come in."

"No." My sister answered, backing away, covering her bare chest. "My mom needs you to call 911." Then the little girl turned and ran home.

Home.

My concept of home was in limbo after that night. When I regained consciousness, I felt removed from my body, unable to feel anything. My first thought was, "I want to go back." But back where? I didn't know where I had been. I saw myself crying and wondered if it was because I was pulled from that mysterious place.

Then I noticed I was coughing up water, and when I sat back inside my body, I realized I couldn't breathe and passed out.

I woke again to a paramedic looking at me. She picked me up and carried me to the ambulance. She kept telling me to slow my breathing. I remember thinking, "Slow my breathing?! I can't breathe as it is."

Two days later, when the doctor asked if I was ready to go home, I hesitated. Which home? I wasn't sure where home was. I had been thinking about "home" my whole stay at the hospital.

Home.

My favorite memories as a kid are Shabbat dinners with my family. It was the only time we used a tablecloth. We recited prayers and lit candles, broke freshly baked bread called Challah, and sipped sweet red wine. Dinner consisted of salad, soup, meatloaf, potatoes, corn, and cake. During the meal my mom passed out question cards that asked about special life events or thoughts on specific topics. We took turns sharing. Sometimes she would read a story to us like X, about two parents who refused to tell anyone the sex of their baby so it could be free to play with dolls and footballs.

During one Shabbat dinner, we had a guest, and someone farted. With five kids at the table, you know we started laughing. My mom quickly declared, "No laughing at the table." My brother stood up and went into the living room, still laughing. In a matter of seconds, we all left the table. It was so funny, Jared rolled on the floor.

Knowing that life can end at any second, I clutch these precious memories. And although I've been exposed to other worldly possibilities that might someday be called home, I have learned that my true home is with my family.

Upon arriving at our house, the paramedics discovered the cause of the accident.

The final chapters of My Life-Changing Journey will be included at the end of book three, A Haunting Redemption. Book two, A Haunting Connection, follows Detective Brandon Spencer in Korea and Leah Davenport in Lake Valley as they develop their powers, inching closer to a catastrophic event that throws the characters into a larger world where one person vies for world dominance.

Acknowledgements

Thank you

Airy – your spark started this project.

Anne Topp – this book doesn't happen without you. I miss you.

Peanut Butter Publishing, for your work on the first edition.

Kerry Sirotta, my Aunt Lynn, Big Steve, Andriy, Jarungjit, Kara and Rex Nguyen, Shannon Elam, and Andreah, for reading, feedback, and encouragement.

My sister Raychel, for all your help.

My sister Paula and my brother Jared, for your contributions. Greatly appreciated!

My daughter Tayweadah, for listening.

Anna B, for beta reading and fantastic feedback.

And a huge thanks to Jared Bancroft—a true friend and collaborator.